Beyond the Gloaming Pass

Rebecca Holmes

Beyond the Gloaming Pass

Copyright © 2023 by Rebecca Holmes

ISBN (eBook 1st edition): 978-1-7389611-0-8

ISBN (Paperback 1st edition): 978-1-7389611-1-5

Published in Vancouver, British Columbia, Canada

www.rebeccaholmesbooks.com

For my mother, Stephanie, who is a greater source of inspiration than she will ever know.

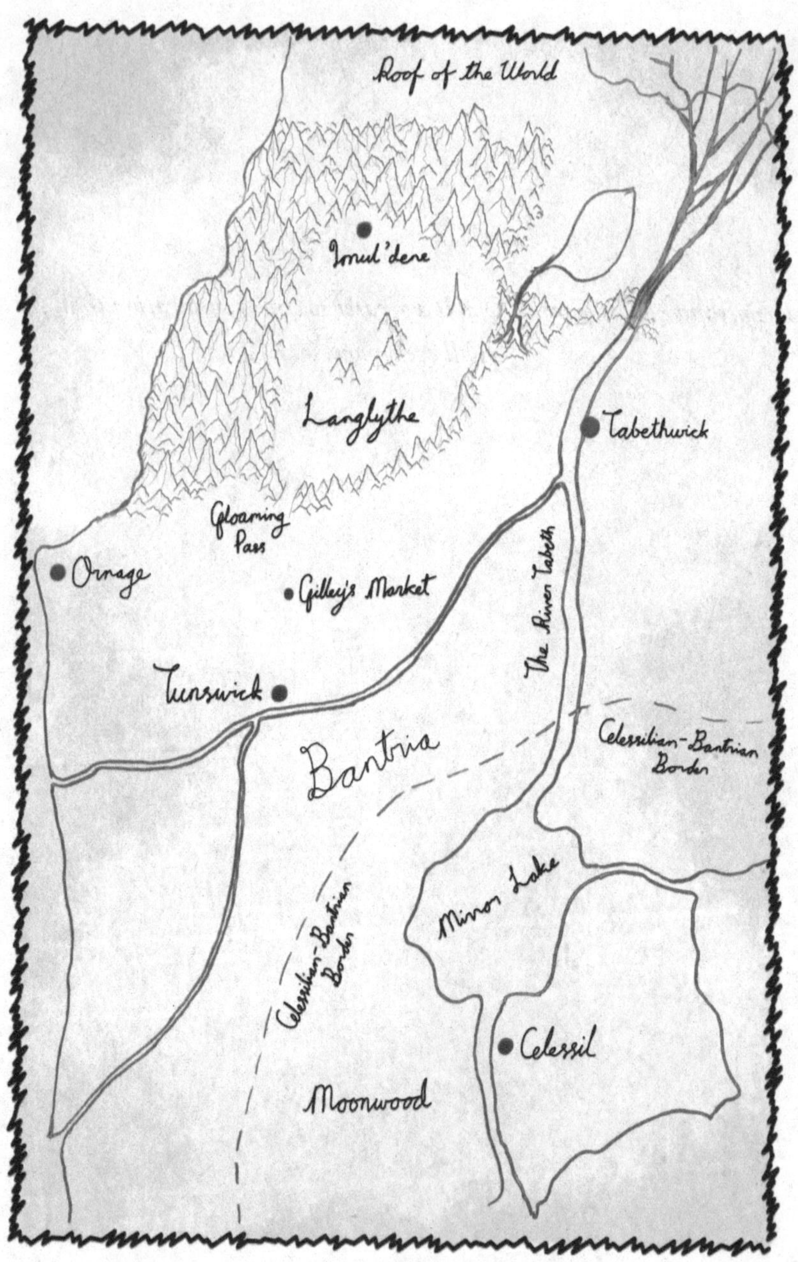

Roof of the World
Ismul'dene
Langlythe
Tabethwick
Gloaming Pass
Ornage
Gilley's Market
The River Tabeth
Tunswick
Bantria
Celessilian-Bantrian Border
Celessilian-Bantrian Border
Mirror Lake
Celessil
Moonwood

Prologue

30TH OF THE TENTH, 1900

Silence ruled. The air lay thick with the emptiness of it. Stillness clutched the lakeshore in a firm hand, as though time and nature paused to take a breath before resuming their endless march. The water lay calm and undisturbed, a black lake in a greyscale world bereft of colour, save the unreachable emerald swirls that curled lazily through the sky. No fish dared to prick its mirror-like surface, no insects hovered above it; a forsaken pool in a forsaken land.

A woman sat on the dry earth by the edge of the lake, her clothes torn and covered in dust, her dark hair tangled. She stared across it without blinking, without seeing; her face deprived of emotion, her mind heavy with thought. A pale glow in the distance caught her attention. Idly, she watched it grow larger as it came nearer, bouncing as the man who carried it made his way around the edge of the lake towards her.

Somewhere in the back of her weary mind, she contemplated running. The thought seemed very far away, as though it belonged to another life, another version of herself. She was vulnerable here, weak and alone, yet she did not run, nor confront him. Just as she hadn't the time before.

"You," he barked. He stopped twenty paces away, his lamp in one hand, the other dragging a makeshift cart behind him.

"Hello, Shavon," she said quietly.

"You're here... *again.*" Both disbelief and annoyance tinged his gruff voice. He frowned at her.

"Yes," she replied, not as surprised to see him as he was to see her. He looked the same, if a little thinner and rougher than she remembered. "Only this time, I will tell you who I really am, and perhaps your next actions will be different."

He stepped closer. She remained still, cross-legged on the ground in a most uncouth manner. Her expression was soft, though all the while those distant thoughts murmured that if he only knew what she'd done...

For she *was* different now; irrevocably so. She could tell he sensed it.

"Durenka-"

"No." She cut him off.

He stared at her, the wreckage of a woman who once shared his village, his hearth. He waited out a long pause before she continued.

"I first came to Langlythe nearly a year ago. I came here to correct a mistake. I came here... to save someone I love." Her voice quavered, barely more than a whisper. "But she... everything..." She swallowed, looking away while she composed herself. Her body tensed as though it caused her physical pain.

"My real name," she said slowly, "is Rubriel."

Her gaze lifted to meet his once more, her voice lowering to a kind of dry resignation.

"I have travelled far, north and south, from Celessil to the Roof of the World and everywhere in between. I have fought, I have killed, I have destroyed. I have *been* destroyed. And yet somehow... I still find myself here in the end, on the shores of your lake, waiting for someone to find me." She swiped away a tear as it welled from her eyelids.

"Rubriel." His eyes widened in recognition, for it was a name he knew well; a name he heard everywhere of late. "Tell me, then," he said, even as it seemed he would prefer not to hear the answer, "why do the spirits whisper your name?"

She studied him again. There was much more than just disbelief in his expression now. His creased brow and tight lips held apprehension, perhaps even fear.

"Because I set them free."

1

Harsh Words

14th of the Twelfth, 1899

"**O**ne hundred gold!?"

Molindra nodded, grimacing as she stirred the pot on the stove.

"Where are we supposed to find a hundred gold? I brought home ten silver last week. *Ten silver!*" Rubriel leant against the cupboards, clutching her temples. Her head was pounding again.

"I will take care of it," Mol said quickly, still not looking up from the stew.

"How?"

She said nothing. The money tugged at her conscience, tucked away in her purse as though it belonged there. It was wrong, what she did, but she hated having to explain herself all the same.

Rubriel knew her silence for what it was. "Please do not say you have been stealing again."

Molindra set the wooden spoon down a little harder than necessary. "It was the only solution I could think of, alright? Mr. Edson left his wallet in his coat pocket. I saw it on the way out and took a hundred to pay off the debt. No more."

Rubriel gaped in disbelief. "Your boss fires you for illegal use of magic and fines you for the damage to company property, so you *steal* from him in order to pay him back? Good grief, Mol–how is that a solution?"

"What would we have done otherwise? You are between jobs and barely making enough to cover the rent, as you pointed out. And don't tell me it is going to get better. You have been saying that for twenty years *and it never does.*" Sparks flew unbidden from her fingertips, speckling the cutting board in embers. She hurriedly tossed it in the sink and doused it in water. "Argh!" she cried, her desire to throw something tempered only by fear of what else she might accidentally unleash.

Rubriel winced. "I am trying. Work is always slow over Solstice. We just need to make it through the next few weeks-"

"Always just about the present with you," she interrupted. "What about the future? We cannot keep on living like this!"

Rubriel rounded on her, glaring across the kitchen table. "No, what we cannot do is keep getting into trouble. You have been caught out with your magic too often lately, and you stole from your employer right after you set fire to the factory. You are the first person he will suspect when he realizes the money is missing!"

"I can't control it, Rubriel! You know I can't! I never had the practice. My medication leaves me feeling half dead and it still isn't strong enough. I need *help!*" She trembled, fighting back the desperation bubbling up inside her. Tears stung her eyelids, and she shook them away irritably, disappointed in herself for getting emotional.

"I cannot *fix* this!" Rubriel threw her arms wide. "I am trying *so hard* to get you your education. I'm exhausted–I can scarcely keep this roof over our heads, yet you keep making things harder for me!"

"This isn't about you!"

"It was your idea to move to Bantria; your idea to set your sights on the most prestigious school in the world instead of living somewhere affordable. But you can't keep a job, so I have to pay for it all - in a country where my profession is redundant and my options are reduced by half just by being a woman."

Mol blanched. "Are you really blaming me for all of this?"

Anger brought a rare flush to Rubriel's cheeks. She seethed behind a clenched fist, her dark brows knotted over the bridge of her nose.

Mol inhaled sharply. "If you hate it all that much, why are you even here? I did not ask you to look after me. Go back to Celessil and have fun making horseshoes, or whatever mind-numbing work a blacksmith does these days."

She started. "You want me to leave?"

"I don't know! It sounds like you wish you'd never come here." An uncomfortable, prickling wave of raw energy took hold of her. She shuddered as she fought to contain it, panic rising at the threat of losing control over the storm inside her. "I can't be around you right now," she snapped, and tore out of the tiny kitchen.

Rubriel heard the front door slam behind her. She snatched the pot from the stove, the stew hissing in protest as it boiled dry and stuck to the bottom, ruined.

Molindra flew down the street like a madwoman, beyond the last few houses and out into the blustery twilight. She waded into a snowdrift up to her elbows and sobbed, the snow rapidly melting as her energy seeped into it. It ought to have been freezing, yet her skin burned with feverish heat. She dug further into the powder, smothering her need to combust, until her nerves cooled and the patch of ground where she sat revealed bare, dead grass.

She looked around, calm enough to take notice of her surroundings and scowl at the unreasonably cheerful snowmen leering at her from behind picket fences and half-buried gardens. The sun bathed the clouds in orange and pink as they raced by. She stood, weary now, and straightened her skirts, the fabric barely damp despite burrowing in the snow moments earlier. Her steps carried her back the way she came, but she stopped. Her heart began pounding again. Where was she to go? *You keep making things harder for me...* Rubriel's words sent a stab of pain through her chest. That wasn't fair. She couldn't go back to the house and face her–not yet.

The streets of Tunswick were not safe after dark, but she needed to be alone–and having shed her excess energy, she began to grow cold. She headed for the library. Its quiet aisles and musty scents of old books and worn leather brought her comfort in times like these. The escapism of reading a good book, losing herself in the details of someone else's life, calmed her when nothing else could, but her favourite part of the library was the maps.

They occupied a small section near the back of the old brick building, ranging from recent, detailed drawings of Bantria's road and rail network, to centuries old sketches of the Eastern Continent, yellowed and crumbling under their protective glass. Maps, in all forms, fascinated her. She would trace their lines and landmarks, imagining herself travelling from place to place. What must it have been like for the first cartographers to see and document it all for the first time?

All the library's maps, new and old, shared one area of uncertainty. A blank area north of the Gloaming Pass with no detail ever recorded by pen and paper, a land secure within its mountainous shell, untouched and unknowable. She knew the stories–myths, really–about a land of the dead; an evil, haunted place cursed with endless night. Superstition, surely, but fascinating all the same. She thought suddenly of the poster she'd found pinned to the community notice board outside this very library three weeks ago.

Pioneers and Explorers Wanted!

Shrouded in mystery and fear, the secluded land of Langlythe lies right on our doorstep, within the embrace of the Gloaming Mountains. We fear what we do not understand. Now is the time to venture beyond the Gloaming Mountains and enter the heart of the unknown in the pursuit of knowledge, trade, and extended wealth. Compensation will be shared between all successful contracted parties upon their return, ranging from two thousand to six thousand gold depending on the quantity and quality of information obtained. Findings that serve the financial interests of the employer will attract the highest reward.

Speak to Murdoch Vesner, Merchant Guildmaster, for more information.

Business District Guild Hall 3
Rensworth Square
Tunswick

Rubriel had scoffed at it, then. "Murdoch Vesner is a filthy rich man who expects people to sell their souls for a piece of his fortune. He'd rearrange this entire country to suit his own purpose if he could," she had remarked. "Come on, we are not so desperate as to need his money. It is a false promise, anyway. No one goes to Langlythe." With that, she'd steered Mol back towards home and never mentioned it again.

She raced outside. Scanning the notice board, she found the paper still hanging there, weathered and half hidden behind a festival poster, but still readable. She unpinned it and retreated to the map corner, reading the words again and again. Two to six thousand gold. A sum like that would see her enrolled at the University of Esmara, a prestigious school of magic at the scintillating heart of the Western Continent. A new world across the sea—and the fresh start she and Rubriel had dreamt about for years. Could she fulfil the guildmaster's request?

Rubriel stood on the station platform, her jacket wrapped tightly against the morning's chill. She hung back as passengers filed out of the train cars, waiting for the throng of people to disperse enough to spot her sister. A porter at the far end unloaded baggage, stacking suitcases in a neat line to await their owners. She recognized Gwendolen's suitcase as one of the first to be unloaded, distinctive thanks to its bright purple canvas embroidered with white carnations. She stood by it, grinning as her sister stepped down from the carriage and caught sight of her.

"I would know that luggage anywhere."

"Rubriel! How are you?" They embraced warmly.

"I am well," Rubriel replied—a little unconvincingly, as Gwendolen pulled back to study her face.

"You look tired. How come you have a suitcase as well?" She nodded to the worn leather case sitting beside her.

"I have not been sleeping well. I... was hoping to share your hotel room whilst you're here?"

"Of course!" Gwendolen brightened. "In fact, I was hoping you would. It has been too long."

Together they lugged their bags out of the station, where Gwendolen hailed a carriage to drive them into the centre of town. Winterfest decorations were already beginning to infiltrate much of the township, with wreaths of holly and fir cones on every door. Bright coloured ribbons and tiny lanterns hung from the eaves, while men climbed ladders on the corners of each street to decorate the trees with yet more ribbon.

"I had best talk to the festival committee once we have dropped off our things," said Rubriel.

Gwendolen made a face.

"I am sorry to run off, but they always need someone for odd jobs. I need the money." She sighed. "We will have plenty of time to catch up tonight, I promise."

"Are you sure you're alright?" Her grey eyes filled with concern, sparkling beneath her long lashes.

"Molindra and I had a fight. I... said some things I shouldn't have." She rubbed her forehead. "Please, can we not talk about this? I just need some space."

In truth, Molindra hadn't come home after their argument. Rubriel waited up most of the night, nauseous and angry and replaying the conversation over and over in her head until the sun came up. She had left a note on the mantelpiece and gone straight to the train station, even though her sister hadn't been due for another two hours.

The carriage rolled to a stop. It wasn't a large hotel, but inside was comfortable and warm. A porter took their luggage while Gwendolen checked in, making sure they would have room for two. They were shown to the suite at the end of the ground floor corridor, pausing to admire the collection of oil paintings along the way, each depicting a famous political or academic figure from Bantrian history.

The suite overlooked a garden from a beautiful bay window. Two beds, each heaped in white quilting and overstuffed pillows, sat on opposite sides of the room with a dividing screen between them. An array of candles occupied the top of the dresser inside another festive wreath. She shoved her suitcase into the corner and gave Gwendolen another hug.

"I will try to be back before five," she promised, and went back outside into town with a little more haste than necessary. What she needed most of all was to keep busy. Hard work had a way of calming her mind - the more strenuous and repetitive, the better. Perhaps that was why she took to smithing so well in her youth, back home in Celessil, where artisans and small businesses largely escaped the sting of the industrial revolution which swept Bantria into the modern age.

Bantrians rarely took her seriously when she described her former life, certain in their narrow view of the world that her tale was spoken in jest. She found it easier to keep those details to herself than to endure the skepticism of others.

Staying with my sister for a few days. ~R.

Molindra let out a guilty sigh of relief when she read Rubriel's brief note, realizing she would have the house to herself for a while. She went straight to bed to catch a few hours of sleep, after hiding behind a cart at closing time in order to spend the night alone in the library. The solitude had been welcome, if a little scary with nothing but old books and creaking floorboards for company.

The time had been well-spent, scouring the shelves by candlelight for any and all reference to Langlythe or its inhabitants. She found frustratingly little, other than mention of a second major pass between Langlythe and the Roof of the World, and speculation of numerous smaller, undocumented ones within the caves of the Gloaming Mountains.

Langlythe, she learned, reopened the Gloaming Pass only within the last couple of decades. The most recent map she could find went as far as a small village just beyond the mountainous entrance, then once again faded to obscurity. Vague details of a war some one hundred and sixty years ago also caught her attention, but it was unclear how it started or who was involved. She read of a great fire in Tunswick started by an army of mages, and shuddered to think of it.

It reminded her all too well of her accident. The lab explosion at the University of Celessil which got her expelled in her second year - the reason she remained unlicensed all these years later. It *was* an accident, though a foolish, preventable one; an experiment gone terribly, fatally wrong. Rubriel had stood by her then, even as her parents disowned her and the dean swore she would never set foot on campus again. They left Celessil together, inseparable ever since... until now. *No*, she thought. *I must do better. I will find a way to contribute more.*

The first few days of Winterfest flew by as she plunged into her research, growing ever more certain that Vesner's contract held the key to a better life. Rubriel had never allowed her to think of herself as a burden, but her heated words said otherwise and Mol loathed herself for it. What a wreck she had become! What manner of deranged fool must throw herself into a snowdrift at midwinter to avoid setting fire to the house, or hide in the library after hours to stay away from her best friend? She had fallen too far. It was time for a plan.

2
Happy New Year

Solstice brought brisk, clear skies, and a reprieve from the wind. A fresh blanket of snow lay thick over the ground, disturbed only by the bare frames of the maple trees along the river bank. The river itself had frozen at its edges some weeks ago.

Rubriel crouched amidst a tangled mass of winter vines, deftly picking fingerfuls of dark purple berries to fill the basket beside her. It was a task better suited to children, who would wriggle their way into hard to reach spots, no doubt stuffing as many berries into their mouths as into their baskets, but she wasn't in a position to say no to simple, harmless work which earned a few extra coins. What she lacked in flexibility she made up for in self-restraint, already onto her fourth basket. Besides, Mrs. Houte's winterberry pie was a local legend. It wouldn't do to spoil dessert.

She huffed into her cold hands, uncurled herself from the ground and stretched, before gathering up her baskets and trudging through the snow with them. Her borrowed horse waited in the shadow of a tree. She frowned. There was too much to carry. Two bundles of kindling, bound neatly with rope, waited to be taken back to town. A fair few extra twigs had lodged themselves in her hair and the hem of her skirt as well, she was sure.

The horse gave her a look that suggested he would really prefer not to have two bundles of kindling and four baskets of berries strapped to his back - but he let her, grudgingly. She spared him the awkwardness of carrying her as well and walked alongside the horse back the way they'd come, towards Tunswick's chimneys and peaked roofs.

Houses squished closer together the further they went, leaving narrow brick-lined alleys between the rows of stout dwellings. The town centre bustled, the tread of hooves and booted feet turning the snow to brown slush. People scurried this way and that, full of purpose and festive spirit now that Solstice night was upon them. She kept her horse on a short lead, murmuring reassuring words to him as he tossed his head nervously at the sight of the lamplighter's long pole reaching up to illuminate the street.

They passed under a small arch, into a side street which ran down behind the town hall, towards the back door into the kitchens. She took her bounty inside, hauling the kindling onto a pile in the corner of the stone cellar. The berries she brought up to the kitchens proper, where Mrs Houte weighed them eagerly and pressed a few coins into her palm for the trouble.

"Oh, I almost forgot!" Mrs. Houte trilled. "Here, a ticket to the celebration tonight. You deserve a slice of my famous pie." She winked.

Rubriel thanked her before returning the borrowed horse to his stable.

The sun had almost set as she made her way back to her sister's hotel, avoiding the attention of wellwishers and festive characters determined to spread cheer to anyone who would listen. She would be glad in another week, when Winterfest finally ended and things would go back to normal.

Would things go back to normal, though? She had not seen nor spoken to Molindra since that night and spent the customary week of year-end reflection trying her hardest *not* to think very much at all. What did she have to be especially thankful for? It stressed her, the sense of an *obligation* to be happy, and the impression that her lack of festive spirit served only to make her more of an outcast than she already was.

For my sister's sake, I will try, she promised herself. She knew what tonight's performance meant to Gwendolen.

Her sister sat by the window, tenderly tuning and polishing her violin with an almost dreamlike expression, lost in thought. She paused as she heard her sister enter the room.

"You're a bit late, Rubriel," she said, raising a brow.

"How can I be late? The festival goes on for another week yet!" Rubriel reminded her, leaning playfully on the edge of the simple wooden screen which divided the room in half.

"I thought you would be here for tea. No matter, I suppose." She set aside her violin and stood, looking Rubriel up and down. "You will change though, won't you? You look like you're wearing half a bush."

Rubriel burst out laughing. "Yes, yes—give me time! I've been busy. Collecting berries, gathering firewood..." Her expression turned mischievous. "The wood trolls were most unhelpful, you know! One of them dragged me several feet through the snow before I could convince him that fallen branches and kindling were all I was after."

Gwendolen rummaged through the wardrobe. "Wood trolls!" She snorted. "Honestly, Rubriel—you are much too old for such nonsense."

"Never!"

At last, she found what she had been looking for. "Ah, here we are—what do you think?"

She laid an exquisite evening gown upon the bed; royal blue silk, pleated with a short train at the back, a wide open v-neck trimmed with flowery white lace and a prominent artificial rose blooming on one shoulder.

"A little extravagant, don't you think?"

"Of course! I am singing the Anthem. It is an honour and I must dress accordingly." She grinned and returned to her violin. In a lilac tea gown with her unwound long black hair falling gracefully over one shoulder, she looked every bit the lady of leisure at the moment.

"Fair enough."

It was tradition for the Anthem of New Beginnings to be sung when the clock struck midnight. Each year, the city chose someone to perform the Anthem outside the city hall, welcoming the new year for an audience of thousands. Gwendolen's growing fame now afforded her the honour.

Rubriel ducked behind the screen to change, finding that she did indeed have many twigs and thorns stuck to the sleeve heads of her jacket. Her brown quilted skirt was damp all around the hem, with round wet patches on her knees where she'd knelt in the snow.

She grumbled to herself and flipped open her luggage, pulling out her own evening attire - the same modest sage ensemble she wore every year - and petticoats. Oh, how she hated petticoats! *Why wear three skirts when one will do?* She changed and stepped out from behind the screen, turning to check her work in the mirror.

The reflection looking back at her was a near opposite of her sister: shorter, strong and muscular, with her black hair coiled high on top of her head in a practical style held tightly in place with an excess of pins. Her smooth, unblemished skin was the colour of fresh cream, the lack of telltale fine lines giving her a more youthful appearance than her years demanded. Kind, silver-grey eyes glimmered beneath bold, expressive brows with a sparkle of sincerity.

She grimaced at the sight of herself in a gown. It made her feel conspicuous, vulnerable even, though of course that was silly; she would stand out far more by not at least attempting to dress like the other women, and she was more than capable of defending herself if she needed to.

"Would you like to borrow my cape for tonight? You will get cold when we head out for the fireworks."

"Thank you, but I will just wear my coat. I am not fond of capes. It is too hard to conceal my knife underneath."

Gwendolen laughed. "Rubriel, no respectable woman brings a *knife* to Solstice dinner! Whatever do you think is going to happen?"

"I am no respectable woman, Gwendolen. I am unmarried and childless; I work odd jobs to pay my own rent and put food on my own table. I live with another woman because no man will have me. *You* can break all the rules and get away with it because you're famous and talented and unreasonably beautiful, but I'm still making a living by doing the jobs no one else wants. And to answer your question, wherever men, merriment and vast amounts of alcohol meet, you never know what might happen. Experience has taught me it pays to be careful."

"You are very capable," Gwendolen said kindly, regretting her earlier comment. She stood behind her in the mirror and put her arms around Rubriel's waist. "I would never let you run short. You know that, don't you?"

"I know," she replied. "But Molindra is the only true friend I have. My prospects have never been great, but her situation is much worse. I will never really abandon her."

"And yet here you are. Are you two still fighting?"

"We haven't spoken."

Gwendolen gave her a knowing smile but said no more. Now wasn't the time to voice her disapproval over her choice of company.

Rubriel bid her sister good luck for her performance and crossed the street as darkness fell, making her way to the town hall alone. She fingered the single ticket in her pocket guiltily. Would Molindra make it downtown for the fireworks?

Her stomach churned and she felt the sudden urge to scream. This was a terrible way to start a new year. Sitting through Solstice dinner would be torture, but she could hardly pass up the opportunity for such a fine meal at no charge.

With a heavy sigh, she resolved to return to the house as soon as Anthem was over. Let her first act of the new year be one of apology.

Two guards nodded a greeting as she approached the massive oak doors of the town hall. They were bundled up, their woolen uniforms smartly tailored in navy blue. Each hung a decorative sword from his belt on one side and a pistol on the other. Rubriel doubted they knew how to use either weapon.

In that sense, Gwendolen was right: what was there for them to worry about tonight, besides the odd drunken reveller? They accepted her ticket and motioned for her to enter with a muttered, "Merry Solstice," as she passed, her skirt rustling stiffly.

Inside, a serving woman led Rubriel down the central aisle formed between the sea of tables and chairs. "How many people are in your group?" she asked with a cheerful smile.

"Just me," Rubriel replied, with a look that told the woman she didn't need any sympathy on account of being alone.

"Very well." The woman nodded. "Come this way, please."

She gestured for Rubriel to take a seat at a table on the far left of the room, where a number of other solo partygoers were already seated.

"Good evening!" a beaming, white-haired man called from across the circular table. "Welcome to the outcasts' table!" he said dramatically. Several people chuckled.

"So this is what they do with folks unfortunate enough to be attending alone—lump them all together at a table in the corner of the room and hope they get along." She laughed, taking her seat between a wiry gentleman on her right and the only other woman at the table, who wore bright turquoise and altogether too much makeup.

"Unfortunate, you say? Nay, I consider myself most fortunate indeed to be seated at this table. You never know who you'll meet. I've met some jolly good folk here over the years. Too bad I never met myself a wife, eh?" He chuckled again and took a deep gulp from his goblet. "The name's Benny. Miss, uh...?"

"Rubriel. Just Rubriel. Good evening to you."

"Good evening indeed," he echoed. Several others at the table nodded in polite greeting. "Where are you from?"

She gave a sly smile. "I've lived in and around these parts for twenty years, Benny. Whatever do you mean?" The feigned innocence of her pointed remark should've halted that line of questioning, but he didn't take the hint.

"But before that," he pressed. "Rubriel is not a Common name, and you gave no surname. Are you-"

"Yes," Rubriel interrupted. "I am from Celessil originally. And before you ask..." She reached under the pleated neckline of her bodice and lifted her glowing sildion pendant for them to see.

Benny stared open-mouthed until the woman next to her glared at him from under her dramatic kohl-lined lids. "That was rude!"

Rubriel waved her hand vaguely in dismissal and reached for the nearest water jug.

"You do not care for wine?" asked the man to her right.

"I do not."

"Henry Wilcox." He offered his hand.

Brash though he was, Benny was right about one thing. Rubriel heard such interesting tales from the unlikely mix of people seated at that table as the evening progressed.

Mr. Wilcox, she learned, made his living sourcing wild medicinal herbs for the Tunswick infirmary. He knew every species by leaf shape, colour and scent; as well as exactly where to find them in the wild and the best time of year to harvest them. The search took him to remote locations. He entertained everyone with a tale of rock climbing to pluck a herb which grows only on the cliff faces of the Gloaming Mountains, earning gasps when he revealed how he'd broken his leg in a fall and survived only thanks to the milestone he carried with him that day.

"What is a milestone?" Rubriel asked as he finished his tale.

"To all but the most discerning, it appears as a regular stone. However, a milestone is bound to a specific location and allows a person–plus anyone, or anything, they are holding–to be transported immediately to that location in a time of need. They are extremely expensive - as with anything involving mage services," he grumbled. "So unless you are especially wealthy, you reserve it for emergencies. It saved my life that day."

His tale earned murmurs of approval and respect from many at the table. Rubriel tucked away the information to share with Mol. Knowing her, she'd see making milestones as a business opportunity and dive headfirst into learning how to make them to sell on the grey market, adding to her long list of illegal ventures as an unlicensed mage.

You should not encourage her, Gwendolen would say. *You fill her head with crazy ideas, then complain when she gets you both in trouble!*

There were several good reasons why mages were the highest paid profession in the world. For one, magical talent was hereditary; either someone possessed the raw energy or they didn't. Like Molindra, most who did traced it back to Celessilian heritage.

Second, it took years upon years of study to refine that raw energy into something useful–and safe.

Third, due to the potential for misuse, the industry was heavily regulated, with a strict pathway to registration. At least, that was the Bantrian government's official reasoning behind the law. In reality, the exclusivity of magic had far more to do with capitalism than public safety.

Despite hailing from Celessil herself, Rubriel did not possess a single drop of raw energy in her veins, as far as she knew. One of the many qualities which made her an outlier in both her homeland and here in Bantria. She'd asked Gwendolen about her lack of raw energy once as a child - one of the few childhood memories she could recall with any clarity. Her elder sister had just smiled sweetly and reassured her that it would develop when she was much, much older. She was still waiting.

A bell clanged from upfront. Standing center stage, a twig of a man in a gaudy blue and purple suit cleared his throat.

"Good evening, ladies and gentlemen! Merry Solstice to you all. Please welcome your most generous host for this occasion, Mayor Graeme Soupe!" He bowed with a flourish and retreated to the side as the mayor of Tunswick took his place on the stage. Graeme Soupe was an aging, pompous sort of man with a thick grey beard. Tonight he wore a deep blue jacket and matching pants with gold buttons down the front of his overly tight waistcoat. A brooch bearing the Tunswick coat of arms—three stalks of wheat under a beaming sun—adorned the huge lapel. His deep, rich voice boomed as he addressed the audience.

"Good citizens of Tunswick, welcome to our Solstice celebration. Tonight, we bid yesteryear a fond farewell and open our hearts and minds to the birth of a new year and a new century; the year 1900!" He paused as the crowd cheered.

"Thank you for being with us tonight. In a few moments, the kitchens will deliver a most magnificent feast. We warmly invite you to load your plates and fill your goblets with the finest food and drink Tunswick has to offer. Don't be shy!" he boomed, earning laughs from a few people. "Of course, tonight would not be possible without our generous sponsor - Mr. Murdoch Vesner of the Merchant Guild!" He paused again, and Rubriel scowled.

Of course that man would use Winterfest to bolster his own reputation.

He dismissed the applause. "Thank you, thank you. Dinner will be served shortly. In the meantime, how about a cheer for the men and women who have worked so hard the past few weeks to bring Winterfest to life? Ladies and gentlemen, our provisioners, our decorators, our cooks, performers and stewards."

Rubriel's table and a few others scattered around the hall clapped enthusiastically. Others seemed slightly uncomfortable.

"We wish you all a very Happy Solstice. Please enjoy the evening. Thank you." The mayor concluded his speech with a gracious bow before disappearing through a side door. He and his family had their own private booth a level above with an aerial, unobstructed view of the stage.

With that, a team of servants carried in four enormous tables clothed in white. They arranged them lengthwise across the stage so that they spanned its entire width. A few moments later, the procession returned, each pushing a wooden trolley laden with serving dishes and platters, bottles, pots and tumblers, all covered.

With practiced efficiency, they unloaded their delicious cargo, setting the table in minutes. Half of them left with the trolleys. The remaining six, all dressed in white with alternating blue and purple aprons, took up positions behind the impressive banquet and began removing lids and covers. Steam and mouthwatering smells billowed into the air. Hungry murmurs and gasps ran through the crowd. The brightly clad announcer returned.

"Ladies and gentlemen, please rise and form a line on the left side." A sweeping gesture had them filing one by one onto the stage, where a smiling server invited each diner to take a warm china plate before moving on to choose from the amazing selection of hot foods.

"What may I get for you?" a serving girl chirped as she smiled politely at Rubriel.

Her eyes widened as she took in all that was on offer: three huge turkeys, each seasoned and stuffed a different way; a leg of lamb drizzled with mint sauce, baked potatoes wrapped in bacon and cheese, medleys of mixed green vegetables and carrots; jugs of rich, hearty gravy and a pot of ham and bacon soup.

"A generous helping of lamb, please," said Rubriel. "Some of each of the vegetables. And a little soup on the side. Don't forget the gravy!"

The announcer's voice rang out again. "Kindly return to your seats via the right side. Orderly, please."

It always amused Rubriel how structured these events were. They usually had several more of these processions, inviting people back for seconds and thirds at regular intervals until all the food disappeared.

Bantrian culture frowned upon wasting food, yet served it up in abundance at times like these, flaunting its agricultural wealth for all to see. Prime, fertile land stretched between Tunswick and Tabethwick to the northeast, its rolling hillscapes forming a belt below the Gloaming Mountains. Their crops were the envy of the Eastern Continent, their animals fatter and better bred than that of any other nation.

Rubriel ate modestly, though she did return on the final round to sample the winterberry pie. Her appetite was especially modest in comparison to Benny, whose third serving left him so full and so drunk he could hardly move.

After a couple of hours, all twelve servants returned to take away the empty crockery. They carried away the tables and swept and wiped the floor until no trace of the feast remained. The mayor once again took to the stage, beginning his customary long and somewhat tiresome speech reflecting on the trials and triumphs of the year gone by. A few people stifled yawns. Others absently swilled their glasses, waiting for him to finish and the *real* entertainment to start.

The gas lights dimmed as the mayor's speech ended. The sleepy crowd perked up as musicians took to the stage, led by Gwendolen, who perched elegantly on a stool at the forefront, while the others formed a semicircle behind. Her silken train tumbled to one side, looking truly resplendent as she rested the violin against her shoulder and lifted the bow. The room fell silent.

From the very first note, she entranced them. She began with a warm, sweet tune, stirring feelings of lightness and freedom. One by one, other instruments joined hers in perfect harmony, sweeping the whole room along on a merry journey. Hearts swelled with joy; happiness flowed unburdened and free as the tempo increased and people clapped along.

Rubriel couldn't help but smile as Gwendolen's gift captured the essence of the festival. Gracious, buoyant and feminine, she was the perfect lady–everything Rubriel wasn't. Sometimes she wondered how she could possibly be related to someone like that.

Still, Rubriel was not without her talents. It wasn't that she felt over-shadowed or jealous. No, Rubriel simply preferred to keep her skillset to herself. Hers weren't the type of skills she wanted to be famous for–indeed, she would prefer never to become famous at all, having witnessed the excess of attention and probing questions that followed her sister everywhere she went. Solstice Berry-Picker definitely wasn't a noteworthy title. Her intensely private self liked it that way.

3

A Damper on Potential

Molindra shivered as the rumble of applause filtered through the windows of the town hall to where she stood, huddled against the bricks. Pulling her hood further down over her ears, she made her way around the back of the courtyard and waited. Soon, partygoers would spill from the hall in a jumble of colours and laughter and wine, filling the cobbled space before her for the Anthem, and the fireworks. The first dazzling explosion was her cue to leave.

She breathed into her stiff hands and tried not to feel guilty, wishing she could conjure a small flame to warm herself. Remembering she couldn't do that in public served as a painful reminder of precisely why she had to go. Raw energy prickled uncomfortably under her skin, adding to her nerves, begging for release.

She briefly withdrew her last vial of damper drought from her pocket and scowled at the foul, herbal tonic under the streetlamp. *No. Never again.* She stuffed it away in disgust. Her raw energy was much too strong to smother like that. To *waste* like that. It had become a disease, making her twitchy and mentally unstable, when by rights she should be an elementalist in full bloom by now.

By law, unlicensed mages were prescribed damper drought twice daily to suppress raw energy and prevent the use of magic—intentional or otherwise. She'd stopped taking it three days ago; the day she made her decision to sign Vesner's contract. The dull slowness of the tonic had gradually faded, leaving her with a desperate desire to unleash the pent-up storm inside her, and a strange, almost giddy lightness. What might she do with her considerable gift, given the chance to practice and refine her craft?

Oh, the possibilities! Another shiver ran down her spine, this time in anticipation. She would grab her things as soon as the clock struck midnight, when the celebrations captivated all of Tunswick, and set out for the unknown.

She needed that reward. One way or another, she would get Vesner the information he wanted, and he would reward her with the means to get away from here - far, far away to Esmara, where she would study anew and live a life of true potential. She knew the substantial sum for Esmaran tuition would never be hers without substantial risk. In Rubriel's absence, she spent the last few days planning her journey north to the Gloaming Pass—and beyond.

She peered up at the clock tower. Another ten minutes. Keeping her head lowered, she leant against the wall with her hands in her pockets; a nobody, hoping to catch a few moments of cheer before the new year dragged her back into the cogs of daily life.

Rubriel was much better at this kind of thing, she thought with another pang of guilt. Her reputation preceded her. Stark, bleached hair gave her a distinct appearance, and she often caught wind of rumours and suspicion as she passed people in the street, each keeping a wary eye on what she'd get into next. It wasn't that her plan was illegal. Dangerous, probably. Foolhardy? Rubriel would surely think so. She swallowed, fearing that Rubriel may never forgive the manner of her departure, nor the long years spent trying to keep them afloat until now.

Cheers broke the silence as partygoers poured out of the town hall and into the courtyard at five to midnight, some skipping with excitement, some stumbling and bumping into one another. She squinted at the faces, desperate to catch sight of Rubriel and also desperately hoping not to. Could she really disappear without saying goodbye? After being near inseparable for years?

It is for the best, she reminded herself, over and over, but she couldn't tear herself away from the courtyard. She was tired of being a burden, tired of being whispered about and drowning her sorrows in drink and poor company. And she *was* a burden to Rubriel, however much her friend steadfastly insisted otherwise. A different side of her broke through that night, the bitter taste of resentment bubbling to the surface for the first time. It was time to take responsibility for her own future.

"Ladies and gentlemen, please join us in the courtyard for the birth of the New Year."

Mayor Soupe gestured for them all to rise and head outside. Standing, Rubriel stretched her spine and waited for the hall to empty ahead of her. Benny tripped over his own feet as their dinner companions ushered him from his seat, where he'd been snoring for the last half hour at least. Even Mr. Wilcox looked ready for bed.

She followed the throng outside into the chilly night and looked up at the stars. Clear skies, a scrumptious feast; her sister could not have asked for a better Solstice night to perform the Anthem. She mingled her way about halfway across the courtyard, then turned back to face the hall. A bright light shone from the balcony above, illuminating the mayor in his bright blue suit and the hourglass of white sand perched on the railing for all to see. Behind her, the clock tower's hands nudged towards midnight.

"Behold, the sand has nearly run out!" The mayor beamed, clearly enjoying the theatrics. "The Winter Solstice, and with it, the end of the 19th century, is upon us. I wish you all a bright and prosperous year ahead. Now, it is with great pleasure that I invite Gwendolen Starsinger to grace us with the Anthem of New Beginnings."

Gwendolen stepped into the light, taking his place. Under the stars, she looked even more resplendent than she had earlier. Her sildion pendant hung freely at her breast, bathing her in its dazzling moonlight. She raised a hand in silent greeting and stood, letting a hush sweep over the crowd in anticipation of that first perfect note. Rubriel wondered if she was nervous. Then she parted her lips and sang.

The Anthem began low and quiet, though somehow Gwendolen projected her voice right across the open air to capture them all. The words of the traditional melody melted hearts and opened minds until not a soul could shift their tear-brimmed eyes from her face. Her song swelled higher and higher as the notes poured from her, laced with power and emotion, building and building as she drew to the climax.

On that final high note which she held and held, the hourglass ran out, the clock tower chimed, and fireworks erupted from all around the central courtyard. People shouted and cheered and hugged one another as the bright lights soared into the air, greens and golds and blues raining down in a scintillating storm of colour.

"Happy New Year!" Gwendolen beamed, waving down at them with both pride and relief.

Molindra tore herself away from the scene. She had lingered too long and now she was crying. Swatting the tears from her cheek before they froze, she hurried away, disappearing down a side road towards the sleepy suburb where they lived. She saw no one as she half strode, half ran from the town centre, the revellers all too drunk or too in awe of the display to care as the fireworks continued to boom and burst around them.

Hinges creaked as she burst through the little picket front gate, puffing and fumbling in her pockets for the keys to the house. She cursed under her breath. Of course - *of course* - she'd managed to lock herself out.

Groaning, she ran around the side of the house to the kitchen window, running her fingers around the ice at the edges of the glass. There was nothing she could grab to pull. With a surreptitious glance over her shoulder, she gathered her raw energy. Maybe she could create an air current that would suck the window open? She held her hands as if to draw something towards her. The glass shattered.

Well, she supposed that was as good a solution as any. She scrambled through awkwardly, trying hard not to cut herself on the broken glass as she dropped one knee, then the other, onto the countertops of their tiny kitchen. Her footsteps crunched as she felt her way along the peeling wallpaper towards her bedroom. An overstuffed satchel sat on the bed-cover, filled with all supplies she could think of needing. She grabbed it and wrestled the straps over her shoulders.

In truth, she knew little about what to expect. She had never made such a journey before, alone and on foot, and what she would find beyond the Gloaming Pass was difficult to imagine. That was the point, after all. The Merchant Guildmaster made her objective clear enough; a full report on natural resources, supply and demand, major cities, trading hubs, transportation routes and climatic conditions. Extra points for obtaining samples or statistical data.

After signing the contract, she left with no specific instructions besides an unhelpful, incomplete map and a meagre advance for the purchase of supplies. It didn't sound that difficult; mostly just talking to people, observing and writing notes, yet Vesner gave her an entire year to return with her findings.

"Who's there?" Rubriel's voice rang out suddenly.

Molindra froze. Heart pounding, she thought frantically for something to say, some way to get through this without causing unnecessary pain. She came face to face with Rubriel in the short hallway, looking every bit as guilty as she felt.

"Mol?" Her knife was drawn, her brow furrowed with caution and surprise. "What is going on? I saw a broken window. Did someone..." She looked around, her confusion turning to fear as her keen eyes rested on the satchel. "We parted on a sour note last week. I... just wanted to tell you how sorry I am for the things I said, and to wish you Happy New Year." Her eyes searched Molindra's face. "What has happened?"

"I- I have to go. Sorry about the window," she added uselessly, her stomach flipping over and over.

"Go where? Mol, please don't go yet. We need to talk."

She gripped the doorframe to steady her nerves. "What more is there to say? You've had enough. So have I."

"That's not true." Her voice cracked.

"Well, you do not need to worry about me anymore," Mol said firmly. "It is time I went out and forged my own path."

Rubriel balked. "What? How?"

"I cannot live this life anymore, Rubriel! It's crushing me. I'm sorry." She pushed past her and out into the yard, before heartache could steal her courage.

"Wait." Rubriel ran after her. "Wait!"

She stopped and clenched her fists, her raw energy prickling all over again, tormenting her.

"Where are you going?"

Say it, Mol. Just say it. She raised her chin and swallowed. "I am going to Langlythe. To fulfil the Guildmaster's contract."

"What? No—no, we talked about this. That poster is a scam. We know next to nothing about that place, what dangers might be waiting."

"I know as much as anyone. I have studied as much as I could find." She bit her lip as a sob escaped her. "Rubriel, come with me," she burst out, not able to contain the thought any longer. "We should be doing this together. I am so much more than I've become living here. You are too and you know it. Leave with me tonight. Become a part of something bigger. Work that actually *means* something."

"You can't do this! Do you not think there must be a reason why we know so little about Langlythe? Why no Bantrians travel there?"

"If we succeed, the reward is beyond generous. It would pay my tuition in Esmara. I would finally be a true, licensed mage and leave behind all of this mess. Is that not worth some degree of risk?"

"Not if you die in the process!" Rubriel's exasperated tone raised her voice to an uncomfortable volume. "Vesner doesn't care about the people he hires. He is offering a small fortune in compensation because he doesn't think anyone will return to claim it! *Think,* Mol. Those posters are designed to manipulate us, preying on the desperate and the ambitious to recruit for an impossible task."

"And what does he get out of it if no one returns? Explain *that* to me!" Rubriel shook her head.

"Imagine if we were the *first,*" Molindra urged. "What if we succeeded in documenting what no one else has? We are not spies, or diplomats, or cartographers, but we work well together and we think outside of the obvious. That is our strength and we'll go far because of it."

Those heart-wrenching words stung with years of pain and frustration. A bitter dread grew in Rubriel's core.

"There has to be another way. I'm sorry for what I said. I will try to be more supportive, help you start your own business, like we talked about. The opportunity will come to you. Be patient. Please do not risk your life over this."

Mol's voice softened. "I am tired of being patient. I'm tired of waiting."

Anger began to simmer. She straightened, gripping the straps of her satchel. "This is no life. I've had enough of people treating me like a lost cause. Whispering about me like I'm some kind of diseased lunatic. Forcing me to take medication just so I'll be 'acceptable' to society!"

"Mol..." Rubriel spread her palms. "I know," she said sadly. "I understand-"

"No, you DON'T! You clearly don't! How could you know what it's like to live with this storm inside you, this constant battle to keep it in check? What it's like to be disowned by your family and carry a stigma everywhere you go? You have no raw energy. You barely even remember your childhood. Reputation means nothing to you!"

Rubriel gaped.

"But I know damn well what I am and who I should be. I am done letting people and money and petty rules hold me back. Nobody is going to stop me. Not even YOU!" The door slammed as she stormed for the gate.

"Molindra, wait!"

Rubriel chased after her. She made to grab her arm before Mol could close the gate behind her, but it burst into flames. She lurched backwards to avoid being singed by the sudden inferno that ripped into the old picket fence.

Molindra stood beyond, staring back at her friend with a mixture of anguish and disappointment.

"Molindra?" Rubriel called in disbelief, trapped in the front yard of her own house as the fence burned.

She turned her back and walked away.

"MOLINDRA!"

She did not look back.

Sobbing and dumbfounded, Rubriel could only stand and watch her disappear through the plumes of smoke.

"Fire! Fire! Quickly, bring water!"

The cries from down the street brought Rubriel back to the present. Suddenly realizing the danger, she rushed to help. Within minutes, five guardsmen arrived at the scene, hurling buckets of water to smother the flames.

"Ma'am? What happened?"

"An accident," she said numbly.

"Are you hurt?"

Someone I trusted just tore a piece out of my soul and vanished into the night. Yes, I'm hurt. She fumbled for words. "Thank you, for…" Her eyes darted around hopelessly. "For saving what's left of the fence, I suppose."

4

A Long Journey North

"**Y**ou intend to move out?"

Rubriel's landlord reacted with no small amount of surprise when she paid him an early morning visit on the first day of the new year and announced her intention to stop renting the cottage.

"I must leave Tunswick at once. It is a family emergency, of sorts."

His bushy moustache curved as he pursed his lips. "Well, it's not my business to pry, but I'll be needing to inspect for damages before you go in any case. I trust you will be in town for a couple of days yet? We are barely past Solstice!"

She winced a little, handing him a pouch containing twenty gold pieces - the sum total of her savings, withdrawn from the bank as soon as the first teller opened his window. "Here. This should cover my final rent payment and the repairs to the fence. I am sorry to cut this short, but I really must be going immediately."

"Repairs to the f-"

"Good day, sir," she said, already at the door. "Thank you for the use of this fine dwelling. It has been a pleasure doing business with you." A farewell nod, and she was down the stairs out of his office before he could say anything more.

Truthfully, he had been a fair landlord; forgiving of a late payment or two occasionally and glad to be of help when the roof leaked or the pipes burst. She had not been looking forward to that conversation and was glad to put it behind her. Her courage wouldn't hold indefinitely. She needed to be hot on Molindra's trail out of town before she had time to lose her nerve.

Next on her mental list was to pay Vesner a visit. *That greedy bastard had better be at work today,* she thought grimly. How she despised the man! Yet, her current predicament required her to feign civility long enough to get information out of him.

The business district was on the opposite side of town from where she lived. Turning her collar against the bitter wind, she followed the flow of traffic towards the river. Brown slush squished under her boots, a combination of manure and chimney soot. She darted between the parade of wagons as she crossed through the city centre at noon, its populace well awake now and bustling about, getting in each other's way.

At the stone arch marking the entrance to the business district, she paused to get her bearings. This part of town spanned much of the riverside, with a mixture of warehouses, factories, and large stately offices which served as headquarters for the various guilds that regulated trade, manufacturing, transport and other such functions. Barges clustered in the port. Somewhere in the distance, a whistle signalled a freight train's departure.

Thankfully, the northerly winds blew much of the factory smoke away from the city, and the air - though far from clean - was less unpleasant than it might have been. She grunted. This wasn't a part of town she enjoyed visiting, but it was also hard to avoid. Most of the lower-middle class came to work here.

She dimly remembered the years she spent working for one of the last remaining independent blacksmiths - and the only one willing to take on a female apprentice, even though she had more experience than her master. That was nearly two decades ago now. They mostly made garden tools, kitchen implements, boat knives and the like, but every so often a client would request a truly unique piece. Her master, well aware of her superior skill when it came to weaponry, would leave those to her.

He took all the credit, of course, but Rubriel's talent earned their business a reputation which kept it afloat for several more years until the mass production of everyday tools finally killed their profits for good.

She followed the road downstream, past the rail yard and the freight offices, and turned right into Rensworth Square. A blackened statue of Simon Rensworth, founder of The Trans-Bantrian Rail Company, stood watch over the guild halls as their architects attempted to outdo each other over the years. Each building became grander and more daring in its design than the one next to it.

Hall Three, the Merchant Guild, stuck out for its terracotta brick and tiling, constantly being scrubbed back to bright orange by a gang of street boys. They only worked as high as the second floor windows, however, which left an odd stripe of grey-brown dirt below the roofline.

Someone left the building as she approached, holding the door for her as she stepped between the thick, round columns flanking the entrance. Above the doors, a gold-inlaid placard read, "*Trade Never Sleeps ~ Guildmaster Murdoch Vesner, 1894*". She scoffed, earning a scowl from the bespectacled gentleman behind the front desk.

Inside, the vast hall was open to the public, where people chatted in groups and looked down from the mezzanine above. A pedestal and seating occupied the back of the room, an auctioneer's gavel resting in its place. Her boots clipped on the polished wood floors as she approached the front desk.

"The Guildmaster's office, please?"

"Guildmaster Vesner is not taking any appointments today," replied the man, his spectacles bobbing as he wrinkled his brow. "The earliest would be-" he scanned through his open appointment book "-the seventh."

"I cannot wait until the seventh. I really must speak to him today," she pressed, draping an arm confidently along the countertop. "This will not take long, I assure you."

"Miss, I am under strict instruction that the Guildmaster is not to be disturbed. I cannot let you in without an appointment."

She donned her most winning smile. "I have known Mr. Vesner for years, since long before he became Guildmaster. Five minutes; all I ask. I am sure he will not mind."

He sighed, frowning, before he reluctantly directed her upstairs to the back of the building.

She steeled herself, going over in her head what she needed to say without getting emotional or angry. Her knuckles were about to rap on the Guildmaster's door when she heard muffled voices and paused. Joking, laughter, glasses clinking–apparently Vesner had company. She tapped smartly on the wood.

"Yes, what is it?" came the impatient reply.

She took that as an invitation to enter, and found Vesner in the company of two other men, lounging in blue velvet chairs, each with a glass of liquor in hand. *Typical.*

"Who sent for you?" Vesner demanded, slurring his words ever so slightly. He reclined in the chair with his feet on the desk, his already rotund belly straining at the front of his gold-buttoned waistcoat as he puffed himself out even more in her presence.

"Pardon the interruption. I must speak with you," she told him as calmly as she could, ignoring his brusqueness and the sickly smell of alcohol mixed with polished wood.

"Well then? I'm all ears," he said with an arrogant smirk.

One of the others snickered, taking a sip.

Rubriel remained in the doorway. "It is about a contract. A reward poster you had displayed on the community notice board outside our local library. You seek explorers to bring you knowledge of Langlythe." She clenched her jaw, suppressing her annoyance.

Vesner's beady eyes roved up and down. He was a pig when he was sober, but when he was drunk... "And what makes you qualified and up for the task?"

"I have no interest in the contract. I do, however, know that a Celessilian woman signed up and left last night - alone. No escort, no instruction - nothing from you to ensure her safety or success."

He snorted.

She waited.

"And your point?"

"My *point*," Rubriel snarled, "is that my friend is in danger - thanks to you - and I need you to tell me where she's headed."

"Langlythe. Obviously." He gulped another mouthful of brandy.

"Not too bright, this one," chuckled one of his companions.

Vesner seemed about to dismiss her entirely, but his drunken gaze lingered on her breast and the loop of silver chain escaping between her buttons. He looked thoughtful for a moment, fingering his ginger beard.

"Open your jacket," he slurred.

"Excuse me?"

"Undo the buttons. I want to see your sildion pendant."

She declined, instead reaching under her collar and retrieving the glowing stone by its chain.

Vesner's companions looked disappointed, but his lips quirked into a half smile as he devoured the sight of it with lustful eagerness.

"I will tell you what I told her, provided you sign on as well." He withdrew a piece of paper from a desk drawer and pushed it across the table.

"Read it thoroughly. Sign it when you're done. I accept no responsibility for your safety. Compensation will be at my sole discretion upon your satisfactory performance." He rattled off the disclaimer with utter disinterest.

She scanned the contract, hoping for something to guide her towards Molindra's trail, but nothing of use stood out amidst the deluge of legalese.

"*Compensation shall be offered to the undersigned contractee upon their return, only in the event that the contractor deems their contribution full and satisfactory,*" she read, frowning. "Nowhere does it stipulate what manner of contribution is required. I will *not* sign this, but rather implore you to do right by those you have already contracted. Surely it is in your best interests to see them return, if you need information from Langlythe so badly."

"Heh," he grunted. "If they don't return, I've lost nothing. If they do, I'll have valuable knowledge with which to expand the merchant empire. A win either way." Another aggravating smirk.

Rubriel's eyes narrowed. "Who put you up to this?"

"Just what are you implying, woman?" quipped one of his companions, glaring at her over the rim of his glass.

"I know you, Vesner, and I smell a rat. What do you really get out of this?"

He breathed deeply, appearing to consider her question without quite meeting the intensity in those piercing silver eyes. "I do believe we are done here." His meaty hand slapped on the desk. "Good luck." He raised his glass in a gesture dripping with sarcasm. "Now, where were we..."

He turned pointedly away, diving once more into conversation with the other men.

She left without another word, fuming. What a waste of time! The sun was already sinking low in the sky, and would soon dash any hopes she had of being away before nightfall. In a foul mood, she jostled her way back to the house one last time, earning shouts from carriage drivers as she darted out in front of them and dirty looks from those she overtook on the pavement.

Rubriel always liked to be prepared. She kept her travelling essentials packed and ready all the time, just in case. Mol enjoyed teasing her about being ready to flee at a moment's notice, as if something terrible was always right around the corner. It only took her a few minutes to gather the supplies she needed. She swapped her skirts for a pair of thick woolen breeches, threading a leather belt through the loops and tucking the bottoms into her best pair of hunting boots, along with a small knife.

Persistence beckoned her from the bedroom wall. A fine sword, forged and shaped by her own hand, rested proudly in its scabbard above the bedhead. Waiting for her to have need of it.

Unlike the thin, curved rapiers favoured by the Tunswick guards, or the blunt, flexible instruments used in fencing, this was a solid, dependable blade, modelled after the famous swords of old and perfectly balanced for her reach and strength. She lifted it from its bracket almost reverently and strapped it to her belt, its weight strangely comforting where it rested against her leg.

She fastened a cloak across her breast, hitching it up over the voluminous sleeves of her jacket, and stepped outside; ignoring the peculiar looks she received from her neighbours as she strode towards the edge of town and set off along the north road.

Molindra brushed straw and bits of sawdust off her clothes and stretched. It had been an uncomfortable night, spent in a barn a mile or so north of Tunswick. Anxious to get away, she had covered the distance through the night, until the cold got too much and she had to find shelter. Farm buildings like this one were scattered throughout the countryside; it was a good distance away from the house and contained enough happily chewing cows to mask any sounds she might make.

She did not summon flame for fear of turning the whole structure to ash–it wouldn't be the first time–and instead curled herself into the straw with the blankets from her pack wrapped closely around her. Her sleep had been fitful, and now she was tired and sore. Now the sun had risen, she needed to press onward before the owners of this barn came to tend to their animals.

She headed in her best estimate of due north. She checked her compass for agreement, frowning that it seemed to be veering off towards the east most of the time rather than pointing directly north. The wintry countryside was both peaceful and unforgiving; quiet as a whisper to her ears but a bitter trial to her body as she waded through a foot of snow that showed no sign of melting any time soon.

Travelling along minor roads through the countryside, there were few landmarks besides the assortment of barns, silos, sheds and farmhouses, which all started to look the same. In the distance, the Gloaming Mountains formed a solid wall of rock at the boundary of the fertile plains, their upper halves shrouded in thick clouds. Whether her questionable compass agreed or not, that was her destination.

As the watery sun began to sink low in the sky, she came upon an old watchtower atop a slight rise. It was perhaps the height of four or five houses, a mostly wooden structure built over the top of the original stone base. A pointed roof covered the viewing platform at the top, which was otherwise exposed to the elements on all sides.

A handful of towers like this one were dotted across the plains, Molindra knew. Originally built to watch over the prized farmland of the Bantrian interior, now they housed a handful of families and served as a meeting spot for local farmers who came to trade with one another or settle disputes. Hopefully, she would find a proper bed for the night among them.

A cottage nestled in the snow at the tower's feet. Beside that, a larger two-storey building proclaimed itself the Watchful Inn. A warm, inviting glow emanated from the front windows, but the door was shut and didn't budge when she tried the handle. She knocked, hoping the only inn for miles around wasn't full. That would be just her luck. A bolt released and a pair of wrinkled eyes peered out at her.

"Good evening. What do you want?" He eyed her suspiciously.

"Good evening, sir. I would very much like to find a bed for the night, and a hot meal, if I may." She glanced around, uncertain. "This is an inn, yes?"

"You travel alone?" he asked with a frown.

Molindra looked at her feet. "Yes."

He studied her, seemingly about to shut the door in her face.

"Please," Molindra begged. "I will not cause you any trouble. It is freezing out here, and I have walked a long way to get this far."

He nodded reluctantly. "Well, it's no use you standing out in the cold. Come inside. Let's take a better look at you."

He was an older man, greying at the temples and weatherbeaten. Likely he'd lived out on the plains his whole life. "Are you hurt?" he asked.

"No."

Her skin prickling at the sudden warmth, she followed him into the small common room, where three other patrons occupied a table nearest the kitchens. Candles provided the only light, and the smells of smoke and cooking filled the dark yet cozy space. He led her to a chair by the hearth, where an open fire crackled and soothed her frozen bones. He disappeared into the kitchen and she heard him talking in hushed tones to his wife. She strained to hear more, but couldn't make out the words. What were they worried about?

"Thomas Buckle," he said, offering a brief handshake and sitting in the chair opposite hers. This is my wife, Martha. What should we call you?"

"Molindra. Just Molindra. I'm Celessilian."

"You are very far from home, dear," Mrs. Buckle said gently, offering her a bowl of hot soup. Molindra accepted it gratefully, smiling up into her round, weathered face.

"How awful for you to be out here by yourself." She leant closer. "Are you running away from home?"

"What?" Molindra paused with the spoon halfway to her lips. "No, no, nothing like that," she spluttered, suddenly realizing what they both assumed. "I'm headed north. For work."

The couple exchanged a glance at that. "And what manner of work would that be? We do not wish to be associated with anything illegal, if you take my meaning," Tom said. He looked ready to shoo her from the building. His wife laid a steadying hand on his arm.

"No," Mol replied. "I have been sent to Langlythe by the Merchant Guildmaster in search of information and trade opportunities."

By the expressions on both their faces, she immediately regretted revealing that much.

"Forgive my saying so, but you're either brave or insane to be doing that. That land is better left untouched."

Molindra frowned. "What do you mean?"

"Merchants enter through the Gloaming Pass every so often. They always get turned away at the first town, something to do with a stream they are forbidden to cross. It is a dark place; unnatural, haunted."

"Haunted?"

"Look, what I'm saying is others have tried before you and they come back frightened, and none the wiser but for vague warnings about the stream and the danger beyond it. I have a bad feeling about this. I'd stay well away if I were you."

She fell silent, thinking it over as she drank her soup. "What about other ways through the mountains? What if I were to bypass whatever happens in that village to turn people away, straight into unchartered territory?"

Tom sighed. "In theory, yes," he said, humouring her for the moment. "I know of one such pass to the northeast of here. It is a five-day journey, but it winds its way up and tunnels through to the other side. I have... seen movement up there in my youth, before I met Martha and settled here."

"Where does it lead?" Molindra pressed.

Tom shuddered. "I have not been all the way through. I once saw people on the mountainside—people who were not from our side of the ridge. I tried to follow them. The tunnel was dark and cold and confusing. I lost them and turned back. There was something unsettling about it."

"Thank you," Molindra reassured him. "I think this might be exactly what I need. The soup was delicious," she added to Martha, who exchanged another worried glance with her husband.

"I'll be taking the lads their meal now," she said, standing up. "You are welcome to stay for the night, though we do not have any spare rooms. We'll make you as comfortable as we can here by the fire for half the usual rate. I'm sure you'll feel better after a good night's sleep out of the cold." *And reconsider your next move,* were the words she didn't need to add.

"Mornings are wiser than evenings, as the saying goes," Tom agreed, as Mol fished in her purse for the money.

"How much?"

"Make it fifty silver."

She counted the coins into his palm while Martha returned with a bundle of blankets and a thin pillow.

But even as Molindra nestled into the warmth of the fire and drifted to sleep, she thought only of mountains and dark tunnels. And she wished, not for the first time, that Rubriel was here to discuss it with her.

Gilley's Market was relatively quiet today. In the springtime, the village north of Tunswick was literally a living market. The hive of stalls buzzed as farmers from miles around came to sell their harvest. Its cobbled streets would be thrumming with activity as buyers bargained for the best price on fresh seasonal produce. Merchants haggled. Coin purses rattled.

Rubriel had often found work at Gilley's Market in one form or another. Sometimes stallholders hired her to provide security at the busiest times of year; others she worked alongside the stallholders to fulfil a backlog of orders. She loved the upbeat atmosphere and energy of it, loved watching people and breathing in the wonderful fresh smells of fruits and vegetables, breads and cheeses.

Today, though, the array of goods was markedly different, with fewer patrons. Rubriel had never been to Gilley's in midwinter before. The stalls displayed tapestries and carvings, wool blankets and clothing, dried meats and preserves. She still found plenty of familiar faces. Stallholders caught her eye and waved at her approach as she made her way down the street, pausing to ask if anyone had seen Molindra pass through this way.

It would have been a logical place to obtain supplies for a long journey, she thought. She intended to do exactly that herself before moving on. The market took up most of the village. It *was* the village; the handful of dwellings and establishments existed for the sole convenience of those who came to trade.

It took a little over an hour for Rubriel to walk from one side to the other. Pleased as they were to see her, and she them, none of her acquaintances were able to provide any information about Molindra. They just hadn't seen her; not since last spring, they said. Unsure what to do next, Rubriel tried to focus on provisions for the road north. She distracted herself with a mental list, swallowing down the knot of guilt tightening in her throat. Food for the journey. A place to sleep for the night. Beyond that, who could say?

With her hands in her pockets, she wandered down the lane of open tents and heavily laden tables. A raven landed on the pointed peak of one and cawed at her noisily. She frowned at it, until a friendly voice caught her attention from the next tent.

"Hey hey! Good to see ya, Miss Rubriel!"

"You too, Dennis!" She beamed at the kind-faced baker, with his curly blonde hair tied back and his blue and white striped dusty apron. His was one of her favourite stalls at which to work a shift. "How's business?"

"Good, good! Folks are always hungry for bread." He clapped her on the shoulder. "Anything I can help you with?"

"Well, yes, actually." She hesitated, but Dennis was a good man and the closest she had to a friend in this village. They had been on first-name terms for years. "It's about Molindra. She is missing. I know she will head toward the mountains, but no one I ask has seen her since she left on Solstice night. I am worried about her. Very worried."

Dennis frowned and nodded thoughtfully. "If I knew something that might help you, I'd be the first to offer it, but I've not seen nor heard nothing."

She forced a smile through her grimace. "It's alright, but I need to stock up for the journey. I am going after her."

"What happened?"

Rubriel swallowed. "She and I... did not part on friendly terms." The anguish hidden behind her eyes said the rest.

"I'm sorry to hear that. You two looked practically inseparable all the years I've known you." He gave a sympathetic smile. "I know many folks thought her a troublemaker, but I saw something different. She had real spirit about her. Always seemed too big for us."

Rubriel stared out into the busy street and bit her lip, not really seeing it at all.

She nodded slowly. "Yes. Yes, she did."

The raven cawed again right above them, breaking her reverie.

"Shush!" she hissed at the ceiling. Dennis chuckled.

"Well, I'd be only too happy to provide all the food you need for your travels. Half price, just for you. Don't tell anyone, mind!"

"You are too kind. Thank you." She filled a bag with fresh bread and paid him.

"When you find Molindra, be sure to come back in the spring!" he called out as she left his tent and started towards the nearest inn. It was too late in the day now to resume her journey; she'd have to stay the night and make an early start in the morning. Crows descended in numbers now, pecking over the spoils of the market that littered the street, preening themselves on the peaks of awnings.

Guiltily, she remembered that she'd left without saying goodbye to her sister. Her suitcase was still in Gwendolen's hotel suite, having run home and spent the rest of the night preparing to go after Molindra. She shook herself. Nothing could be done about that now. She was tired and sad, and what she wanted more than anything was to relax at the inn with a mug of something hot and comforting before she slumped into whatever bed she could afford for the night.

Dawn brought with it the sounds of chatter and chores. Doors opened and closed in the hallway beyond her thin-walled room. She washed thoroughly, not knowing when the next opportunity for a bath would be. As she dressed, she mulled over the advice given to her by a merchant she'd encountered in the common room the night before.

Near to the border, you will find a village more like ours. Mornik lies just beyond the pass; I suggest you rest there and purchase what supplies you may. They are as close to welcoming as you will find in Langlythe. Still, keep a low profile. They will not like you crossing the stream. Adopt their manner of dress. Hide or discard anything that is not locally made. Speak only if you have to, for your accent will give you away. Ideally avoid towns, avoid caves, avoid venturing too far into the wilderness. Keep your sildion pendant covered. That jewel is like a beacon in the dark.

She hoped Molindra had received the same advice, though it was clear she had not come this way. She'd asked around enough; everyone insisted they had seen no one like her friend's description. Downstairs, she devoured a hot breakfast of eggs and thick, buttery toast. She ate fast, not wanting to waste any time. Molindra was three days ahead of her at most.

She paid the innkeeper and thanked him.

"I'd think you were mad heading to Langlythe at any time of year, but midwinter? You'll be lucky to have any feeling left in your toes by the time you reach the pass." He folded his arms.

"I'll keep that in mind." Rubriel shrugged.

He waved her off, muttering to himself. And as Rubriel reached for the door handle and glanced back at him, a strange sensation tingled at the back of her neck. As though she were about to cross a line; a fundamental line that would alter the future–alter *her*–in ways that could not be undone. For all her years, her life had been one of limitations and boundaries. *We are more than we've become, living here,* Molindra had said. Rubriel hoped she was right - for both their sakes.

She pulled her cloak tighter around her. Light, cold snow drifted through the air. What would the weather be like beyond the pass? North–surely it would be colder still to the north. Yet no one had mentioned any possibility of the Gloaming Pass being snowed in. Strange.

She had only a handful of information about her destination, and even less idea how she would pick up Molindra's trail when she arrived. She knew only that it would be dark and foreign and she'd have to be constantly on the alert. Her country upbringing in Celessil's woodlands would serve her well.

On impulse, she turned back and asked the innkeeper for pen and paper. She penned a quick note to her sister, begging forgiveness for her sudden departure and attempting to reassure her that all would be well in the fullness of time. She scarcely believed that, but it would do no good to have Gwendolen worry without the means to assist. Assured by the innkeeper that he would see her letter safely posted, she set off again at a brisk pace, eager to make up for lost time.

5

A Voice in the Dark

Somewhere inside a complex cave network deep within the Gloaming Mountains, Molindra was completely and utterly lost. She must've taken a wrong turn somewhere - or several. The dim light emitted from the smoldering tip of her makeshift torch hardly made an impact on the gloom, and every passage, every hollow, every rock looked the same. The air hung thick and stale, and carried no sound save for the grinding of Molindra's boots against the grit-covered floor. Stupid, so stupid to get lost.

Stick to the widest path, head upwards, not down, and don't turn unless it is the only option. That had been Mr. Buckle's advice when she pressed him for more information. She convinced him to provide directions to the cave of which he spoke, though no amount of cajoling would persuade him to accompany her. It seemed twists and turns in every direction were the only option most of the time, however—and the cave walls were so close together in parts that she was beginning to wonder if she'd found the right cave entrance to begin with.

Cursing to herself, she kept going, willing the torch to burn brighter. The flames responded to her, but she struggled to concentrate on keeping them burning while also trying to navigate. Why hadn't she thought to bring a gas lantern, like a sensible person? She tried lifting her sildion pendant out from under her neckline, but its white light was too small to reach very far, and only made it harder for her eyes to adjust to the dark.

Perhaps it was her imagination, but it seemed like the darkness was getting *thicker*, resisting her efforts to illuminate the way. She skidded on a loose stone, sending pebbles rolling downhill as she steadied herself. Down. Wasn't she supposed to be going up? Carefully, she trod a little further, wondering if she should abandon this path or keep going.

A damp, slimy rock made the decision for her. She didn't see the slippery surface until she was already sliding on her back down a steep slope, twisting sideways and tumbling through some unspeakable muck before landing in a shallow pool of filthy water. With a groan, she pushed herself up onto her knees and fumbled for the torch, extinguished now, wiping the muck off her face with the other hand. Filth clung to her sodden cloak. Her tailbone had slammed into the rock as she fell; she'd have an impressive bruise in the morning.

That's if she ever found her way out. Limping to her feet, she peered into the gloom, trying to make out where she was. The water, it seemed, remained shallow, and she only had to take a few sodden steps before clearing it.

A chill brushed past her. A breeze? Interesting. That would mean she was close to the surface. Encouraged, she made her way further away from the pool. She couldn't see far enough to know how large this chamber was, or where it might take her. The chill came again, stronger this time—enough to make the hairs on the back of her neck stand up. In the distance, she could've sworn she heard a faint whisper of air. She moved a little further... and froze.

She heard it before she felt it; the whispering grew into a steady hiss which got louder, closer—until a sudden chill wrapped roughly around her and sucked the breath from her lungs. A strange haze clouded her vision. She could see nothing—not even her own trembling hands as she tried to will the torch back to life. It was as if the darkness had become so thick that it pressed inwards, smothering her light source faster than she could produce it. The harder she tried, the more it resisted.

Her heart began to race. Something was very, very wrong in this place. Swallowing her panic, she turned one way, then the other, searching in vain for something, anything, which might help her get her bearings.

There was nothing to see, nothing to smell, nothing to feel, except… except that deathly chill which wrapped around her again, squashing her, freezing her to the core. She struggled to move, to break its hold, but the cold stiffened her bones and she couldn't shake it off.

Another wave hit, this time encircling her throat, choking her, hissing in her ear. She gasped for air, panicking and grasping at nothing. Spots bloomed before her eyes as she retreated deep within herself, trying desperately to focus on drawing up her raw energy. She spread her palms, willing the flames to spark between her clawed fingers, urging it to grow brighter.

The hissing turned to a screech as her fire swelled, pushing her unseen enemy back into the darkness. Sweat beaded on her forehead. She whirled around, letting the fire illuminate her surroundings as the warmth banished the stiffness from her bones. Coughing, she saw a huge chamber with high-ceilings, its walls ending somewhere far beyond her line of vision. Her muscles ached. She had to make a move before the flames drained her reserves, while they still offered her some protection. She dared not extinguish them.

Slowly, steadily, she placed one foot in front of the other, the need for haste at odds with the immense concentration required to keep the fire burning without fuel. Another hiss startled her. She braced herself, listening for its approach. Her panic willed her flames higher, throwing them forwards as the deathly chill swept in. There was a flash and a piercing screech as it recoiled from the fire, whooshing back into the darkness. Encouraged, but shaking with adrenaline, she drew more heat into her palms.

She could do this. She would make it. She began to move forward again, faster this time and ready to fend off another wave.

"Well done," said a voice in the dark.

Molindra stopped dead. "Who's there?" She whirled around, seeing no sign of the speaker.

No response. It grew darker, and she realized with a start that she'd let her flames drop.

"Let us try four, then." The voice echoed smoothly through the caverns, seeming to come from every direction at once.

Before Molindra had time to react, her invisible foe began sweeping in again, from both sides this time, threatening to crush her in its frigid malice. She felt it from the right first and met it with a handful of fire, lunging out of the way as another one came from the left. She spun and flung a thin stream of fire towards it, listening to the dying screech as the thing retreated. Four, that voice had said. Four what? What were these things?

They returned at her back, stronger, sharper this time. She turned and struck with both hands, a wave of light and heat chasing them away. Fire splashed in all directions, and she jumped backwards to avoid setting herself alight. Several small patches of flame lingered on the ground, burning without fuel, until her power drained from them and they went out.

"Potential," the voice in the dark murmured.

Apparently not at all concerned that she was fighting for her life. Indeed, it sounded rather amused.

"What *are* these things?" Molindra shouted.

"Gloom spirits," the voice replied silkily. "Now, eight!"

Fear turned to anger, and anger fuelled her power. She cast a sweeping, burning arc onto the ground, encircling herself with flame and light. Her focus shifted from her palms to the circle of fire around her, pouring into it as much energy as she could muster, until it rose into a solid wall. She could hear the spirits circling, hissing and spluttering their rage above the crackling flame. They couldn't reach her so long as her wall kept burning.

All at once, the spirits leapt. Her flames wavered as the rush of cold and darkness ripped past them, upward and out of reach. In the firelight, she saw them more clearly; formless shadows that writhed angrily against the ceiling. An otherworldly screech rattled her to the core as they swooped down towards her.

Blind and desperate, Molindra threw her circle skywards, spreading the flames haphazardly through the chamber. The spirits slammed into the fire, pressing, crushing with more force than their incorporeal state should allow. Her knees buckled under the strain. With a defiant yell, she threw the wall of fire outwards again, expanding rapidly in every direction and filling the entire chamber with light and searing heat. The spirits screamed and fled. She fell to her knees and plunged into darkness as her fire went out, exhausted.

"Enough!" she breathed. "What do you want?"

Shaking, she tried to rekindle the fire in her palm, but could only muster a few glowing embers. Years on damper drought had wrecked her stamina and control. Such a burst of exertion drained her in moments, leaving her with a feeling not unlike the aftereffects of a half-mile sprint.

Raw energy was a talent that had to be constantly honed and strengthened, a muscle that needed exercise lest it become stiff and unwilling. Frustrated and angry, Molindra fought back a fresh wave of panic. Her life now depended on the very skillset Bantrian law forbade her from practicing. If the gloom spirits came back again, she would not have the strength left to repel them.

"What do you want from me!?" she raged again, scanning the darkness for her leisurely tormentor, who remained invisible.

"You are an infant, playing with the power of an elder," said the voice in the dark. "Take this. Find me on the outside, and I may grant you what you seek."

There was a chink as some small object landed at Molindra's feet.

"If I knew how to get *outside* I would be well on my way!"

Her ears strained, but heard no further response. And Molindra got the impression, though she hadn't seen anything, that the owner of the voice had left.

She stooped, patting the ground for whatever it was that fell, until her fingertips touched something small and hard that sent a peculiar pulse of energy up her arm. She jerked away in surprise, bending down closer and this time using the fabric of her sleeve to pick it up.

It could've been a stone, except that it was *harder* than stone, *colder* than ice, and somehow *blacker* than the cave's unyielding darkness. A gem of some sort, then. By the strange, unnatural disturbance emanating from it, a powerful one. Though she didn't see how it would help, she pocketed it.

She managed to light her fire again, just enough to show her the way forward, and she ran for the far end of the chamber. Finding a small opening, she hoisted herself onto a ledge and scrambled up a steep, narrow path. The climb was awkward, and she dropped onto all fours for stability, making a terrible noise as she kicked loose stones tumbling down to the bottom.

No further spirits harassed her as she dragged herself to the top, panting heavily, and at last drew a glorious breath of fresh air. The way out. She followed the last passageway around a corner, then stopped in her tracks as the cave came to an end.

She stood on a rocky outcropping in the mountainside, mist hanging lightly over a vast, ashen landscape below. The lamplights of a small village gleamed in clusters in the distance. A starless night, empty but for the way the sky pulsed with a brilliant green light. It swirled and rolled overhead in graceful waves, arcing through the void, twisting and fading to black, only to rise again from beyond the horizon.

It had never occurred to Molindra that Langlythe was far enough north to see the northern lights, if that was indeed what they were. Something about the speed with which they danced through the sky didn't seem quite right. For a few minutes, the mysterious beauty of it bewitched her, calming her nerves after her narrow escape.

"Magnificent, is it not?" The voice from the cave returned, hollow yet powerful.

Molindra spun, startled, and froze.

The speaker took the form of a man, yet no living man could seem both solid and insubstantial, made of shadows with abyssal eyes like those that watched her now. He was cloaked and hooded in black, a silver mask jutting across his face where nose and cheekbones should have been. The metallic pattern extended down his collar and across his shoulders as a broad, heavy mantle. A coat of blood red flashed from beneath and fell right to the ground. He regarded her coolly.

"Who are you, wanderer?"

She found it unreasonably difficult to speak. "Molindra. Of… of Celessil."

"Just, 'Molindra'? Not, 'Elementalist?'"

"No." She grimaced.

"Why have you come to my lands." It wasn't so much a question as a demand. His gaze could have stripped her bare.

His lands...? Oh, this was bad. Instinct begged her to flee, but she stood on the edge of a sheer drop, the only way down being a steep and narrow path. She would have to talk her way out of this.

"My quest is exploratory," she said eventually. "I mean to study these lands. To–to understand them. I am not your enemy." She hesitated. "As far as I know."

"Do you think you would still be alive, if you were my enemy?" A smooth, idle challenge.

Molindra swallowed. "What–*who* are you? What do you want from me?" She could feel her power stirring again, energies tingling at her fingertips, though she doubted it would do her much good. *His* power was cold and deadly, like nothing she had encountered before. It rippled off him in waves.

"I am Zildred, Master of Imul'dene. I have ruled Langlythe unchallenged for nearly two hundred years."

She bowed hastily. "I didn't know... Of course. I mean no disrespect, or harm - I know very little of this place."

"That much is obvious," he chided. "Nevertheless, you are of Celessil, and may be of some value to me."

Mol bristled. There was a very intense pause.

"You will return with me to the capital," he decided, starting down the slope, his heavy cloak trailing behind him. He simply expected her to follow.

Free from his withering stare, Mol regained some of her composure. *I did not come this far to be ordered around,* she thought angrily.

Without taking any more time to properly consider, she leapt over the cliff, pulling up a strong upward draft to lessen her fall. She hit the ground harder than she would've liked, scrambling to her feet and turning to sprint in the direction of the village she'd seen from above. Out of nowhere, a hand grabbed her arm and yanked her back. She gasped in horror. Zildred's gloves were trimmed in polished steel; thin, intricately crafted plates shaped to mimic skeletal fingers. When he spoke, his words sliced directly into her thoughts. She winced painfully.

Your boldness brought you here, but you remain only because I will it. Do not run from me. I will find you with half a thought.

He released her and strode away, not looking back.

This time, Molindra reluctantly followed, trying to rub some sensation back into her arm and chase the shadows out of her mind. Her flesh was numb where he had touched her. She realized she was shaking, with cold and with a new kind of insecurity: an uncanny sense that her thoughts were not entirely safe in her own head. As she trod the dusty road that cut through a flat land of bare earth and rock, under a starless emerald sky, she couldn't help but wonder what on earth she was getting herself into.

6
Solemn Walls

The Gloaming Pass was not at all how Rubriel expected. The uphill slope was more gradual and the road much wider; she'd imagined a steep, narrow trail zigzagging between peaks. This was a carved path; a long, mostly straight canyon cutting right through from one side to the other, part natural, part man made. Great cliffs towered on either side, joining in a massive overhead arch in some places. The well-formed road was broad enough to be an arterial trade route, though she saw no one travelling this way but herself.

She understood now how the pass couldn't be snowed in. The cliffs and overhangs kept the road sheltered. Despite the long shadows cast by its imposing formations, the chill had lessened considerably. It was also getting darker - rapidly. Rubriel couldn't locate the sun to know whether nightfall was indeed approaching, or if Langlythe's perpetual darkness began abruptly at the border—and she was about to step over it. How long would it be before she saw the sun again?

Her insides squirmed a little at the thought, and she shoved it down. A tumble of questions replaced it. What kind of food could be grown in a land without sunlight? If there were plants, how would she learn which were safe and worthwhile to eat? What about grass—if there was no grass, surely there were no grazing animals either?

Curiosity and unease accompanied her right to the end of the pass, where the cliff walls opened out, providing a clear view of a heavy, starless sky. They swept downwards and flattened, leaving Rubriel suddenly feeling conspicuous as she crested the hill and saw the road descending into a valley transected by a great stone wall.

A concave, three-faced wall angled towards the bare rock face where the pass opened out. The earth had been deliberately cut and squared off to form a tight, impassable junction on either side. Its imposing presence would give even an army pause, but the iron gates stood wide open, and the wall - though clearly designed to host a military garrison in the past - was deserted.

Alert, she approached the gates, hand close to the hilt of *Persistence* as she listened into the forlorn stillness of the place for signs of life. She jumped at the sound of a hammer striking metal, peering around a pillar to find a small encampment on the other side. A handful of workers laboured over half-built foundations; others dug and ferried dirt in hand-drawn carts.

A supervisor barked an order every so often, in a language Rubriel could not understand. Their native tongue, she presumed. Of course! She should've expected Langlythe to have its own dialect, isolated as it was. Another potential complication.

A few pairs of cautious eyes looked up as she approached the work site, but never paused in their work. They remained focused and efficient; a coordinated unit under the watchful presence of their superior; solemn, dedicated. For some reason, that bothered her. It wasn't that she expected a welcome, nor had she expected outright hostility, but to receive no reaction at all felt strange. Then again, merchants did pass this way on occasion, like the trader who had told her about Mornik. Perhaps travellers were not so unusual after all.

She hurried onward, afraid to look back in case they changed their minds and ran to apprehend her. The road continued its descent into the valley. A damp chill of mist, mixed with the half light of dusk, made for limited visibility despite her above average night vision. The area on either side of the road was bland and bare–though she could make out a few spindly tree trunks here and there.

She longed to reach Mornik. Walking alone in this empty, barren place left her exposed and insecure. Each of her senses was on high alert. Ahead, the slim, leafless trees thickened into a tangled nest of branches and trunks. The road crumbled to nothing as she reached the wooded lowlands. The path forward was marked by a single standing lamp.

Rubriel paused to examine it. No ordinary lantern, this. It consisted of an upright pole with a forked basin at the top, holding a glowing crystal. Intrigued, she peered closer, noticing how the light held a faint golden hue. Its brightness held perfectly stable without flickering. Interesting. She guessed that a lamp such as this needed no gas or heat to keep alight. She hoped they lit the path all the way to Mornik.

Ahead, the trees were no more than fifteen feet tall and branched only at the top, giving the pathway a cramped, narrow feeling. Their blackened bark glistened with an oily green moss. Closely packed branches and sticks arranged in parallel formed a narrow walkway, wide enough for two to walk abreast at most. She pressed the pace, eager to get out of here. How far must she trek through this musty, oppressive forest before she reached the village?

She drank a few gulps from her canteen without stopping, briefly regretting that she hadn't made camp and rested within the relative safety of the Gloaming Pass. Still, the more ground she covered, the better her chances of finding Molindra sooner rather than later. What exactly she would say to her when she found her was another matter entirely.

She lost count of how many crystal lamps she passed. Her legs began to tire and she slowed, longing to sit down and rest. A variety of unseen creatures went about their lives within the thicket. She'd heard evidence of their presence; a rustle here, a twig snapping there. Whether any would threaten her if she came upon them, she didn't know. Instinctively, she felt it would be safest to keep on moving, even if her lead-weighted feet disagreed and the fog upon her mind thickened as she grew weary from her constant vigilance.

Just when she feared she would be forced to make camp after all, the chimneys and shallow roofs of Mornik loomed up ahead. Twin crystal lamps marked the simple gate into the village beyond. A sentry watched Rubriel's approach from a raised platform, assessing her over the pointed tips of the poles lashed together into a crude fence.

He cleared his throat. "Hold, traveller," he called down to her, his voice thickly accented. "Your name?"

"I am Rubriel. I am looking for a friend who I believe came this way recently."

The sentry leaned forward, resting his arms in the gaps between pole-points and crossing them in front. He eyed her curiously. "And your occupation?"

She sighed. "Factory worker, former blacksmith." She shrugged. "Solstice provisioner."

He raised a brow at the latter.

"For now, I am simply tired and hungry. I need a place to rest most of all. Will you allow me to enter the village?"

"You may pass," he said, waving an arm towards the gate. A second man whom Rubriel hadn't seen opened it from the inside. She inclined her head, unsure of the proper greeting. He returned the gesture stiffly.

She turned back to the sentry. On the inside, she could see him properly now, illuminated by the crystal lamp on his platform. His body language told her well enough that he didn't consider her a threat. He wore a long black overcoat, belted at the waist and parting below to reveal close fitting pants and tall leather boots underneath. A maroon collar stood tall up the back of his neck, curving around to join with the black mantle that squared his shoulders. His dark hair curled unkempt around his stubbled cheeks.

"My friend... she is about my height, green eyed with ash blonde hair. Have you seen a woman like that?" She may as well ask.

The sentry, however, wrinkled his face. "Blonde?"

"Oh," said Rubriel, taken aback. "Light coloured hair, not white, but the colour of straw."

"Never seen someone like that in my life."

Right. Perhaps they had no word for 'blonde' in their language, if all Langlythians are as dark-haired as those I have encountered thus far.

He must have caught her confused expression, because he cocked his head and asked, "You know nothing about these lands, do you?"

"No," she admitted, suddenly feeling very naïve. "I would be grateful for any knowledge you are willing to share with me."

"Wade, take my post," he ordered the man who had opened the gate. He was clothed in the same manner, but without the maroon collar.

The sentry bounded swiftly down from his platform. "Is a long, uneventful shift, and I am bored. Tinoti, Sentry of Mornik. Maybe we will entertain each other for a moment. Come." He waved his arm for her to follow.

Mornik stood on either side of a shallow stream, the two halves connected by a single narrow bridge constructed with the same thin, blackened planks as the fence surrounding the village. Huge frogs croaked in deep, throaty voices along the muddy banks. Simple cottages sheltered Mornik's human residents, arranged in groups, each with a shared central yard. Rubriel followed Tinoti into the township, such as it was. There were only a few people around, but one detail she noticed immediately: men and women dressed alike, in the same manner as Tinoti, grey or black without exception. She wondered why.

"We do not see many foreigners," Tinoti said. "Those who come usually do so only to trade for trinkets. They stay here, in this... visiting house." He gestured towards a two-storey building up ahead. "You may do the same."

"What manner of trinkets?"

His brow furrowed. "Aside from food, many strange things. Coloured stones, broken crystal lamps, sometimes a dagger or hunting knife. And always, they offer nothing but handfuls of gold or silver disks." He shrugged. "Why would we want those?"

"You mean coins? Money?" She grinned.

He grunted, not understanding and not wanting to.

She didn't push it. Instead, she regarded the 'visiting house' before them. It was nothing fancy, but it seemed maintained well enough, at least from the outside. Lights glowed from within.

"Go inside." Tinoti waved her off. "You will want to sleep, yes? Trade your trinkets and be on your way."

"I am not here for souvenirs," she replied, slightly irritated by his dismissal. "I intend to pass beyond Mornik. I must find my friend."

"Foreigners do not cross the stream," he snapped.

The sudden change of demeanour surprised her.

"You stay here, then you go."

She blinked, unsure how to respond, while he grew distracted by a creak from the front gate.

"I must return to my post."

She stared after him for a while, shaking her head before heading into Mornik's idea of a lodge, where an unmanned desk occupied most of the small entryway. Muffled sounds came from behind the door on her left. To her right was an open arch that led to a stairwell. A crystal lamp on a small iron stand illuminated a bell on the desktop. She was contemplating whether she should ring it when a woman bustled in from the adjacent room.

"Greetings." She peered up at Rubriel expectantly from behind the desk. She was very short. "Need something?"

"A room for the night, please."

"The night? How *long?*" The small, shrewish woman pointed over her shoulder to a clock hanging on the wall. Her voice was so heavily accented it took Rubriel a moment to register what she meant. She glanced up at the clock - and then looked again, for it made not the slightest bit of sense. Twenty-six numbers marked its dial, and the hands pointed to what she could only interpret as quarter to twenty-five.

"Erm, a full cycle?" she managed, gesturing to the clock with a circular motion.

The woman nodded. "You must write here." She lifted a leather-bound book and flipped it open, pointing to the first empty row. "Your name."

Rubriel took a pencil, then hesitated. Was it wise to leave a record of her passage? Not much she could do about it, she thought, and wrote, scanning up the list as she did so to check for Molindra's name. It wasn't there, of course; Tinoti had said that no one of her description had entered the town. He had no reason to lie...as far as she knew.

"Room five." The woman held up all five fingers on one hand and pointed to the stairs with the other.

Rubriel nodded her thanks.

The narrow staircase creaked awfully underfoot. Room five was at the end of the hall, the door left ajar. Inside, the room could almost pass as a lower class Bantrian hotel room, containing a single bed covered with a wool blanket, a table and two chairs, and a door which led to a small washroom. Another nonsensical clock shattered the brief illusion of normalcy. It was also completely dark. She slumped onto the bed, wincing as she sat on something hard–the key to the room. She grunted, going to the door and locking it.

Looking around again, she spotted a wall fixture beside the bed. A soft fabric tube that reminded her of a sock covered an iron bracket similar in style to the lamp on the front desk. She pinched the top and pulled it off, revealing a glowing crystal beneath. Its pale, straw-coloured light brightened the room, instantly making it more appealing. The bed cover was a soft cream-beige, matching the drapery that hung over the one small window in the back of the room.

At the foot of the bed was a chest of drawers; she took the last of the bread from her pack and stowed the bag inside for now. Chewing thoughtfully, she mulled over what she'd seen. Folk here were not exactly hostile, but there was something unsettling about the way they regarded her–or indeed, ignored her. Tinoti had seemed willing to help at first, if somewhat mockingly, but her intent to pass beyond Mornik had struck a nerve with the sentry and caused him to abandon her rather abruptly.

A long yawn reminded her of how badly she needed sleep. Pulling off her dust-caked boots and stripping down to her undergarments, she crawled under the blankets. She left her sword by the bed, within arm's reach. Then, as an afterthought, she reached up and stretched the sock back over the crystal lamp. Its glow faded, leaving her alone with her muddled thoughts and growing insecurity until tiredness overtook her.

Despite his threat, Zildred did not accompany Molindra all the way to Imul'dene. He left her at the crossroads just outside Ashpul and told her to climb the central plateau. That, she could see from here, was the glimmering light on the horizon to the northwest, a city built on a shelf of land that jutted out and towered above the level of its surroundings. It was perhaps half a day's journey.

How he intended to ensure she followed that path was not clear, but she assumed it had something to do with the many pale shades that had begun following her from a distance. They hovered like wisps of grey cloud, insubstantial and silent, yet alive - in so far as a spirit can be thought of as alive.

She took the left fork in the road, glancing back towards Ashpul and wondering if it would be safe to stop and rest. She hadn't eaten or slept since before she entered the caves. Her energy reserves had yet to recover from the fight, leaving her exposed out here and acutely aware of how vulnerable that made her. Instead, she ate what she could on the move, deciding that if she could make it as far as the start of the climb onto the plateau, she would rest there.

What am I doing!? The thought chilled her to the bone. She wasn't really going through with this... was she? Walking, all the way to the capital city of this strange land, and for what? *I may grant you what you seek,* Zildred had said, but what did he believe she wanted? More importantly, what did he want in return?

Molindra reasoned with herself that making an enemy of him would be most unwise, but every other instinct urged her to run as far away as possible. She flinched every time a spirit hovered too near, ducked at every shadow cast by the emerald lights.

The journey itself was hard going. She had already covered many miles, all day - or perhaps all night. The sky remained the same, and she had lost all concept of time. She pulled out her compass. It pointed due north now, as a compass should. Had she imagined it before, when it seemed to be veering eastwards?

Her weary self doubted everything now. She was no longer in control. It was disappointing to think that her whole life had been this way; a long trudge through the dark to meet the demands of someone else. Always someone with more power and respect in this world than she would ever have. Had she ever truly been free to make her own decisions?

Mud from the caves still caked on her boots, her knees—even her hair, which had partially pulled loose from its tight braids, bore a stiff coating of grime. Her cheeks reddened, even with no one around to see the state she was in. At home, the neighbours would roll their eyes and mutter about her under their breath, until Rubriel glared at them in that thoroughly disapproving way of hers that made people feel ten inches shorter.

She could almost feel Rubriel's disapproval on her as she walked, taking in how rapidly her plan had gone astray and raising an 'I-told-you-so' eyebrow before reassuring her that everything would be fine as long as they kept their heads down and kept on working. Molindra didn't believe that any more. Working harder kept them alive, but it wasn't a *life*.

Perhaps she could still salvage something out of this expedition. She did, after all, have an open invitation to Langlythe's capital city – somewhere she doubted any Bantrian had visited before. What better opportunity to gather the kind of information Vesner wanted to fulfil her contract?

7

Spirit of the Stream

R ubriel slept longer and deeper than intended. When she awoke, she nudged the drapes aside to find - much to her surprise - that it had come light. Partially, at least. Thick clouds with an unhealthy greenish appearance smothered the sky, but some light still filtered through, making it considerably brighter outside than when she arrived.

She went to the washroom and ran the tap over the basin. The water ran clear with no smell. It seemed normal enough, so she splashed a handful over her face. She dressed, mulling over the beginnings of a plan in her head.

First, she needed a meal and supplies for the road. That meant finding a market. Surely there must be one? Tinoti had mentioned foreigners trading for food. After his eagerness to point out just how little she knew, she fully intended to not only browse the market, but to observe closely. Watching how people do business can teach one a lot about a culture, and she was determined to learn more about them.

Feeling conspicuous, she left the lodgings and wandered the dingy village square, if one could call it that. This was nothing like the bustling, cheerful Gilley's Market she was familiar with. There were no stalls as such. Instead, a few tables positioned underneath the window ledges held various items, while the occupants leaned out of the windows trying to catch her eye.

The locals ignored this behaviour, heading for a specific building further up with the appearance of a small warehouse. She leant against a wall opposite, trying not to draw attention as she observed people come and go, entering through an arched doorway with empty boxes and returning with them full of goods. She wasn't close enough to identify the contents, but she did discern that the haul seemed very... uniform. Each person went in with the same size box and came out with the same items packed inside.

As much as her curious mind wanted to investigate further, the locals shooed her away when she attempted to follow them inside, telling her she had "no allocation," and pointing sternly back towards the visiting house and the dismal window-sellers. Reluctantly, she headed back for another look at their wares, having dismissed them earlier for offering nothing of any practical use - just trinkets, as Tinoti had said.

"Do you have any food?" she asked a startled woman with a window ledge full of broken crystal lamps.

The woman opened her mouth too wide and closed it again, surprised by the question, and pointed back to the visiting house.

"No." Rubriel shook her head. "Food for travel, not to eat here."

"What have you to trade?" she said, uncertain.

"I can pay you in coins-"

The woman huffed, and Rubriel changed tactics, realizing that wasn't the answer she wanted.

"Or I have this."

The woman's eyes lit up as Rubriel produced a mechanical pencil from her pocket. "Wait a moment," she said, disappearing from the window and returning with a small cloth bag. She studied the pencil more closely. "It is made in your lands?"

"Yes." Rubriel offered a smile, pleased to have read the situation correctly.

"I will trade you for this," she said, offering the bag for Rubriel to inspect. She peered inside, finding a staple food somewhere between peas and lentils; small, hard, yellowish grains of the kind that would lend itself well to soup. So long as she had water, fire - she could make a basic meal with these, though she would have to ration it to last more than a day or two.

She moved on, trying to ignore the suspicious and sometimes disdainful looks the locals threw her way as she dawdled. These people were uniform in both appearance and behaviour, and very purposeful. They didn't *window shop* like she was doing, nor could she hear much in the way of social conversation. They went about their business in a quiet, dignified way.

She must seem awfully indecisive to them. Lost, maybe. Loitering, even! Rubriel didn't feel threatened as such; just a strong sense that everyone would be much more relaxed if she left, almost as if she threatened their orderly, prescriptive ways.

She rolled her shoulders. So far, she had achieved very little, and there didn't seem to be anything else of use to trade here. She wandered further down the street but found nothing of interest - merely a few old homes that couldn't be more than one or two rooms each. No shops or craftsmen, no workers or industry of any description. Perhaps the true village centre was across the stream?

She headed towards the croaking frogs and the smell of wet earth, trying to find a clear vantage point to see how far the village extended on the other side. Movement caught her attention, and she paused to admire a particularly loud frog sitting by the murky water's edge. Huge, dark green and glistening like the moss from the trees, it swelled as large as her full hand span as its throat ballooned in and out.

Her stomach let out a growl of its own, and she found herself wondering what frog meat tasted like as she followed the stream down to the unimpressive bridge, slightly arched and made out of the same dull, blackish wood from the surrounding forest.

A sign right before the bridge issued a warning, in foreign words written with chalky white paint. Below it hung a second, smaller sign with the notice again in Common: *Do not interrupt stream.*

She chuckled to herself at the odd choice of wording. Why were the locals so protective of this stream? The shallow water barely maintained a current and held too much dirt and algae to be fit to drink. She didn't see what difference it would make if she disturbed the water.

"Can you not read?"

She whirled as Tinoti marched towards her, looking decidedly irritated.

"Of course I can read. I have done nothing wrong."

"Stay away from the stream. On this side only."

Rubriel couldn't hide her growing exasperation. "I'm afraid I cannot stay on this side. I must find my friend." A thought occurred to her. "If she did not pass this way, there must be a way around the stream. A way to avoid crossing it?"

"No!" he barked. "No going around, no crossing deeper into Langlythe. Is for your own good as well as ours."

"Can you at least explain why?"

He huffed, hesitating to respond. Whether from discomfort at revealing more, or lack of the right words, she couldn't tell. "It is the southmost spirit border. The Spirit of the Stream sees all who pass."

She blinked.

"You are naïve of our ways - and dangerous, I think. Take your rest-" he nodded towards the visiting house "-and begone from this place."

She had no choice but to take his advice. Her stomach growled and echoed her general ill temper, reminding her that the possibility of a meal at the inn might not be such a bad idea.

Thwarted for now, she investigated the ground floor of the visiting house, finding a mess hall with several long tables and a board indicating the next serving would be at thirteen o'clock. A glance at the *very* unreasonable clock behind the reception desk told her that was about thirty minutes away. She was beginning to doubt if there was anything reasonable at all in this mudhole of a town, who counted time in twenty-six hour days, didn't understand the concept of money, and were obsessed with protecting a supposedly haunted stream.

She sat down miserably at a table in the far corner, away from the gaze of distrustful eyes, keeping her chin lowered and missing Molindra something terrible. Oh, what she would have given to have Mol sitting at that table so they could figure this out together. Instead, she had a bowl of steaming mushy peas, headless charred morsels of small fish, and a mug of some strange smelling herbal tea, which she couldn't quite force herself to drink.

One thing was for certain: she had to cross deeper into Langlythe if she was to have any chance of finding Molindra, and to do that, she needed a disguise. Her dark hair and fair skin were not unlike theirs; perhaps with a change of clothes, she could pass for a local well enough to cross the bridge without their noticing. What was this *spirit,* though? If such a thing truly existed, would *it* recognize her through a disguise?

Feeling a little better for having eaten, she headed back out amongst the cluster of cottages, away from the market. A common pathway led to each entrance. They had small windows - if any - and no back doors. She spotted a more promising dwelling right at the back. A larger house, different from the rest, with a lean-to on one side covering a trapdoor.

Breaking and entering wasn't usually her style, but of all the crimes she could commit in her determination to cross the stream, it seemed the most harmless. The irony of it was not lost on her. Not even two weeks ago, she yelled at Mol for stealing her way out of a sticky situation. Still, she could think of no better option.

With a look over her shoulder to check no one was looking, she ducked under the roof and crouched to examine the hatch. She tugged and found it unlocked. Thrilled by her change in fortune, she lifted it higher and slid carefully into the opening, easing down the first few rungs of a ladder. It was dark, and she closed the trapdoor behind her to let her night vision take over.

Just a storage cellar, and an empty one at that, save for a few muffled rustlings that indicated the presence of mice. The far end, however, held exactly what she wanted: a stairway up into the house. She paused and listened hard to make sure the rooms above were unoccupied. The door above the stairs creaked open in a very uncomfortable way as she pushed through to the main interior of the dwelling.

It was not at all what she expected. Thin wood planks lined the walls, hung with thick drapery for insulation. Two large carpets covered most of the stone floor, each black with a rich burgundy emblem in the centre. The furnishings had a style all their own, favouring metal over wood and decorated with engraved patterns.

A side room held a single bed, well made up with warm covers. Inside a woven basket, she found the clothing she needed. She grabbed an overcoat and a pair of pants, and a plain black mantle like all the villagers seemed to wear. She quickly checked the contents of the drawers but found nothing of interest - certainly no weapons, or anything that resembled a map. She would have to try to conceal *Persistence* under her purloined clothing somehow. Doing her utmost to leave the house as she found it, she bounded back down into the cellar.

She felt safer in the dark, always had. Having such exquisite night vision gave her an edge in places where most would stumble blindly; she took comfort in being able to see those who could not see her. In the absence of raw energy, it was arguably the only remarkable quality she possessed, and she clung to it as a lifeline.

In the privacy of the cellar she changed into the black pants, which were too long but succeeded in covering her boots. The coat was surprisingly heavy, the thick fabric embossed with a subtle damask-like pattern. It touched the ground, but hung open below the level of her hips so as not to impede movement. The pointed sleeves covered the backs of her hands. With the buttons done up and the mantle over top, it completely hid her Bantrian clothing. She felt strange.

She stuffed the rest in her satchel. Yes, that was going to be a problem, too. She hastily looked around for something else, settling on a drawstring sack of about the right size. Shaking the dust from it, she emptied the contents of her own bag into it, then rolled up the empty bag itself and shoved that in too.

By now she had lingered long enough and it was time to get out of this basement before someone returned to the dwelling above. On the climb back up, she paused at the top to listen before she squeezed out through the hatch and stood, slinging the sack over her shoulder. She needed to look like she was on some mundane errand.

Someone spotted her. "*Lok avanh*? Stop!" a familiar voice said as a man strode towards her. It was Tinoti. "What were you doing in my cellar? Are you-"

He cut off as he recognized her. "Are you *stealing* from me? And after I bid you welcome?"

"Quite some welcome," Rubriel muttered. "Tinoti, I mean you no harm. I would gladly pay you for this," she reasoned, gesturing at her purloined clothing.

He ignored her. "Return what you stole at once!"

To her surprise, he also carried a sword beneath his coat, though his was a lightweight, less traditional form than her own.

"Surely a few items of clothing are not worth bloodshed," she said, one hand held up in a placating gesture while the other hovered near her own weapon.

"Not just clothing, is it? You mean to sneak across the water!"

"And you are duty-bound to stop me, that much I understand." She studied him, weighing her options. She could take him if she had to, but she had no desire to try to fight her way from one side of the village to the other if he raised the alarm. Were all the villagers similarly armed?

"Why, Tinoti? What is it that you fear? I already told you I mean no harm. I am simply passing through. Let me be on my way, and you will soon forget I was ever here."

"It is our sole purpose to prevent the likes of you from crossing deeper into Langlythe," he seethed. "Leave this place the way you came. Let it be known in the lands to the south that we do not tolerate trespassers. I will not warn you again."

"Very well." She sensed the stealing was of no consequence to him, as long as she disappeared. "I will leave without further trouble, but I'll not be undressing in front of you."

"*Cem,*" he scoffed. "If we ever see you in Mornik again, we will kill you on sight. Understood?"

She inclined her head in ascent. "You have my word."

He escorted her to the gate under tense silence. Folk scowled as they passed. He wrenched open the gate and all but shoved her through, watching her go from the frame of the open gateway.

He yelled at her back in his own language, and she kept walking, stopping only once she rounded a bend in the narrow path and was safely out of sight within the thicket of spindly trees.

If she couldn't go through Mornik, she would go around, hacking her way through the undergrowth if necessary. Surely there was another way? She waited, half expecting Tinoti to follow and ambush her. She was, after all, still wearing his clothing.

After a few minutes with no sign of him, she moved on, relying on her heightened senses to detect any sign of someone creeping up on her. Only the faint rustlings of creatures in the undergrowth reached her ears, the creak and sigh of branches densely intertwined.

She stepped off the path, wincing at the crunch of twigs snapping underfoot. It would be impossible to move quietly here. But, if she veered off the path, she could perhaps skirt around the outside of the village and cross the stream without them knowing. *To the Floor with subtlety*, she decided, and pushed her way into the scrub.

It was slow going. The ground was treacherous, abruptly giving way into mud holes that clung to her feet. More than once she disturbed a snake and watched its black tail disappear into the tangled mess of wood and leaf litter. She had no idea if they were poisonous - and no intention of putting it to the test. Eventually, the trees began to thin out. If she paused and listened, she could hear occasional sounds of human life from some distance away.

Altering her direction to keep the village to her right, she continued until she came to a clearing of sorts. The stream was just ahead, the trees mostly absent along its banks. It was narrower here than where the bridge crossed, and even more shallow. She could probably jump across without touching the water, if that helped.

Rubriel knew spirits were real. She'd read about them, heard the folk tales about haunted caves and the like, but she'd never actually seen one. They were considered bringers of ill health and misfortune, but they did not kill, as far as she was aware.

She sensed something. A sound? Perhaps just a feeling. It didn't matter. She tensed, listening, then whirled to the side just in time as Tinoti launched himself out of the bushes to tackle her. Twigs clutched at her where she fell. She tore herself from them to fend off his assault. They tussled in the scrub.

"Why won't... you just... leave?" he said through gritted teeth.

"What is... the spirit?" she demanded as she struggled for the upper hand. She managed to bring her knee up to kick him in the groin. With a moan, he rolled off her. She scrambled to her feet and drew her sword, pointing it at his throat. "Tell me the truth!"

"No!" He retreated until he found his back against a tree. There was fear in his eyes - fear and a hint of desperation.

"I do not want to hurt you, Tinoti," she said, following him. "But I will if I have to."

"You do not understand. The spirit is more than it seems. You will find only death in the lands beyond."

"You would kill me for trying to cross and yet you pretend you want to protect me?"

"You are not giving me a choice!"

"I don't care." She was so close to the stream, close enough to turn and leap across. Perhaps she could outrun him on the other side.

"You do not understand. I'm... not protecting you. I'm protecting myself." He swallowed, wincing at her sword tip still hovering below his jaw. "The spirit watches. They all do. The Master of Imul'dene sees all through their eyes. If - if I let you cross-" he squirmed uncomfortably "-he will kill me, and turn me into one of them."

At that, Rubriel pulled away, allowing him to sit up more. "All the more reason why I must find my friend. She sounded braver than she felt.

"If she truly went that way, she is most likely captured already-"

"-I have to try," Rubriel snapped.

"Then I must continue trying to stop you."

Their eyes locked for a moment.

Then she flipped her sword over in her hand and stabbed down through Tinoti's foot. He howled in pain and surprise.

"For what it's worth, you tried to stop me. It is not your fault I made it impossible for you to follow."

She turned and ran, sprinting to clear the stream in a flying leap, landing in a crouch. She pushed to her feet and lunged toward the trees. The whoosh and splash of water made her turn back.

A tall form hovered above the stream, dripping with malice. Water seemed to flow up through its hollow body and run down its sides, down its face. It stared at her, watery appendages lifting from the stream in a slow, threatening way; poised. She gaped over her shoulder as the spirit began to froth and boil. It hissed and bubbled. She ran.

To her horror, the spirit left the confines of the stream and chased as she tore through the slalom of spindly trees - trees that ostensibly squished much closer together now she was in a hurry. A snapped branch grazed her cheek. The spirit roared like a sea storm behind her, leaving a watery wake. It was gaining on her. She fled as fast as she could, half running, half climbing, hoping it was limited in how far it could stray.

She realized with a start that she was approaching the edge of the forest. The trees thinned out onto a wide open space. She spotted movement up ahead and skidded to a halt. Heart in mouth, she turned back.

The spirit drew nearer. She heard its gurgling, boiling wrath; she saw its watery form slipping between the trunks, closer and closer to the edge of the forest. As it reached the treeline, it melted away, soaked into the earth and disappeared.

She sank down in the grey-brown dirt and cupped her head in her hands, shaking. That had been much too close.

And this is only the outskirts... She couldn't help it; it was dread she felt now - dread and hopelessness. She wanted to scream at the absurdity of it, to scream at Molindra for overreacting as she always did and dragging her into a bigger and bigger mess.

She sat there for quite a while, hunched in the dirt at the edge of the forest. At least with the black clothing she'd stolen, against the dark earth, she would be difficult to spot. Perhaps that was why they all dressed alike. Slowly regaining a measure of courage, she looked up. She gasped at what she saw.

The sky, all swathes of emerald, rolled in silken folds overhead. They curled and intertwined, ebbing and blooming, flowing lazily across a sea of blackness. Every so often, an aurora cast a faint, shimmering emerald light across her face. She smiled, even as tears stung her eyelids at so beautiful a sight.

8

Durenka

Ten thousand steps. Turn in, loop back. Climb, climb. Look from the shelf. See.

The spirits' tormenting whispers did nothing to lessen the monotony of the climb, the burn in her calf muscles, and the misery in her heart as Molindra ascended the central plateau. The blackened stone staircase was the largest she had ever seen, not just long but wide - as wide as the farm cottages back on the snow-covered fertile plains she'd left behind only a few days prior.

Each carved step cut deep and low into the rock. Not a test of strength, but a trial of patience and endurance; one that actively sought to dent her resolve around every turn, where she faced a long line of stairs as high as the one she'd just climbed.

The stairway began its ascent straight towards the base of the great shelf of land, then turned to run parallel along its side before bending inwards and climbing back on itself within the underbelly of rock. Crystal lamps, Molindra deduced, hung from the walls of the tunnel on each side every twenty steps. She used them to pace herself. Every hundred steps, a massive square column split the staircase in two, set diagonally such that its four corners faced outwards.

Outside, the steps had been worn and dusty, but inside the stonework remained crisp, though equally deserted - apart from the five or six spirits that still followed. The confined space made them follow closer now, though they mostly floated behind; every so often one rushed past her whispering those same words on a phantom wind:

Ten thousand steps. Turn in, loop back. Climb, climb. Look from the shelf. Seeeeee...

They would loop around and swirl behind her as if herding her towards her destination. It was both irritating and unsettling. More than once, Molindra entertained herself with the idea of hurling fireballs at them, but this place was already well lit; unlike the gloom spirits of the Gloaming Mountains, these, apparently, did not fear light. Perhaps instead, she could blow them away with a breeze. Perhaps she would accidentally create a wind tunnel and crack her skull against the cave's next abrupt change in direction. What peculiar twist of fate had led her here?

At the base of yet another flight of stairs, she finally slumped against the wall, looking up in dismay. The spirits swarmed around her, hissing in warning. She tried to ignore them, but they pressed closer, seeming to solidify. They had her cornered. Their whispers became almost maddening, urging her forward, threatening. She was unsure if these spirits were as capable of hurting her as the gloom spirits had been, but she felt their cold forms buffeting her, trying to push her onwards.

She wasn't sure what made her do it. Her hand drifted into her pocket and grasped the object within - the cold obsidian-like gem she'd picked up in the caves. She'd all but forgotten about it until now. Her fingers clasped tightly around it in an almost involuntary motion; the cold bit into her palm, its power reverberating in her bones.

"I need - to catch - my breath. Leave me alone," she ordered.

And the spirits obeyed.

To her surprise, they retreated immediately at her command, seeming to fade as they slid backwards down the staircase, then stopped. Molindra quickly let go of the stone as a sudden jolt like lightning lanced up her arm. The spirits hesitated, seeming for a moment to be as confused as she was. Slowly, they began to reform and drift back towards her, though more cautious and subdued than before.

"Interesting."

She jumped, putting her back to the wall and leaving black soot marks where her fingers touched.

"I suggest you refrain from using abilities that do not belong to you," said Zildred.

How is it that he can just appear wherever I am? Mol thought in alarm. She noticed that on this occasion his form seemed rather indistinct, not unlike the spirits themselves. What *was* he?

She could've sworn he looked right to where the stone sat inside her pocket. Yet, even if he disapproved of her clutching it, he expressed no desire to take it back from her.

"What is this?" she asked instead, opting to hold the gem aloft and study it. No more than the length of her finger, it swallowed the light from the crystal lamps within its abyssal depths. Her arm tingled uncomfortably.

"Keep it hidden," he said, holding back the spirits that now clustered around him.

"*You* command these spirits. Is that why you left this stone for me to find? To make them vex me?"

He ignored her question. "There are three more flights. At the top, you shall find the gates of Minnorak. My men are expecting you, and will send you by wagon to Imul'dene."

"And why do I want to go there? Why should I do as you say? I see nothing in this for me." She readied fire to defend herself, but Zildred remained still.

His voice was calm; smooth and unhurried. "You possess a great deal of raw energy, but you are weak and poorly trained. You may prove yourself useful at the mage's academy. If you do not, I will... dispose of you."

A shiver ran down her spine. She could hear the hammering of her own heart.

"Climb the stairs," he commanded, and vanished.

If Mornik was a makeshift trading post, Ashpul was a rigid military compound. The difference was startling. Though not a large settlement, Ashpul consisted of four stone corner towers, square and solid, with rows of tents arranged neatly along either side of the main road. From there, the road curved to the north and split in two directions.

It was perhaps the most important crossroads in Langlythe, for the two roads travelled around opposite sides of the central plateau and its five volcanic peaks, north-west and north-east respectively for many hundreds of miles without any further intersections or connections between them, until they met, finally, in the three-tiered city of Imul'dene. Walls ran parallel to the road between Ashpul's towers, leaving only two possible approaches from the outside. The place had a decidedly unfriendly air.

Rubriel lay prone on the ground, observing from a distance across the vast, mostly flat expanse of land. It was dark permanently now, save for the brief flickers of emerald from overhead. She was again grateful for her night vision, though she beheld a disturbing sight. Spirits drifted restlessly up ahead. These were not like the spirit of the stream, but rather soft, indefinite shapes; like wisps of cloud given mostly human form. And there were hundreds of them.

Subtly, she studied them, trying to discern a pattern to their movements. Some drifted in groups of two or three; others alone. They were spread out, covering an expansive area around Ashpul's perimeter and along the road.

The Master of Imul'dene sees all through their eyes...

She now understood Tinoti's words. These spirits acted as sentinels. Why feed and equip human patrols for rotating shifts when the dead could watch tirelessly? It made sense, and she shuddered at the thought.

She glanced nervously behind her. Were they looking for her? She suddenly wished she'd put a lot more ground between her and the edge of the forest, the last place she'd been seen. She wouldn't be that hard to find, not with so many of them out here and nowhere to hide. Where was there to go, if not towards Ashpul? They didn't *need* to look for her. They could just wait, knowing that sooner or later, hunger and thirst would drive her towards the nearest settlement.

For all her urgency to move on, a moment of hopelessness seized her and struck her numb. She lay face down in the dirt and shivered. She couldn't help it. She was alone and frightened and she didn't know what to do. *What would Mol do?* Was she out here somewhere too, facing the same fears?

A light flickered in the distance. Looking up, she saw a small group of people making their way along the road, away from Ashpul. They each carried a lantern, a soft white glow illuminating their footfalls. A few of the spirits glided towards them and hovered either side in silent observation. The man who led them stopped and threw back his hood, holding up his lantern as a spirit approached closer, perhaps to speak with him. It seemed reasonable to assume they could.

A thought occurred to her as she watched. Even the spirits needed light to see clearly. Rubriel didn't. Molindra had tried to describe it to her on numerous occasions; how normal eyes could only just make out shapes in the darkness, how night could engulf and disorient her. Rubriel found it impossible to imagine a night without the many subtle shades of grey that she could discern as easily as daylight's true colours. It was, perhaps, the only magic she possessed. For now, she decided it would have to be enough.

She waited until the group had taken their lanterns far enough away, sweeping a few spirits along with them. Bravely, she stood. The nearest spirits were a few hundred feet away. *I can walk past them,* she thought firmly. *They will not see me. So long as the darkness remains, I will always see them first. I can do this. I will go around.*

She moved swiftly and quietly, the ground so dry and hard as to leave no trail. Maintaining roughly the same distance, she circled around Ashpul to the south. Fewer spirits drifted this way.

"Durenka!"

The shout carried. Rubriel crouched and waited. It looked like the same group from earlier. Apparently, they had also circled around, but in the opposite direction. Perhaps there were human patrols after all.

A woman ran towards them.

"Durenka! *Lok avanh?*" The man spread his arms, seeming irritated.

The woman called Durenka spoke, though Rubriel could not make out the words, foreign or otherwise. She looked to be apologizing.

The man scolded her in Langlythian and they carried on with their patrol.

Rubriel also moved on, following, but staying clear of, the road that led out of Ashpul to the north, towards the crossroads. The road was wide and well formed here, much like that of the Gloaming Pass; cobbled with edges marked by stone slabs. It crested a slight rise and split in opposite directions, continuing long and straight with no signposts to indicate how far to either destination.

Neither way looked any better than the other, but the eastern fork would, at least, take her further from Ashpul. In the absence of any clue to Molindra's whereabouts, she had nothing better on which to base her decision. She'd be glad to put that place behind her. She chose the right fork.

Rubriel, like any other civilized person, took weather patterns for grant-ed. Bantrians never failed to complain about the weather when it didn't suit their particular interests, which - now that she thought about it - was most of the time. How many times had she listened to chatter in the streets, cursing the cold and wet every winter, only to beg for rain a few months later when the summer sun scorched them to drought? The weather influenced everything from the neighbour's mood, to her daily routine, to outright survival with its constant shifting patterns.

Only now, in its complete absence, did she fully appreciate its impact.

Here, the weather did not pose an inconvenience, or a guiding force. The air possessed an unnatural stillness, and a dryness that made it feel emptier than air should be. There were no clouds in the sky to give rain, nor did the sun ever pierce the emerald-swathed darkness to provide light or warmth. The temperature barely changed. Counting the passage of hours or days proved impossible through simple observation. It was very, very wrong.

Wrong, like the rest of this situation, Rubriel thought bitterly. She lay flat on her back, arms folded across her lap, gazing up into what should've been a starry sky. Her lower half was covered by the thicker, but smaller, of the two blankets she had; the other served to cover the ground beneath her.

She'd lost track of how long and how far she'd walked from the crossroads. The barren landscape all looked the same, apart from a slight upward gradient. It had been hardly noticeable until she looked back and saw how the road sloped away into the distance. She kept off the road, of course, but she need not have bothered; it was deserted, like everything else in this miserable country.

The journey outlasted her food and water supplies. She had veered away from the road then, knowing that she wouldn't make it much further without finding sustenance. Eventually, she found a lake of sorts; small and shallow near the edge, but clean enough to drink. It also contained fish.

A walk around its perimeter revealed a discarded fishing net. She repaired it as best she could and threaded it between two sticks - she'd had to walk for hours to find those - and practiced snaring the lake-dwellers as they fed on whatever algal nourishment grew on the rocks. She did catch and eat the odd one, steeling herself as she gagged on its raw, slimy flesh. Collecting enough wood to start a cooking fire had proven impossible.

The dried peas brought from Mornik were not much better. They had to be soaked for a long time in cold water to soften them enough, by which time they were little more than a bland, gritty mush. It tasted disgusting.

Doubt gnawed at her. If Molindra came here for research, as her contract stipulated, would she not travel from town to town as Rubriel was doing? Had she found a way to bypass the Spirit of the Stream altogether? It seemed likely, given the absence of information about her in Mornik. If she came to Langlythe via another route, where would she go next?

Rubriel's confidence faltered. Could she even be certain Molindra made it to Langlythe at all? What if she changed her mind, and had been safely waiting at home all this time? Worry, along with the constant growling of her empty stomach, kept her awake despite her tiredness.

She saw him approach long before he spotted her; the man with the buckets. She rolled onto her side and watched him make his way around the far side of the lake. Checking fish traps, she realized belatedly.

Should she run? Her interactions with the locals thus far had proven unhelpful at best. Run where, though? She didn't know where she was. Her journey across the plains left her starving and miserable. She didn't have a plan anymore.

Unfortunately, she needed help. And so she let the man with the buckets find her. Two buckets he carried - one in each hand. That seemed rather optimistic.

"Ah," he said, noting first the sorry excuse for a net swaying in the water, his eyes glancing over the rest of the camp until they found Rubriel herself, still crouched on the blanket. "So it is you who stole my missing fish trap."

"And attempted to repair it," she said dryly, mimicking his accent the best she could.

He frowned. "Not from Andorlai," he guessed.

Her heart sank, though she didn't know where that was.

"A runaway?"

She said nothing, unsure how best to respond.

He shook his head. "No, do not answer. Seen that look before."

"Who are you?"

"Shavon," he replied, "Fisherman." He removed his hood and lowered the mask that covered his nose and mouth. She noticed the peculiar gesture he made with one hand, curling it upwards to press the side of his flattened palm to his chest as he introduced himself. "And you?"

She hesitated, opting to borrow the name from Ashpul. "Durenka. I am... lost," she admitted.

"To wander without reason is a dangerous thing." He moved closer, studying her with dark brown eyes. "By the look of you and your use of Common, I would guess you fled Minnorak, or perhaps Imul'dene itself. Whatever your reason, it is best left unspoken."

She started.

"Advice, though: do not keep running. You are not the first, nor will you be the last. Your time will be short if you continue to chase freedom. Go into town and get to work while you still can. Dissolve yourself into the grind until it seems you have always been part of it."

"Are they searching for me?" Her palms pressed into the dirt.

He shrugged. "Probably. Depends what you did, I suppose."

Her eyes narrowed. "Is there a reward?"

"What?"

"You are not just fishing. There is no way you get enough fish out of this lake to fill two buckets. You are looking for me, and pretending to be helpful so that I'll go back with you to wherever you came from and you can turn me in." She wasn't wanted for some crime, as he assumed, but if the spirits were looking for her...

He almost laughed. "A decent idea. Alas, I have never heard of you, nor seen your likeness posted anywhere in Andorlai." To her astonishment, he handed her a bucket. It was, in fact, nearly full. "Carry these, help me skin and fillet them. Next time, you also bring two buckets. Contrary to what you think, there are multiple lakes and more fish than I can collect alone. This way."

She stood and stared, dumbfounded, holding a bucket of fish with a blanket still tangled around her ankles. "I am supposed to just... trust you? And - and work for you?"

"You are doomed either way," he said matter-of-factly. "May as well have a decent meal first."

She looked down at the bucket of fish. Some were still twitching. "And what do you get out of this?"

He frowned as though that should've been obvious. "To fulfil my quota early and take a *waik* of rest."

She didn't understand what he meant by this, but couldn't ask more without giving herself away. "Alright," she said reluctantly. "But if I sense even one hint of a trap, I run."

He scoffed. "Do not worry. That large sword you carry has not escaped my notice."

She plodded after him. The heavy, awkward fish buckets made it difficult to walk with any haste. Carrying two would be easier than one, she decided, but it sounded like Shavon wanted her to be seen working for him. It was risky, but he was right - she would not get much further on her own. Convincingly playing the part of a local labourer could yield helpful information and, as he suggested, a decent meal.

They walked in silence, Shavon pausing only briefly now and then to let her catch up. She kept stopping to swap the bucket from one side to the other until both arms ached equally. The discomfort occupied her mind, away from darker thoughts. If Molindra had made it to Langlythe at all, she had disappeared without a trace. Rubriel didn't want to think about what that meant.

Andorlai came into view as they crested a rise. A larger settlement, well populated and structured with stone-lined streets and crystal lamp posts on every corner. Unlike Mornik, Andorlai was open and sprawling, much like the vast emptiness on which it was built. Shavon brought her to a yard dominated by four sturdy triangular structures. Each hung many rows of headless fish from its struts; the first stage of the drying process. Two figures worked on one of the frames, hanging a fresh batch of fish by their tails. Shavon surveyed them in passing.

"Another four frames dried, that should make eight by the tenth *yirst*; two buckets fresh, looking for another two and two by *waikevi*. Barely enough." He muttered as they walked, leading her to a long workbench in a corner of the yard that reeked of fish.

Rubriel couldn't help wrinkling her nose as he set down the bucket, handed her a knife, and began to use his own to remove head and tail and deftly separate fillet from bone. She watched him prepare the first couple in a matter of seconds, fascinated even if the smell made her queasy.

He shot her a sideways glance. Shrugging, she grabbed one of the slimy creatures from her own bucket and attempted to follow his movements. It was much harder than he made it look. The slippery skin slid out of her grip. She made slow and clumsy progress, finishing one fish for every five of his.

They worked in silence for a couple of hours. When the last of the fish had been filleted, he laid the meat onto a broad tray and told Rubriel to dump all the waste back into the buckets and clean the bench.

"What to do with the waste?" she asked, eager to be rid of the foul-smelling slop.

"Gut and bone is to be ground into fertilizer. Take it to the mill. That way," Shavon replied, pointing.

When she returned, he had gone and taken the fillets with him. She wandered between the drying racks, in varying stages of progress. How much fish did it take to feed a settlement this size? Her experience helping the festival caterers told her a great deal more than was currently hanging here to dry.

She found a tap to wash the slime from her hands and decided to poke around what she assumed was Shavon's residence, helping herself to some clean clothes (they were all the same; how would he know the difference?) and seating herself by the glowing coals in the hearth.

He scowled to return and see her sitting idle, but only said, "Come. The kitchens are not far," and withdrew again from the house.

They walked to a mess hall far larger than the pitiful Mornik visiting house, where the people of Andorlai gathered to dine on the fruits of their labour: platters of roasted fish, seasoned with salt and eaten alongside minted peas boiled until just soft. Rubriel was so hungry she could've eaten three times her share. It was simple food, but cooked so nicely and so comforting to an empty stomach.

She noticed with interest that the servers dished up exactly the same amount to every plate; sometimes a little less for the young or the elderly, but never more. With all the talk of allocations and quotas she'd heard so far, it seemed unwise to ask for seconds.

There were maybe fifty people in the hall between the two long tables, holding quiet, careful conversation in a mixture of native and common tongues. They spoke mostly of labour and production, equipment needing repairs, how long until the next supply train from the north. Rubriel listened to it all, piecing together as much as she could and trying to glean the meaning of the unfamiliar words from the context.

The subdued atmosphere struck her the most. A meal like this in Tunswick would've been a prime opportunity for gossip and small talk, especially once the ale began to flow and tongues loosened. The people of Andorlai, it seemed, favoured silence even in the company of others. Not that she minded; the less she had to talk, the less likely she was to slip up and break her cover.

Some unspoken signal had the hall emptying, and she followed Shavon back through the streets, hoping that he did in fact mean for her to sleep under his roof. Inside, he put her mind at rest when he tossed her two tightly rolled bundles.

"There is no spare bed, but I imagine my hearth will still be more to your liking than cold earth by the lakeshore." A rare smile warmed his stony expression.

"Thank you," she said, and meant it. Perhaps, if she could just stay here and regroup for a few days, she could pick up Molindra's trail and pursue her with renewed vigour.

"*Yirstevi*, we return to the lakes. Let us hope your filleting skills improve quickly in the next few *waik*."

9

Arrivals

FIFTEEN YEARS EARLIER

"Here it is, finished!" Molindra announced, springing up from the corner where she'd been occupied for quite some time. Her frazzled hair hung loose from her braids. Dust and soot smeared her clothes from the dirty workshop floor.

Rubriel looked up and wiped the sweat from her brow. "Where? What?"

Mol grinned playfully. "Behold, my masterpiece!" She extended her palm to reveal the item she had been working on.

Rubriel stared at it, frowning. "It's very small."

"It's a ring, silly. Look." Mol held up the metal trinket, twirling it so Rubriel could see. Two spirals curling in opposite directions, the thin - somewhat crudely shaped - metal slivers interlocking where they met. "I don't know how jewellers have the patience to do this all day. This small stuff is just so fiddly to work with."

"Agreed," said Rubriel, taking the ring and studying it up close. "I definitely admire the skill and detail jewellers put into their work, but I'm quite happy to leave them to it. Are you going to wear this, then?"

"We're both going to wear it. Here." Mol twisted the two spirals, separating them into two identical rings. She gave the other half back to Rubriel. "I enchanted them too, you know."

"You're not an enchantrist." Rubriel crossed her arms, puzzled. There *were* such mages in the West, she knew. They could trap energy inside objects, such that their contraptions could operate all on their own. Whatever Molindra had been doing on the floor, it definitely wasn't enchanting.

"One does not need magic to give an item a unique purpose." She grinned playfully and slid her half of the ring onto her finger.

"Very well. Do I want to know what you 'enchanted' them with?"

"A promise," she replied with a shrug.

Rubriel's face wrinkled. "That does not sound like a valid enchantment. Is it?"

"Maybe it is, maybe it isn't," Mol said, twirling a lock of hair mysteriously. "I guess we'll find out someday. What are *you* working on?" She nodded towards the glowing forge.

A sigh. "This."

"*Another* sword? You made three this month already! For yourself, that is." She watched as Rubriel stepped back and went through a series of experimental swings.

"I'm still not happy with it. I cannot seem to get the balance exactly how I want."

"You are a fine weaponsmith, Rubriel, but do you not think you might be trying a little too hard? I'm not convinced the perfect sword exists."

"I'm starting to agree with you."

"I admire your persistence. That might be a good name for it, if you ever finish a sword which meets your high standards."

Rubriel set the blade down on the bench, and Molindra bent over to study it closely. "You put a sharp edge on this and everything!" She ran her finger gingerly over the steel.

Rubriel shrugged. "You never know."

Mol laughed.

"I've always thought it was more about the fit; both what feels familiar and what suits your reach, strength and style of fighting. But then, what would I know? I'm not even a proper mage. I am quite literally here just to keep your forges burning and your troughs full of water. And even that is technically illegal."

Rubriel winced at her bitterness. "Do not say that. We are making good money here. We *will* get to Esmara someday." She held up her right hand and wiggled her ring finger. "I promise."

There are worse ways to earn your keep, Rubriel decided, than trap fishing. As the days - or *yirst,* as the locals said - went by, she found herself sliding into a kind of wholesome routine, the physical labour and repetition a soothing balm to her troubled mind. She and Shavon visited the lakes frequently and usually returned with four buckets' worth. They had set extra traps since her arrival, and she marvelled at just how bountiful the fish supply was. What would happen if they someday ran out?

They always prepared two buckets fresh for the mess hall, while the remaining two were added to the drying racks. A total of four buckets fresh per *yirst* and twelve frames dried every month was the quota shared between the full fishing group, which made more sense once Rubriel realized that a Langlythian month was only fourteen days long.

The concept of the quota was simple in essence: Imul'dene decided how much they had to produce. If they fulfilled it within the timeframe, the people's needs would be met. If they didn't... well, Rubriel didn't know exactly what would happen then, but the threat of falling short drew enough tension from the locals that she understood the consequences must be dire.

She also understood why Shavon had been so eager for her aid. There was no benefit to exceeding the quota, and with her help, the fishing group met theirs ahead of schedule. That meant downtime for all concerned. As long as the capital never learned they had an extra labourer, the quota would likely remain the same. Apparently, head counts didn't occur very often, and it wasn't uncommon to send a few people out of town on those occasions in the hope of having the bar set lower.

Fear of running short was a feeling she knew all too well, yet she found unexpected comfort in the sense of shared responsibility among these people. For once, she wasn't alone in her struggle to survive, and only now did she fully appreciate what a burden that had been. It was selfish, she knew—selfish that she might *enjoy* herself here, after begging Molindra not to go. The idea of venturing out again remained too overwhelming, and so she stayed in Andorlai and played her part ever more convincingly.

Often, she would volunteer to run errands for Shavon or the other fishermen, because it gave her an excuse to explore other sections of town. She kept quiet and focused so as not to attract undue attention, all the while listening keenly for as much knowledge as she could glean from those around her. She hoped in vain for word of someone matching Molindra's description, unsure what it was she hoped to hear.

The locals spoke in a bizarre mixture of native and common tongues that was hard to follow. The Langlythian language was harsh-sounding and direct, much like its culture. She inferred what she could from the context and gestures accompanying unfamiliar sounds, slowly piecing together a mental dictionary. Her own conversations she kept as short and as few as possible. It stressed her, measuring every word and speaking with such a distinctive accent, but she managed. Plenty of people in Andorlai never uttered a word.

She also learned to measure time as they do, since day and night were meaningless here; in one *yirst,* people slept twice, ate four meals, and worked two full *waik,* or work shifts. A year lasted twenty-four months, which she supposed made them roughly the same length as a year by any other calendar.

Gradually, she became aware of the supplies trickling down from the north. Stone slabs, barrels of gravel and cement arrived by wagon and piled up on the east side of town, where an area of land had been marked out and groomed as a future worksite. Beasts of burden drew an open cart of dark, knotted logs in from the west - off the central plateau, apparently. Rubriel learned that most of the wood supply came from there, as much of the plateau held cultivated forest nurtured by natural rainfall.

"For the growing house," Shavon told her when she asked him about the supplies. "Andorlai is centrally located near the crossroads, but unproductive. Our land is too barren, and completely dependent on the mages for rain. This town exists mostly to process resources obtained elsewhere. The growing house will create... conditions, that will enable us to grow our own crops."

Rubriel was fascinated. "You will be able to grow food inside this... structure?" She thought the concept resembled a greenhouse, but without sunlight, she could not begin to guess how it might work. Light from the crystal lanterns - *celairs*, as the locals called them - was surely insufficient to grow crops.

"Indeed, so they say. Will be the first of its kind."

Does it truly never rain here? she thought, amazed. *Do they really get all their food brought in from elsewhere, apart from the fish we catch and dry every day? What a strange feeling, to be at the mercy of others for something as vital as water and basic food supplies.*

Her mind rippled with a hundred other questions, which she kept to herself, but continued to mull over as she worked. Her filleting skills had indeed improved; she no longer had to concentrate over every stroke of the knife, leaving her thoughts free to speculate about this strange new world.

The first of the overseers arrived a short while later, their deep maroon mantles and crisp authority instantly catching the grey town's attention - and obedience. They visited each section in turn, calling muster outdoors for what could only be described as a mass reshuffling of duties. Those deemed best suited to the new task were pulled from their regular routine and sent to begin construction, leaving the rest behind to continue to meet their quotas.

No one, it seemed, was exempt. Even children were put to work one way or another, be it simple tasks such as counting nails, or to replace grown men and women in the kitchens or tailors, whose strong arms were better utilized elsewhere. If this frightened them, they did not show it.

Rubriel, much to Shavon's dismay, was among those sent to the new worksite. Already he'd grown too comfortable with her aid. Back at the house, he muttered his distaste for how much harder they would all have to work to make quota now they were so many hands short.

"Perhaps the build will go quickly," she said, "and you will not be without us for too long."

Of course, I did not mean to say "us", she thought later, finding herself mixing and pouring mortar and cement amidst a frenzy of activity. *I cannot possibly stay that long.*

She reminded herself, again and again, that Durenka wasn't *real*, that her life here was a lie waiting to be discovered. She was only passing through, looking for a friend who may or may not wish to be found. And yet, it was so much easier to focus only on the packing of bricks and mortar, the tools in her hands and the structure slowly taking shape.

In that much, at least, she felt she understood these people. Shavon complained quietly to her alone, but they were just words - he would never voice those feelings publicly, nor take any action to provoke change or disruption, for that was not the Langlythian way. They didn't wish for things they could not have.

The wagon ride was incredibly boring. Molindra shared the vehicle in which she travelled north - little more than a box on wheels - with many sacks of coal. This left her with a corner space just big enough to kneel on the floor and peer out through a broken board.

Other wagons accompanied hers, each pulled by a heavy beast with thickset horns curved forward towards its bovine snout. On the back of the nearest beast, she caught a glimpse of the rider controlling it. He - or she - it was hard to tell - sat sideways on a raised saddle, holding the thick ropes of the beast's harness.

Strong animals indeed, to carry both wagon and rider up an incline as steep as this. For steep it was; the road wound ever higher and higher, snaking its way up into a mountain range of triangular black peaks, bereft of plant life or snow. The latter she found strange. They were certainly high enough - and cold enough - to be under permanent snow cover. Instead, the rocks glistened, damp, or perhaps frozen with a thin coating of dry ice. Emerald reflections played upon them.

She bumped and jostled miserably in the small space, her legs stiff and cramped after many days of walking. How much longer before the wagon rolled to a stop? She longed to get out and stretch.

In her mind, she ran through a hundred possibilities of what awaited her in Imul'dene, none of them good. She wasn't a prisoner - not exactly; her escort did not treat her as such. Nor could she leave of her own choosing. The wagon door was barred while they were moving, else the coal would tumble out on the steep incline, and hers was in the centre of the group, surrounded on all sides.

There had been no sign of Zildred since their encounter on the stairway to Minnorak, but she was quite certain she would see him when she arrived in Imul'dene. She had something he needed - or he *thought* she did - but what? Several times during the journey, she'd taken the dark stone out for another look, then hurriedly put it away again. Something about it made her extremely uncomfortable.

The terrain began to flatten and the road widened. Peering out, Molindra saw a high wall that spanned the gap between the rock faces on either side. A wrought iron gate stood open, broad enough for several beasts to pass through abreast. Inside, they stopped and unhitched the wagons; the contents efficiently unloaded and counted. She jumped as one of the riders unbolted the door of her own wagon. He jerked his head to indicate she should climb out. Stiffly, she crawled from the space and flexed her sore muscles.

The lower level of the city rolled out long and narrow before her, the rough buildings to her left stacked one on top of the other up the side of a cliff, closely packed together. To her right, it opened out a little more with the buildings mostly at ground level, then ended abruptly in a long iron railing which provided the only barrier between the slum-like dwellings and the sheer drop below. Thin streamlets ran beneath and plunged over the edge into a depthless fog. Crystal lamps lit either side of the road with their pale light, each fixed atop a thin stone pillar.

Her escort followed that widest of roads, leading her deeper into the city, past a deep canyon in the rock. The cliff face split part way down the middle, each half peeled back to make way for the waterfall which tumbled into the pool at its base. They paused at a corner in the road, where a branch angled upwards and climbed towards the water's source.

Another man, hard-faced, stiff-mannered and clothed head to toe in deep maroon, met them part way up. Her escort handed her over without a word, and her new companion took her even further up, into the Middle Tiers of the city. While the Lower Tiers had been dishevelled yet functional, the Middle Tiers had the look of a much larger city that had been forced against its nature to occupy a series of canyons and grudgingly gone about it in the most space-efficient way possible.

Built in layers, each structure was partially set into the rock, a complex network of stairs, bridges and mechanical lifts joining one house to the next and each row to the one opposite. The vertical arrangement gave it an overcrowded, yet organized, feeling. Molindra's tired legs screamed in protest as they climbed higher still. She almost immediately lost track of the route they took, worrying that it would be next to impossible to navigate her way down again on her own with any kind of urgency.

They followed a metal walkway to a square platform at its end, suspended from above by a sturdy cable and pulley system. She couldn't see much of how the platform operated, but it began to lift almost immediately as they stepped onto it, up the remainder of the sheer cliff and out of the canyon.

The platform jerked to a stop as it reached the enclosed upper landing, where she was again handed off to a new guide - a woman in brilliant red. A heavy gold mantle covered her shoulders in intricate, almost lace-like metalwork, and a deep ruby medallion hung above her breast. Mol knew straight away that she was mage - likely a high ranking one at that.

"Molindra, I assume?"

Mol opened her mouth, then shut it again when her Middle Tiers escort answered from behind. The mage hadn't been addressing her at all.

"Elementalist, and Celessilian. To be taken to the academy for evaluation."

"I am well aware," the woman said curtly. "You are dismissed." She frowned at Mol with intense disapproval before turning on her heel. Mol followed her wordlessly outside.

The High Tiers of Imul'dene took her breath away.

The heart of the city had the luxury of an expanse of flat land which ran alongside its mountainous backdrop. Glacial falls cut neatly down from a crater lake somewhere deep in the ranges, flowing cold and crisp beneath two stone bridges that joined east to west. Sparsely snow-covered peaks pierced the emerald sky. Mol hadn't realized just how high up they were until now.

Heavyset, angular buildings straddled both sides of the river, each one tall enough to house at least six floors or more. They increased further and further in height the deeper into the city they went, such that each rooftop would provide an unobstructed view of all those below it. Figures in varying shades of red moved to and fro on the roofs, seemingly unfazed by the height. Spirits surveyed the streets, clinging to whatever protrusions they could find.

Right at the end of the long cobblestone road stood what Mol instantly deemed to be the most intimidating citadel in existence. Semicircular stairs knelt before its base. Perched arrogantly above all the rest, its single central spire was the tallest of them all - absurdly so.

They turned off that path however, instead taking a different road further east into a walled off complex that distinguished itself as the mage's academy. Front and centre, a courtyard held a menacing statue of a giant bat in the middle of a stone basin that looked like it should have been a fountain, but wasn't. The ring of tall, turreted buildings of varying heights was clearly arranged in three distinct sections, representing different divisions.

She guessed the one on the right belonged to the healing science, given the plaque fashioned after a human heart that hung above the entrance.

The one on the left was less obvious at first, until she spotted two mages who appeared to be sparring without any weapons. They were kinetics, hurling stones at one another without touching them - an extremely rare type of raw energy that Mol had only read about.

Her guide bypassed both of these and took her to the largest building directly ahead. She stepped inside an assembly hall with smooth, polished floors. Rivulets of water ran down grooves in the walls, collecting in some unseen reservoir underneath. They crossed the room into the corridor beyond, taking the first door on the right and descending a spiral staircase below ground.

The mage lit the way with a small flame in her palm, which she extinguished when they reached the bottom. There were no crystal lamps here. Mol squinted into the darkness. Before she could begin to make sense of her surroundings, the mage shoved her forward onto her knees. There was a thud and a grinding sound behind her.

"Argh! What...?"

No response.

She turned and realized she was alone, though she couldn't see anything at all. Focusing, she gathered fire into her hand, the way the other mage had, although Mol's was unsteady in its intensity. With the flame held aloft, she found a bland chamber, empty of everything - including a way out.

That's impossible, Mol thought rationally. *It's just hidden.*

She went back to the side where she had entered and ran her fingers carefully over the stone slabs, feeling for any irregularity or crack that would indicate a concealed door. She searched every inch of the wall and found nothing, then started on the wall at the other end in case she'd got disoriented and chosen the wrong wall. Nothing at that end either.

Starting to panic, she lashed at the wall with a burst of fire. This was an elementalist's tower; perhaps this chamber would respond to the elements? Her blast glanced harmlessly off the stone. She tried air next, pushing and pulling on the current to try to sense a draft passing under or around a blocked exit. She even tried to produce water. Elementalists could learn to condense moisture out of the air into a sizable amount of pure water, but she had never mastered the technique. The most she ever got was a few drops, and it hardly seemed worth the amount of effort.

She knew she overused fire, but it came most naturally to her and responded to her emotions. Anger fuelled her now as she blasted the walls again and again. She even tested the floor and ceiling for some kind of hidden activation or switch, until her body trembled with fatigue and hopelessness began to set in. Belatedly, she realized she should have concentrated on extracting enough water to drink instead of wasting her energy on ineffective fire streams. That was the sort of basic survival measure that Rubriel would think of right away. *What else would Rubriel do?*

Molindra knelt on the floor, closed her eyes, and focused on her breathing. Rationally, she knew the Langlythians wouldn't have gone to the trouble of bringing her all the way here only to leave her to starve to death in this chamber. They had some other purpose or task in mind - Zildred had said as much on the stair to Minnorak. He also said he would dispose of her if she failed. Was this room a test, then?

Her raw energy fizzed and spluttered in her veins; she'd overused it, and what remained was hard to control. It was a strange feeling, like working a limb so hard the muscles became temporarily weak and shaky. She could afford to rest.

She tried to meditate like she'd been taught long ago, but the fizzing inside her sent her thoughts wayward. Instead of centreing herself, she noticed subtle details of the environment - the temperature, the amount of moisture in the air, the small currents she was making with each exhale. In the silence, she could sense the network of energy all around her, becoming more aware of her elemental affinity than she'd experienced before. She sat in quiet contemplation a while longer, until her observations were interrupted by the grinding of stone against stone and bright light flooding the chamber.

A mage stood in the open doorway, the celair he carried illuminating his red garb and glinting off the ornate detailing of his mantle. His overcoat fell to the floor, sewn of thick dyed cloth trimmed in gold and buttoned at the waist. The buttery celair light reflected as gold off the pale flecks in his brown eyes.

Squinting, Molindra got to her feet. "Who are you and what is going on?" she demanded. "I am tired of being hauled from place to place with little to no explanation."

The newcomer briefly assessed her ragged appearance with the singed and dusty patches of her clothing and smirked. "This is a sparring chamber. You were brought here to expend whatever pent up energy you amassed in transit before meeting with me, lest you make a mess in my office."

Molindra huffed. "And you are?"

He raised a hand to his chest, turning the palm inwards. "Elementalist Gal'denan, High Mage of the Academy. And you are Molindra of Celessil, supposedly here to... *study* us." He chuckled.

Mol scowled.

"Instead, we will attempt to train you. An untrained mage is a danger to herself and no use to anyone. I will oversee this myself, though you are a little old... probably older than you look, too."

I'm only forty! Molindra seethed. She was still young by Celessilian standards, though he wasn't wrong in his assessment. Her mind whirled. Angry though she was, she saw the opportunity beckoning her with a gilded hand; too good to be true.

"What do you want of me in return? I have no gold to pay you - I would not be here if I did. I should like to understand why you saw fit to kidnap me and bring me here when Imul'dene clearly has no shortage of mages."

He raised a black eyebrow. "That constitutes kidnapping where you come from? You truly have no idea how lucky you are." He sighed. "Indeed, your purpose here depends entirely on how you perform."

"But-"

"You are extremely unlikely to learn more unless you demonstrate a high degree of worthiness and obedience, so do not ask. For now, a room has been prepared for you upstairs. You may rest for six hours, then we will talk."

Chastened, Mol followed him to the third floor of the complex, too weary and upset to take much notice of where they were going. A servant led her the rest of the way, into a circular room with a bed and a prepared bath. Food and clothing had been laid out as well.

Not bothering to check if the door had been locked behind her, she stripped off and eased her aching body into the hot water. She groaned, loosened her braid and dipped her head under the water, massaging the dirt out of her scalp. The water soon turned murky with dust. She leaned over the edge and grabbed the bowl of minted peas from the counter by the wall and devoured it, still in the bath, hot and ever so slightly sweet to taste. There was meat, too - red meat on the bone. She dried herself off and finished it.

She thought about crawling into bed as is but decided against it, worrying that someone would come for her and find her naked and unprepared. Instead, she opted for the chemise and drawers that had been left on the bed, placed the boots to the side so she could put them on in a hurry, pushed everything else onto the floor, and climbed beneath the covers.

Training as an elementalist. *Here.* Was that not the ultimate purpose of her expedition, to fund her missing education? Langlythe, it seemed, would give her that, only she feared she would not learn the cost until it was too late.

10

The Price

"Energy can be neither created nor destroyed. As mages, we simply manipulate it in ways that others cannot."

Gal'denan paced the small study as he lectured Mol on what he considered to be the fundamentals of their craft.

"Each of us has a certain reserve of raw energy inside us; energy with the potential to transform as we see fit. However, our true strength and skill lies in drawing upon external sources - the energy present in our environment. Avoid depleting your inner reserves. Even if you ate solidly for a week, you would still exhaust them relatively fast, leaving you at risk of overexertion. Instead, use them as a catalyst, then let nature do the rest."

That makes so much sense, Molindra thought. She sat quietly and waited for him to continue.

"Raw energy is just that - unrefined potential present in variable amounts in a mage's blood. The differentiating factor is how we shape and express that energy - the concept of affinity. Do you have any other affinity besides the elements?"

"I have some affinity for healing, I think. But the elements respond most naturally to me."

Gal'denan nodded. "Indeed, elementalism is usually paired with healing to some degree. The traits are co-inherited. Though it is, of course, possible to be born a dedicated healer."

Despite her initial reluctance, Mol was fascinated. Celessil taught magic as an art form; here, it was a science. She'd never thought of her own energy reserves in such a physical sense before.

He stood straight and faced her from across the workbench, clasping his hands together expectantly. "Let us start from the beginning, then: what can we do with air?"

"Draw heat from it to make fire, draw moisture from it to collect water," Molindra answered.

"Those are things we *extract* from the air. What do we do with the air itself?"

She thought for a moment. "Currents. We add or remove energy to manipulate air currents, creating winds or updrafts."

"And what are the side effects of doing that?"

She frowned, unsure of the answer.

"The energy we add or remove is heat. It is as you said before; draw enough heat from the air and it will cool, potentially yielding precipitation or at least condensation. The heat we extract then provides a significant amount of energy that has to go somewhere. The clever elementalist uses that by-product to their advantage."

"That sounds like the opposite of what I said."

His eyes gleamed. "The result is the same. I am simply giving you a more complete way to understand it."

Molindra nodded slowly. "I once tried to cool the auditorium by pulling the warmth out of the air and releasing it through the window. Only there was too much energy - I lost control of it and it... umm... exploded." She winced, regretting bringing up the accident that got her expelled. "I think I understand why now, at least."

Gal'denan merely chuckled. "Good. Now, let's move on to the others. What can we do with earth?"

She cocked her head. "I've... never done anything with earth."

"That is not surprising. Of all the elements, earth is the least useful, yet it does have some agricultural value to us."

Since when were mages involved in farming? "What?"

He rubbed his chin. "I see this is a new concept for you. Put bluntly, without elementalists, Langlythe would starve. We stimulate the soil to produce nutrients, allowing crops to grow on land that would otherwise remain infertile. We monitor soil temperature and moisture, and bring rain to areas where it does not rain naturally."

She couldn't help but gape at the newfound insight.

"Which brings me to our next element: water. The hardest to manipulate, and yet arguably the most important. For our purposes, water can be thought of as similar to air, but the energy involved is far greater. Drawing or adding energy to or from water can alter its flow and temperature and, at the most extreme ends of the spectrum, will cause it to freeze or evaporate. Water in its liquid form is the best external source of raw energy we have."

"It's more complicated than that though, isn't it? Water never behaves the way I expect."

Gal'denan didn't answer. Instead, he took out three pewter mugs and lined them up on the workbench between them. He poured an equal amount of liquid into each; one clear, one thicker and slightly yellowish, one dark brown with the unmistakable smell of ale. "Try drawing the water out of these cups."

Frowning, she held her hand over the first one. The clear liquid readily lifted until she could cup it in her palm. Focusing on keeping it contained, she held it as a sphere, like a fluid snowball. Then she tipped her hand over and dropped it back in the cup.

"First point to note: water responds to you directly. You were able to pick it up without heating or cooling it, as though it were an object. It was heavy though, wasn't it?"

Mol nodded.

"Try the next one." He indicated the mug of ale.

As before, she held her hand over the mug and concentrated on pulling the liquid into her palm. It responded, though a little less easily. She caught it and flipped her hand over. To her surprise, the ball of fluid was as clear as the previous one. She peered into the mug. Dark sediment mixed with a small amount of liquid left behind, concentrated into a sludge in the bottom.

"Second point: you can affect *only* water. The water itself responded to you, but the alcohol and sediments mixed in with it did not. Try the last."

Mol pulled on the liquid in the third mug. And pulled some more. Nothing happened. "What...?"

"Third point? Some liquids don't contain water at all. This is one of them."

She held the mug at eye level, tipping it towards her and studying its contents. "It's oil."

"Yes. Swamp moss oil, to be exact; used by alchemists as a carrier oil, but of no use to an elementalist."

She sighed. "But how-"

"How is this relevant?" He smirked. "Be mindful of what liquids are around you, and what gets left behind when you take the water away. Now I have one final experiment for you. Go back to the first mug, the one with pure water. Pick up half of it."

She gave him a wry look. The water rose as before in one perfect sphere. She dropped it and tried again, concentrating harder on affecting only some of it and leaving the rest behind. It was surprisingly difficult to separate in her mind. The sphere elongated but didn't break. She let it go.

Frustrated, she began to draw energy from the air around her and focus it into the water, warming it. It stretched further. She kept going, determined to thwart him and prove that she could. Steam began to rise. The globe of water split in half. It splashed into her palm and burnt. She cursed loudly, shaking her scalded hand.

Gal'denan only laughed. "That... was an interesting strategy. The point is, water sticks to itself. Why it behaves that way for us is unclear, but it is important to realize that you cannot use raw energy alone to draw a sample from a body of water. Heating the water makes it easier to separate, but harder to control, as you discovered."

Mol glared at him. Her palm throbbed; the reddened welts would surely blister.

"That will be all for now." He handed her a pitcher. "Go and make some ice for that hand, then practice using our fifth element."

"Fifth? What fifth?" she grumbled.

"The product of the other four. Life, Molindra. Heal yourself."

With that, he turned away, leaving Molindra with an empty pitcher, a scalded hand, and a bruised ego. Dejected, she grumbled her way back to her own chamber. It was perhaps her fourth or fifth day in Imul'dene - she was struggling to think in twenty-six hour cycles - and her first proper lesson.

Up until now, her meetings with Gal'denan had been nothing but a barrage of questions about her past tuition and experience. It left her humiliated and feeling woefully inadequate, though as time went on she realized that his sarcasm and slander were directed more at the manner in which she had been taught than at Mol herself. Still, he didn't spare her any embarrassment, and today was no exception.

She frowned at her reflection in the jug, her fine features and daintily pointed nose comically distorted in the convex shape. The dark roots of her natural hair colour were beginning to show against her scalp. Her scalded hand dipped in and out of the water and froze the droplets into small pearls of ice to soothe the burn, finding instant relief.

She flopped backwards onto the bed and rubbed her eyes. A smile played at the corners of her lips. It felt good to learn; to be encouraged to practice her gift, after so many years of smothering it with tonic and suffering the instability that came with unreleased raw energy. Things may not have turned out quite how she intended, but she had to make the most of this opportunity.

Molindra found herself with an hour or two to spare. While the other mages eyed her suspiciously from time to time, she was mostly free to go where she pleased within the academy grounds, so long as she appeared on time for her scheduled lessons. She left her apartment on the third floor and wandered downstairs, pausing in the entryway to listen to the relaxing trickle of water running down the wall. Other wings of the building branched off from here. One led to a mess hall; another to the sparring chambers below ground.

She chose a route she hadn't explored yet, through an arch and across a short hallway to a room filled with tall shelves of books. Fascinated, she ran her fingers along the spines, slightly disappointed to realize she couldn't understand the language. She opened a few at random, flipping through the pages, hoping she might come across illustrations or diagrams.

Here and there, spirits occupied empty shelf space, curled up tightly between rows of books. Their presence startled her more than once, as she reached up to replace a volume and caught the flash of movement as a spirit slid out of the way, retreating further into the dark recesses of the library. They seemed mostly content to avoid her, however, so she tried in turn not to disturb them, though she wasn't sure she would ever get used to the sheer number of them lurking throughout the city.

She'd taken to hiding the black gem in her dresser whenever she went out, in the hope the spirits would be less inclined to follow her around. It worked - for the most part - except that she would return to find her apartment full of them instead, and have to sleep with them watching her from every crevice.

As she wandered the aisles, a smaller room off to one side caught her eye. A writing desk in the middle held various drawing instruments. Cabinets stood against each wall, their open drawers full of scrolls neatly rolled and bound with twine. Curious, she selected one of the newer-looking ones and untied it, rolling it open on the desk and placing a paperweight in each corner.

A grin spread from ear to ear. The paper held a complete map of Imul'dene, drawn precisely to scale with labelled buildings and landmarks. She glanced over her shoulder. Did *all* these scrolls contain maps? There must have been twenty at least.

Excited, she checked a couple more. These drawings were more technical in nature – blueprints of some kind. She didn't recognize the structures, but this was perfect. What if she finished her training as an elementalist *and* brought Vesner the information he wanted? She would have to make time to study the map in more detail and practice redrawing the outline from memory. Surely he would reward her handsomely for such a treasure!

From then on, she returned to the cartography room every chance she got. Her lessons grew more and more gruelling as she progressed, leaving her with less time to study the maps than she would've liked, but she could hardly complain. The difference in her control and stamina compared to just a few weeks ago was astounding. As she grew in confidence, the manipulation of energy came ever more naturally to her, such that she barely had to think about lighting her way with a small flame, or condensing moisture from the air into thin crystals of ice.

In a way, she felt cheated. Twenty years it had been since she was expelled; twenty suffocating years, scraping together a living under the belief that enrolling at a foreign university was the only path to develop as a mage. Now, in less than two months, she had more than made up for lost time. It was *easy*. Shockingly so. Why had she allowed herself to waste so much of her life smothering the raw energy that came so naturally to her?

Rubriel never believed there was any other way and so she hadn't either, until the bitter truths of their fateful argument before new year pushed her to take drastic action. Sometimes she found herself fuming at Rubriel for being content to let them both struggle for so long. She would lie awake, running over and over their reunion in her mind. How she would share news of her good fortune and lift a heavy weight from both their shoulders. Except, no matter how she tried, the conversation always turned sour in her mind, and she couldn't stop the resentment leaking through.

Must I go home at all?

She still studied the maps, exploring the city and collecting as much local knowledge as she could, but as time went on, her resolve to bring it back to Vesner waned. What was there for her in Tunswick, really? Rubriel was better off without her.

She was so distracted by her brooding thoughts that she didn't hear Gal'denan come in.

"Still planning an escape route?"

She jumped. "I..." Her cheeks heated as she glanced down at the map in front of her. "Maps of all shapes and sizes have always fascinated me. This is quite the collection." She flashed him a smile, letting the paper roll up as she lifted the paperweight.

He checked his watch. "Yet you are here as an elementalist, not a cartographer, and you are running late. Were you not reminded of the need to set out early to reach our destination?"

"Oh!" She got to her feet at once. "We're trekking into the mountains. That is today–I mean, now. This... *waik*."

He pursed his lips, the corner almost quirking into a grin. "Come on."

They left the academy grounds and took a steep trail north out of the city, where it cut between two peaks and branched out into a cavern on one side and further ascent on the other. They entered the cavern, each lighting the way with a small flame as they moved further from the opening, until they reached a large frozen pool.

Gal'denan turned towards the wall, scanning along the side of the pool until he reached a firepit. He tossed the flame from his palm into its centre, igniting the coal waiting there. The fire cast long, dancing orange reflections across the surface of the ice. He indicated for Molindra to do the same on her side, revealing the full expanse of the pool between them. It was easily the size of her apartment and too deep to see the bottom.

"What is this place?" asked Mol, frowning at the two pre-prepared firepits.

"This is nothing more than it seems; a repurposed cavern. I brought you here to test your abilities."

She tensed. "What manner of test?"

He moved away from the fire to stand looking down the full length of the pool. "The hollow is ten feet deep at its lowest point, and frozen all the way through. Your task is to melt the ice."

"As in, melt a hole down to the bottom?"

"Melt all of it."

She turned bone white, even in the firelight. "Melt the whole pool? That is crazy!" Her heart thumped. "There is no way I can melt that much ice at once!"

"You can. I froze it three yirst ago."

"You are stronger than me!"

He raised a hand to stop her protest. "I also have your blood test results."

She looked momentarily confused until she remembered the blood sample she'd given about a week ago; a test that could measure the relative strength of a mage's raw energy. She swallowed. "And?"

"Your readings put you in the top one percent."

"Out of how many?"

"Out of every elementalist on file, including me. It is time you showcased the true depth of your ability."

He spoke matter-of-factly, but this new revelation only served to worsen Mol's rising panic. "That's... too much energy. Where am I to find that much heat?" She blurted out the question, more to stall him than anything else.

"From the fires, of course–and all around. This should tax you only mildly. All you are doing is moving energy from one place to another."

She reached out with her awareness, sensing the potential within the glowing coals and the air above them, even the rock overhead. She pulled on it, holding her breath, and felt it respond; a great cloud of energy ready to do as she willed. Its magnitude terrified her, and the ease with which it responded reminded her suddenly of her accident all those years ago, when her plan to cool the university lab on a hot summer's day had incinerated it instead. She let go, horrified, and the flames momentarily swelled in each firepit.

"I need a minute." She gasped and ran to the cave entrance.

Gal'denan followed. "What is it?"

"Just let me think!" she snapped.

"You need not *think* about it any harder. Molindra, the elements do not respond to intellect. They respond to emotion. Do not think; react."

"Easy for you to say," she muttered, massaging her temples. He reached out, and she swatted away his hand. "I said let me think!"

"Get angry. Channel it."

She ignored him.

With a sigh, he returned to the pool and waited while she fumed and paced outside.

She was more than strong enough to do what he asked—that was precisely what frightened her. It was dangerous to *react* with raw energy, to channel the surge of bottled up emotions inside her into the environment. All her life had been spent learning to suppress that desire—for her own safety, and that of everyone she knew.

How could she explain that to Gal'denan, who had clearly never held back a day in his life? Mages here had blast-proof practice chambers. They were allowed—no—*required* to create entire weather systems just to keep the country alive. How could she compete with that?

Or perhaps it is time I let go of the past, she thought. *If he truly wishes to see the depth of my potential, he will also see my potential for destruction. For once, it won't be my fault.*

She marched back into the cavern. Standing at the end of the pool, she grasped the twin fires and sucked energy into them until the flames turned blue and touched the ceiling. In one swift movement, she ripped all the gathered heat from both of them and threw it into the ice. It cracked, hissed and dissolved, leaving the firepits empty and a faint haze of smoke hanging over the water.

"There you go." Gal'denan acknowledged her work with a satisfied nod. "Well done."

She stared at him like a threatened buck, nostrils flaring.

"What?"

"Forget it," she muttered. *Sometimes I hate how terribly practical you are!*

She whirled to march for the exit. Then turned back. Glanced from Gal'denan, to the now-liquid pool and back again.

With a snort, she strode back to the water's edge. She reached into the water and stole the heat from it, hurling it back onto the coals. The water crackled as it froze. The flames soared again and licked the stalactites overhead.

"You want to see what I can do?" Her voice echoed off the rocks. "Watch me go too far. Watch the collateral damage pile up. Then tell me not to 'think' about what I'm doing."

"Challenge accepted." A frustrating grin and a twinkle in his eye told her was looking forward to it.

11

In Need of Rain

Rubriel hadn't meant to stay in Andorlai for so long. Since the advent of the growing house, she'd worked so hard as to have neither the time nor the energy left to think of anything else. The entire town had been swept into a frenzy of gathering and building. The overseers missed nothing; she couldn't help but be swept along with it, even though she kept a travel pack hidden in Shavon's house in preparation for a hasty departure.

Having proven to be strong and efficient, whatever doubts people may have had about her origins were forgotten. They relied upon her more and more as the growing house took shape. It had four full-height walls now, and they had begun to angle the thick wooden beams of the ceiling frame across from one wall to the opposite. They were heavy to lift and awkward to position, even with the aid of ropes and pulleys. Progress was slow but steady.

By the end of her shift, they started to bring out metal plates and bolts to cover the ceiling on the inside, coated in a fine crystalline substance and polished to a mirrorlike finish. These would reflect light and warmth down onto the plants, they said. Light would be provided by a series of hanging crystal lamps with a white-yellow hue. The growing house was set to become the brightest building in the whole of Andorlai, a veritable shining masterpiece against an otherwise desolate backdrop.

The overseer called for the change in shift. Rubriel slid gratefully down the ladder from the rooftop to head back. Trudging past the waste pile, a distinctly round shape caught her eye. Anything in the waste pile was fair game; it wasn't uncommon to see people routing through it, making off with useful scrap material. She paused for a closer look. Amidst the offcuts of wood and misshapen bricks, she found several circular segments of wood, sawn off the end of a log that was too long.

On impulse, she selected two the same size and carried them with her. Too tired to stop at the mess hall and eat, she went straight back to Shavon's house and collapsed in front of the fire.

She woke to a growling belly and the sounds of Shavon working outside. He must have returned from the lakes while she slept, cleaning and filleting in the yard. The stench of fish nearly made her wretch as she leaned through the door to talk to him.

"Did you catch many?"

"More than I could carry," he replied glumly, not looking up from his work.

"Do you need help?" she asked, hoping he would say no. Hauling fish guts around was the last thing she felt like doing.

"Not from you. Go to the mess hall and eat. You're no use to anyone passed out with your head in a bucket."

He wasn't wrong, but it bothered her nonetheless. The demands of building the growing house put an increasing strain on everyone who still had a quota to meet. Every able-bodied man, woman and child had already been put to work; there were no extra hands to be found to spread the load. They could only push through and hope for a reprieve at the end of the project.

She didn't go straight to bed after supper. Instead, she went to the alcove where Shavon kept his tools; where she had also been gradually stockpiling bits and pieces of discarded building materials for an idea that

had been simmering in her mind for some time now. She cleared a space
on the floor and began.

Some time later, the result of her efforts swam groggily back into view as
Shavon shook her roughly awake.

"Durenka, you are needed at the worksite. The overseers are looking
for you."

She jumped then, dislodging a smattering of wood splinters from her
lap. She'd fallen asleep with her back against the wall, still holding the
rough stone she'd been using to sand the wooden wheels of her creation
- a contraption that Shavon frowned at curiously.

It had a simple upright frame, holding two rectangular wooden crates
with no lids, one above the other. A long piece of metal bolted to the
back afforded stability, attached at waist-height to a horizontal bar that
would serve as a handle. And at the bottom, the cart rested on two large
wheels, fashioned from the rounds she'd picked up earlier and mounted
on a simple axle.

Shavon kept his frown, but the corners of his mouth began to turn up
at the side. He pushed the cart back and forth experimentally.

"It is a little stiff," she said, "but those crates will each hold twice as
much as a bucket, no?"

He sighed. "You are a strange woman, Durenka. But thank you." He
smiled with his eyes if not with his lips. "Now go to work," he insisted;
grumpily, but not without affection.

Her muscles protested with overuse that day and her head throbbed
from lack of sleep, but she felt strangely content as she held mirror tiles
in place while they fastened them to the ceiling. Each tile was about the
size of a hand, smooth and polished. There were hundreds of them. The

building was in its final stages, and she'd helped Shavon in the one small way she could think of to repay him for the kindness he'd shown beneath his hard-faced demeanour.

They wanted the structure completed five shifts from now, the overseers said, for the mages were to arrive to enrich the soil and bring rain in a few days' time. Seeds would be brought down off the Plains of Kalakat with them, and were to be planted under the mages' supervision so they could report back to the capital.

Just a few more days, then. It was a fool's hope to believe that the mages from Imul'dene might somehow bring news of Molindra. More foolhardy still to hope that Molindra herself might be with them.

An elementalist from the south trains with them, rumoured to be the most powerful Imul'dene has produced for many years.

She'd revisited that snippet of conversation a thousand times in her mind. *An elementalist from the south...* she had to know who that was, though she was afraid of what it might mean if the rumours were true.

The arrival of a trio of elementalists might have been a relief, but their mode of transport was disturbing. They flew into Andorlai, each on the back of a great and monstrous bat, membranous wings stretched as wide as a carriage and landing smoothly beyond the worksite. The creatures glared with beady black eyes as the riders slid from their backs, walking forward on unsettlingly humanoid clawed hands and feet. Sharp, elongated fangs protruded from the upper jaw, and a swelling at the root of each suggested their bite would be venomous, like a snake's. Molindra wasn't with them.

The workers downed their tools but kept a wary distance. Even the overseers stood to attention. It was clear the new arrivals commanded a great deal of respect among the people of Andorlai, and rightly so, if they were to bring the only source of rain that kept the town alive. Rubriel watched as the trio spoke briefly with the overseers before they were shown to the newly completed growing house, inspecting the structure in silence as the overseers pointed out the finer details of the construction.

Eventually, the mage named Merrick - who appeared to be in charge - gave a satisfied nod. She and her fellow workers were dismissed, while the mages conditioned the rough clumps of dry earth that would soon become crop plots within the building.

Rubriel would've liked to stay and watch, but the overseers ushered her away with the rest and gave her a much less interesting task; clearing the gutters and preparing the water reservoirs to receive several days of solid rain. Armed with rough-bristled brushes and brooms, they swept dust from the roofs of homes and cleared drains of debris. Half pipes ran along the eaves and fed into covered stone tanks through a fine mesh filter, dry and clogged with dirt waiting to be brushed clean.

It wasn't until their work was done and Rubriel woke from a few hours' rest that the rain finally came. A cool breeze arrived first, blowing a layer of cloud down from the mountains. The wisps thickened into broad sheets that gradually dropped lower until they smothered the emerald sky and covered the full extent of the settlement. There they seemed to pause, before releasing a uniform, measured shower, as though the volume and quantity of water droplets had been precisely calculated. Perhaps it had.

The rain pooled at first on the surface of the parched, unyielding earth. It mixed with the former layer of dust, setting the cobblestone pathways awash with blackened mud. It splashed down the sloped roofs and through the gutters, filling the reservoirs with a steady trickle. Rubriel contemplated from the window, thinking that it would probably take several days of steady rainfall for it to properly absorb into and moisten the soil. Several more to provide enough water to last the town until next time the elementalists deigned to visit.

She was keenly reminded, as she and Shavon set out for the lakes and the rain abruptly stopped, that this was no natural weather event. Apparently, those responsible did not bother to extend their influence much more than a hundred feet beyond the edge of the town. When they returned, the rain had eased, as though the mages had foreseen the need to slow the pace so as not to overwhelm the drainage. She wrestled in her mind to accept the idea of something so naturally unpredictable being forced to behave in such a rigid and measured manner.

It lasted about a week. During that time, the freshly enriched, moistened soil in the growing house planters was sewn with many seeds, the bravest of which already pushed the tiniest green sprouts up into the light by the hour of the final inspection. The town jittered, decidedly on edge. Merrick conversed at length with one of the overseers. The other two paced the fields, if you could call them that - empty, barren land beyond the growing house, currently unsuitable for anything.

Except, perhaps, further development. A sharp bell toll gathered all within earshot to the centre of town at Merrick's behest. Shavon had gone fishing alone; Rubriel had been called to help clear the last of the building tools and leftover resources away from the worksite. Cautiously, she followed along, not quite understanding the air of foreboding that seemed to hang over them. The build had been a success. Surely Imul'dene was not *displeased* with the result?

"Where are the rest?" Merrick addressed the gathered townsfolk from the central square, the other two mages and their great bat mounts waiting behind him. "Overseers, rally the rest of the people!"

The maroon-clad figures nodded their assent and strode off in different directions.

"This project," he continued, "has exceeded expectations. Already, the first crop seedlings have sprouted in the growing house. The productivity of this region is set to expand in ways we have never seen before." He paused then as more people filed into the square. The translucent form of a spirit caught Rubriel's eye as it floated past and settled to his right, though he gave no indication of having noticed its proximity.

"As such-" He held up a hand to ensure he regained the increasing crowd's attention. "As such, the project shall progress immediately into the second phase. Three more growing houses, each twice the size of the first, shall be constructed on the remaining land immediately beyond Andorlai's northeastern edge."

A wave of palpable unease washed over them at this proclamation, eliciting gasps, murmurs and muffled cries.

"The plans will be dispatched from Imul'dene immediately, with the required resources to follow. Completion is due upon our return in sixty *yirst*."

A bitter mumbling from the side drew Rubriel's attention.

"Twice the size, in the same amount of time? Imul'dene cares not if we starve." The man in question muttered angrily, a look of utter distaste upon his sharp features. Dark circles beneath his eyes betrayed a chronic lack of sleep. Unfortunately, one of the overseers heard him.

"What did you say?" she demanded of him, pushing her way towards the disgruntled speaker. Others readily backed away from the confrontation.

But he'd clearly had enough. He raised his voice, interrupting Merrick's speech. "I said, Imul'dene cares not if we starve. They will work us to the bone to feed their army while we are still left with *nothing!*"

His outburst was met with a moment of terrified silence. Rubriel knew he wasn't alone in that sentiment, but he *was* the only one brave enough - or foolish enough - to speak it aloud.

The overseer seized him. Holding a knife to his throat, she looked up at Merrick for confirmation.

"Take him away." He sounded almost bored.

The overseer led the protester away at knife point, still hurling insults to the world at large. People hurriedly moved out of the way, huddling closer together out of fear and a desire not to be associated.

"Listen carefully," Merrick called out.

Rubriel let the crowd move in front, though none seemed particularly eager to push forward. She came to stand behind a taller person and hid her face from view, suddenly grateful for the mist that still swirled in the wake of the elementalists' work and provided reason to keep her hood up. Spirits drifted in off the plains and settled on the rooftops, watching with idle interest from above.

"Does anyone else wish to voice their opinion?"

No one uttered a sound.

"Good. There are plenty enough of you here to complete the growing house while maintaining town provisions, as you have already proven once," he said pointedly. "Now -"

"Hold, Merrick," a cold voice said. The crowd flinched.

Clad fully in brilliant red, wreathed in shadow and terrifying, the Master of Imul'dene appeared abruptly before them. A mantle of needle-like spines draped across his shoulders and extended down both arms, every bit as lethal as they were decorative. Even Merrick looked nervous now.

"Andorlai has been long without a headcount," Zildred announced. "I see many more in this courtyard alone than are recorded as fit for work." His abyssal gaze surveyed the quiet, nervous townsfolk, seeming to linger where Rubriel stood hidden amongst them.

She cast her eyes downwards beneath her hood, willing herself to go unnoticed.

"Merrick, you will initiate a headcount immediately. All quotas shall be re-assigned before work commences on the second growing house."

"Of course, Master." Merrick bowed and withdrew.

Satisfied, Zildred took one last look over the crowd, again looking right towards Rubriel.

A shiver ran unbidden down her spine. She avoided his gaze, but she felt in her bones that he somehow knew who she was, that if she did not leave immediately, he would find her.

"That is all," he said finally.

The forest of people began to split up and she realized he was gone, though the spirits remained on the rooftops. A knot of panic tightened in her stomach. Heart pounding, she tried to move with the throng, though she did not know where to go. She half-imagined that the spirits were aware of her presence and pressed close to the shadowed walls; though the dead should be no better equipped to pierce her charade than the living. She felt their attention all the same.

Like a ghost herself, she flew in the direction of Shavon's home, straddling the line between efficiency and urgency in her pace, knowing only that she had to get out of Andorlai and as far away as possible. To run and jostle people would only make things worse, and she was not so desperate as to flee without basic supplies. She had not forgotten the days spent starving and alone before Shavon found her, and she did not know how far to the north she must walk to reach another settlement.

He would still be by the lakes, she hoped. Better that he not know of her departure.

She ripped her meagre stash from its hiding-hole beside the hearth and slipped out into the deserted yard. It would not be long before the fishermen returned. She would head south, away from the town, then circle back north at a distance. No sooner had she rounded the corner, however, than she ran face to face with Shavon, nearly dislodging his full cartload.

"There is to be a head count. Now." She gulped.

"Durenka, you cannot leave," he reasoned, confused by her urgency. "There are always those that try to cheat the quota and hide; it will only be worse when they find you. It is too late to run."

"I can and I will." Her face darkened, walking past him with more confidence than she felt.

"Durenka."

She sighed in dismay and kept walking.

"Durenka!" He ran to catch up with her. "Did you not hear? Where are you going?"

She pulled him aside. "The success of the growing house has drawn too much attention. It is time I moved on."

"Success that you were very much a part of."

She shook her head in protest.

"You are an integral part of our workforce now. No one here doubts you. You must know that." His eyes searched hers for an explanation. "Stay and be counted. The best way to remain invisible is to keep on working."

"I cannot do that."

"Why not?"

"It doesn't matter," she muttered, pushing past him again, weaving along the edge of town between closed up homes. He followed and she quickened her steps, ignoring his pursuit until he ran and grabbed her roughly and shoved her into an alcove.

"What did you *do?*" he growled.

"Shavon, please-"

"*What did you do?*"

He looked as though he would strike her, but she jumped back out of reach. Her hands flew to the belt she'd strapped on inside her overcoat and drew her sword part way, the blade she had forged herself in Tunswick's smithies glinting in the dark.

"Do not make me draw this upon you. You would not be the first person I have hurt for their own safety."

His face flushed with anger, but slowly his aggression faded at her words. A pallid dread washed over him instead as he seemed to realize the implication.

"The Master himself is looking for you."

It hurt to leave this way. It hurt to lie. Shavon had befriended her in his own way; used her to offset his own workload but also shown her kindness. She would not put him in unnecessary danger.

"I believe so," she admitted. She owed him that much truth, at least. "Now let me go..."

"Why did you come here?" He ran to catch up to her again. "Durenka, you cannot just come and go."

She ignored him.

"We need your help!"

The note of desperation stopped her.

"Durenka does not exist." She sighed at his bewildered expression. "I am sorry, Shavon. I am not who you think I am. Believe me, I have wanted to tell you everything on several occasions. You deserve to know. But no good will come of it."

He shook his head slowly, swallowing. He did not understand, but what could he do?

In the distance, they heard the overseers approach, barking orders to the townsfolk. On impulse, she took his hand in her own and squeezed it. "*You* must go," she murmured. Her expression softened, apology in her eyes. "Thank you, and be well."

With that, she was gone swiftly, slipping into the vastness of the dark and out of sight. Glancing back, she saw he stood there still, staring in the direction she'd gone. His eyes could not pierce the thick darkness. Had he seen, he would have urged her not to go so far east, but his gaze was unfocused, uncomprehending. Rubriel hurried away into the unknown.

Molindra sat in the window, nursing a water droplet between her fingers. She rolled it back and forth, thoughtfully watching her reflection swim and distort. It was cold outside, but her room was comfortable, thanks to the fire she had learned to keep burning permanently in the hearth. When she first set out, it had taken all her focus to summon enough flame to defend herself from the gloom spirits that haunted the Gloaming Mountains. Now, something as simple as keeping a hearth burning was trivial.

She returned regularly to the cavern above the city, freezing and thawing the ice pool over and over until she could do so comfortably.

For all Gal'denan's arrogance and sarcasm, she couldn't deny he was a good teacher. He never tried to restrain her. Instead, he pushed her harder and harder until she stretched out to the limit of her power. Once she reached that point, her fear of it subsided, leaving her calmly in control for the first time in her life. She could shape it and tame it as she wanted, flaring or tempering the raw energy in response to the environment as though it were an extension of herself.

Not that he wasn't strict with her. He was a ruthless opponent in the sparring chamber, where they fought almost daily. Poor judgement or lack of concentration on her part was rewarded with burns, scalds, frostbite or a lungful of water - all of which he then left her to figure out how to heal by herself. Occasionally - but not often - she had the satisfaction of catching him off guard, only to face a retaliation so swift and fierce that she always seemed to come off worst.

The rest of her training was spent with other elementalists, manipulating weather in the courtyard; or in the healer's wing, studying anatomy and physiology and dissecting a gruesome array of body parts, animal and sometimes human. She didn't want to know where they came from.

Healing she still found difficult. It wasn't nearly as simple as the elements, all a matter of pushing and pulling and heating and cooling. Living things had to be stimulated to heal via their own natural processes, and that meant holding a clear understanding of the energy flow within living tissue while she worked. To heal was to tap into the body's own mechanisms for growth and repair, channeling raw energy to accelerate the process. She found it both fascinating and frustratingly complex.

A cool breeze rippled the heavy drapery hanging to the side of the open window. She inhaled deeply, watching the quiet streets below. The air felt heavy with moisture, the emerald sky overhead mottled by a rare thin mist.

She wished to see it better. The large window permitted her to climb through easily, and the generous ledge that ran along the outside of the wall seemed almost built for this daring purpose. She welcomed the cold as she hoisted herself up onto the roof and climbed to its apex, suddenly desperate for open space and fresh air to cleanse her thoughts. The sky pulsed slowly.

There was another emerald land out there, far to the west; the true Emerald City of Esmara - the city of her dreams. How marvellous it must be to stand on an ivy-covered balcony and see green, so much green! Green in the hedge-lined streets, green climbers curling up walls and over roofs, green in the pampered trees between every house and estate. Dense shrubbery, perfectly trimmed to exotic shapes. A big blue sky, vast and clear. How she missed the feel of the sun on her face, the softness of grass underfoot, the scent of spring flowers on the breeze!

Esmara felt that much closer now - and that much further away. Another few weeks here, months at most, and she would no longer need to worry about tuition. She could take a ship to Esmara as soon as possible and finally become a licensed mage without having to save thousands and thousands of gold for the hefty fees.

There was nothing to fear anymore. She would find Rubriel and explain her peculiar good fortune and all would be forgiven. They could sail away and start over, just like they always wanted. Her chest swelled with joy, even in the darkness of the present. Her blood tingled with energy.

She looked up. Suddenly she wanted rain, wind, a storm - as though she could blow away the shadows and see into the future beyond. The clouds answered, sweeping in and thickening until they poured. She opened her mouth, tasting the rain, savouring the wild, ruthless sensation of the wind battering her and soaking her to the skin.

Lighting forked. Cries of surprise came from somewhere below, but she heard nothing, lost in the thrill of her own unleashing and the infinite power of nature that would always, always answer her. She let the rain slow to a light drizzle, the sky clearing as she did so, clouds dissipating as quickly as they had come. She stood there a long while at the edge of the roof, tired now but content.

"Molindra?"

The thin, raspy voice startled her so much she almost fell as she spun. It was a spirit who addressed her, faintly outlined as a human head and torso floating a foot or two above the rooftop. Its dull, translucent form seemed weary in its approach, as though too weak to speak to her across any distance.

She suppressed the desire to back away, her euphoria rapidly fading. She knew that the spirits roaming Imul'dene weren't dangerous, but to touch one was never a pleasant experience. This one curled an indistinct appendage tentatively around her arm, seeming to gain some small strength from doing so. Mol shuddered.

"You are wanted in the citadel," it said. "Go now to the Great Hall."

"Now..." she said numbly, half to herself.

"Of course." The spirit released her and floated away.

She hugged herself. Whether from the spirit's touch or the rain, she was chilled to the bone. She slid carefully down off the roof, taking one last look back over the city as she did so, but saw only dark stone wreathed in false hope far below.

12
The Secret Springs

I t was cold and bitter. An eerie wind whipped between the rocky hills, stirring ribbons of fine grey dust that swirled across the cracked earth. Rubriel stepped as lightly as she could, ever watchful for signs of life that could only mean trouble on her long and perilous walk. The wind's rush could so effortlessly mask the sound of footsteps, or the sound of stones dislodged by someone - or something–waiting to spring upon her from behind a great mound of rock.

More than once she herself ducked for such cover, preparing to be ambushed. There she would crouch still and silent, sword in hand, hardly daring to breathe until she was certain that whatever disturbance had caught her attention was nothing but a cruel trick of the landscape. She had strayed too far from the road. This was a wild place, a dangerous place. It seemed as if the land itself were hostile to her.

But not empty. No, she had the growing feeling of being watched as she scrambled her way over razor-sharp rocks, going slowly to maintain her footing. Sheltering in the shadow of a boulder for a moment, she stopped to get her bearings. Northeast. She needed to head due north, but the terrain was too steep and it pushed her further and further to the east, towards the junction where the Gloaming Mountains met the Ice Divide.

The latter was the highest mountain range on earth. It formed Langlythe's northern border and stretched all the way to the west coast, creating a divide, as the name suggests, between it and the eternal winter at the Roof of the World.

The mountains weren't what worried her most. It was a single, thin spire that bothered her, rising steeply from the jagged floor of the valley and reaching almost high enough to touch the violent flashes of emerald overhead. The upper part was surely man made, but its lower two-thirds blended and intertwined with the rock such that it was impossible to tell from a distance where the earth ended and the tower began. It resembled a massive stalagmite in a crater of smaller ones.

There was something about it that made the hairs on the back of her neck stand erect. That, and the occasional sound like wings flapping and claws scratching against stone. Something definitely followed her.

She paused to take a brief sip from her canteen and grimaced. She was lost - again. The canteen would run dry within a day, with no sign of water for miles around. She kept going, not daring to let her guard down lest whatever was stalking her chose to take advantage, trying to veer north as much as possible, searching for a way to climb up and out of the labyrinthine valley.

An echoing screech sent her ducking for cover. She looked up to see a formation of formidable dark shapes pass overhead. Bats, she realized - giant bats like those the mages had ridden to Andorlai. These were riderless however, and they circled back around. Hunting. Quickly and quietly she darted to find better cover. Had the flying beasts picked up her scent?

They passed again, four of them in all, low and close enough to see the grisly dark fur that covered their legs and underbellies. A second ear-splitting screech told her she'd been found. Cursing, she drew her sword and ran, glancing over her shoulder to see them circling round towards her position. Lack of visibility from the ground made her an easy target from the sky. She had to get to a better spot, where she could measure the bats' approach and fight somewhat on her terms.

She vaulted over a boulder and ducked as one of the creatures swooped low. A second dove towards her but swerved harmlessly away before it came within striking range. She sprinted again, uphill to where those strange jagged rock formations grew smaller and a sheer cliff face marked the edge of the sunken valley. She spun to face them. At least now they could only approach from the front.

They came as one, four of them in all, swooping down at speed - a steep dive they couldn't pull out of. Rubriel swung and shredded the wing of one and left a shallow cut along the body of another. The other two landed with a thud behind her as she spun out of the way. They stalked forward on all fours, black eyes gleaming hungrily.

The one on the right lunged for her first. She dodged but lost her footing as the second slashed at her with its front claws. It leapt for her as she went down, but Rubriel's quick reaction saw it collide with her sword-point, impaling itself under its own weight.

Seeing its companion fall, the first bat retreated slightly, giving her time to heave the corpse off her body and wrench her blade free of its chest. *No blood,* she registered in alarm. Her blade glistened instead with a viscous, clear fluid.

She faced off against the final bat. It was far more cautious now, its moves almost calculated, searching for her weakness with an uncanny level of intelligence. She was quick enough to counter its attacks, but every swipe from the creature drove her further out into the open as she fought to avoid those bloodthirsty fangs and claws.

Too late, she heard the heavy flap of wings at her back. She whirled around as another bat - the one she'd cut earlier - collided with her. Its taloned feet dug painfully into her shoulders as it lifted her off her feet.

She narrowly kept a grip on her sword as it hoisted her into the air, her own legs flailing uselessly as she tried to wrestle free.

The bat swayed in the air as she threw it slightly off balance. Under the sideways momentum, she swung herself upward and grasped the bat's leg higher up. With a cry of pain from her clawed shoulder, she heaved her right arm and stabbed at its belly. It screeched and flapped wildly, but did not let go. She'd only managed a shallow wound.

Panic set in as she tried again and again, her strength failing as the bat carried her further and further. Then, with one last desperate lunge, she managed to puncture the taught membrane of the bat's wing. It screamed again and veered sideways, struggling to stay airborne as more of that strange, clear fluid oozed from the tear. They tumbled out of control, plummeting towards the ground dizzyingly fast, each wrestling for the upper position until they landed with a heavy thud against the unyielding earth.

Rubriel cinched the better landing, but she'd lost her sword in the descent. It lay just out of reach. She attempted to roll towards it, but a sharp, unbearable pain stopped her as the bat's two elongated fangs sank deep into her upper arm. The fiery sensation swallowed her shoulder and spread across her chest as though she'd been doused in burning oil. Her head swam.

She moaned in agony and terror as the second bat arrived. The pair of them loomed over her, ready to devour her... until a long pointed object flew out of nowhere and took one of them right in the head. A human battle cry followed, and a man with an immense shield appeared, brandishing an expertly crafted spear with great skill. From the cover of his shield, he drove the last of the bats away from her, until a dying screech told her he'd finished it off some distance away. She tried to sit up and immediately changed her mind.

"Don't move," the stranger said.

She blinked against her starry vision as he came nearer. She wanted to thank him, but the ground spun beneath her and her arm stung with a sickening pain. No sound came out when she opened her mouth. She saw him squat and thought he would help her up, but instead he grasped her collar firmly in one hand and held a small vial of liquid in the other.

"You have been poisoned with bat venom. We both know you won't make it out of here alive if I don't give you this antidote. Tell me why I should."

His accent was like no other she had heard in Langlythe, or anywhere. The pitying look in his eyes told her that despite his demanding tone, he would prefer not to let her die. Her lips moved in vain; only a faint rasp escaped her. Fading fast, she instead dragged her good arm up across her chest. It was so heavy to lift, her bones made of lead. Shakily, her fingers delved below the neckline of her torn garments and tugged her sildion free. He squinted at the sudden brightness.

"Celessil," she managed weakly. "I'm... Celessil..."

He nodded once. His thumb flicked the vial open and he tipped the contents between her pale lips.

She gagged - even swallowing stung - but the relief that followed was immediate, like a cool, cleansing wave sweeping the fire from her veins. She relaxed finally, breathing hard as sweat beaded on her forehead and the colour slowly returned to her cheeks.

"Thank you," she said after a time, her vision clearing enough for her to study the face of her rescuer. He was clothed in typical Langlythian garb, a hood and scarf obscuring his hair and most of his face, but the deep green eyes of a young man looked back at her between the folds of fabric. The skin surrounding them was a rich golden tan, his brows the colour of warm oak. "Who are you?"

"I am Rascovor Garvin Mytholi, of Esmara," he said. "Just call me Scoe. I am sorry for testing you like that. It is rare to find a friend in these parts. I took a risk in revealing myself to you." He shuddered. "I don't think anyone deserves to die by those monsters."

"And yet they ride them," she thought aloud, remembering the mages in Andorlai. She tried to sit up and again regretted it. The dizziness threatened to return the moment she lifted her head. "I am Rubriel, or sometimes Durenka, depending on the circumstances. You saved my life. I am very grateful that you came along when you did."

"That a Langlythian name?" asked Scoe, curious. He unwound the scarf covering the lower half of his face and wrapped it as a crude bandage around the bite wound.

She flinched. "Durenka is, yes," she said through clenched teeth. "I adopted a secondary identity in order to travel more freely here. My colouring is not so different from the native population, so long as I keep this covered." With her good hand, she tucked her sildion away again.

Scoe frowned thoughtfully. "How exactly did you end up out here by yourself?"

She huffed a laugh. "It is a long story. I could ask *you* the same question."

"I'm not, strictly speaking, alone. My friends are out here somewhere, hunting for supper. I stayed behind to guard their way back. I'm not subtle enough for them, apparently."

Rubriel glanced towards the shield he'd been using earlier. It was broad enough to cover his full body with a tapered bottom edge and a notch in the upper right corner for bracing a spear. Scuffs of frequent use marked its surface, but it was obvious he took good care of it. Many comments sprung to mind, not the least of which involved that shield and its likeness to someone's front door, but she wisely kept them to herself.

Instead she asked, "Is there any fresh water nearby, or someplace relatively safe? My wounds need tending, and I'll likely need a few days to properly recover."

Scoe blinked. "Right!" he said, ending his momentary distraction. "We do actually have a camp of sorts inside a hidden cave. It isn't terribly far, though it is uphill. If you think you can stand, we should start making our way there. It is quiet for now, but I wouldn't want to risk more bats showing up."

"Thank you," she said again, smiling. What a relief it was to find herself in friendly company!

The walk was a slow but tolerable one. Rubriel limped slightly from the fall and remained weak from the aftereffects of the poison, but mostly able to support herself. She braced herself against Scoe now and then for a brief respite, while he assured her somewhat apologetically that they were almost there. They were out of the valley now and into the foothills of the ice divide.

There was no sign yet of the cave he'd mentioned, but Rubriel was just glad to be out of that horrid maze - a place Scoe informed her was very appropriately named the "Jagged Labyrinth".

He led her to an unassuming gap in the hillside. A shallow channel underfoot held a slight trickle of water. They followed this upwards, twisting further into the base of the mountains as they went until they came to the water's source - an apparent dead end where the rivulet seeped between the stones from higher up.

He nodded towards the bank on their right. "You first," he said, hoisting her up to grab the ledge and pull herself to the top.

She winced from the strain on her injured arm, but managed to get a leg up and swing her weight over the threshold.

Scoe unstrapped his shield and hurled it up after her, then bounded up himself with seemingly little effort. He was a good ten inches taller than her. They'd reached a path of sorts, which ducked beneath an overhanging boulder and threaded into the mountain proper. At the end was a shabby wooden door, old and sad like it had stood there forgotten for at least a hundred years. Scoe knocked twice and pushed it open without waiting for a response. It groaned softly on its rusted hinges.

An aging man in a patched shirt and dark grey pants stood to meet them in the passage beyond. His face was a mixture of concern and distrust as he looked Rubriel once over and frowned at Scoe for an explanation. He was taller than her by a hand span with thinning auburn hair, greying a little at the temples.

"Adam, this is Rubriel of Celessil." Scoe introduced her with a hint of pride. "I found her besieged by bats in the Jagged Labyrinth. She suffered a bite, but I gave her Grace's antidote mixture. Now we know it is as effective as the one the twins stole from that mage. I'm sure they will tell you all about it," he added to Rubriel.

The older man seemed to relax a little. "Adam Carter." He extended a hand in greeting.

"Pleasure to meet you," said Rubriel, grasping it. His handshake was firm, reassuring.

"This cave system houses a secret spring, believed by most to be uninhabited. We are safe here, so long as it remains that way. You are welcome among us, Rubriel."

"Scoe saved my life." She glanced at him and smiled. "It feels good to meet a friendly face out here. Thank you for having me. I am sure we will have lots to talk about!"

"I'm sure we will," Adam agreed. "Are you well?" he asked, indicating her injured arm.

"Well enough, thanks to Scoe, though it is still painful."

"Grace will help you with that. Come, meet our other companions."

She followed him down the cave passage until it opened out into a generous chamber, high-ceilinged with several rounded doors set into the smooth rock walls. The sound of flowing water drew her attention to the far corner, where fresh water tumbled gracefully down from the ceiling to collect in a clear, deep pool.

To the right, several rugs in varying shades of faded red covered the expansive floor. Sewn together from numerous old remnants of much grander rugs, it seemed. There wasn't much furniture; just a few rickety wooden chairs and an old table which, if the collection of mismatched objects occupying its surface was any indication, served a variety of functions.

Three people bounded eagerly to their feet upon seeing her. Two were dark-haired men, tall and slender and almost identical. Brothers, most certainly, if not twins. They couldn't have been much beyond eighteen years.

"Meet our twin scouts, Daelin and Dornir," said Adam, giving one of the boys an affectionate clap on the shoulder. They grinned at Rubriel in unison.

"Ultimately, you will learn to tell us apart. I'm Dornir," said one of them.

She noticed a queer gap along the arch of his eyebrow, as though he'd somehow accidentally shaved a stripe through it which had never grown back. It was as good a way as any to distinguish them.

"Rubriel." She offered a handshake to each of them, which they returned a little awkwardly.

Footsteps echoed from an adjoining passageway, and a kindly woman of about thirty came to join them. She smiled prettily.

"Rubriel, allow me to introduce you to Grace. My niece—and a skilled herbalist."

"How lovely to welcome someone new. I hope you'll be comfortable here, Rubriel. It's not much, but it is home, for now," she said cheerfully, flicking a bang of gold-brown hair out of her eyes as she made to embrace Rubriel in a friendly hug. She stopped herself as she saw Rubriel's bandaged arm.

"Oh! You're hurt." Her voice was full of concern. "You'll have to let me see that. Is it very sore?"

"I'm alright," Rubriel said, but she let Grace sit her down on one of the upright chairs and inspect the makeshift bandage.

She clicked her tongue. "This is very dirty. I'm going to have to wash this properly."

"Scoe and I did the best we could. There is no water in the Jagged Labyrinth."

"I sacrificed my scarf to staunch the bleeding," Scoe said, striding over to join them. "It works well enough in a tight spot."

"Scoe, fetch me some water, would you?" Grace said, trying not to sound impatient. She hastily cleared a space on the table and rested Rubriel's forearm over the ample bowl of water Scoe brought from the spring. She began to wash and flush the bite wound, Rubriel flinching as much from the icy cold water as from the pressure on her injury.

"Glacial waters," Grace said apologetically.

Not surprising. The water flow probably originated high up in the Ice Divide. Rubriel took another look around the cave. The pure serenity of the waterfall was enchanting, its sound peaceful and gently reassuring. It seemed at odds with the harsh world outside, the emerald arcs ricocheting overhead. This unlikely band of foreigners were lucky indeed to have this precious resource to themselves.

"Tell me about this place."

"The water here is the purest you'll find in Langlythe - or so I'm told," said Grace, with a glance at the twin brothers. "We enjoy relative comfort here because of it. It is wholesome to drink, to cook with, to bathe. Even if it does take a very long time to heat over our small fires."

"What?" Rubriel looked sideways.

"We have to keep our campfire small, otherwise this cave gets too full of smoke. You should see how grumpy Scoe gets when we stoke it too high!"

"I heard that," Scoe called out.

"Don't make the warden angry," teased one of the twins.

"Have you seen the size of his spear?" said the other.

Scoe fell into an easy banter with the two younger men. Rubriel enjoyed listening to them, relaxing more than she had in a long time.

"Those two are natives," Grace said, following her gaze. "Born and raised in Minnorak. They can be boisterous at times, but they mean well. Their knowledge of these lands has been a great boon to us."

"How come they're with you?"

Grace smiled knowingly. "Well, as you can probably already imagine, they are not fond of rules, and Langlythian society is full of them."

"Rules that no one dares to break."

"Indeed, but they did. I'm not too sure of the details, but apparently they were marked for a lifetime occupation that did not appeal one bit. They up and left that city on a shelf. Been living in the wilds ever since. That's how we found them - or rather, they found us, since they do so enjoy boasting how they saw us a mile off. They showed us to this place." She patted the skin dry and unravelled a clean bandage.

"Why are *you* here? It seems like you've been here a long time."

"My uncle has been making the journey out here every few years for as long as I can remember. Bantrians are superstitious and afraid of these lands, as you know, but it is more than that. There is a troubled history between our people and theirs. My uncle told me there was a terrible war in the past, in the 1700s I think. Tunswick was nearly wiped off the map.

The only reason it still stands is because allies from the west arrived at the last minute and were able to push Langlythe back through the Gloaming Pass. That's why Scoe is with us. He is from Esmara."

Rubriel looked again at Scoe, taking turns now at sparring with the twins. He was tall, built like he'd trained in melee combat ever since he was old enough to hit things with a stick. She watched his style, how he focused more on defence and gradually wore down his opponent. The twins were quick and nimble, but Scoe stood firm and blocked them with ease; neither of them making much progress past his ridiculous shield.

"My uncle considers himself a self-appointed spy, coming here to observe and watch for any sign they might be plotting against us. In my youth, he was always back home within a month or so. My own first two excursions were like that. But this time everywhere we looked he found cause for concern, so we stayed longer... and now we've been here almost a year." Grace finished setting Rubriel's dressing and sat back in her chair.

Rubriel's tone grew skeptical. Grace made her uncle sound more than a little paranoid. "What exactly is the real concern? This country is wild, unnatural and brutal at times but - are you saying there is a real possibility of threat against Bantria?"

Grace sighed apologetically. "It would be best if you asked Uncle directly. He and Scoe do all the analyzing. I... prefer to stay out of it."

Rubriel wondered if she was ashamed to say so. "Thank you," she said, indicating her newly bandaged arm. She was looking forward to a few good hours of sleep.

Standing, Grace led her through to a small room where a wonderfully inviting sleeping bag was already laid out for her. "I shall fetch you clean clothes and something to eat," she said and was gone, leaving Rubriel alone to contemplate all she'd just learned.

Molindra pounded on the door to Gal'denan's office.

"Alright, come in. Knocking harder will not make it open faster," he scolded as she burst through, looking ready to incinerate something.

"So this is what I've been training for. To–to retrieve some ancient artifact from *inside* the Roof of the World. This is why you had me melt and refreeze so much ice over and over again."

"Indeed." He swivelled to face her and waited, not sure what she wanted from him.

"What I practiced on is nothing compared to the crater of a volcano!"

"You will not be alone."

She exhaled sharply. That wasn't the assurance she wanted.

"Sit down, Molindra."

She did so, trying to straighten her thoughts into the questions she needed to ask. "This artifact... how do you know for sure it lies beneath the crater lake?"

"Two hundred years of research and exploration. We found reference enough to determine its location among our oldest archives. Do not forget there are spirits dwelling here today who lived many centuries before you and I were born. They have been able to confirm much of what was written."

"What else do we know about it?" she pressed.

"There will be a vault of some kind – a door, a chest–that requires equal and opposite energies to open it."

"Equal and opposite... as in fire and water?"

He shook his head. "This vault predates even the earliest elementalists. Its lock is thought to require raw energy in its oldest, purest forms. Dark and light; ludion and sildion."

Molindra lifted her sildion pendant out from under her mantle. "I am to use this, Celessil's sacred gift, to open a vault that clearly is not meant to be found?"

"Yes, alongside its counterpart." He paused, and a brief flicker of indecision crossed his face. When he continued, his voice held an unusual sincerity. "Interaction between the two is poorly understood. Our opportunity to study it has been limited, but channeling equal and opposite energies at the same time will not be without risk. It would be... unnatural, to say the least."

"Could it kill me?"

He looked away, straightening the papers on his desk. "Truthfully, I do not know."

13

Friendly Exchange

THE FABLE OF THE GATE

*I*n the year 1677, a young Celessilian mage set out on a long and perilous journey to the Roof of the World, in search of an ancient gateway rumoured to be buried there beneath sixteen centuries of ice and snow. As an elementalist with a particular talent in incendiary arts, Sil'celes believed her ability to generate her own heat and melt the ice beneath her feet would defeat the unforgiving frost.

A few weeks earlier, a kinetic mage set out from Imul'dene with the same intent. With his ability to lift and displace many times his own weight, Deizil believed he would make short work of the snow and ice that barred his way and uncover secrets lost since before time was counted. Alas, while he cleared snowdrift after snowdrift, he was no match for the harsh conditions of the North and its constant blizzards. Though he tried again and again, the roof's icy shingles refused to yield to his touch, and he would be forced to retreat, exhausted, to his packed snow hut; only to find the way once again buried in snow come morning.

At first, Sil'celes made quick progress towards the fabled buried glacier beneath which the gateway was thought to lie. With the heat of her own raw energy swelling around her like a furnace of hot coals, she barely felt the cold and no blizzard could touch her. But once she reached the foot of the glacier and sunk her hands and her power into its base, she was soon overwhelmed by the sheer volume of snow that covered her prize and was forced to retreat, exhausted, to her packed snow hut; only to find what little progress she had made obliterated come morning.

When at last their paths crossed, there was, at first, suspicion. By what path would a man of Langlythe find himself beyond the mountainous walls of his dark homeland? And yet, as they talked, they found that they were not so different; for the languages of northwest and southeast once shared a common mother tongue. They agreed that if they worked together, they might complete the task that had defeated each of them alone.

Deizil cut and shoved the snow aside. Sil'celes melted deep into the ancient ice. And as the water hissed and pooled below, they saw it for the first time: the World Gate, carved of marbled stone, a great doorway standing alone in its magnificence. The height of two men and the width of four abreast, it towered over them as they descended into the icy crevasse.

An inscription scrawled across the top of its curved frame in that old ancestral language. Together they took its meaning: the World Gate connected all the doors of the world as one, that any might come and go between lands as they please. The gate had long been sealed, however; not merely lost to the ravages of time, but purposely locked and buried at the time of the Great Segregation. Its key lay hidden elsewhere.

Deizil and Sil'celes made camp together that night and pondered what to do about their discovery, for returning with news of the Gate to either country would surely spark a race for the key. And what would their present day independent races do with such a power?

In the end, they made a pact. They would never speak of their discovery, nor record it in writing. They would return to their respective lands unsuccessful in their search and allow the World Gate to remain nothing more than a legend, for no one faction of man could be entrusted with the power to come and go as they please and not use it for dominion over others. And so they parted, never again to meet. Sil'celes kept her promise and carried the secret of the World Gate to her eventual grave. Deizil did not.

The next few days passed comfortably. After long weeks on the road and as many more watching her back while pretending to be someone else, Rubriel was glad of the chance to finally relax and take some much needed rest. She exchanged tales of her adventures thus far with her new hosts. They listened with interest, as she was the only one of the five to have travelled through, and spent any significant amount of time in, the various settlements along the road from the Gloaming Pass. The twins were most impressed that she had managed to blend in for so long and learn as much as she had. Daelin and Dornir had been living outside society for the last three years and never set foot in a village other than to steal food or supplies - a skill of which they were unreasonably boastful.

Grace, she learned, was born in Tunswick and grew close to Adam for the latter half of her childhood after her father died. She studied herbalism from a young age and worked at the infirmary, tending wounds and minor ailments with trusted tonics, tinctures and poultices. She recalled that they sometimes used a miniature setup of mirrors and lamps to nurture some of the more delicate herbs indoors - a concept not unlike that used in Andorlai.

Scoe, meanwhile, was born to a wealthy family. Wanting to see more of the world, he had crossed the sea from the Western Continent and docked at the port of Ornage, the only well-established trading hub between the two continents, where the distance by ship was shortest. The city was a bustling centre of commerce, where suppliers and businessmen gathered in spacious trade halls to spread their merchandise in grand displays, hoping to attract the rich and powerful buyers from the West.

From there, he took the main road to Tunswick. He had actually spent quite some time in Tunswick the summer before last, getting to know the locals and unfamiliar customs - and ultimately befriending Adam and Grace. The three of them had made the initial journey into Langlythe together, through the Gloaming Pass before the construction began behind the outer wall. They had bypassed Mornik and the spirit of the stream altogether, instead attempting to head due north and ending up very, very lost - or so the twins liked to remind them.

The camp had a loose sense of routine about it. Scoe trained daily, running through a sequence of intense exercises and stretches to keep his muscular form toned and supple. He never missed an opportunity to spar with the twins or occasionally with Adam if they were around, but more often than not they left the cave soon after rising. They did not return until what their stomachs somehow universally deemed "supper time" - even though it was impossible to tell when night replaced day. Adam's old pocket watch had ceased to keep time a while ago.

Adam spent much of his time observing the surrounding lands. The cave entrance faced south, but if one were to climb higher and scale the slope towards the west, they would come across a rocky outcropping from where they could see far across the cultivated Plains of Kalakat below. He spent many hours here alone with his spyglass, watching unseen as Langlythe's agricultural communities cultivated their hardy crops.

The arterial route to the capital ran through here, far in the distance. Sometimes, when the air was particularly clear, he could just make out the silhouettes of a patrol or caravan making its way to or from the great city of Imul'dene. Rubriel couldn't help but wonder what it was he was waiting to see.

She asked him about it after supper, joining him where he sat warming his hands by the fire.

He wore a hooded, thoughtful expression. "The Plains of Kalakat are the only other fertile land they have besides the Central Plateau. This area supplies food and textiles to most of the country. You can learn a lot about the state of a nation by watching its people."

She agreed.

"An army would also likely march this way, as although the distance is greater, the road is much wider and easier for a large contingent to travel than the narrow slopes of Coal Miners' Pass."

"You speak as though we are at war, and..." She thought for a moment. "That has happened before, hasn't it? Grace mentioned something. She said that Langlythe all but destroyed Tunswick a long time ago."

"Indeed, the Sudden War of 1742," Adam said. "Called so because it ended so abruptly. My great-grandfather was mayor of Tunswick at the time." He sat back and folded his hands in his lap.

"What really happened?" Rubriel asked.

"A bitter struggle for the then newly opened Gloaming Pass. Langlythe would have broken through if Esmara had not arrived to aid us from the West. Yet while we drove them back through the pass, they sent an aerial legion in secret; a host of mages mounted upon great-bats. They bathed Tunswick in flame before the alliance knew what was happening, then retreated to their dark lands, sealing the Gloaming Pass behind them."

The events Adam spoke of were a hundred and sixty years ago, yet the bitterness remained fresh in his words. He spat distastefully.

"So Langlythe retreated, just like that - cut themselves off from the outside? That seems like an odd choice, under the circumstances."

"Aye, an odd choice - a coward's choice. They sacked our city for spite and ran, denying us a fair shot at revenge. Bantria has never forgotten." His eyes narrowed as they met hers. "This land is evil, Rubriel."

She said nothing. Adam's brief version of history indeed sounded horrific, but she struggled to reconcile the notion of *evil* with the common people she had laboured alongside.

"The pass was reopened fifteen years ago," Adam continued. "Tunswick was on high alert. We stationed patrols along our side of the pass and doubled our military presence. That is why there are so many watchtowers dotted throughout the fertile plains. Our farmlands are the envy of the Eastern Continent; it isn't hard to imagine why Langlythe wants to take it for themselves. The pass was gradually widened - by them - over the years, and relations remained extremely tense, but there has been no attack. At least not yet."

"And you believe there will be soon," Rubriel said thoughtfully.

"It is not a matter of *if,* but *when,*" he replied gravely. "There is every indication that Langlythe is preparing for war on a grand scale."

She was reminded suddenly of the protester in Andorlai. Hadn't he claimed they were using the growing houses towards feeding an army?

Sleep eluded her after that. She tossed and turned under the thin blankets; this new, nagging worry holding sleep just beyond reach. As always, her thoughts strayed back to Molindra. She'd told the story the day she arrived - the salient points at least - but none of them had any news to give, good or otherwise. It was beginning to feel as though her friend had disappeared into thin air.

She nursed the spiral ring on the ring finger of her right hand - something she caught herself doing a lot lately - until she finally dozed off, only to be woken a few hours later by the sounds of Scoe running through his daily routine. Yawning, she padded out to the main chamber to watch.

His discipline reminded her of her old instructor. That had been many years ago, but she remembered his lessons like it was yesterday.

Observe your opponent every chance you get, he would say. *Both in and out of combat. The key to a combatant's strengths and weaknesses can be*

*hidden in the smallest details; a favoured limb, an opening left unprotect-
ed.*

Rubriel flexed her injured arm experimentally. The wound had healed
nicely; the muscles felt stiff and awkward from lack of use, but the
soreness of the bite itself had all but gone. She found another of Scoe's
blunt practice weapons - a piece of repurposed junk, really - and began
to run through her own set of moves.

"Would you like to spar?" asked Scoe. "If you're healed enough, that
is."

"Why not?" She moved away from the pool to stand opposite him.

They began with the basics, Scoe clearly holding back out of concern,
but the last of her stiffness soon melted away with the warmup. He
pushed harder then, picking up the pace, and she responded in kind.
Her movements were swift and precise, a practiced and balanced blend
of speed, strength and deadly accuracy. The rhythm was ingrained in the
very fibre of her being. It returned to her as naturally as a bird to flight,
sliding smoothly from one quick stroke and parry to the next.

Whatever Scoe had been expecting, he was taken by surprise. He held
his own until she managed to trip him and sent him sprawling uncere-
moniously on his back.

"Blazes, Rubriel! Where did you learn to fight like that!?"

She chuckled. "I was a sparring champion in Celessil for four years
running. Swordplay is an important part of our culture, especially in the
city. Hundreds of people gathered ringside to socialize and cheer for their
favourites. There were tournaments held all throughout the year; I rarely
lost." She offered a hand and pulled him to his feet.

"I can see why," Scoe remarked, grimacing as he rolled his shoulders
and rubbed the soreness from his back. He took a bottle and filled it from
the spring, splashing the sweat from his face and taking a deep drink.

Rubriel rummaged for a mug among the cooking supplies and knelt to do the same.

"What about you? It is not often I come across another trained in the old ways."

"We have compulsory military service in Esmara. Our units prefer firearms, of course, but our enchantrists developed shields that can stop a bullet, and so we learn both ways."

"*That* can stop a bullet?" She raised a brow at his ungainly shield where it rested against the wall.

"No." He chuckled. "I did not bring an Esmaran war shield with me to Bantria. Can you imagine the looks on their faces at immigration if I had? I hardly expected to need one! But then I ended up here, and that... well, that is a door."

Rubriel burst into laughter.

His cheeks flushed. "It was a difficult situation!" he protested. "That door saved our lives, so I modified it to suit. It is not easy to find good doors around here."

She laughed even harder. "You said good doors."

"*Shields!* Good shields, damnit!"

"Alright, I will stop teasing you," she said smugly.

She grew serious. "It is one thing to fight for sport and entertainment. But fighting in the real world, where sometimes the only option is to take a life or lose your own, is another matter entirely."

Scoe nodded. They sat together at the edge of the pool, listening to the refreshing trickle of the glacial waters tumbling down the far wall.

"I understand. I have seen battle before; bandits, outlaws, gangs. Training prepares your body, but it doesn't always prepare your mind. There is no shortage of violence in fair Esmara." He sighed.

"What really brought you here, Scoe?" Her pale grey eyes settled on his face with a kind and curious gaze.

Scoe forced a smile. "Cold feet," he said, his embarrassment returning.

Rubriel grinned. "You were to wed?" She nudged closer so no one else could hear.

Scoe nodded. "Yes. It, ah." He struggled for the right words. "It was just too big and scary all at once. I panicked. I didn't really mean to leave; I just needed some space." He rubbed his forehead.

"What is she like?"

"Tall, strong, curly brown hair and blue, blue eyes. I've known her since I was a boy. We trained together, studied together. Our courtship was... encouraged," he said awkwardly, taking another swig from his water bottle.

"Encouraged by whom?" Rubriel frowned, the slightest twinkle of mischief in her eyes.

"Her father. And, well, most everyone really."

"Sounds like you spent a lot of time with her."

"Yes. Until one day my father took me aside and told me the King wished to offer me his daughter's hand in marriage." The words tumbled from him in an untidy cascade. He grimaced.

"Your betrothed is a princess?" A cheeky grin spread across her face.

"The one and only."

"Well, do you love her?"

His jaw dropped a little, not expecting such a direct question about his feelings. He wrestled with it internally. Rubriel just waited.

"I think so," he conceded. "It's just..." He gestured with one hand to make a point and then dropped it. "It is a lot of responsibility. I'm not sure I'm ready for that. For having everyone watching me, following my lead, expecting - even though they do already. I must sound like a fool to you."

Rubriel smiled and prodded his knee with her own. "While running to the other side of the world and holing yourself up in an ashen wasteland may have been a slight overreaction, I understand."

Scoe laughed in spite of himself. "You do?"

Rubriel looked thoughtful. "I suppose I have always played the part of the responsible one, but in reality? I've always been running, moving, sidestepping. I cannot seem to put down roots, or… *be* anyone, or anything in particular. I become whatever is needed to survive, and what I've discovered is, that is not always someone I like."

"You seem very in control."

"Do I?" she asked. "Because lately I feel that control slipping away, like I'm a slave to this quest, and the harder I try to find Molindra, the harder it gets." She shivered, changing the subject. "I had a man who called himself my betrothed once. He waited nearly ten years for me to set a wedding date. I never did."

"What happened?"

"I cared for Avorell, but it wasn't love. He loved an idea of me, of who he thought I would become as his wife. It just never felt right, though I did a poor job of explaining why not. I began to resent him. I am glad I left when I did."

Scoe pondered this for a while, his fingers tracing half circles on the rim of his empty bottle. He was only twenty-two, but he'd known Lady Morgrian since they were children. He tried to imagine what that would be like, to have her silently drift off in some other direction while he clung to the future for which he'd always hoped. He missed her more than he wanted to admit.

"Do you have family back in Celessil?" he asked instead.

She took a deep breath before answering. It had been many years since she'd spoken so candidly about her past to someone new. But Scoe was a good man, easy to talk to, and she found herself enjoying the openness of their conversation.

"No. My sister left shortly after I did. She is a talented musician with the most beautiful singing voice I've ever heard. She is famous in the East." She smiled fondly, remembering. "If only you could hear her sing, Scoe. There is magic in her melodies; I am sure of it."

"I should like to," he said. "Do you think she'll ever travel to the West?"

"That is her plan, someday." She frowned slightly. "Soon, I hope, if Adam is right about the rumours of war."

"What about others?" He paused. "Forgive my ignorance, but... I am not sure how the sildion thing works, but if your parents, grandparents, went back to Celessil, they'd still be alive? I assume."

She chuckled. "Yes, but... no. It is true that those who reside within the sphere of influence of our mother sildion are exceptionally long-lived, but my sister raised me on her own."

The frankness with which she said that startled Scoe. "Oh. Sorry."

Her brow rose and fell in a nonchalant dismissal.

"But... well, someone must have given birth to you. You didn't just drop out of the sky."

"As far as I know!" she exclaimed, enjoying Scoe's bewilderment.

He laughed before he caught himself and grew serious again. "Sorry. That must've been hard."

She shifted uneasily. "I suppose it was, as a child. Sometimes people would ask well-meaning questions and I wouldn't have the answer, since Gwendolen would never talk about it. They thought me strange. But I got used to it, grew up, lived my life. I learned to deflect the questions I didn't want to answer. Knowing my bloodline isn't going to change who I am today. Is it?" The single eyebrow quirked almost to her hairline told him that she still wasn't taking this conversation entirely seriously.

"I don't know. Most people seem to have at least some desire to understand where they came from." He shrugged and grinned.

"I think it matters more when you're younger. I'm well beyond repair as far as parental guidance is concerned." She grinned back, and they both laughed some more.

Miles to the north, in a tower overlooking the mage's courtyard, Molindra prepared for her journey.

The disgruntled way she stuffed her necessary belongings into her travelling pack betrayed her resentment of the mission before her. The slight tremor in her fingers as she shook her temperamental compass gave away her nerves.

"Useless thing," she muttered. The compass *looked* fine enough; fashioned in gold with a fine needle and elegant letters, but it steadfastly refused to point north.

"Let me see that," Gal'denan said curiously.

She shrugged and handed him the compass.

He twisted it in his fingers, watching the needle spin wildly. "How did you come by this?"

"I bought it from a shady dealer. He claimed it was a high-quality piece. I should've known better. It doesn't even work." She shot it an accusing look.

But Gal'denan looked thoughtful. "No, I believe it does, in fact, *work;* though perhaps not in the way you expected. Which way does it point when you hold it?"

"It varies. On my journey here it pointed north like a compass should. But now it points east, east-north-east I suppose. I don't see how that is useful."

"This compass does not tell you which way is north; it tells you which way you are going."

Molindra returned a very puzzled expression.

"I have no cause to make any journey, so in my palm it cannot point anywhere. But you? You are destined to travel east, through the Ice Divide. This compass will always point toward your destination, no matter what route you take." He handed it back to her, and sure enough, the needle swiveled to the east.

"It knows where I am going… even if I don't. I'm not sure whether to find that comforting or intrusive."

Gal'denan laughed, and Molindra scowled.

"I assume you or one of your companions has been supplied with a piece of darkstone, in some form?"

She started, reaching for the obsidian-like gem in her pocket. She'd never mentioned it to him, or anyone else for that matter.

"No, I do not wish to see it." He recoiled, stopping her. "And you think your *compass* is intrusive. Still, I suppose if you have been carrying both stones on your person all this time with no obvious ill effects, the odds of you being incapacitated from channeling both are somewhat reduced."

His sarcasm hit a nerve.

"Must you look down upon everything that I do?" she hissed back at him. "I am not your project, nor your pet."

"It is not your use of magic I find amusing, but your naivety. And yes, I rather think you are." His smugness made her want to smack him.

"What is the use in honing my skills if it only serves to erode my freedom?" she muttered as she threw the pack over her shoulder and marched from the door.

"Such is the price of power, Molindra. The more you have, the less it belongs to you."

She hesitated. "And you? How come *you* are not joining me on this expedition?"

"I am untrustworthy."

She blinked at his nonchalant reply, spoken with not a trace of bitterness.

"With an artifact as potent as the one you seek, it would be all too easy from my elevated position to take control. It is as I said; I am the most powerful mage in this city - save Zildred himself - and kept on the shortest leash."

She said nothing. She had already considered that possibility; not to seize power in Langlythe, but to take this artifact - whatever it was - for herself and flee.

He mistook her silence for want of further proof. "Why do you think Merrick is so keen to assist you? He has designs of his own, though he lacks the courage to follow through."

"Hmm." She feigned disinterest, even as further ideas sprouted in her mind. "Farewell then, I suppose."

"Good luck," he returned pleasantly, going back to his work as though they had spoken of nothing weightier than the best way to brew tea from swamp moss.

14
Roof Shall Fall

"I wonder if the twins found anything. They've been gone a while," mused Scoe as he watched Grace stirring a pot of stew over a handful of glowing hot coals.

"Indeed," she said. "Do you think we should be worried?"

"No. No, I'm sure they're fine. Those two have a knack for avoiding trouble by an extremely thin margin." He peered through a tiny gap between his fingers for emphasis.

"Or just extremely lucky," Adam grumbled. "We could use some of that luck on a hunt. What that stew needs-" he took a sniff "-is a good bit of rich meat."

"Agreed." Grace sighed.

"I miss Esmaran food," said Scoe. "The rich flavours, the spices. Fresh fruits bursting with juice. Meat and vegetables fried in oils until the outside is crispy and golden..."

"Ooh, stop it!"

Rubriel listened quietly in the background. Food was always a favourite topic of conversation with those three. They could go on like that for hours. She smiled. Grace was a fine cook, and she did her best with what food they could find. She had a quiet positivity about her which Rubriel admired, a stark contrast to her uncle's pessimism.

"These aren't really peas though," Scoe was saying. "They're too solid. More like lentils."

"Since when were you an expert on vegetables?"

He did not finish his thought, for at that moment Daelin and Dornir returned to the camp, out of breath like they had been running and a troubled look about them.

"What is it?" Adam asked, rushing to his feet.

"Mages. Elementalists," said Dornir, puffing. "They passed right by us, headed northeast."

"Towards the Ice Divide," Daelin finished for him.

"How many?"

"Eleven. Their leader is high ranked. And with him - a woman with hair the colour of parchment, exactly as Rubriel described."

Rubriel started. "Molindra! I must go after them. She is in danger."

"Is she, though?" Dornir cautioned. "She did not seem to be in distress."

"How can we be sure she is not a danger to us?" Daelin added.

"There must be an explanation," Rubriel insisted. "You only saw them from far away, did you not?"

"Yes, but-"

"Molindra is like a sister to me, Dornir," she snapped. "We have had our quarrels, but I cannot believe she would throw her lot in with them from choice. She does not like to be controlled. She would never betray me like that."

"In any case, we must be extremely cautious," Adam interjected. "Follow them if you will; take Scoe with you. We should learn what they are up to. But Rubriel," he said sternly, "you must not be seen."

She huffed in response, his condescending tone grating against her nerves. They downed their meal and began to make preparations at once, not wanting to get too far behind. Her stomach churned at the thought, the first news of her friend in nearly four months. The idea that Molindra was working with Langlythian mages wasn't new to her. She'd grown accustomed to it since first hearing the rumour in Andorlai, but the group's apparent destination was troubling.

What did they seek at the Roof of the World? It was a frozen wasteland of mountains, ice and avalanches whose only inhabitants were the scattered frostmen tribes and the hardy beasts who bore adaptations to such a climate. Daelin and Dornir were to accompany them as far as the caverns beneath the mountains. Scoe and Rubriel would be on their own from there.

"You will likely need to barter safe passage and supplies from the frostmen in order to survive up there," Daelin had explained. "And that will be better accomplished without a Langlythian escort. They will not take kindly to the intrusion from Molindra's party. Those mages will take what they need from the frostmen by force."

Rubriel winced at that.

"I hope you realize just how powerful they are. Even one mage is fearsome in combat, but *eleven*? No doubt they could turn all that ice to steam if they wanted."

Grace packed some rations along with a small pot and a dozen matches, while Scoe found them blankets, a compass, and equipped himself with two fine daggers. Rubriel still had the black overcoat she'd worn when she fled from Andorlai. For the sake of warmth, she put it on over her own wool blazer and breeches, Grace having since mended the torn sleeve from the bat attack. When Scoe emerged, he had the same idea, for he also donned the Langlythian coat and hood he'd been wearing when she first met him.

Worry gnawed at Rubriel's insides as they bid Adam and Grace farewell. She could tell the others thought her foolish, that her feelings blinded her from the truth, but they hadn't lived with Mol for twenty years. It was her nature to be swept up in the moment and carried along a path without thinking of its destination, only to wake up and realize her error half way and scramble to find her way back.

Rubriel had pulled her out of such situations several times in the past. The stakes hadn't been as high, then - alcohol, money, or dishonour thanks to Tunswick's more nefarious underground groups of rebel mages and smugglers living outside the law - but rarely life and death. Never a brewing storm between nations.

The four of them climbed down from the cave entrance and the twins led them to the east, following a narrow ridge which circumvented the rim of the Jagged Labyrinth's vast basin. They hugged the cliffs on their left and kept a fair distance between themselves and the party of mages up ahead, far enough behind to remain out of sight, but not allowing them to get so far ahead as to lose their trail.

Uneven stones made the path rough underfoot, and the steep descent into the labyrinth on the right meant they had to watch their footing. One misstep could easily lead to a sprained ankle - or worse.

To the south, the great spire loomed in its ominous way, towering over them even from their vantage point at the lip of the basin.

"Daelin," murmured Rubriel, "What is that thing?"

"That would be the Lone Peak," he replied. "One of the oldest structures in Langlythe, carved from the giant rock formation that gives it its name. The platform at the top holds the great ludion, or *Morkile-ne Nect*, as my people sometimes refer to it. We know that it is probably at least nineteen centuries old, but its origins - and function - are not well understood."

"It makes me uncomfortable. There is a strange energy coming from up there."

"Of course there is. The great ludion's energy is that of the dead. I have never been up there, but the stone is said to be three times the height of a man."

"And what exactly *is* ludion? The word would translate to darkstone where I come from, but I have never heard of such a thing."

"Some would indeed call it a stone. Some call it a jewel. Others say it is raw energy in solid form, or the opposite of raw energy, but that doesn't make a lot of sense to me. There are a great many rumours about it and very little science. They say that the Master of Imul'dene draws some or all of his power from it, and that part I do believe."

"Do I want to know who he is?" She frowned doubtfully.

"Someone you should hope you never meet. He has control over all the spirits of this land and uses them to maintain a constant vigil over his domain. He is also capable of maintaining his own physical presence in multiple places at once, and can rip the thoughts, feelings, memories straight out of your head with merely a touch. There is no shortage of reasons why people fear him."

Rubriel grimaced. She looked up at the Lone Peak once again and decided that the white snow and freezing temperatures beyond the Ice Divide, however unpleasant, would nonetheless be a welcome reprieve from Langlythe's oppressive darkness.

The journey was not as much of a reprieve as they'd hoped. Daelin and Dornir turned back at the mouth of the ice caverns, leaving Rubriel and Scoe to brave the slippery way forward alone. The vast, interlinked caves of the Ice Divide made Scoe's compass a true necessity if they were to avoid losing their way. Spearlike protrusions of ice hung from high arched ceilings. Even the smallest sound echoed all around, forcing them to slow to a quieter pace and lose further ground to their quarry.

They stopped for a brief rest by a partially frozen pool and quenched their thirst on the clear waters. It stung their throats on the way down and sent a brief but painful ache across their foreheads. They ate a little of their packed rations and took turns at getting an hour or two of sleep each, but it wasn't long before they were again up and moving.

The first beams of arctic daylight broke through the cave exit after about two days of hard travel. Its brightness brought tears to their eyes after so many months in the dark, a little disorienting at first. A stinging wind whipped across their faces as they staggered out into the foothills, sinking up to their knees in snow as they looked around for confirmation of where the mages had gone next.

They found it a short way to the north. The previous night's snowfall had erased any trace of footprints, but the path the elementalists had melted and refrozen into the snow was still visible as a trench several inches deep.

With their hoods pulled close and their scarves wrapped securely up over their noses and ears, they quickened their pursuit, hoping to regain some ground while the conditions were more favourable.

Far from Esmara's subtropical climate, Scoe felt the cold much more keenly than Rubriel did, though even she could not recall ever trekking through quite this much snow before. He was both fascinated and appalled by the stuff, how it shifted uncomfortably under his footsteps and stuck in clumps to his boots, making his movements clumsy and awkward.

Rubriel told him stories of Tunswick winters as they went, how the children filled the fields with snowmen every Solstice while the sweepers cleared the roads of snow twice a day or more to make way for horse and carriage.

Scoe could scarcely imagine living in such conditions for a week, let alone an entire season.

The Roof of the World was a solid land mass extending from the upper reaches of the Eastern Continent, and though parts of it were below sea level, the climate kept the ice permanently frozen. A massive lake dominated its more southern regions, off which most of the native peoples made their livelihood. Further north, the terrain grew steeper and far less hospitable, filled with mountains and glaciers much too dangerous to climb.

The pole itself was thought to be flat, but no successful expedition had ever reached it; save, perhaps, among the hardy native tribes, who were far better adapted to the ways of the arctic.

The mages' trail continued further to the north and once again began to climb. Rubriel and Scoe hoped it would lead them close to one of the frostmen villages, where they might restock their supplies for the rest of the journey and find a warm bed for the night - if the frostmen were agreeable. Rubriel knew little of the northern tribes. They kept to themselves, far from modern civilization, continuing to live off the land as they had for centuries.

If she was being honest, she was not at all confident that she and Scoe would be welcome here. Given a choice, she would have preferred to leave the natives well alone, but they both knew that wasn't an option if they were to travel further north and make it back alive.

As if to prove a point, the sky darkened and the wind blew stronger. Huge snowflakes began to fall, swept along far and fast in the growing gale and smothering what remained of the trail. They stumbled on doggedly for as long as they could, just a bit further and a bit further, shielding their faces and desperately peering into the storm for signs of life, a glimpse of a road, shelter - anything.

"This is impossible," Rubriel said in dismay, raising her voice to be heard over the howl of the wind. "We're going to have to make shelter and wait this out."

"Make shelter?" said Scoe. "How exactly do you propose we do that?"

"We dig into the snow and make ourselves a burrow. We won't be able to make a fire, but we can cover the entrance behind us to keep the wind out, and the snow will trap some of our body heat inside. Anything is better than being out in this. I'm freezing."

Scoe's teeth chattered. "I'm so cold I can hardly think straight."

"You must keep moving, no matter what. Start digging with me and don't stop until we have a hole we can both crawl into. And keep talking, even if you're tired. You have to fight that fogginess you're feeling. It is very important."

She spoke in a firm, even tone, but she was worried about him. His lips were turning blue and he'd been getting increasingly sluggish and clumsy in his movements. The fast-falling snow sat loosely on the ground and proved difficult to work with, falling back into the hole they made as fast as they could scoop it out with their frozen fingers.

"Push it all to this side," she suggested, shoving her weight behind a pile of snow and compacting it into a wall against the prevailing wind.

Scoe followed her lead, and soon they had a bank tall enough to crouch behind and catch a respite from the gale, at least.

"Did you hear that?"

"Hear what?"

"I thought... barking. In the distance," he mumbled.

Rubriel strained her ears and listened.

"Maybe I'm going mad," said Scoe.

Then they both heard it; the rustle of someone approaching, footfalls muffled by the snow until the natives were right upon them.

These men were stocky and broad-chested, their lilac-hued skin hardened from life in the frigid north. Each wore thick furs and hide and carried a spear almost as long as he was tall. Others carried bows with quivers upon their backs. Knives hung from their sturdy belts. Behind them, several wooden sleds pulled to a stop by shaggy, wolf-like animals, who growled at the newcomers' approach and pawed warily at the snow.

The leader of the hunting party stepped forward, and the others immediately moved to guard his flank. More emerged from the blizzard to encircle the intruders and cut off their escape route from behind. Rubriel and Scoe stood slowly from their miserable shelter and raised their empty palms in surrender, looking from one fierce pale face to the next until the big man in front spoke at last.

His deep voice cut cleanly through the wind. "For what reason do two Langlythian stragglers wander ill equipped through the Frostfells? Speak."

"We are not of Langlythe," Scoe answered, slowly. "I am Scoe Mytholi of Esmara; this is Rubriel of Celessil. We…" His numb, sleepy mind struggled to find his next words.

"We trail a party of mages headed towards the Roof," Rubriel finished for him, "but we are lost in the storm and in desperate need of shelter. Please, we really need your help."

Murmurs ran through the group surrounding them. The leader surveyed their foreign clothing and pathetic attempt at a snow cave and spat his distaste.

"Bah! Those treacherous bastards outnumber you six to one. If you seek confrontation, then you are fools; if you are a friend of theirs, you are no friend of ours!"

His men shook their spears in agreement, a bitter look in their eyes.

"Fools we may be," she acknowledged, "but we mean you no harm. I swear it." She carefully lifted her sildion from her breast with frigid hands. Its bright light dazzled against the blustering white, and the big man's brows lifted at the sight of it.

"Langlythe threatens my homeland too. We are a friend to the tribes of the north and would seek your counsel. Please. My friend won't last out here much longer."

He nodded warily. "Maybe you are, maybe you aren't. Chief Selch will decide what to do with you."

With that, the tribesmen parted and ushered Scoe and Rubriel towards the sleds. Their weapons were confiscated and their hands bound in rope before they were piled onto the back of the sleds with the rest of the hunters. The wolves took off, straining hard against their lashings under the extra weight, barking as they gathered momentum. They drove against the biting wind, deeper and deeper into the northwest.

The storm was beginning to settle by the time they reached the tribe's village. A strange stillness greeted them. Women and children peeked timidly from the doors of their snow houses as the party made its way towards the chief's pavilion - a snow house bigger than all the rest. They passed the remains of a family dwelling, its snow blocks caved in and melted, its hide floor and fur bedding burnt and charred. Ash and soot stained the nearby snow. Scoe and Rubriel exchanged a grim look.

The hunting party disembarked their sleds and began to unload. Their leader - whose name they learned was Ik - brought the two of them through the entrance tunnel into the chief's meeting place. It was surprisingly warm inside the giant domed structure, warmed by the body heat of many people inside and insulated by the thick snow blocks that held its shape.

Chief Selch sat cross-legged at the back of the room atop a bearskin rug. He stood as they approached, and they saw that he was wounded; his right arm bandaged and held in a sling, the side of his face reddened and sore with recent burns.

"Welcome home, Ik. Who have we here?" he asked, nodding at Scoe and Rubriel, who kept their eyes lowered respectfully and made an effort to appear as non-threatening as possible.

"We found them wandering below the foothills, claiming to be tracking the same party of mages that raided us."

"Langlythians?"

"They say they are not."

"Well?" said the chief. "What have you to say?"

Rubriel chose her words carefully. "I am Rubriel of Celessil. This is Scoe Mytholi of Esmara. It is true that we travelled through Langlythe - through the Ice Divide - to get here, but we do so only because we fear what those mages are planning. We have reason to believe that Langlythe intends to wage war to the south, and even if we cannot stop them, we at least need to know what they want at the Roof of the World. I do not think they would send so many elementalists at once unless they are expecting a battle - or intend to melt a great deal of ice - and that worries me either way."

The chief's expression grew dark. "They came to our village three days ago, demanding transport and supplies for their journey in exchange for the chest of gold they brought with them. It has been a rough season for us, and we had not the resources to spare for such a journey. When we refused, they destroyed my daughter's home and threatened the same fate to our entire village if we did not give them what they wanted. They took our food, our sleds and our furs and left us with next to nothing, save that chest of gold."

He spared a glance across the room where the chest still sat, unwelcome and unwanted. "We have no use for gold. It will not keep our bellies full or our houses warm."

"I'm so sorry, Chief," said Rubriel - and she was. The fear and anxiety that had twisted in her gut since Molindra left had begun turning to anger - a dangerous, ruthless kind of anger, simmering beneath the surface. "Do you have any idea what they're looking for?"

"An artifact of some kind. A formidable one. There are ancient things buried within the Roof of the World - things that are not meant to be found." The chief scowled.

"Scoe, the snowmelt from the Roof - it feeds the rivers that flow down through the Fertile Plains. If they melt the ice caps, the town of Tabethwick and all its fields will flood."

"Then we have to stop them," said Scoe. "Chief Selch, will you help us go after them? Put a stop to their plans before they can hurt anyone else?"

But the chief shook his head. "As much as I would like to see Langlythe brought down to size after what they did, we are not equipped for such a confrontation, and neither are you. We are in for a rough year ahead as it is, and I do not wish to see any more lives lost."

"Untie them," he said to Ik. "If you wish to continue your pursuit, we will not stand in your way, but I cannot spare any more supplies nor able hands to go with you."

Rubriel bit her lip, but nodded in understanding.

"Thank you for hearing us out. I am sorry for your loss." Scoe bowed.

With that, they were dismissed. "What'll we do now?" asked Scoe as they made their way out of the hut and followed one of the chief's men to their sleeping quarters for the night.

Rubriel had no answer. The storm had lifted for now and the peach rays of sunset pierced the clouds, but they both knew it would only get colder and more dangerous as they headed further north, for the Roof never felt the soft touch of spring and the ice never melted there.

The morning lifted Scoe's spirits a little. Bright daylight - the first true daylight he had seen for many months - drew a smile to his face as a brisk, clear sky greeted them. They set out at an easy jog, following a road of sorts; a route well used by dog and sled.

Rubriel remained quiet and brooding beside him. He felt for her, though he could scarcely imagine how it must feel to have known someone as long as she had known Molindra and then have that person act in such an uncharacteristic way. Rubriel still had faith in her best friend; he could see that hope lingering there. She wanted to believe that Molindra would never have hurt or stolen from those tribes people, that she was here against her will. Scoe wasn't sure what he thought anymore.

They made it only a few hours before the clouds rolled in and the first flakes of snow began to fall. By now, their noses were already red from the cold and their toes had numbed in their boots. They kept up the pace for as long as they could, knowing that if they slowed, they would soon be forced to dig in and lose precious time. But as the snow intensified and the wind sent brutal lashings of ice against them, their progress slowed to a trudge.

"Rubriel, we cannot keep going like this," Scoe shouted from beneath his hood. "Not without proper clothing and supplies. This bitter wind will be the death of us."

"What choice do we have? If we stop now, we'll never make it in time."

"If we keep going, we might not make it at all! We should turn back to the Ice Divide. Make camp on this side of the pass and lie in wait for their return. Molindra's company will surely go back the way they came."

"And what then? What if something happens to her? What if she isn't even with them when the company returns? What happens when Langlythe gets hold of this 'artifact' and uses it to-"

The barking of dogs and a spray of loose powder stopped them as a lone sled rushed downhill toward them, turning and skidding to a halt. A familiar pale face eyed them from beneath a heavy fur hood. "I will take you," said Ik. "Climb on."

They stumbled aboard the small sled, just big enough for the two of them to sit comfortably behind Ik's driving position.

"I brought some spare furs from my household. You may borrow them for the journey."

"We are most grateful!" Rubriel could scarcely believe their luck. "Thank you."

With pelts to keep them warm and the sled flowing swiftly across the tundra, they made up considerable ground. Their quarry was a day ahead of them at most, and with Ik's sled and mastery of the terrain to guide them, they might just have a chance of catching up before the mages could melt through the Roof. And if they did? Rubriel had to admit she wasn't sure what she would say to Molindra given the chance, or even if she would have the opportunity to speak with her.

Was this a rescue mission, or just another of Mol's great schemes blown way out of proportion? Would Rubriel talk some sense into her, persuade her to come home and leave the Langlythians to their search among the ice caps? *It's not going to be that simple*, she thought. Because it wasn't just about Mol anymore; if the mages really did intend to melt as much ice as Ik's people said they did, the consequences for Tabethwick would be devastating.

15

Key to the Continent

The Glass Lake wasn't made of glass - not really - but the sharp, transparent quality of its icy rim made it seem so. Nor was it truly a lake, for the extinct volcano's crater was filled with years of snow and debris, frozen solid and unmelting.

"We're here," Merrick announced, their trek up the mountainside ending in a near-vertical surface up ahead. The party of eleven had taken turns clearing the path, rotating in pairs these last few days; except for Molindra, whose strength they were saving for the final task that lay just beyond the crater wall. They took a moment's pause. Merrick walked around the outside aways, Molindra in tow.

"We cannot climb over this," she said, peering up at the crater rim above them.

"No," he agreed. "The floor of the crater is much lower on the other side. Even if we were to make our way to the top, we would be faced with a sheer drop."

"So we tunnel straight through. There are areas here-" Mol pointed to a lighter patch "-where the wall is only ice, and we can melt our way in. We are so close." Her face set in determination. "We will retrieve the artifact and be gone from this place!"

"Indeed," he replied evenly. Merrick was a difficult man to read.

The mages organized themselves, forming a semicircle around the spot Molindra had indicated. She placed one fingertip against the ice and channelled heat to that precise location, until water ran down her palm and a small but distinct hole appeared in the surface before them. She stepped back, joining the others, and together they focused on that one spot.

The hole deepened and spread. A cracking sound followed as the rapid heating of the ice caused jagged fissures to radiate out from the centre. The energy intensified to a palpable heat, and the hole widened rapidly into a nearly cylindrical tunnel. Water gushed forward and turned to steam at their feet. The sides of the tunnel cooled just as rapidly upon removal of the heat source and froze into a firm structure, wide and tall enough for them to pass through in single file.

Just like that, the way into the heart of the Glass Lake, untouched for centuries, opened to them.

Merrick went through first, testing the footing on the other side of the tunnel. He nodded to the rest of the group and clamoured down from the entrance. Mol pulled her furs tighter across her chest and followed. There was still a drop by a few feet from the opening into the vast basin of solid ice within the crater. The sky overhead was a clear, pale blue, and the sun glistened bright and sparkling off the walls. She shielded her eyes as she walked towards the centre.

"How far down do you suppose it is?" she asked of Merrick, who was pacing the distance from the midpoint to the rim and measuring the radius against its height.

"Hard to say," he said. "At least this distance again before we hit rock, based on the overall size of the crater. Perhaps more, if it turns out to be especially deep. We have our work cut out for us."

"I hope she's as strong as they say she is," one of the others muttered.

Molindra ignored her. That ice was now all that stood between her and this "artifact", and with it, the key to their freedom. She did not know what manner of ancient treasure was buried here - none of them knew exactly - but it was either very valuable, very powerful, or both to warrant such a large expedition. Their instructions were to return with it to Imul'dene with all haste.

Molindra had other ideas. Away from the eyes and ears of Langlythe, she spoke plainly to the group - a group of elementalists she and Merrick had hand-picked for their strength with fire. But that wasn't the only trait they all had in common. Each of them harboured a secret resentment, a bitterness towards their superiors; a shared motivation - whatever their individual reasons - to exit Langlythian society.

Yes, they would find the artifact, but Molindra promised they would take it south instead, across the Ice Divide into Bantrian territory, from there to sail down the coast and beyond the reach of either nation.

Merrick was a stoic, reserved individual, but he had been kind to her during her training and she had come to rely on him. She wondered at his own reason for wanting to leave. He was affluent, high-ranked, and apparently in good standing. It would take years for him to reach a similar standard of living elsewhere, starting from scratch. Like most Langlythians, he kept his feelings to himself and never shared any details with her.

Nevertheless, having him on her side was the one thing that had kept her sane these last few weeks. She could not have planned all of this without his support.

"Alright, same as before," he was saying. "Form a circle around this point. Keep your area of focus small and keep working downwards until we hit stone. Molindra, let us begin."

She looked at the ground, to the tiny hole marked in the ice no more than a finger's width. She fixated on it, concentrating a stream of heat to that one point until it formed a soft, visible glow. The others joined her effort and together they guided the energy downwards, melting the dense ice layer by layer. The melting point dropped out of sight as they progressed deeper.

Mol closed her eyes to visualize it better. The deeper they went, the harder it became to maintain focus, and the more energy it took to overcome the ancient cold of the mountain's heart.

"I can't go any further," Molindra said.

"We've reached the bottom," Merrick agreed. "Now, hold your focus and begin to push out to the side. Carefully; we do not wish to collapse the ice beneath our feet."

Expanding the hole proved far more challenging. Not only was the focal point, far below them, out of sight, they now had to hold focus on a larger area. It was difficult to hold the vision steady.

"Do not try to melt evenly around the whole circumference; focus only on a line right in front of you. Pull the melt back towards you in segments."

They kept working for a good twenty minutes. From the surface, there was nothing to see, but Molindra could feel the ice separating from the rock; she knew they were making progress, albeit slowly. There was a cracking sound. Suddenly, the ice around the entry point splintered and caved in. They stepped back hurriedly, but the hole remained confined to the centre, an arm's length across and filled with slush and broken lumps of ice. Mol peered cautiously over the edge.

"Is it enough?" one of her companions asked.

The man beside her took one of their hiking poles and prodded below the surface. He shook his head. "It is too deep. I cannot see or touch the bottom."

"We would have to further melt those chunks of ice before one of us could swim down there, and in doing so, we risk collapsing the entire crater beneath us. Some of us will have to stabilize the outer rim while the rest continue to warm the water. We will have to balance our efforts, as we will be opposing one another."

Mol disagreed. "This is not going to work. We don't know how deep that hole really is, nor have any idea what to look for down there. What if the artifact is lodged inside the rock, or there is a whole cave system to navigate? We need to melt through from the top down and expose the whole surface. That's why there are eleven of us. This was never going to be as simple as drilling straight through."

"If we warm the whole lake, the sides of the mountaintop and the glaciers will melt as well. We will not be able to stop until we have drained the entire crater," Merrick warned.

She swallowed. "Then we melt it all. This is a turning point for all of us, for our futures. Starting over somewhere new will not be easy. It will take guts and determination. I should know; I've tried before. This is but our first test. If we let the mountain defeat us, what chance do we have against those who would hunt us down?" She looked from one face to the next. Murmurs ran through the group. "The sun is bright above us; we have all the energy we need. What say you, Merrick?"

All eyes turned to him.

"We melt it all," he said grimly.

"Melt it all!" they echoed, with raised fists and renewed vigour. They reformed into a broader circle, arms linked, and looked to the sun.

The sled raced across the ground. The dogs barked and churned up the snow, their muscular bodies and strong legs making short work of the distance and growing incline. Rubriel and Scoe hung on tight to the back of the sled, the wind whipping around them as they went.

They were close to the Roof of the World now - so close. They had already begun to climb the base of the mountain. The sled would take them as high as the dogs could safely travel, Ik had explained, until the ascent becomes too rocky and too narrow; then they must continue on foot to the summit and the Glass Lake.

"Why did you decide to help us?" Rubriel had asked of him during the one brief stop they made to rest and water the dogs.

"Because I saw in your eyes something the others did not," Ik answered earnestly. "I saw compassion; a kind of sadness and fear for something far beyond yourselves. Chief Selch is doing what he believes is best for our people. But I also believe you are only trying to do the same for yours."

"Will you not be in trouble?"

Ik shook his head. "Our chief is a good man, an honourable man. It is our people's belief that a man should trust his deepest instincts, for that is where we feel the will of Mother Nature guiding us. My divergence will be forgiven, for I sensed strongly that Nature meant for our paths to cross. Why else would She have sent the storm that brought us together, not once but twice?"

Rubriel had questioned then why Mother Nature saw fit to hinder her and Scoe's ascent, not Langlythe's, but she kept those thoughts to herself out of respect for Ik and his kindness, for it would not do to gainsay a culture and beliefs she knew so little about.

The pace slowed as the terrain became uneven and slippery underfoot. Boulders protruded through the snow covering, bearing icicles and posing a threat to the dogs' footing and sled runners alike. And from higher up they began to observe a curious phenomenon, for a thin trickle of water ran down here and there from above, carving a narrow indent in the snow as it went.

By now, the dogs could go no further. They left the sled in a more sheltered spot and proceeded on foot, noticing more and more that the ice above them seemed to be melting unnaturally fast for early spring.

Scoe regarded the mountainside with a worried expression. "They're already here. We must hurry."

They picked up the pace, stumbling and sliding a little. Ik climbed with the aid of two long poles, each with a sharp spike on the end for better purchase on the frozen ground. He handed one of them to Scoe, who was having the most trouble, and the three of them trekked towards the outer wall of the Glass Lake.

"Look there!" Rubriel pointed to the hole in the side of the crater rim, where the human-sized tunnel cut through the ice.

"Blazes, they're *inside.*"

Sensing no time to waste, Rubriel all but sprinted the last few metres to the tunnel opening.

"Be careful..." Ik's voice trailed off behind.

A gust of uncharacteristically warm air greeted her as she peered cautiously into the tunnel. A bright light shone from the other side. Its floor was wet and slushy.

Scoe looked down at his feet. A curious maze of white lines zigzagged through the ice beneath him. They seemed to reach up from below, anastomosing with one another and spreading incrementally across the surface. His eyes widened. "Rubriel..."

"What?"

She looked back, and at the same instant there came a cracking sound, a rush of water, and the entire mountainside collapsed beneath them. The ground shattered and crumbled, chunks of ice rushing downward and sweeping Rubriel and Scoe with them. Ik thrust his pole straight down with all his might. It found purchase somewhere deep below. He clung to it, and Scoe to him, who barely managed to catch Rubriel on the end of his own pole before she tumbled out of reach.

She clung desperately to the shaft as a great wave of water rushed over her and submerged her completely. Scoe lost sight of her. Ik was doing everything he could to maintain their footing as more and more of the ice split and slid away. Rubriel resurfaced from the torrent and gasped, still clinging to Scoe's pole, and she lunged to grab it higher up. Scoe pulled, and she scrambled until he could grab her arm. Ik stumbled as his hold weakened, and Scoe thrust his own pole into the ground to steady them.

The ice below melted so fast from within that they were visibly sinking lower and lower, all three of them soaked to the bone. There was a roar and a clap like thunder, and the whole mountain seemed to shudder as it shed the last of its icy mantle, water gushing over the rim of the crater and nearly taking the three of them down with it. They held on, barely, until at last the eruption stopped and they collapsed in a heap, spluttering and battered.

The mountainside was unrecognizable. They sat on bare rock, the skeleton of the mountain and its crater fully exposed. The crater rim seemed much shorter and wider now, such that they could climb to the top and peer over the edge. No trace of the tunnel or the ice from which it had been carved remained, but for the sound of flowing water continuing somewhere far away.

Wearily, Rubriel led the way up on all fours. Scoe put a finger to his lips, reminding them of the need to be quiet and cautious, for the ordeal they had just survived was not a natural event. She eased up to the edge and looked over. Her breath caught in her throat.

Ten mages stood in a tight circle inside the crater below. An eleventh with ash blonde hair stepped forward to examine something on the ground. They had found Molindra, and they were much too late.

The last vestiges of steam rose from the naked stone at the bottom of the crater, laid bare for the first time in centuries. Several of the mages dropped on the ground to rest, while others bent forward with their hands on their knees, breathless and yet relieved. The final push that tipped the ice melt over the rim of the cauldron had taken more out of them than they anticipated.

Now, they surveyed the results of their labour. The stone beneath them was abnormally flat; cut and shaped by man or magic, while towards the edges of the crater, the rocks held a more uneven, natural arrangement. And right in the centre was an ornate rimmed square embedded in the rock, etched in cold iron like the lid of something, and much too small to conceal a passageway.

Molindra stepped forward and knelt to examine the markings. An ancient inscription engraved in ornate lettering decorated the inside of its iron borders:

No life without death; no dark without light.

Only one who wields both in equal splendour shall hold the key to the continent.

It was written in an old dialect, far predating her native modern Celessilian tongue, but close enough to understand. Two smooth indentations, suggesting a hand should be placed on either side of the plaque. *Only one who wields both...*

Shivering, Molindra wrestled her sildion out from beneath her furs and lifted the chain off over her head. With the other hand, she drew the dark stone from her inner pocket. She held the two gems out in front of her and looked from one to the other, feeling an odd polarising sensation as the power within each stone throbbed and intensified. Almost by reflex she held them further apart from one another, understanding in her peculiar discomfort what Gal'denan meant by equal and opposite forces.

She stiffened, partly from the sensation and partly with nerves. Slowly, she lowered her arms, forcing her hands closer together. Her companions backed away. The stones repelled each other fiercely, but she fought through it, carefully and deliberately pressing each against the indentations on the plaque. She dared not open her fists as the hollow shape suggested, for the gems would leap from her hands in opposite directions if she let go.

It was enough. As soon as she touched the metal, intense pain shot down her arms like a jolt of electricity and then winked out as the clunk of an age old mechanism sounded from beneath the plaque.

She yelped, casting the dark stone away and clutching her sildion pendant, trying to steady herself. With shaking hands, she felt her way around under the rim of the plaque until she found a grip and pried the lid open, her fingers aching. It was no more than a lockbox, a cleverly concealed chest with a seal that very few would possess the means - let alone the knowledge - to unlock. The compartment inside was small and shallow, lined with ice crystals despite the solar inferno moments earlier. And in the centre...

"What is it?" asked one of her companions, peering forward anxiously into the box.

"A..." she trailed off as she drew the ornate metal object from the vault and held it aloft. "A key?"

She frowned, and a brief shadow of doubt crossed her face as she scanned her surroundings, thinking at first to see a hidden door with a fitting lock. There was no such thing, however.

She shook her doubt away. "We have done well. This key is ours now, and with it, we shall forge our own path. The inscription referred to it as the key to the continent. We will find its lock on our own in time, and it will bring us the freedom we so desperately desire."

No one answered. The group had fallen strangely quiet.

Molindra stood there, staring at the key in her hand and finding that she had little clue what to do next, and exhaustion was rapidly catching up with her. "Come," she said finally. "We must move; find warmth and shelter before we freeze. I have not the strength for more fire in this bitter cold. I doubt any of us do after that."

She started towards the crater wall, looking up at the rim which, although much diminished from its former frozen height, would still require a boost in order to climb up. Looking back, she stopped. No one else had moved. No one would meet her eyes.

"Merrick!" she called, louder. "We must go."

But he did not follow her. She almost thought a brief flicker of apology crossed his face before the silence broke.

"You have done well, Merrick. We have what we came for." Zildred materialized before them, and with a mere glance in her direction, his kinetic energy wrenched the key from Molindra's frozen grasp.

Scoe grabbed Rubriel and jerked her back from the edge. "Are you mad?" She'd almost lept out into the open. "There is nothing we can do. Watch and wait."

The three of them crouched behind the crater's rim, listening and stealing brief glances at the proceedings below. They were rather exposed up there, and could not risk peering over the edge for too long, lest one of the mages look up and spot them. But they heard enough of what was said, heard Molindra scream in rage and despair as her former allies abandoned her. The walls of the crater were too steep, and even at full strength, no elementalist could tunnel through solid rock. They had left her there to die.

Scoe and Ik helped Rubriel climb over the edge and lower herself into the pit. They remained on the outside and she went forward alone. Molindra was on her knees, covering her face with her hands and weeping bitterly. There had been many a time over the past years when Rubriel would have run to comfort Molindra, to console her in failure and forgive her latest string of mistakes. Even that morning, as fearful as she had been of her friend's role in this destructive affair, she had still imagined their reunion would be a relief above all else.

But now that she was here... Rubriel couldn't go to her. The wild-eyed, frantic woman that paused in her sobbing and saw her standing there wasn't someone she knew. She wore the deep red of Imul'dene's High Tiers beneath her stolen fur cape, a decorated red and gold mantle fastened about her shoulders. The colour dominated her, taking away from the delicate beauty of her ash blonde hair and fine features. The sharp, angular silhouette of her bodice hardened her appearance, and she seemed all the more foreign and wild in her despair.

Rubriel wore a twisted expression. When she found her voice, anguish tainted her words. "Molindra. What have you done?"

She struggled with her response. "I... this wasn't supposed to happen... Y-you found me. You followed me all this way."

Despite all their years, it had somehow never occurred to her, after the last words exchanged over the burning fence, that Rubriel would try to come after her. Perhaps at the time it hurt less to believe they were finished.

"Of course I came after you!" Rubriel burst out. "I left Tunswick the day after you. Not a single day has gone by without me worrying about you, or replaying our argument over and over in my head. I travelled through the Gloaming Pass. I crossed miles and miles of unforgiving ground until I finally saw you and gave chase to the Roof of the World. The more I learned of Langlythe, the more I dreaded learning of your fate; the more I lay awake imagining horrible things. And I was right to, wasn't I?"

She paused, her eyes darting wildly around the empty crater. "Tell me you didn't come here for personal gain. Tell me you didn't melt the Roof of the World and condemn Tabethwick to flooding and desolation. Tell me you didn't provide our enemy with a weapon to conquer the East."

Mol looked stricken. She wanted to say that she had no choice, that she had been forced to come here, but Rubriel's words stung, and for the first time she felt the heavy weight of guilt settle on her heart. "I don't know," she said, frightened. "I never thought-"

"You never do! You act without thinking and get yourself in too deep before you understand the consequences. I can't *do* this anymore, Mol!" She turned away and sighed, pinching the bridge of her nose. Anger tore at her. Disappointment too, and fear of what would happen when they returned south. She wanted to scream.

"Are you going to leave me here?" She knelt on the ground still, forsaken and forlorn in her defeat. Rubriel would leave her too, she thought, and she would freeze as the frost returned; too drained to keep herself warm and without supplies to restore her energy. Perhaps she deserved it.

"No, of course not." Her voice broke. "Let's go."

Scoe and Ik heaved them both over the rim of the crater and the four of them began a tense, weary descent. There was no sign of the Langlythian company. Nevertheless, they wouldn't feel safe until they were far away from Roof, travelling by sled in the opposite direction until they found themselves back in friendlier climes. No one said anything as they flew south. Only the din of the dogs barking accompanied them as their paws pounded through the snow.

16

Homeward

Ik took them as far as the edge of the tundra, where the snow became too thin for the sled. Here, they bade him farewell and continued on foot. Soon, they found themselves immersed in the boreal forests of northern Bantria, following a rough trail that kept pace with the river Tabeth from on high. Light rain filtered through the needles of the tall spruce, the ground moist and moss-laden underfoot.

Here the land had embraced the throes of spring, blooming and bright green with new growth. It looked to have rained solidly for quite some time, judging by the mud and marshy areas lower down, and the roar of the river current some fifty feet off to their left.

The misty rain had been pleasant at first; a refreshing drift under the warm, humid conditions of the fifth month. Now it soaked through their clothing, leaving the three of them damp, uncomfortable and irritable. They thought they were probably about a day from Tabethwick - perhaps two - and the thought of spending another night out under the spruce with wet boots, wet blankets, wet everything was not even remotely appealing.

Scoe grumbled that it would be impossible to get a campfire going without dry kindling, though Molindra thought that she could, only she would have to maintain it constantly, she said, and the wood would mostly smoulder and smoke.

Rubriel continued to avoid conversation. The numbness she had felt earlier continued. Whenever she opened her mouth to speak, her feelings would either spiral deep into anger and hurt so thick she could choke on it, or flee far out of reach and beyond her own observation. There did not seem to be an in between.

As they descended into late afternoon, the thickening foliage forced the trail closer to the river's edge. They could see its great bulk through the trees, swollen and enraged, its monstrous brown waters ripping and tearing at the muddy banks on either side. The relentless current had already claimed an unlucky sapling; its roots pulled free and dragged downstream to become snagged on a rock lower down. The water frothed over and around it, picking up speed the further down they went.

Alarmed, they pushed further back into the trees, trampling through the undergrowth in order to stay on higher ground. It was exactly as they had feared: the river Tabeth was fed by several glaciers originating at the Roof of the World. The sudden artificial melt had to go some-where, and with this part of the country already in its wettest season, the banks would do little to stop flood waters sweeping through Tabethwick township.

Those fears peaked when, as dusk fell, they reached a clearing in the woods and found it occupied by a sprawling refugee camp, erected by those who fled the rising waters five days earlier. Forlorn, tired faces peered at the three strangers as they wound their way slowly through the tents. Here and there, a family huddled around the dying embers of a campfire. Mothers took refuge in the back of their tents, hushing and singing to wailing children. Husbands and fathers tried to patch up their shelters in preparation for another long night ahead.

The air smelled of damp and misery. These people had been ill pre-pared, no doubt grabbing whatever they could and running for higher ground. Some had been lucky enough to load their provisions and treasures into a wagon; others had escaped with nothing but the clothes on their backs and whatever they could carry on foot. There were horses tied up at one end of the camp, but not enough by far to carry so many.

Rubriel caught the attention of a refugee in passing. "Excuse me. Is there someone in charge here?"

He pointed wordlessly towards a grey tent a few pegs down. A couple sat outside, their hands each wrapped around a mug. They pressed close together upon a wooden trunk, trying to keep warm.

They looked up as the three of them approached, offering tired, but warm smiles.

Rubriel noticed he wore a uniform; dark blue with gold buttons and belted smartly at the waist, though mud stained the bottoms of his trousers just like her own.

"Greetings, sir," she said, offering him a slight bow. "I am told you are in charge of this camp."

"Indeed, such as it is. My men and I led the evacuation efforts. And who might you be?" He had the tone and confidence of a man who was used to giving orders. His wife sat modestly beside him, her beady eyes studying them closely.

"I am Rubriel of Celessil. This is Scoe Mytholi of Esmara, and... Molindra, an elementalist. We have been travelling south along the river for some days. With the state of the Tabeth, we feared something like this might be afoot. What happened in town?" She knew she wouldn't like the answer.

The sergeant's wife continued to stare as he crafted his response, frowning at their strange attire - especially Molindra in her Langlythian red. She herself wore a dark purple gown which, under different circumstances, might have been rather beautiful. Rubriel wondered if she had been attending a social event of some sort when the chaos started. Now the hem of her skirt was torn and stained, with bits of leaf and twigs threaded in through the lace.

The sergeant let out a long sigh. "It happened very quickly. The Tabeth was swollen already after the heavy rainfall this spring. We had built up the banks with sandbags, as we do every year, but it wasn't enough to contain a deluge such as this. It was like an entire winter's snowmelt reached us all at once. The water rose so fast, we barely had time to load the wagons before the streets were knee deep." He took a sip from his mug.

"Those on the other side of the river took refuge in the villas further uphill; the rest of us had no choice but to flee into the woods in search of higher ground. Many folk lost everything they had. Two good men lost their lives trying to save their livestock. More have since fallen ill with pneumonia, and we fear for them without proper shelter and warmth. We can only hope that aid will reach us soon; I sent two officers riding south as soon as they were able. With any luck, they will return soon and bring relief from Farlow."

"That is awful," Rubriel said. "I am so sorry. We are only passing through, but if there is anything we can do to help, we would be grateful to spend the night and do what we can in the morning."

The sergeant nodded. "You are welcome to stay, though we have little room. Just don't go stirring up any trouble," he warned. "These people have been through enough already, and empty bellies make for short tempers."

"Does anyone here have a bow and arrows? I could hunt for some game - the old-fashioned way."

He frowned. "I doubt it."

"I can shoot, but not in the dark," Scoe said, with a sideways glance at Rubriel.

The sergeant stiffened slightly, and he remembered that firearms were illegal among civilians in Bantria.

"I come from a military background in Esmara," he clarified, and the sergeant relaxed a little.

"I could help build up the campfires," Molindra said from behind them. "Dry the wood, warm the tents."

"I don't think that is necessary." Rubriel cut her off, a little sharper than intended. "Come, let us lay out our beds for the night."

Mol followed silently.

The sergeant gave Scoe a questioning look, and he sighed in response. He wondered if it was wise to leave the two of them alone.

"Pardon me, I should have introduced myself earlier. Sergeant Edward Hedgling." They shook hands firmly. "What brings you to the East, Mr. Mytholi?"

"Please, call me Scoe."

"-Scoe, then. If I may speak plainly, you keep some rather unusual company, and travel a strange route at that."

He seemed to be making conversation, but Scoe caught the wry note of suspicion underlying. "I think it is fair to say this is not quite what I had in mind when I crossed the ocean," he said, in an attempt to lighten the mood.

Hedgling didn't catch the intended humour.

Scoe softened. "If it is any consolation to you, I think you should know that the flood was not a natural event. My friends and I tracked a party of Langlythian mages to the Roof of the World. They were searching for some kind of artifact buried under the Glass Lake and melted a great deal of ice in the process. I wish we could've stopped them, but they outnumbered us and are far too powerful. There was nothing we could do."

"Langlythe, you say?" Hedgling's eyes lit up, and he pursed his lips thoughtfully.

"Yes, sir." He lowered his voice, glancing over his shoulder to make sure no one else was listening before he continued. "I do not know the purpose of the artifact, or what exactly they intend to do with it now they have it in their possession, but I don't think it will be good. I have been through Langlythe myself, in secret - and they look to be preparing for war."

"And if what you say is true, Scoe, and Langlythe is responsible for our current and future plight, why is it that you travel with one of them?" Hedgling threw a pointed look in Molindra's direction.

She had already settled down for the night, but Rubriel sat upright still, her blanket in her lap, watchful and restless even in the safety of the camp.

Scoe sighed. "She is our prisoner, of sorts. She was with the group of mages at the Roof, but they betrayed and abandoned her when the deed was done. When we confronted her, she came with us willingly. Now we take her back to Celessil to face judgement. They were both from there originally."

"How can you be sure she won't turn on you?" The sergeant frowned. "How do we know she won't turn this camp to ashes, given the chance?"

Scoe shook his head. "It is not like that. Those two have known each other for a long time. Langlythe used Molindra and cast her aside as soon as she served her purpose, as they are wont to do. She is clearly heartbroken, wracked with guilt over the part she played, but Rubriel is too angry with her to see it. In any case, I do not doubt that she will submit to the laws of her home country without complaint, for she believes she deserves to be punished."

"And you do not?"

Scoe did not answer right away. He often felt like the mediator between them, observing both sides without the emotional ties to cloud his judgement. "Truthfully, I am not sure. She has been involved in a wrong-doing with terrible consequences. I think she made some bad decisions and acted selfishly, but... Naturally, everyone will look for someone to blame, and find it in her; but I have seen what Langlythe is really like, and I do not think the fault ultimately lies with Molindra."

Hedgling made no further comment, but Scoe could tell the news had unsettled him. He hoped it had not been a mistake to confess Molindra's involvement. To him, it seemed better to speak plainly and address the truth as it surfaced, than fuel further suspicion with efforts to conceal the facts. They talked a little more before he bade the sergeant and his wife good night and went to join the others. Rubriel was still sitting up.

"Get some sleep," he insisted. "I do not think we should stay here too long come morning."

Scoe woke just before dawn. He blinked, rubbing the sleep from his eyes as he looked around to find the two bedrolls next to him were empty. They had slept behind a tent rather than under one as there were not enough to go around all the refugees as it was. A few others were already up and moving about, taking advantage of the clear weather while they could to tidy the camp and hang damp clothing and shoes out to dry.

"Scoe!" Rubriel hissed.

He jumped.

"Start packing up. We need to leave as soon as possible." She crouched low in the long morning shadows, her eyes darting warily from one tent to the next.

"What's wrong?" Scoe whispered. "Where is Molindra?" He pulled on his boots and started rolling up his blanket.

"Waiting in the forest. I had to leave her outside."

He jerked back in surprise.

"Scoe, there is a rumour going around camp that we are responsible for the flooding. I overheard a group talking about taking revenge into their own hands - five men, maybe six, armed with knives, if not more."

"Damn it!" Scoe cursed under his breath. "I shouldn't have trusted Hedgling. I thought he deserved to know the truth."

Rubriel shook her head. "This isn't the sergeant's doing; these are ruffians - the kind who live by laws of their own. I have seen that look on a man's face many a time in the back streets of Tunswick. They demand blood, and right now they care little about whose it is."

"Which way?"

"Over there. We'll exit the camp to the north the way we came in, then circle around to the west, where Molindra is hiding. Be on your guard. They may try an ambush, and we need to make sure Molindra doesn't do anything stupid."

They picked their way through the village of canvas and poles, weaving in and out such as to make their hasty departure less obvious. Luckily, most of the occupants were still asleep, and those who were awake took little notice. Once under the cover of the forest, though, they moved faster. Rubriel didn't think they'd been seen, but her senses were on high alert all the same.

"Stop." She motioned for Scoe to join her crouched in the bushes.

"Trouble?" he whispered.

She nodded and peered silently through the undergrowth.

"Let go of me! Don't make me hurt you," Molindra's voice warned.

A man scoffed. "*Now* you don't want to hurt anyone? You should've thought about that before you flooded us out."

Others jeered and spat.

Edging closer, Rubriel could see two of the men with their backs turned about twenty feet away; another two had Molindra by the arms, while the fifth - the one who spoke - held a knife to her throat.

"We'll make you pay for what you did to our homes, Langlythian scum!"

Scoe signalled to Rubriel and pointed to the two thugs closest to them, indicating they should take one each. They split up and moved in behind the tree trunks. Their targets were too preoccupied to notice them before Scoe snatched the one on the right in a stranglehold while Rubriel knocked the one on the left unconscious with a swift blow to the temple.

"What the...?" The man with the knife spun in surprise, but Rubriel wasn't looking at him.

"Go on," she said to Molindra. And without another word, Molindra set both of the men holding her alight, their clothes igniting down their backs and sending them running through the forest, cursing and rolling on the ground. Rubriel drew her sword, but the ringleader was already gone, running back in the direction of the camp.

"Do you think more will come after us for that?" asked Scoe.

"I don't know, but let us not wait around to find out," Rubriel said. They took off, ignoring the trail and cutting straight through the forest to the southwest. Only when the camp was a good twenty minutes behind them did they stop for a rest, and Rubriel ventured to ask if Molindra was alright.

"I am fine," she said. "I could have handled them myself, but I didn't want..."

"It is fine."

"I am glad you got there when you did. Thank you."

Scoe winced at the tension between them. Rubriel continued to lead the way, and she did not see - or chose not to see - the pained expression on Molindra's face, or the way she trailed gloomily behind, scarcely lifting her head. If they had found a moment alone, he might have sought to offer her some words of comfort, though he wasn't sure what he could say to make it any better, and in any case the opportunity never arose.

They rejoined the path as it circled around the valley and wound downhill along a low cliff edge, where they hoped it would join up with one of the major roads south. There was a small village just beyond Tabethwick where, if they were lucky, they might be able to find a carriage to take them the rest of the way - or close to the Celessilian border at least. It was a common stopover for travellers between the two major cities; Rubriel and Molindra had picked up a ride there once before, years ago.

Even on the high ground, the particularly wet spring had left its mark. A huge bite of the earth had slipped away up ahead, taking a young spruce with it and exposing tangled roots and layers of clay beneath. It had eaten most of the trail's width, and the earth was soft underfoot. Rubriel edged around the slip, looking back as she reached the other side through the gap left by the fallen tree.

She gasped. Tabethwick lay stranded in the distance, muddy water almost up to the eaves of the dwellings, the pointed roofs in shades of brown and green all that could be seen above the flood level. Debris lay scattered throughout; floating or washed up against the walls of buildings. Only the villas on the far hillside remained untouched, the mansions of the well-to-do surveying a grim lookout over the lifeless, washed out streets below.

Molindra stifled a sob; tears streamed down her face. The final, flooded reality in front of her condemned her as surely as if the noose were already around her neck, and she was afraid. Horrified. Guilt crushed her, and her mind began to spin unhealthy thoughts - thoughts that she deserved to be left for dead in the empty crater, that Rubriel's stiff mercy and Scoe's calm kindness were too good for her after the suffering she'd caused.

The cold, saddened faces in the refugee camp tormented her. She wept for them, wept for their ruined lives in the valley below, wept for her own miserable fate. Most of all, she wept for the death of a friendship, and a companion of whom she would never again feel worthy.

There was indeed an empty coach waiting when at last they reached the village. Its driver was part of the relief effort and would be returning empty to Farlow on the morrow to pick up additional supplies. He agreed to take the three of them. Farlow was only half a day's journey by coach; from there, they would seek transport for the far longer journey south to the Celessilian border.

It was a route less commonly travelled, as Celessil had strict rules about who they allowed to enter the country and for how long. Rubriel and Molindra could enter by birthright, but Scoe would have to acquire the appropriate papers when they arrived.

Fortunately, their luck held for once, and they had not been more than a day in Farlow before they were assured of a ride, not just to the border but all the way to Celessil City itself.

They asked around town if anyone knew of someone who might be travelling south. The grocer knew a man who lived on a farm some twenty miles away, but that wasn't nearly close enough to their destination, and in any case, he had already left for the week. The butcher and the proprietor of the Ramble Inn were no help either, so they decided to go straight to the livery stables.

They had no money to pay for a coach, but often in small towns like this, a livery would earn most of its income from travellers passing through. One of the stableboys or perhaps the wheelwright might know of someone headed in the right direction.

As they passed the coach house, Rubriel noticed an old carriage being prepared in the yard. Age had faded its dark green paint, but the crescent moon symbol of her homeland was clearly visible on its door just below the window. It was missing a wheel, and Rubriel caught the eye of the man working on a new one and asked if he knew to whom the carriage belonged.

Charmerie was her name, and she was staying upstairs until he finished the repairs. The wheelwright said she would most likely be down in the afternoon to check on him, if they wished to come back later to speak with her.

Charmerie, it turned out, was an old Celessilian making her final journey home after a lifetime in Bantria. She was a kind and caring woman, who at first glance looked no older than Mol or Rubriel. Her face was unlined but for the crow's feet etched around each of her eyelids, but her world-weary eyes with soft blue irises betrayed her true age, in the peculiar way that Celessilians age in spirit, but not in body.

Her clothes were pristine and well-tailored, her navy blue suit and matching trilby suggesting that she had enjoyed a comfortable lifestyle. She agreed to take them with her at once, glad of the company on such a long ride, and filled the journey with the telling of her life story.

She had left Celessil alone in her twenties; rather unusual for a woman in those days, but she was an elementalist - though not a very good one, she laughed - and had been able to support herself without too much difficulty as a result. She married a doctor, had four surviving children and sixteen grandchildren, all grown up with families of their own now. Her husband had passed nine years earlier, and now at last she had come to realize it was time to go home. She was a hundred and two.

Scoe listened in awe, baffled at how someone could be so old and so young at the same time. Rubriel marvelled at how at peace Charmerie seemed, how open-hearted and kind she was, even as she said goodbye to all that was dear to her. She couldn't help but feel a pang of envy for their new friend and the golden simplicity of a life like that.

Where did I go wrong?

17

The Council of Celessil

Dawn extended its first golden peach rays over the treetops. The morning chorus of chipper birds joined the song of an early rising choir, drifting from behind the closed doors of a breakfast eatery. It had been Mol and Rubriel's favourite for exactly that - eggs and toast on the upper level at sunrise while the choir's harmony lifted them from slumber.

Today, their voices sounded sombre. Today the first light judged and decided, sharp beams of orange and vermillion writing their verdict in the streets. Rubriel lost track of how long she had been walking the paths of an old life, reading lines of memory on the white stone walls of every building, the bark of every tree. Scattered remnants of the past lay out for her to relive for the last time, swept away as she archived them all in the deep recesses of her mind.

They had crossed the border two days prior, reaching the city proper not until dusk due to the delay in getting Scoe's visiting papers in order. Foreign travellers were a rare occurrence, but he eventually received his pass, stamped and sealed with a fourteen day allowance. What happened next had been woefully unpleasant.

Having finally arrived, Rubriel wasn't entirely sure what to do. Scoe would need an inn for the duration of his stay; she supposed she may as well stay there herself, since she had neglected to keep in touch with any of her former acquaintances who may have otherwise offered her lodgings.

Dread had settled heavier and heavier over her the further they went. How long could they turn a blind eye to Mol's guilt before the true word of her deeds in the north came out and brought her to justice? She walked sullenly behind them down the street - afraid, and perhaps in denial.

They'd not made it more than a few blocks before a night patrol stopped them, asked to see Scoe's papers, and arrested Molindra on suspicion of treason as soon as they realized who she was. Word, it seemed, travelled faster than they did. Worst of all, she did not go quietly. Her knees buckled; she sobbed and begged Rubriel to defend her.

Rubriel had said nothing.

She howled as they took her away.

It was as though a piece of Rubriel died that night. She and Scoe were also taken for questioning, and they spent the night sitting in the court offices, numbly telling the same story over and over and each producing their written statement. She included every detail of the overheard conversation between Molindra and the other mages - and the subsequent betrayal.

But even if her intentions were not treasonous, there was nothing Rubriel could report which would prove Mol hadn't knowingly created a flood that decimated a populous area of an allied nation as a mere side effect of her quest for personal gain.

A summons from Elder Berren arrived first thing in the morning. By now, Rubriel had been awake more than twenty-four hours straight, and her eyelids drooped with weariness. For all his years, the Elder was not a patient man, and she knew it would be improper to postpone their meeting - especially given the calibre of news she brought.

His estate was not far, centred behind the formal council building amidst a sprawling, lush garden of all-colour roses, vine covered archways and ancient statues in pristine white stone. The mansion itself was more modest in size, built in late 18th century style with tall round pillars marking each corner of the steps leading to its grand entranceway.

She had visited a handful of times in her youth, the pleasant light and airiness of the place not quite allowing her to forget that she was essentially visiting royalty, or as close to it as remained on the Eastern Continent. Bantria had abandoned its monarchy quite some time ago, but while Celessil elected its twelve Council members by popular vote, Elder Berren had presided over them as the head of that council for longer than anyone could remember. He alone had the authority to overrule the majority if necessary - though it seldom happened.

After the formal pleasantries were exchanged, they took tea in the sitting room. With only the butler in attendance, he welcomed her like extended family. She recounted yet again all she could remember of her journey through Langlythe and the Roof of the World. He looked exactly as he always did; steel grey hair which lay neatly against his skull, strong jawline and bright, intelligent eyes with deep crevasses in the corners that creased further as he listened.

Their relationship was a strange one, familiar-yet-distant. At times, he spoke to her almost as a father might, yet the difference in status meant he never acknowledged any connection with her in public, and she was never quite sure where the boundaries lay, even when they were relatively alone. She was never with him unchaperoned, and she did not recall exactly why she and Gwendolen had come to know him as anything more than the ruler of their country.

The finding of the key, he said, was of great concern; more so if Langlythe already knew the location of its lock. He had his suspicions on the origin of both, but would say no more of it until his scholars had done their research. All would be presented before the Council meeting tomorrow; she and Scoe were both required to attend and contribute as they may.

To Rubriel, he offered a guest room in his own estate. She felt bad for Scoe in accepting it, though she could hardly refuse. She hadn't seen him since they first arrived at the courthouse, and as a rare foreign visitor with no money on him, he would not have an easy time finding a bed for the night. The Elder assured her he would be taken care of, however, and with that moment of relief she had retired to her appointed room on the second floor.

She hadn't been able to sleep. Thoughts of Mol milled and frothed until she gave up trying to rest and wandered outside. Celessil summer nights were balmy and often more pleasant than the heat of daytime. After the cold north, the heat was hard to get used to, even having grown up here.

Upon hearing that she would be visiting with the Council of Celessil, the ladies of the Elder's household had loaned her a suitable outfit, made of the lightest silvery silk with an asymmetric panel of traditional olive green down the front of the bodice. A fine veiled hat and gloves accompanied the ensemble. Her country's colours seemed both foreign and familiar, like an old skin that didn't quite belong to her anymore.

She meandered away from the main street and down towards the river. The docks were quiet this early, the little fishing boats lapping idly in the current. Upstream, a lone fisherman cast his line into the green water. Further down, a couple walked hand in hand across the arched stone bridge, talking softly.

On the other side of the bridge, the road slid into the Moonwood, where it branched into the tiny woodland hamlets scattered throughout. She had grown up in one of them - a lone cottage, really - where they kept their own animals and lived off the land, venturing to the city only once a month or so to stock up on anything they couldn't make, grow or borrow.

When she was nineteen, she crossed the river permanently and moved into an apartment near the university. Alive with the newfound hustle and bustle of city life brimming with possibilities, she threw herself into a broad spectrum of study - language, history, science, as well as many practical skills. It was here that she first discovered her fascination with metallurgy, a study which led her to its application in weaponsmithing and ultimately learning to fight with them.

Her feet took her unbidden that way now, towards the arena which had once been the most exciting place in her world. Like many of the buildings in the older parts of Celessil, Stadium Liza was constructed from mammoth slabs of white stone, chipped and cracked with age in places now reinforced with additional wood framing. Circular in shape, the outer wooden parts opened doors onto great curved staircases that rose to the upper levels, then cascaded down in concentric rings of tiered seating to the combat surface in the middle.

Swordplay had been refined and dramatized into a traditional Celessilian form of entertainment, as much about artistry as it was a sport. Contestants fought with blunt - but very elaborate - weapons, in annual tournaments that drew crowds in the thousands.

Rubriel had once been the star of the show.

Points were scored for forcing your opponent into a compromised position, but that alone was not enough to win. You had to do so with style. She had mastered that art; the perfect balance of skill, speed, and showmanship. She had won the championship four years in a row. The crowd had cheered for her then, chanted her name, carried her on their shoulders on a victory parade through the city.

She remembered it like it was yesterday, relishing the forgotten flame of passion reignited for a moment, before it blew away on the present-day breeze. She was also the *last* champion. The tournament had been shut down in 1880, citing a growing trend of too many injuries and one unfortunate fatality as the competition reached its peak intensity.

Now, the stadium seemed somewhat forgotten. A crumpled poster hung from the door advertising something called "cricket" to be played the following week, tickets selling for twenty silver apiece for those who wished to spectate. Everything had changed.

Rubriel felt so naïve. When she and Mol left here together twenty years before, she believed they would find a fresh start in Bantria away from the painful reminders of their past. Mol's parents had disowned her when she was expelled from the University of Celessil. Her combustion of the auditorium - accidental though it was - caused enough notoriety that people shook their heads and muttered whenever they saw her.

Rubriel had been at a loss, both personally and financially, since without the annual tournament she had lost both her passion and her source of income. They had thought - no, assumed - they would always be inseparable, making a comfortable life for themselves somewhere new, secure in the knowledge that so long as they were together there was nothing they could not overcome.

How very wrong they were! Life had only grown harder, and somewhere along the line, she and Mol had stopped communicating. And even though Rubriel knew well that she needed to visit Mol in prison and talk to her - *properly* - the mere thought of that conversation terrified her.

The clock tower tolled once in the square. It was still too early to attend the Council, but she headed back in that direction anyway in search of Scoe. To her surprise, she found him sitting on a bench outside the council building, gazing up in awe at the Tower of the Moon and its scintillating jewel high in the sky.

"Couldn't sleep either?" she asked, sitting beside him.

"I did at first, but woke early. Decided to go for a walk, see the sights, as it were." He nodded once at the tower. "There is something I certainly never thought to see up close in my lifetime," he said, his eyes wide with wonder. "It is breathtaking."

"It is," she agreed. "The original Council hall was inside it, as was the Elder's residence and that of most council members. But the tower is so old - built at the time of the Great Segregation - that in the late 1700s they decided it was unsafe having so many people using it. They relocated those who worked and resided there to separate buildings, and now the tower is mostly off-limits."

The shaft of the tower rose far above the rooftops; windowless, like the sturdy trunk of a magnificent tree. Its top branches opened out into a nest of silver leaves and vines. In the centre, those vines twirled around the largest sildion on earth - the *Vanassildion*, or 'mother lightstone'.

"I have heard the words, 'Great Segregation' a few times, but not having grown up here, I don't know what it means," said Scoe.

"That is when the world changed. The 'known world' at least; the West and the East had not yet discovered one another. It marks the fall of the First Ancestors and the rise of men and women as we know them today, and the start of our Eastern Calendar."

"Why 'segregation'?"

Rubriel frowned. "Because it is also said that the Gloaming Mountains arose at that time, separating Langlythe from the rest of the continent. But that is more legend than fact, and heavily tainted with superstition. Any Bantrian will tell you that the mountains were purposely put there to *contain* Langlythe, but there is no proof of that, or even if the land there was dark before the segregation or became that way afterwards. We know so little of our own history, yet many will speak as experts in worldly matters as though the past has no relevance in the present. Sometimes I think there is still some ancient mystery out there that will someday reveal itself and play us all for fools."

Scoe blinked.

She chuckled. "That was very philosophical of me, and too complex an answer for this early in the morning." As if in agreement, the clock tower chimed again.

"Another hour," Scoe mused, "assuming we are both due in at the same time?"

Rubriel nodded. "I am sorry I left you yesterday. I had meant to help you find a place to stay, but the Elder summoned me before I even left the courthouse, and his is not an audience one should neglect."

"It's quite alright," Scoe assured her. "I did not have to look for a hotel. After they were finished interviewing me, one of the officers escorted me to that guest house right there." He pointed across to the other side of the council building from where they sat. "He said the Elder had instructed that I should be accommodated there for the duration of my visitation with the Council."

Rubriel looked relieved. "I did not even know there was a guest house attached to the council building. I suppose that makes sense; we must host delegates from Bantria from time to time. In any case, I feel a little better knowing you are being looked after."

Scoe gave her a pointed look, summoning the elephant she had been trying very hard to ignore.

She sighed heavily. "I don't know what to say to her, Scoe. "I feel sick thinking about her trial and what the verdict might be. But how can I convince the court of her innocence when I am not convinced of it myself?"

"Mol had no better idea what she was getting into than you or I did when we crossed the Gloaming Pass," Scoe reminded her. "We just had to react, to do what we could to stay safe in very unfamiliar circumstances. Surely you can forgive her for that."

She looked hurt. "It is not a simple matter of forgiveness. The problem is trust. I feel like I do not know her half as well as I thought I did."

Scoe just nodded in response and wisely fell silent. They both needed a clear head for the imminent meeting.

He had also been given fresh clothing in Celessilian colours for his appearance before the Council. Apparently, they were quite particular about how one should dress and behave. He straightened his borrowed vest nervously as it came time for them to go inside, hoping he wouldn't make a hash of it somehow. "Shall we?" he said, proffering his arm, and together they walked with elbows linked through the grand double doors of the council building into the foyer beyond.

There was a tree in the centre of the room, a glass dome overhead providing sunlight to its waxy green leaves and an octagon of white stone housing the soil for its roots. They were greeted promptly as they entered by a uniformed guard, who took their names and escorted them through another set of double doors and down a short hallway. Rich oak panels covered everything, and their footsteps echoed off the polished floors. Their escort knocked smartly at the entrance to the meeting hall itself.

"Enter," a voice boomed from within, and he swung open the doors to admit them. "Your guests; good sirs, ladies - Rubriel of Celessil and Rascovor Mytholi of Esmara." He bowed from the waist and exited, leaving the two of them standing at the foot of a long table with thirteen chairs.

The room wasn't overly large, but it was a little intimidating nonetheless, with its exceptionally high ceiling. Unlike the foyer, this room had no natural light. Huge olive and silver flags hung from the walls on both sides, and the open ceiling space accommodated a chandelier of many, many candles. Elder Berren sat alone at the head of the table opposite them, flanked by his ten council members down either side. Two extra chairs, different from the rest, had been placed at the near end of the table, and the woman nearest them indicated that they should sit.

"Welcome to our guests," the Elder said, with a practiced mix of authority and warmth. "The Council has been briefed on your journey and the dangers you have faced; we thank you for your attendance on such short notice."

Rubriel nodded once in assent.

"There is much to discuss, and much we would hear from each of you directly regarding what you have witnessed. I would like to start, however, with the most pressing of matters, which is that of the key you claim Langlythe recovered from the Roof of the World. Please, recount what you saw." He gestured for them to begin, and eleven sets of eyes turned in their direction.

Rubriel cleared her throat. "They found the key deep inside the volcanic crater they call the Glass Lake. The Langlythian mages melted through the wall of the crater and right down to bedrock in the very heart of it, which is what caused the flooding. Scoe and I were nearly swept away as the water heaved out of the crater. Underneath, there was a small vault of sorts, and M-"

She hesitated, then recovered. "They used two gems to open it. One of them was a sildion pendant. The other I could not get a proper look at, but I think it may have been ludion, because her hand shone dark when she pressed it against the plaque."

"Was there an inscription?" interjected one of the council members.

"There was, but I do not recall the words."

"A pity," he said, but waved it off. "Please, continue."

Rubriel grimaced. "The lid opened and only the key was inside, but I did not see the key at all; I only know it was a key from what was said..." she faltered again, shuffling uncomfortably in her seat.

"But it was Molindra who held it," Scoe jumped in, rescuing her. "I could talk to her, if you will allow it; see if I can gather a description."

"That may be useful," said the Elder, "but she has been of no help whatsoever since we brought her in. What makes you think she will talk to you now, if she did not open up for the entirety of your journey south?"

Now it was Scoe's turn to be uncomfortable. "I apologize; I mean no disrespect. It is just that..." He licked his upper lip. "I think, under the circumstances, she may be more likely to talk to me one on one. I have no history with her. I met her for the first time crying in the snow, having been rejected by everyone she knew. Perhaps she will trust me sooner than anyone from her former life."

The council members exchanged murmurs and glances. Scoe wrung his hands nervously under the table, but to his credit, he managed to keep his face even.

"The young man has a point," said the man to the Elder's right, then whispered something inaudible.

"Very well," the Elder said finally. "Scoe will meet with Molindra at the conclusion of today's session. Guards will be present in the hall, but otherwise the two of you will be alone. Make it count."

Rubriel hadn't realized she was holding her breath. "Thank you," she mouthed sideways to Scoe, almost weeping with relief.

He returned a sad smile, squeezing her hand. There was a weariness to her today that was more than just lack of sleep. It seemed to have cast a shadow over her all of a sudden, and the meeting was far from over.

In the absence of further insight on the key, the topic switched to Langlythe itself, and what the pair of them gleaned about the state of the country from their time there. Rubriel recounted what she had seen and heard, Scoe supplementing from time to time with his own experiences. It was well into the afternoon before they adjourned.

Rubriel disappeared almost as soon as they left the building. She didn't say where she was going and Scoe did not ask, inferring that she wanted to be alone, so he headed back to his accommodations to eat and refresh a little before going to the jail.

18
Severed Threads

Their appearance before the Council turned into a series of meetings which dragged on for days. Scoe and Rubriel saw little of each other outside of those sessions, each of them hurrying off in opposite directions in the latter half of the day for one reason or another. Rubriel was still staying at the Elder's estate, though she secretly wished she was also accommodated in the council guesthouse with Scoe.

While she knew she should feel honoured by the arrangement, she couldn't help but wonder what the Elder really thought of her and her role in all of this. She also knew he would ultimately oversee the outcome of Molindra's trial, which made the whole thing rather uncomfortable.

In Bantria, it would surely be viewed as a conflict of interest and improper in a myriad of ways, but Celessil was still possessed of a rather old-fashioned, small-town mentality. Its population was low for its physical land area, and that, combined with an average age of well over a hundred, meant most of its citizens were connected in some way.

All Celessilians had a secondary persona. There was the true self that generally accepted the natural connections between everyone regardless of their station, and then there was the public self, which existed to preserve the level of decorum and hierarchy necessary to keep a civilization functional.

Elder Berren was no exception. Nevertheless, Rubriel found herself going out of her way to avoid him. She made sure to arrive back at the estate before he did and spent her evenings in the garden or the library. Often, she took her meals outside, under the pretense of wanting to enjoy the summer weather, having not seen much sunshine of late. The estate also contained an extensive library with many unique titles; a diversity of topics and writers one simply did not see lining Bantrian shelves.

One afternoon, she stumbled upon a particularly interesting volume, entitled, *The Theory of Equilibria*. She probably would not have been drawn to it if not for the events at the council meeting earlier that day.

Scoe had presented a sketch of the key before the Council, thanks to his apparently productive time spent with Molindra, who had also transcribed the inscription from the lid of the vault as best she remembered it:

No life without death; no dark without light.

Only one who wields both in equal splendour shall hold the key to the continent.

It was that exact concept into which the book delved in great detail. The work was well-reasoned, and the author had referenced other, more factual works where he could, but it was otherwise entirely theoretical, as the title suggested.

In order to examine the theory of equilibria, one must first be introduced to a theory of opposites, she read. *An idea that all qualities in nature come in equal and opposite pairs. Equal, because neither member is superior to the other either in strength or necessity. Opposite, because the two are fundamentally antagonistic to one another.*

The theory of equilibria in its simplest form is thus: In order for the world to thrive, both sides must exist in equal magnitude from all their constituent sources. It must be firmly noted that an individual source should not exhibit both qualities at once. Rather, balance is achieved broadly through a combination of entities which both complement and repel one another.

A later chapter went on to explain how, as thinking, feeling beings, humans tend to project their emotions onto these fundamental qualities of nature, branding them as "good" or "bad" and favouring one over the other. Doing so fosters imbalance, which, in the author's opinion, has been the cause of most conflict and turmoil throughout history. Was that what the vault inscription warned against?

Rubriel found this alternate view of the world oddly comforting. She kept the book by her bedside and referred to it often, finding solace within its calm, measured outlook. *How wonderful it would be,* she thought, *if there were no such thing as good and evil; only balance and imbalance. And how terribly wrong that would make us all if it were so!*

Scoe, meanwhile, spent as much time with Molindra as her guards would allow. She turned out to be more than forthcoming, keen to help in any way she could, and Scoe was there to listen without judgement. The jail permitted her to have paper and pencil, so she drew detailed maps; as much as she could remember of Imul'dene's layout and points of interest.

Between Scoe's visits, she made copious notes on anything she saw or heard which might be useful. They could only hope the court of law would look upon her more favourably when the time came as a result of her cooperation.

The final meeting took place on the tenth day, after a hiatus in which the Council scholar, Eroth, had his team unearth everything they could find on the key and its presumed lock; for surely every key must unlock *something.* There was an air of tense anticipation in the room as they filed in and sat down, Rubriel and Scoe taking their now-familiar places at the near end of the table.

Eroth led the first hour of the meeting, delving into the history of the Roof of the World and the theories behind how the vault came to be buried in the crater of an extinct volcano - and perhaps more importantly, why. He was clearly fascinated by the discovery and seemed to be savouring the opportunity to present his research to the Council, despite the gravity of the situation.

"The prevailing theory, based on the correlation between the tribal tales and the inscription on the lid, is that the key was intentionally hidden far away from its lock by the First Ancestors at the time of the Great Segregation, for they believed no one should have access to it with the world in such a state of conflict." Eroth's pause was met with a few impatient stares from his fellow Council members. Apparently, even century-old folk were not possessed of infinite patience.

"That key is, as the inscription states, the Key to the Continent," he concluded. "It opens the World Gate."

Grave murmurs rumbled along the table at this revelation. Scoe and Rubriel exchanged puzzled glances.

The Elder frowned deeply. "Are you sure of this?"

Eroth nodded. "The drawing we obtained from Molindra matches the diagram and description we found in the old archives. They are one and the same, I'm afraid."

"Excuse me," Scoe interjected. "The World Gate... as in *The Fable of the Gate* - the bedtime story?"

"I know that story too," added Rubriel. "Only in the version I know, they never found the gate and agreed *not* to look for it. Are you saying there is truth to it - that a portal to all the doors of the world really exists?"

"I knew Sil'celes personally; I sent her to the Roof of the World myself," said Elder Berren. "What she told me upon her return aligns with the tale Rubriel - and indeed all of Celessil - is familiar with, though she was with child when she returned and never would speak of the father."

"In the Esmaran version, Sil'celes and Deizil do find the World Gate - by working together. But having found it, they agree not to tell anyone it exists. Sil'celes keeps her promise and as a result her homeland flourishes. Deizil breaks his promise and brings a curse upon his land. Parents use it to teach their children morals." Scoe still couldn't quite believe what he was hearing.

"While the tale has clearly been embellished over the years, it seems the Esmaran version may be more accurate as far as the gate is concerned," said Eroth, re-centreing the conversation. "We have evidence enough to suggest that Langlythe has already found the gate, and sent a team to that specific location to recover the key. This does not bode well for any of us."

"I'm not sure I follow," said Rubriel. "Why should we fear the gate?"

"Because the World Gate is an ancient portal nexus which connects to every other portal on earth. Many people can travel through it at once and land instantly anywhere they wish, so long as the basic gateway structure is present on the other side to receive them. The one beneath the Tower of the Moon, for example."

"So Langlythe is no longer forced to invade through the Gloaming Pass. They cannot teleport in or out of their own lands, but from the Roof of the World? They can strike anywhere without warning and retreat just as easily," Scoe said, understanding.

"And there are many ancient gateways throughout the Eastern Continent - probably more than have ever been discovered. Most of them are in Bantria."

"Can we use it too? Use our gateway to reach the World Gate and seal it off?" Rubriel suggested.

"Only if the way has already been opened," Eroth said.

The extended pause that followed forced him to elaborate.

"While it is not clear exactly how it works, we do know the connection to other gateways can only be initiated from the World Gate. We cannot open our gateway here in Celessil - many have tried and failed. The only way we could travel from here to the World Gate would be to hold our side open after someone has passed through in the opposite direction."

"Essentially, we'd have to ambush an ambush, then risk walking into a trap on the other side. They will have the World Gate heavily fortified by now. What's more, by the sounds of it, there are many of these gateways, and we do not know which one they will use." said Scoe.

"Agreed," said Eroth. "Such an attempt would likely end in disaster."

A fist thumped loudly on the table. "Need I remind you all that Celessil is - and always will be - a neutral territory?" The man who spoke now was tall and broad-chested. He would be fearsome if not for the gentleness behind his eyes that betrayed his curt interruption. "What you speak of are acts of war. We are a non-militant nation! Bantria has ever been our friend, but we have not the numbers to fight on their behalf."

"Calm yourself, Nathaniel."

Everyone turned to the head of the table as the Elder spoke. "You are right, of course. It is not our place to fight in a war between nations, and yet we are not safe from it. We cannot ignore what happens beyond our borders and assume it will never reach us. If Langlythe were to invade Bantria, if the borders between lands were contested and redrawn, what is to say we will not be next? We are an easy target, after all, whether we admit it or not." He paused to let his sobering words sink in.

The man called Nathaniel studied his hands, chastened. Scoe looked sheepishly at Rubriel, but she didn't catch his eye.

"But we *are* their advisors," Eroth ventured. "If we have a duty to our allies, it is to share our greater knowledge. We should not keep this information to ourselves."

"We have only one choice, that I can see," the Elder said. "We must disable or destroy every gateway in the southeast, before Langlythe can use them against Bantria - or us."

Murmurs ran around the table. There were some frowns, some nods.

"Forgive me, Elder," said one of the female Council members, "but it could take many weeks or even months to find and destroy every gateway, and so long as they are on Bantrian soil, we do not have the authority to take action ourselves. We can only make our recommendation to their Prime Minister and urge him to follow it."

The Elder held up a reassuring hand. "And we will. We will start by destroying our own gateway. As our acting ambassador, Nathaniel will ride to Tunswick with haste and implore them to do the same. And in secret..." He paused, and a hush fell once again over the Council.

Rubriel's heart pounded in her chest, though she wasn't sure why.

"In secret, we will dispatch a mole to Imul'dene to sabotage their plans and buy time for Bantria to prepare a stronger defence. This task I entrust to Rubriel."

She blanched. "What?"

Their eyes met across the table, and he addressed her directly. "You know more of their ways than all of this Council combined - more than enough to conceal your intentions. No one must know where you came from. Take back the key, if you can."

"Elder, please. I cannot-"

But the woman on her right shot her a sharp, silencing look. Before Rubriel could protest any further, the meeting was adjourned, and they were ushered out of the hall.

Scoe grabbed her arm and pulled her outside, away from the throng of people in the street. "Rubriel..."

"Scoe I can't go back to Langlythe," she said, her voice shaking. "If I leave now, I won't be here for Molindra's trial, and if I don't speak for her, who will?"

"I will," Scoe said, but she shook her head.

"Scoe, you are not from here. They will not listen to you in a court of law."

"What? That's absurd."

"Yes, maybe," she said in a high voice. "That's how it is here. Say we will be neutral, wise and unbiased; do what feels like the opposite. I might never come back, Scoe. How is sending me undercover anything other than an act of war? If I fail, Langlythe won't hesitate to kill me and take retribution on Celessil as well."

"You've been staying at the Elder's estate this entire time. He sent you because you are the only one with a reasonable chance of success. I do not think he means it as a death sentence. Don't... take it personally." Scoe tried his best to reason with her, but he knew she wasn't of a mind to listen.

"Not for me, perhaps," she replied, trembling.

Scoe sighed and placed a firm hand on her shoulder. "Go to her, Rubriel. Go and make things right between you and Mol, so that whatever happens next you don't have that as a regret."

She took a deep breath and nodded.

"I suppose I should get ready to leave, too."

Then he called after her as she took off in a flurry, not towards Molindra's cell but in the direction of the Elder's estate. "Don't you dare leave without saying goodbye!"

Rubriel returned to the mansion first. She hurried up the stairs past the startled butler and burst into her room, throwing her satchel onto the bed. Sniffling, she packed what few belongings she came with. She threw open the wardrobe searching for her own clothing, only to remember that the maid had taken it away to be laundered. With a curse, she turned to go look for it and ran headlong into Elder Berren, who now stood in the doorway.

"Forgive the intrusion," he said, a tangible note of suspicion in his voice.

Rubriel exploded. "How could you? You heard all about what I went through, what it is like out there. Going to Langlythe destroyed *everything* for me, for Molindra - and now you expect me to go back?"

"The consequences of inaction will be far greater for us all, and there is no one else I would send."

"Then find someone!" she retorted. "I am no soldier. I am no spy."

"You are the greatest swordswoman Celessil has known for generations," he countered. "And you have come to know our adversary, whether you wish to or not."

"It is not the same."

She turned her back and seized her satchel defiantly. "I am done here! I do not want to deceive; I do not want to *kill*. All my life I've been made to believe that my own self worth is dependent upon how *useful* I can be to others. I became skilled and strong and subservient *because that's what other people wanted from me*! But they don't own me. I don't belong to Bantria, I don't belong to Celessil, I don't belong to *you!*" She pushed past him and out of the bedroom.

He called after her, his voice echoing down the long hallway. "Rubriel, where are you going?"

"Away!" She stormed down the corridor. "Away to somewhere new, somewhere where I can just *breathe*, to learn how to be myself and the kind of person I want myself to be. I don't even know who that *is*, Elder!"

A cold fury lashed across his usually calm features. He chased after her, grasping her shoulder and turning her back roughly to face him. "If we do not stop this war, within less than a year there will be nowhere safe for you or anyone else to go."

His tone lashed her with its sharpness. "You alone *know* Langlythe; you have lived among its people. You know its weaknesses, and together with Molindra's intel you have a chance to cripple it from the inside before it can crash down upon us! So tell me, Rubriel: do you wish to be the kind of person who turns her back on a chance to save us all?"

Rubriel glared at him with all her pride but found nothing to say. She'd never seen him so angry. He wasn't wrong, yet she resented him all the more for the fact.

He softened slightly. "We raised you here as one of our own. You bear the gift of our people around your neck. This duty I ask of you in return."

Rubriel frowned deeply. In time, she would recall his words and reconsider their significance. But for now, she merely shrugged out of his grasp and asked, "How am I to get in?"

"The three of you brought back a sample of their dress, and your colouring is close enough to the natives that you can pass as one of them well enough. You have proven so already. You will return in the guise of a High Tiers mage and infiltrate the great city of Imul'dene. Disrupt the chain of command; sow seeds of chaos and dissention. Meanwhile, we will ensure that no portal remains open."

"And you truly believe this will stop a war, not further exacerbate one?"

He sighed, once again wise and fatherly. "No, we cannot stop it. But we can delay it long enough for Bantria to prepare and bring in allies from the west. To give them a fighting chance when the might of Langlythe spills from its borders, so that it never reaches Celessil."

She closed her eyes and nodded solemnly, swallowing her dread. She could have hated him then, but he was still her sovereign, and she thought that he was right in his objective, even if she detested the means.

"Am I to go alone?" she asked, covering her resentment with a steely resolve.

He nodded. "It is riskier to do so, yet you will arouse less suspicion that way. Glean as much strategy as you can from Scoe before you leave, however; he has spent a great deal of time with Molindra since you brought her in, and she has been very forthcoming with information to him. If he were Celessilian, I would enlist him to accompany you, but as a foreigner I cannot place him under any obligation to do so."

She bristled at the reminder, though she had a feeling Scoe would go with her from choice. He was young and braver than her. With his two years of compulsory military service to Esmara behind him, he probably understood the concept of duty to one's country far better than she did.

What is wrong with me? she thought crossly. *Celessil is my home. Was there not a time when I would have done as the Elder asked without question? Am I truly so weary of the world that I cannot muster the courage to fight when it is needful?*

"It shall be done, but first, there is something else I must do."

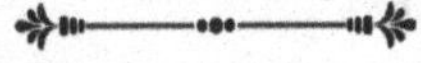

Pale light filtered through the narrow barred window of Molindra's cell. She sat on the edge of the narrow bed wearing a puffy white robe, her wild hair loose about her shoulders. The rich auburn waves which grew from her scalp were the only colour in the bare, sanitary room, rebelling in their unravelled way as they pushed the bleached ash lengths down below her chin; the abrupt colour change a measure of how long since the decision that irreversibly altered her life. Her face lifted from the floor. Heavy-rimmed eyes laced with sadness turned towards the door where Rubriel stood.

Scoe, who sat on a chair outside the bars, followed their gaze, and he rose as Rubriel entered.

"I'll take my leave," he said, looking from one anguished face to another and deciding he best be somewhere else.

Rubriel stepped forward, but did not come so close as to take his seat. For a while neither of them spoke, the air between them thick with emotion.

"I was beginning to think you would not come," Molindra said, standing.

"I nearly didn't."

"Believe me when I say I did not mean for any of this to happen. I hate that I was used and betrayed. I hate that I allowed myself to be caught up in a plot to bring harm to the places we called home. But I do not regret what I gained from it, to be finally comfortable with the full extent of my raw energy; to be in control of it. I am deeply sorry to have dragged you into the mess I created."

"I followed you willingly. I was terrified of what might happen to you," Rubriel said.

"No, you didn't, Rubriel."

She let her words sink in. "You admonished me, told me I was being foolish. You would've had me continue to lead a miserable life while you barely earned enough to cover our rent, let alone save for any kind of future. Then you up and followed me anyway without me knowing." The argument came across calmly, but she couldn't disguise the current of hurt which ran beneath.

"Was that really worth it to you? To trade what you had for life in prison, and multiply your misery a hundred fold with all those in Tabethwick who now suffer because of your actions?"

"And do you really think that would not have happened anyway, with or without my involvement? It has been made painfully clear to me I was nothing more than an accessory."

Mol's hands fisted in the fabric of her gown. "Besides, I have been doing everything I can to help now that I am here. Scoe came with many questions from the Council and I have answered them all with as much detail and truth as I can remember. I do not think my sentence will be for life, especially not with you to vouch for me. You always did have the ear of the Elder."

"Ha! I will not *be* at your trial, Mol. Elder Berren is sending me back to Langlythe to try to stop the invasion. He did not give me a choice. I do not wish to go." She was shaking now, pacing back and forth in the small room.

"Well, I do. *I* would go back and set things right, as I may."

"They would kill you on sight - if Bantria didn't hang you first."

"I am not afraid of dying and I am not afraid of Langlythe. They are just *people* - well, most of them. What I fear is inaction, and that is exactly what I will get. I suppose you think it is a fitting punishment." She folded her arms.

"I did not say that." Rubriel glowered beneath hooded lids.

Mol stood again. "No, but you've thought about it. Sometimes, Rubriel, there is this self-righteous streak in you that makes me want to smash your head against a wall. You say Elder Berren isn't giving you a choice. How much choice do you think I had in going to the Roof of the World?"

"There must have been another way."

"You have no idea what it was like in Imul'dene!" Mol's temper flared, and they were both lucky for her newfound control over her raw energy. "There are no choices. You follow the path that is set for you or you don't survive. Quality of life is directly proportional to how useful you can be and the instant you stop, it's all over."

Rubriel gaped in disbelief. "Really, Mol? I don't understand what it is to live in a society that values wealth above people, to work sixteen hours a day at hopeless jobs at the whim of the rich and powerful because money is the only way out? I lived that life for twenty years. I made myself indispensable to people I despise to give us our best chance. But when I was asked to commit murder or give... *favours* in exchange for your tuition? I still said no."

"What? You never told me-"

"It doesn't matter now!" Rubriel snapped. She looked down at the spiral ring on her finger, gripping it in the other hand and wrestling it free. When her eyes met Mol's again, there were tears rolling down her cheeks. She tried to speak, but her voice abandoned her, and her lips would not form the words she needed to say. Those fine, invisible threads she'd always imagined joining them in spirit were breaking. She tossed the ring through the bars. "This belongs to you."

Mol flinched. "It was a gift. Keep it. Please," she begged.

But Rubriel turned away, and in her anger Mol rushed forward and gripped the bars. "If you truly believe there is always another way then prove it! Run away on your own and see how far it gets you!"

She received no answer. Rubriel left her behind, the threads between them tearing painfully apart as she went, until Molindra felt completely and utterly alone for the first time in her life. The emptiness of the prison matched the sudden, terrible emptiness in her own heart; cold and unforgiving, with the ruins of a lifelong friendship lumped gruesomely before her like bloody sinews.

Scoe waited in the afternoon sun for Rubriel to emerge from the prison. Her face was hollow when she climbed the stairs and saw him, as though a piece of her very self were missing. She said nothing of what had happened below, but he could guess well enough.

"I'm coming with you," he told her.

She nodded grimly and followed him without a word.

He led her to the guest room he had occupied for the last ten days, where he had already assembled most of the supplies for their journey, including the special equipment the Council had provisioned for them: clothing the three of them had brought back from Langlythe, adjusted to serve as their disguise, and two milestones, to be bound to a location of their choosing should they require an immediate means of escape.

Rubriel remembered hearing about milestones from a stranger at the Solstice dinner, a lifetime ago now; a milestone could return them to safety, so long as the binding brazier remained lit. Scoe relayed the instruction given to him, that they must find a hidden location where no one would disrupt the brazier, and where no harm could come of it should the milestones fall into - and be used by - the wrong hands.

They would leave at dawn, ride north along the road out of Celessil, then cut across country to Gilley's Market, where they would leave the horses and continue on foot to the Gloaming Pass and beyond. Scoe brought with him the maps Molindra had drawn and the notes he made on potential weaknesses they could exploit.

As they rode, they formed the beginnings of a plan - a daring plan which would take them to the very heart of Imul'dene.

They travelled light but for their weapons and their change of attire - Rubriel with her favoured sword, Scoe with twin knives and his pistol - "only for emergencies," as he put it - in answer to the obvious distrust encountered in the East at the mention of anything involving gunpowder. They would shed the rest before they reached the mountains.

Rubriel pushed the horses too hard, he felt; even with time short as it was. She'd grown cold and distant since they left Celessil, consumed by the task at hand, or perhaps more by the emptiness in her heart. The chill in her eyes could frost a conversation like a bitter gust of winter.

19

Quietly Destructive

T he Gloaming Pass was so named for the transition as one travelled from the light of day on one side to the depth of night on the other, as though gloaming were a place rather than a time, and to pass through it was to observe a permanent sunset.

It is aptly named, thought Scoe, as the mountain range loomed closer and they baked under the last of the summer heat. This last leg of the journey had been on foot, and rough going, with the weight of the packs they carried and the sun beating down from the cloudless sky overhead. Yet he cherished that heat, even as they neared the shade of the pass, for there was no denying the danger for them both beyond that threshold; the passage from light to dark that may well be a one-way journey.

Suddenly daylight seemed so precious, the chirp of insects and tall grasses a comfort he could scarcely bear to part with. Esmara was a warm country, with long, hot summers and mild winters. He missed it. He missed his love, Lady Morgrian. What if he never saw her again?

Rubriel walked ahead of him in silence. She did not waiver on the threshold, did not pause to reflect until she realized she had left Scoe behind. She turned to look back at him over her shoulder questioningly.

"Sorry," he mumbled, jogging to catch up.

"Scoe." Rubriel took both his arms and turned him to face her, a look of deep concern etched into her brows.

"I was thinking of home," he admitted, glancing apprehensively at the pass up ahead.

"We cannot afford to look back. We must be committed. When we reach the other side, we must each play the role we agreed upon. Make them believe we are on our way home, not the other way around."

"I know," he nodded, grimacing a little. She was right, but a harshness grew in her ever since they left Celessil, a kind of ruthless determination driving her forward. It frightened him, though he did not say as much.

Under the eaves of the mountain, they stopped to change into their Langlythian attire. Both wore black overcoats, breeches and boots. Scoe put on a plain black mantle, gloves and hood, pulling it firmly over his golden hair and fixing his mask up over his mouth and nose so only his eyes were visible. His sun-kissed skin had seen twenty summers too many for the role he was to play.

Rubriel wore Molindra's scarlet mantle and ruby medallion, marking her as a mage of the High Tiers. Most of her skin was covered too, but she needn't have bothered. She looked pale enough already to have spent all her years under cover of darkness.

They trod lightly through the pass as it climbed and narrowed to its apex, where they crouched low and peered across at the immense wall before them, its arched iron gates open, but guarded this time. Unlike Rubriel's prior journey, men and women now stood watch from atop the wall. Where it had felt forgotten and uninhabited before was now fully awake and brimming with activity. There was little chance they would get by unnoticed.

"Look up there," said Scoe, crouching even lower. "Those spyglasses. They will spot us right away."

There were two of them; golden contraptions semi-concealed on either side of the arch from which the guards could inspect any who approached.

"Then we are hiding in plain sight," Rubriel sighed, retreating from the overlook. Out of line of sight, she stood and brushed the dust from the front of her clothes. She fixed her mask across her face, a look of steely determination setting in her heavy-rimmed eyes.

"What are you doing?" Scoe's apprehension rattled in his throat.

"Follow me," she said, and strode out into the open, giving Scoe no option but to go along.

She made straight for the open gate, paying no heed to the guards atop the walls who signalled below at their approach. She raised her hand in a two-fingered salute to the two surly men who stood on either side of the gate. To Scoe's amazement, they returned it, but stopped her anyway before they could pass through.

"Hold, traveller. State your name and purpose," said the more forward of the two, while his companion scrutinized them closely.

"Durenka," she replied. "*Brehan-na Imul'dene.*"

Thankfully, Scoe's face was well concealed, else his surprise at her unexpected use of their native language would have given them away.

"*Ne cembla?*" The guard jerked his chin toward Scoe.

"*Ne gandamire es cembla,*" Rubriel said. "*Lok avanh a'rul kempre-mai.*"

"*Revelair, a'rul spelse.*" The second guard spoke with a palpable note of suspicion.

But Rubriel smiled in return. "Of course we are spies," she said smoothly in Common. "What else would we be doing on this side of the wall?" Her smile did not reach her eyes, and she stared him down as though she outranked them both - which, in her guise as a mage, she did.

With that, he nodded curtly, and allowed Rubriel and Scoe to pass into the encampment beyond.

Encampment was no longer a fitting description, however, for the former construction site had since assembled into a fully functional outpost. An outpost designed for a single purpose: staging an invasion - or warding against one. Three squat towers flanked each side of the short road between the outer wall and the inner wall. Behind them, temporary housing and various training apparatuses occupied most of the space. A mage ran through a series of exercises over a brazier of flame. Men hauled sacks of supplies from a wagon to the warehouse at the back of the compound.

It was not totally dark here, nor did the emerald aurora reach this far south, which left them bathed in an odd sort of half-light that cast long shadows and played tricks on the eyes. Rubriel and Scoe crossed swiftly to the inner wall, taking care not to appear overtly interested in everything going on around them, and passed through the gate on the far side. Fewer watchers guarded this end. No one challenged them a second time.

Beyond the outpost, the landscape remained unchanged from Rubriel's previous journey, though they kept a wary eye out for more foot traffic on the main road this time around.

"I forgot," Scoe whispered once there was no one around, "that you speak some of that harsh-sounding language of theirs. It sounds so strange coming from you."

"You would not believe how many times I mentally rehearsed that particular encounter on the way here," she said. "I don't know *that* much, and I had to avoid getting into any details for which I may not know the words."

"You were unnervingly convincing," he said with a worried look.

Rubriel just shrugged and kept walking. They passed the first of the crystal lamps marking the path through the thicket of blackened trees. She remembered how scared she had been last time, jumping at every snap of a twig; how she'd hurried without daring to stop, desperate to reach the village beyond. A few rustlings in the bush seemed trivial now.

They stopped for a drink, grateful to be alone and take a break from their charade.

"How do you plan to get across the stream in Mornik?" Scoe asked.

"We will simply walk across it like we do so every day," she said. "We know exactly where we're going and we do not question it. That is their way. For now, it must also be ours."

"What if the spirit of the stream sees through our ruse? It chased you before, didn't it? Will it recognize you?"

"I hope not."

Scoe looked unhappy, but he nodded. So far, she had proven she knew what she was doing. He just hoped his own insecurity didn't get in the way. He hoped Rubriel's half-crazed confidence didn't falter.

They arrived in Mornik as what little light permeated the thick sky faded to naught; the sentry who greeted them thankfully wasn't Tinoti. They paused only briefly to eat, deciding it would be unwise to linger in the village. As appealing as spending the night at the inn sounded, they would be better off making camp in the wilderness. Rubriel had left her name - her real name - at the inn once before. Even if the spirit failed to recognize her, it was only a matter of time before someone in the village would.

Interestingly, no guards surveyed the bridge connecting one half of the village to the other. Perhaps with the stronger presence at the Pass, they deemed it unnecessary to monitor such a small, unimpressive entrance. The stream was only a foot deep and slow-moving; the walkway across it a simple boardwalk made from the spindly woods that surrounded them.

Scoe hesitated briefly, letting Rubriel go first. Her boots clipped smartly on the old wood bridge. A fizzing and bubbling to their left made her stop as the spirit's dripping haze rose from the water to glare at her in silent scrutiny.

She turned her head slowly to meet its watery, eyeless gaze and held it. An unseen force subtly rippled between them in response, chilling the air. The sensation passed just as quickly, and she strode across with Scoe at her side, through the better part of Mornik, out onto the open road once again and into the void as the emerald aurora claimed the sky.

The spirit made no move to stop them or give chase, yet Scoe felt there was a lot more to that exchange than a mere look. "What *was* that? We're supposed to be blending in, not engaging in a staring contest with the Spirit of the Stream."

She made no reply to that, at least none that he could see; it was so dark to his eyes now that he could barely make out the ground beneath his own feet. Every so often a bright ripple would afford him an outline of her up ahead, and confirmation that he wasn't about to step into a rut. Otherwise, he was practically blind. A chill wind whipped across the plains. Dust swirled and coated them from head to toe.

"Slow down. I don't see like you do. Let's not get separated."

"Sorry," she said, letting him catch up and linking her arm through his.

"I'd forgotten how much I hate this place. I have no idea where we are, or how much further we have to go - only that we are supposed to head north, which is approximately that way-" he pointed vaguely in front of them "-and that at some point we will find hills, and a steaming bog."

"Shall I describe it to you? It is grey and flat and dusty," she offered helpfully, sounding a little more like herself.

"Mm-hmm. I guessed that."

"We are away from the road in the middle of nowhere, but there are peaks in the distance, and we will soon be walking uphill."

"Peaks... in the distance. You really see that far?"

"Yet I would be lost without you," she said - and meant it.

"I may be of little use to you in the dark, but there was no chance I would let you come back here on your own."

"I am grateful." She smiled wanly and sighed.

They walked for hours. The mountains - despite Rubriel's ongoing reassurance that they were indeed still travelling in the right direction - did not seem to be getting any closer. Their legs ached from the gradual incline, and their clothes were covered in dust. The wind had mostly died away, but they were exhausted.

"No way we will make it all the way to the mountains without stopping for a proper rest. It is much further than I thought," Rubriel admitted.

"Agreed," said Scoe. "I don't much like camping out in the open, but we have been walking all day - possibly more than a day. I have already lost track."

"We are alone out here. From my observations, those who live here do not see in the dark any better than you. Even the spirits can't."

"What about beasts?" Scoe quipped.

"Beasts?"

"We have deserts, back in Esmara. They are home to all manner of dangerous things." He gave an exaggerated shudder. "Snakes, scorpions, coyotes; buzzing, whirring, biting insects; camels... they say never to sleep on the sand, lest you wake up covered in... in-"

"Covered in what?" Rubriel laughed.

"Well, that's exactly my point! Who knows what monstrosities live in these parts? They have human-sized bats for goodness' sake!"

"And how did *camels* make it onto your list of potential monstrosities?"

"Well, I was just-"

"Are you afraid of camels, Scoe? Who would've thought; the brave Rascovor Mytholi, noble soldier and son-in-law to the King himself, will fearlessly face down a colony of giant bats, charge through the snow after a group of rogue mages outnumbering us six to one, yet show him a camel and he goes weak at the knees.”

“Stop making fun of me! I was being serious.” He pouted, but he laughed too, relieved to hear her slide into the comfortable rhythm of their usual banter. In the absence of a better option, they decided they may as well stop there.

“Let’s drink a little and rest our legs,” Rubriel suggested. “I will take first watch and ensure no Langlythian camels try to eat you.”

He batted away her teasing. The sky had brightened a little - enough to lay blankets on the ground and rummage amongst their small stash for sustenance.

“How much water do you have left?” asked Scoe, holding up his canteen.

“Two thirds.” She carefully sealed her own.

He nodded. “We should be fine, as long as we can find safe drinking water when we reach the hills.”

“What does the map show?”

“Not much.” He pulled the rolled up paper from his satchel and spread it before them. “We’re in this area.” He peered at the hand-traced map in the dim light, pointing to the blank space southeast of the central plateau. “There are mountains all along here - five peaks, in a ‘V’ shape - and several ruins. The easiest way into the swamp will be on this side - through the gap between Mount Eils and Mount Yel’ent - but we will have to cross the road to get to it. No streams or rivers marked on here, though.”

“If people once lived in those ruins, they must have had a water source,” Rubriel said thoughtfully.

“Let’s hope you’re right.”

They both startled as a tremor rippled beneath them; a brief moment of instability that passed as quickly as it came.

"Did you feel that?"

Scoe nodded. "Just a small earthquake. I've felt them here before."

"That was... unnerving."

"Even the *ground* is unwelcoming in this place," he grumbled.

They took a few hours of rest. Scoe, despite his unease, managed to fall asleep, but Rubriel could not. She sat and gazed across the vast emptiness, one eye on the horizon, her mind deep in thought. Though they remained undisturbed by both man and nature, the indescribable sense of something being *wrong* persisted. It seemed almost too easy, right from the moment they crossed the Gloaming Pass. There were no spirits on the plains to watch them, but what she felt in the piercing gaze of the spirit of the stream...

I am wanted here; expected.

The thought played over and over in her mind. She didn't wake Scoe for his turn to take watch, and he scolded her when he realized. He grew palpably more worried about her the deeper into Langlythe they went. He wasn't wrong, but Rubriel couldn't find the words to express what it was that gnawed at her.

There were too many pieces in this giant puzzle, too many moving parts all connected in a mechanism that hovered just outside the grasp of her understanding. She was one of those pieces now, and she kept on moving towards whatever fate awaited them.

It took them about three days in all to reach the end of the plains. By the time they safely crossed the road and stopped to sip from a tiny rivulet dribbling its way down a cliff further north, they were parched and out of food. The only consolation was the brightening of the sky, paired with the luminous yellow-orange fungi that grew rampant in the moistening earth, that together made for somewhat improved visibility within the bog.

They needed it too, to avoid stepping in the wells of mud that bubbled thickly, or the hot steam vents that burst unexpectedly from unassuming holes in the ground. A smell like rotten eggs permeated the humid air. Streaks of white, yellow and green mingled on the rocks like paints on an artist's palette. Somewhere in the distance, a geyser spurted a fountain of boiling water every few minutes.

Their most immediate priority was food. Scoe's belly rumbled as a constant reminder of this, as Rubriel's keen eyes searched for anything that might be edible. So far, the only fauna they'd come across were annoying flying insects, and they both knew better than to sample any of the unfamiliar mushrooms in this place.

Scoe stopped by a pool for a moment, mesmerized by a smooth, colourful rock at its edge, patterned with swirls of grey and orange and yellow. He reached down tentatively, wanting to touch it, and immediately yanked his hand away. The "rock" stood up and scuttled sideways under the water, burying itself further into the muddy bottom.

"Crabs!" he called out. "Look for crabs at the water's edge."

Now they knew what to look for, the crabs were easy to spot - if not so easy to catch. Their shells mimicked the painted rocks perfectly, but underneath they stood on knobbly grey legs with thick, muscular pincers. After much awkward poking and grappling, they extracted and subdued four of them, each roughly the length of a human foot. They scanned their surroundings for a spot to make camp. Mist - a combination of fog and fumes, really - seemed to cling to the ground in patches, uneven and treacherous as it wove between pools and fissures.

"What now?" asked Rubriel, holding up their bounty of crabs trussed together with string.

"Head for the cliffs, maybe? The ground should be firmer over there at least, and if we're lucky, maybe we will come across the ruin marked on our map."

With three volcanoes on their right and two behind them, they hugged the earthy cliff and followed it around to the northeast. The vertical face petered out as they went, replaced by the rocky terrain with which they were more familiar, though the unusual colour patterns and sulphuric odour remained.

Then they spotted it - a square opening in the hillside, partially collapsed on one side but still plenty wide enough for a person to walk through. A suggestion of an old path lay underfoot, leading to the entrance. Rubriel paused on the threshold and listened, hearing nothing from within. Scoe glanced nervously at the visible cracks in the stone, and even more nervously at the darkness beyond, before following her into the tunnel.

It was not totally dark inside, however, for once his eyes grew accustomed, veins of raw crystal glowed softly in the walls. The surface had been polished smooth wherever there was a concentration of crystal, as though the natural resource had been purposely left in place to light the way. All was quiet but for the faint drip-drip of water somewhere deeper.

They followed the sound cautiously until they came to a fork in the tunnel. They chose the right fork first, but that soon ended in a collapsed dead end; the left fork kept going much further, and every so often they spotted doors on either side, as though this were some great hallway of underground apartments.

Rubriel pressed her ear to one of them, straining to hear any sound from the other side. An experimental push found this particular door to be blocked from behind. She tried another and another, until they found one that groaned open with an uncomfortable grinding sound that echoed down the tunnel. Scoe winced.

The room beyond was naught but rubble at the far end, but the undamaged part held an old wooden table and two broken chairs. An empty cauldron sat in an open fireplace, a bucket of coal beside it and a shovel in the corner.

"No one has lived here in a very long time, but the hearth seems usable," said Rubriel, peering into it. "Let's make a small fire and cook these crabs. I'm starving."

"I do not like this place," Scoe said warily, not wanting to turn his back to the doorway. "But I cannot argue with a hot meal."

"There is water here somewhere as well. We heard it. Those who lived here must've had a source of drinking water. We shall have to find it."

"Why do you suppose they left?"

"Who?"

"Whoever used to live here."

She shrugged. "I don't know. Look, we don't need to be here for long. It may make sense to bind our milestones here though, since it is sheltered and discreet. We may find enough coal to keep the brazier burning for several days in our absence, if what they say about Langlythian coal is true."

"It'll burn for a week. Should be enough time to get in and out of Imul'dene - assuming we don't get lost in the bog trying to find our way to the sewers." He wrinkled his face. The idea of climbing up through Imul'dene's waste water system was not at all appealing, but it was the easiest way to get to the heart of the city unnoticed, according to Molindra.

After devouring the crab meat, Rubriel took the cauldron and ventured out in search of water. She clung to the darker side of the tunnel, trusting her eyes to see any potential threat before it saw her, and followed the dripping sound until the tunnel turned a corner and opened out into a wider space.

In the middle of this room was a large hexagonal well. A sturdy iron frame arched over it from each corner, bearing the pulley system and an old crystal lamp at the apex, its orange glow faint with age. On the far side of the room was another door, and stairs leading down.

The well was missing its bucket, but the rope felt sturdy enough, so she looped it under and around the cauldron instead, tying it securely so that it would stay upright. The mechanism squeaked as she lowered it slowly into the depths. She winced at the sound, pausing to listen. Was that movement she heard? A voice, even? Her eyes darted anxiously from one passage to the next. What - or whom - had she disturbed? She cursed herself for not even thinking there could be spirits down here, even if the living had long since abandoned these ruins.

She neither saw nor heard anything more, however, so after a few minutes she steeled herself to continue pulling on the rope, trying to retrieve the cauldron as quietly as possible. It had tipped sideways under the weight of water inside and was only half full when it reached the top. Perhaps just as well, given how heavy it was to carry.

Just as she was leaving, there came a clattering sound - the sound of something being knocked over, or bumped into. It came from behind. She hurried back to the room she and Scoe had claimed, set the cauldron on the table and closed the door behind them.

"Water?" Scoe whispered hopefully.

She nodded. "But that's not all, unfortunately. We are not alone."

20

Under the Fells

Several hours later, the squeak of metal and water splashing interrupted their rest. It was Scoe's watch, and he crept across to listen through the door. "Rubriel," he whispered, but she was already awake. He frowned, his hand resting on the hilt of his dagger.

"Someone is using the well," she guessed.

"Do you think they heard you earlier?" He paused to listen again before she could answer, hearing footsteps. They grew fainter however, moving further away until all was silent again but for their own nervous breathing.

"I'm sure they did," she said, "but they don't appear to be looking for us - at least, not yet."

Both too on edge to sleep now, they sat down on their blankets and discussed their options. They could leave now, take some of the coal and try to find somewhere else to build the brazier for their milestones nearer to Imul'dene. That seemed like the safest option, but if they couldn't find a dry and secluded location, their retreat could be compromised.

It would also be a much more arduous journey *out* of Langlythe, since they would have to cross the bog in its entirety, which could not be done quickly in the event of pursuit. If they stayed in the ruins, they could explore further, collect more coal and be certain the fire would last, but risk running into whoever else occupied these caverns. Outcasts, most likely. If so, they probably had their own reasons for not wanting to be found.

In the end, they settled for a compromise; Scoe reasoned that the others only came out to use the well and then retreated in the opposite direction. So long as they avoided that end of the passage, they could explore the other side doors and hopefully gather what they needed to build a proper brazier, then move on.

They held their weapons ready as they ventured out into the hall once again. Rubriel went first and watched Scoe's back as he tried each of the other doors. The first couple wouldn't budge; another opened reluctantly, only to reveal a useless pile of debris.

They were about to move on to the next when Rubriel ducked into the small space behind him and held her finger to her lips. Scoe couldn't see the gesture, but he froze anyway. Someone moved slowly along the passage towards them, stalking them. The doorway was completely in shadow, the nearest crystal vein several paces behind them. The person - or people - did not appear to be carrying a light source.

Trusting the darkness to conceal her, Rubriel stole a peek around the edge of the frame. Two men with masked faces flattened themselves against the wall. One was looking straight at her, but before he could register the subtle shift in the shadows, her keen eyes recognized a distinctive stripe through the arch of his left eyebrow and knew him at once.

"Dornir?" she said quietly.

The young men sprang with their swords drawn, but she backed away without raising her own. "Who's there?" one shouted.

"It's alright. You know me." Heart pounding, she backed into the light of a crystal vein and slowly dropped the mask from her own face.

The twins stopped dead. "Rubriel? Quakes, what are you doing here?"

"What..!" Scoe exclaimed from the doorway, making them both jump.

"And *Scoe?* What... we thought someone was sneaking around in here, spying on us. We were not sure what to do, so eventually Daelin and I - being the designated scouts and all - decided we would go and find out who was creeping about outside our hideout."

"I do not believe our luck," said Daelin. He produced a small celair from inside his coat - an old and dim one - but he held it out to verify the faces of his friends in its pale glow, and they his. Scoe smiled broadly in return.

"It seems we have all been sneaking around each other." Rubriel grinned, and they embraced each other merrily, all the world's weight temporarily forgotten in the unexpected joy of their friendly reunion.

The twins led them through the door in the back of the well room to yet more welcome surprises. Inside was a mess hall with a long table and an oven with a proper chimney. Off to the right was another room, with an actual brazier in an iron stand, already burning. Various furniture, tools and bags were stacked in the corners. And around the brazier, staring at them in disbelief, were Grace and Adam.

"Look who we found!"

Grace ran to embrace the newcomers.

Adam did not rise, for his leg was bandaged and tied to a splint. Even he smiled to see them all together again, though he winced as he pulled himself upright. Soon the six of them gathered around the brazier's warmth, sipping from mugs of hot mushroom broth and exchanging stories.

Shortly after Rubriel and Scoe had left for the Roof of the World, the others had been forced to leave the spring cave. Foot traffic had increased on the roads to the point where it was too dangerous to hunt and gather food from the area, and the four of them had been more than ready to head home. They travelled south, but their journey had taken a turn for the worse when Adam slipped from a rock and badly twisted his knee. He struggled to put any weight on the leg.

They knew they wouldn't make it far like that, so Daelin and Dornir had led them to these ruins. The twins had made their hideout here once before; when they were first on the run, having deserted their obligations in Minnorak.

"Below us, and deeper under the mountain, used to be a mine rich in coal and metal ores," Dornir explained. "The stairs and passages behind us all lead to the old mineshafts. They are not safe. This upper part where we are now used to house a whole community of workers, until Mount Yel'ent erupted and drove everyone out about sixty years ago. A single eruption probably wouldn't have deterred the miners for long, but this one lasted for years. Imul'dene ceased all mining operations in the area. No one has lived here since. This place is 'officially abandoned' - thus the perfect place to live unofficially." He winked.

"So long as said volcano remains dormant." It was Scoe's turn to talk next. In detail, he recounted their journey to the Roof of the World, his first encounters with snow, Ik and the tribesmen who refused to assist them. He told them of the floods, the devastation of Tabethwick and the suspicion from the refugee camp. He spoke mindfully of Molindra and her role in it all, with a sense of wisdom and tactfulness beyond his years.

Rubriel sat silently through most of the conversation, nodding in agreement or adding the occasional comment. The men did not appear to notice the heavy weight that settled on her shoulders at the mention of Molindra, or Celessil.

But Grace did. She took her aside later. "Are you all right?"

Rubriel shook her head. "I have to be. So much depends on what I've come back here to do, and I feel unworthy of it, yet I am told there is no one else."

This part of the caverns afforded them separate sleeping chambers off the hall. Away from the others, Grace spoke her mind with a hint of sharpness that was seldom heard from her.

"I've seen you spar with Scoe and the twins, seen the light in your eyes when you speak of those you care about. Most women in Bantria never have a chance to do anything of meaning, whether they feel worthy or not. I envy you, Rubriel. The ruler of your nation values your opinion! He sees something in you and has entrusted you with a chance to change the course of the future. That *means* something." Her cheeks flushed. She raked her fingers through her soft curls.

"It does mean something," Rubriel responded in a low voice, "but there is a feeling I cannot shake, something dreadfully wrong that I cannot see, like an apple that is rotten on the inside. It would seem like a gift until you bite into it." She paused. "Grace, you may not be remembered for your part in this, but at least you will still be yourself at the end."

Grace sighed. They stood in silence until Rubriel started rummaging in her pack for the cleaner of the two blankets she used to camp outside.

"Take one of these." Grace offered her a much thicker one from her own modest bed. "I'm sorry," she said. "That was unfair of me to say."

Rubriel didn't respond until she was seated on the edge of the old, thin mattress with the faded red blanket wrapped around her. "No, I'm sorry. I am angry and sad and afraid, just as anyone must be with war looming. But I am here to do something about it. I will try to take a little of that fire with me and..."

"And?"

"Wallow less," she finished with a half-hearted chuckle.

They slept better that night than they had in a long time. After a good eight hours of rest, they rose and washed with water from the well. Grace cooked up some mushy peas - apparently they'd managed to pilfer a bagful on their way here - then set about building up the brazier fire with full stomachs. Smoke was a problem, so they ended up rearranging much of the decrepit furniture; pushing the long table up against the wall so the brazier could stand in the centre of the former mess hall, which had better ventilation.

They had quite a bit of extra coal, so they planned roughly how much to keep the brazier burning well and how much they could use for cooking, until Adam gruffly suggested that they simply mount the cooking pot over the brazier. He thought they could keep it going for several weeks at least.

Binding of milestones was a peculiar business, Rubriel thought. They each had a smooth, oval stone with a flat surface, like a river stone, that fit comfortably in the palm. She went first, holding her stone in the heart of the flames with tongs until it glowed hot. Then she closed her eyes and spoke the exact words the Elder had given them:

"With fire to give you strength, remember this place. Remember the warmth, remember the light, remember the air and smoke. Return me here when I call upon you."

It wasn't enough to merely say the words; they must be spoken with love, as though to a living being. She felt she had done it correctly, but there was no visible response from the stone, nor the brazier; she removed it from the flames and held it while it cooled, but the stone itself appeared unchanged.

"How do we know if it worked?" Scoe asked doubtfully.

She wrinkled her chin. "I suppose we won't until we come to use them. We cannot test it, because each stone will only work once."

"I must admit I feel rather silly doing this." Scoe shrugged and held his own stone in the fire. He copied Rubriel, again receiving no confirmation of having accomplished anything.

"This shouldn't work," he protested. "I am not a man of science, nor of magic, but asking an apparently ordinary stone to remember something? That makes no sense, and yet... I felt as though something happened."

"So did I," Rubriel admitted. "We will have to trust that it did. Milestones are real; I once met someone whose life was saved thanks to the use of one. Perhaps we are not meant to understand how."

"Do you remember how to activate it? Put it down first."

"Warmth, light, air and smoke. Remember and return."

He nodded. "Let us go over our plans again." Setting the two milestones aside, Scoe spread the maps Molindra had given him on the table. They were hand-traced, with her own additions and notes in the margins - remarkably detailed.

She made the most of her time there, Rubriel thought, but brushed it aside.

"We are down here right now," Scoe said, pointing to the area labelled 'ruins' between Mount Yel'ent and Mount Mornik further northeast. "From here we head north across the swamplands until we reach the Fells."

"It's called the Painted Bog." Daelin overheard and joined them at the table to listen in. "And the Fells are three huge waterfalls that cascade all the way down through Imul'dene itself. The fellwater, despite its name, is actually clean; it's the bog beneath it that is contaminated."

"Right," said Scoe, "because the sewer outflow is here somewhere, behind it."

"Are we sure there is a way for us to get in?" Rubriel asked.

"That I can personally vouch for," Daelin said. "There is an entrance to the east which leads up to the maintenance tunnels inside the dam, and from there, almost anywhere in the city, if you can avoid getting lost. It is quite the labyrinth."

"Which also brings us to the first part of the plan," Scoe continued. "The dam controls the water volume and flow of the river that runs right through the city. If we can locate the control mechanisms and disrupt it, we will create some serious problems higher up."

"Indeed, if you were to close the dam completely, I imagine most of the Lower Tiers would be rapidly flooded out."

"So we cause a flood, which will draw the attention of the Middle tiers and hopefully most of the spirits as well, but as soon as they realize the dam has been tampered with, they will rush down there to reopen it. We should also disable the mechanism so they would have to repair it first - and then get away into the higher levels as soon as possible," Rubriel said.

Scoe nodded in agreement. "From what Molindra told me, the Middle Tiers will be difficult to traverse. The area is vulnerable thanks to the lifts and pulley systems they rely upon for getting up and down, but I also cannot think of a way to cause significant disruption there without being caught. I think our best option is to bypass the Middle Tiers altogether and follow the aqueducts right up to the High Tiers. According to the map, we should come out behind the citadel."

"Or more accurately, between the citadel and an underground warehouse, set into the side of the mountain. Do we know what they store there?"

"Well." Scoe pulled another piece of paper in front of them and turned it so the others could see. "Molindra did sneak in there once. She said it is divided into sections, like so." He traced the lines drawn on the map, segmenting the warehouse into three parts. "There is food, textiles, and building supplies - cement and such."

"So we break into the warehouse while everyone is focused on the chaos down below and either destroy or contaminate their food stores.

Is that likely to have a significant impact? How many other storehouses are there?"

"That I don't know, and there are no others marked on any of these sketches." Scoe rubbed his chin thoughtfully.

"Dornir and I have never been to Imul'dene... well, not above ground, at least. But, supplies in general are allocated with precision. There is rarely a surplus. Any loss is going to be felt."

They fell silent for a while, deep in thought.

"Is this not difficult for you, Daelin?" Rubriel asked softly. "It is your capital we're talking about, after all."

He waved off her concern. "This country is so unwell it is oblivious to its own sickness. It will have to be fully broken before anyone can begin to fix it."

She frowned, considering this, but before she could ask him to elaborate, they were interrupted as Adam limped into the room.

"You should know that an army marched across behind us as we fled our refuge in the north," he said gruffly. "They make for the ice divide - and the World Gate, no doubt."

Dread swelled in the pit of her stomach. They had expected this, of course, but hearing of it made it all the more real. She nodded stiffly.

"It is likely only a matter of time until Langlythe marches for the Gloaming Pass as well. We must be away from here before that happens, or the way home may close with us on the wrong side."

"We should get ready to leave," Scoe said to Rubriel, and she stood.

"Yes," she said firmly. "There is little more we can do from here. Let us be done with this mission, and hope that Bantria took the Elder's advice and will destroy as many gateways as they can find."

The roar of the great waterfalls diminished all other sounds long before they came into view, for a pungent volcanic mist hung over the Painted Bog, thickest where the Fells tossed plumes of vapour up from the deep pools beneath. Geysers hissed steam into the air as boiling water gushed somewhere underground. Rubriel and Scoe thought it best to skirt around the edge of the bog, following the higher ground to avoid such hazards, though they still passed many a pit of bubbling mud as they went, opaque and viscous like molten clay.

Standing to one side, they peered up through the fog to glimpse where the torrent split, hundreds of feet above, whence it fell in triplicate to crash down into the swamp. Having reached what they felt was the right area, they searched the cliffs on the northeastern side for the tunnel entrance Daelin had described.

Rubriel wrinkled her nose. "That stench is... *very* strong here. More than just sulphur and wet earth. I think we are getting close."

Scoe pulled a disgusted face in agreement. Neither of them was particularly looking forward to traipsing through sewage.

"There," she stopped to watch how the fog parted around a dark opening in the rock, tall enough for a person to walk through. The ground was sodden underfoot. They picked their way over to it and stepped carefully inside, finding a ledge on either side where they could walk along the walls of the tunnel without treading in the refuse that accumulated in the middle.

Scoe shuddered as the putrid smell assaulted his nostrils. Not wanting to fumble in the dark if he didn't have to, he produced a dim celair from his pocket to light their way - one of the ancient, faded ones from the mines. The tunnel only ran straight back into the cliffs a short way before stairs split off from the main sewage pipe. He glanced back at Rubriel.

"We are really doing this," she said, apprehensive.

"Stay together, stick to the plan," Scoe assured her, sounding calmer than he felt. "We've got this."

They climbed. Scoe led the way up the narrow staircase, the walls so close it forced them to ascend in single file, the top of Scoe's head nearly touching the ceiling. The stairs turned ninety degrees to the left and continued up onto an equally narrow bridge that crossed from one side of an open chamber to the other. Below them, Rubriel could see a river of sludge moving sickeningly underneath where they walked.

More stairs climbed higher still, leaving them a little breathless as they reached the next landing. Similar to the first, this one crossed a vast reservoir filled with water - clean water - which poured in through three giant valves on the far side and rushed out somewhere behind them. Halfway along the bridge, it branched out and up into the centre, towards a door that led to another room on the floor above.

Unlike the passages thus far, crystal lamps set into the grimy walls every few paces illuminated this room, with a larger, teardrop-shaped one in the ceiling. Iron grate windows gave a view of the reservoir and its valves below. Something ancient and mechanical occupied much of the floor space, all iron and gears, with three heavy levers controlling it. Rubriel examined them, trying to trace the mechanism back to verify what it might control. The metal was corroded in parts, discoloured by rust and algae and mould; evidently the machine was seldom used or maintained.

"One for each valve, I think," she said. "We must be inside the dam, or part of it anyway. If we close those valves, the reservoir below us will likely empty, but the question is - what will happen further up?"

Scoe indicated yet another set of stairs. "Let's find out what is on the other side of the valves first, then decide if we should close them or open them fully."

As they climbed again and crossed another chasm, they realized they must now be directly under the city. Smaller drains poured water at a steady rate into this upper chamber, which did indeed appear to feed the valves lower down.

They followed the bridge, suspended from the ceiling by mammoth chains, further and further, until they reached another control room. This one contained a single lever in the centre of the room, its mechanism intertwined up into the ceiling. Behind it, a large iron grate looked out into a third reservoir - more like a huge pipe, really - that curved right underneath them and back down to feed into the rest of the system.

"Look!" Rubriel pointed up through the window. A single enormous valve filled the upper end of the tunnel, angled up through its roof. It consisted of several concentric rings, all but closed to permit only a steady and controlled plume of water to pass through.

Hastily, Scoe pulled out one of his maps, studying it under one of the wall crystals. "According to this, the river originates far up in the mountains to the north and runs right through all three tiers of Imul'dene. It follows a single path through the High and Middle Tiers, then splits into three when it reaches the Lower. I think this whole structure is an overflow system, and that valve controls how much excess water gets from the upper levels into the Lower Tiers."

"So if we were to close the three below and open this one all the way..."

"It would overflow above ground and flood everything in between."

Like the previous chambers, this one followed the same pattern of offering another staircase to ascend yet higher still. Rubriel poked her head around the corner and looked up. "We ought to get to higher ground as quickly as possible after we do this. There is a *lot* of water behind that valve; I can feel it."

Once they were satisfied that the passage would lead them out of harm's way, they retraced their steps back down to the first control room with the three levers. Each lever made a forty-five degree angle with the ground and could be pulled in either direction. They deduced that the valves on this level were not fully open.

"Do you think it matters what order we pull them?" Scoe asked.

"No, but we should move fast. These machines are old and stiff; our efforts here will no doubt be extremely loud. While we do appear to be alone in these tunnels, we cannot be sure they won't hear us up above and send someone to investigate." She grasped the lever shaft in both hands.

"Let's pull together and flip it all the way over." Scoe gripped the lever from the other side. "Ready? One, two, three..."

They both pulled hard. There was a crunching, grinding sound of metal on metal as the gears slowly began to turn. They eased the lever upright, then changed positions to push it down towards the floor. Once beyond the apex, the lever moved more easily, and they were rewarded with a reverberating *thunk* as the rings of the first valve closed against each other.

The second lever fell with ease, and they moved straight on to the third. This one stuck half way where one of the pulleys was badly rusted, but they managed to coax it steadily into position.

Rubriel turned to peer through the iron grate. "They're all closed. Let's go."

They bounded up the stairs to the next level, somewhat relieved to see that the water level in the second reservoir had not yet risen significantly. The lever in the second control room was much bigger, and the mechanism attached to it was in poor condition.

"What if it breaks?" Scoe said, glancing nervously at the tangled, corroded knot of gears, chains and pulleys.

"The idea is to destroy it," Rubriel reminded him. "We force it open and then we break it on purpose. It will take months to repair something like this."

Scoe flinched a little at her ruthlessness.

Not only was the lever larger, it had further to travel. They stood on either side, grasped the shaft in both hands, knees bent, and heaved.

The lever didn't budge.

"Harder!" Rubriel urged. They pulled again with all their might. The ancient mechanism screeched in protest. "Come on!"

Scoe growled and heaved, moving it an inch or two. He changed positions, climbing astride it for better leverage. They pulled and pulled and pulled, until the gears shuddered and the lever gave another few inches.

With it further off the ground, Rubriel ducked underneath it and pushed up. "Come on," she growled again through gritted teeth. "We did not come this far to be bested by a stupid... rusty... lever!"

With a mighty shove, the lever groaned its way to vertical. Machinery wailed. A roar of water intensified as the valve opened part way and the torrent swelled.

"We're making progress," Scoe said, panting. "I pull, you push."

They braced themselves. Scoe pulled down with every ounce of strength, his knuckles white and veins protruding in his neck. Rubriel threw her weight behind the lever, pushing furiously. Slowly, it began to move. Then, with a horrid crunching and scraping, it fell all at once. Gears splintered and broke where they rusted, sending bits of metal flying. Water thundered through the valve and sprayed into the control room, soaking them. So much water. The stone shuddered.

Scoe gaped at the enormous tide pouring in, as though they had removed a plug from the bottom of the ocean. Cold water filled his boots. He looked down and gasped.

"Scoe!" Rubriel's shout was almost lost in the din as she realized the same thing.

"We need to go up, now!"

He splashed his way towards the stairs. The water was rising insanely fast - faster than they could climb, until they were half walking, half swimming up the tunnel as the turbulent rush chased them. It pushed them all the way to the highest layer of the system before the water finally slowed, leaving them to crawl up the last few steps and spill in a gasping, sodden heap into the High Tiers' underground plumbing network. They took a few moments to recover, watching as the water level slowly receded back the way they came.

Scoe emptied the water from his boots, grimacing as he put them back on. They wrung as much water out of their clothes as they could. Rubriel checked her inner pocket to make sure the milestone was still there. With their coats damp and crumpled and their hair dripping, they could not help but be conspicuous to anyone who should catch sight of them once they finally made it above ground.

Now they faced a new network of tunnels, filled with pipes of varying diameter. Their surroundings were drier here, at least. They followed a straight path away from where they came up, remembering that the warehouse marked on Molindra's map was at the back of the city, but they only got so far before they were forced to make a choice between going left or right. Both directions looked the same from where they stood, but if they were right about their current orientation, the right fork would take them closer to where they needed to go.

At first, they thought it was a dead end, but an alcove to the side held a ladder leading to a circular iron trapdoor in the ceiling. Carefully,

Scoe climbed the ladder and paused, tilting his ear upwards to listen for sounds of life overhead. He heard little, so he unlatched the door and pushed it open by a sliver to peer through. Light and fresh air greeted him as he looked across a narrow street at ground level between two large buildings. He nodded to Rubriel, and they climbed up out of the hole and replaced the cover.

She stood against the wall and looked up. The citadel loomed over them from its intimidating height. Opposite, a back entrance to a large, featureless rectangular structure, set into the mountainside, that could only be a warehouse.

They were exactly where they wanted to be.

21

The Citadel

The city was oddly quiet, Rubriel thought, considering the mayhem they just instigated with the water system. She supposed those higher up were simply not yet aware, but couldn't help wondering if their manipulations had less impact above ground than anticipated. Without finding a suitable viewpoint and looking down from on high, it was impossible to gauge the effects of their actions.

Inside the warehouse, they hid behind a stack of crates while a group of people worked in an aisle further down. Goods were being shifted from the wider walkway down the centre and stashed on the shelves with great efficiency by a team who had clearly done this many times before. After a while, the sounds moved to a different aisle across from them, and Rubriel and Scoe scurried across to the other side to better observe.

The workers did not appear to hear anything, making too much noise of their own to detect an extra set of footsteps. They loaded goods onto a cart with four wheels, too wide to fit through a normal doorway, which meant they would have to leave via the warehouse's main entrance and avoid passing by Rubriel and Scoe's hiding place.

Once sure they were alone, they set to exploring the place. The warehouse itself was immaculate. The stone floor had been regularly swept; overhead signs labelled each aisle, indicating what was stored where, and the shelves were relatively free of dust. If they had a resident population of vermin, it was well-controlled.

What mattered most, however, were the food supplies, located toward the front of the building in the section immediately behind the double doors of the main entrance. Here they found bags and barrels of dried peas, flour, tallow and various herbs. Another area, segregated at the end of an aisle, held cheeses, meats and vegetables, kept cold atop long trays full of ice.

They looked at one another, unsure how best to proceed. The most obvious tactic would be to set fire to the warehouse, but with the building itself made of stone, and the shelves all metal, a fire would not spread easily by itself. Originally, they had thought to contaminate the food stores, but with everything so well packed and clean, it would take far too long and risk them getting caught in the process.

Voices and rattling from beyond the doors startled them, and they hurried away from the entrance into the third major section at the back of the warehouse. Hiding amongst rows of textiles, furs, leathers and chemicals, they listened as another pair of workers came in to retrieve supplies.

"Most of this is at the back," one of them said. "Soap, oil, a bolt of undyed cloth..."

Scoe's eyes widened. Wordlessly, he pointed at the shelf across from them, stocked with cakes of soap in varying sizes.

Rubriel nodded and crept further down the aisle, squeezing, as quietly as she could, through a gap in the shelving and putting a full bay of fabric bolts between them and the pickers.

Crouched low as they were, an unexpected warmth caught their attention. The source was a horizontal slit in the back wall of the warehouse, glowing orange as hot coals smouldered low in the furnace behind it. An idea slowly took shape.

"Most of the materials in this section will burn easily," said Scoe once they were alone again. He took the lid off a barrel and sniffed, wrinkling his nose. "If we mess things up a bit, knock stuff onto the floor and douse it in the contents of these barrels, we can use the coals from the furnace to start a substantial bonfire. It is unlikely to spread to the other wings, but the heat and smoke trapped in here will ruin a lot of the food, anyway."

She glanced around. "We will have to work quickly. If only the water problems would cause more of a stir. They might stay out of the warehouse for a bit."

They set to work. Anything they could easily push off the shelving ended up on the floor. Rubriel found more coal in the first wing and piled that on the floor too, for good measure. Scoe, meanwhile, was organizing the barrels. They were heavy and awkward to manoeuvre, though they worked as efficiently as they could. A shout from outside startled them.

"I'm not finished!" Scoe's heart pounded as he tried to work faster.

On impulse, Rubriel took off her red mantle and tossed it aside. "Keep going. I'll distract them."

Before Scoe could argue, she dashed out through the back door into the street where they first came in. She hugged the wall until she could peer around the building and see who was out front. A small man with a handcart stood in front of the double doors, fumbling with the keys on his belt. She squared her shoulders and strolled out to meet him.

"Have you seen what is happening in the Lower Tiers?"

He looked up and frowned.

"It is all flooded! Underwater! Something is terribly wrong."

He blinked, then suddenly realized her clothes were all wet. "I must see this for myself." He strode away, leaving his cart behind.

"Oi!" came another man's shout. "What are you doing? Get back to work!" He scowled at Rubriel, pointing to the servant's entrance to the ground floor of the citadel and leaving her no choice but to hurry inside.

She found herself in a corridor with workrooms branching off on either side. It was noisy with the sounds of scrubbing and pounding wet fabrics. Anxious, she strode past the open archways, keeping her head low and avoiding eye contact with those busy laundering garments. She made it to the other end, only to squish herself into a corner and hold her breath as an overseer entered, willing him not to spot her.

Heart racing, she watched him stop on the threshold to talk to the workers. If he turned back this way, he would surely see her. She desperately needed to get back to Scoe, but right now she needed a place to hide, and a moment to think.

She slipped through the door from which the overseer emerged, up the steps and around a corner into another long corridor with many rooms - living quarters - opening off it. A mess hall branched off at the far end and a stairwell led to the second floor.

There were spirits *everywhere*. Some clung to the ceiling; others hid in the spaces under and between furnishings, or curled around light fixtures. They paid her no heed, or at least, if any of them thought her presence suspicious, they made no sign nor attempt to alert the living occupants.

Rubriel considered going back. Would she run into the overseer before she reached the exit? Had Scoe succeeded in setting fire to the warehouse? And if he had, where was he now? Lacking a better option, she followed the stairs up to the second floor. She knew there were various balconies and outcroppings on each level; perhaps it would be possible to climb down?

The second floor was even busier. Groups of red-clad individuals occupied rows of desks, or stood in small groups deep in conversation. She continued up past them to the third floor, panicking now, to hear raised voices coming from the next room.

"... A flood, you say?" said a woman's voice, followed by irritable footsteps as she strode over to a large window on the northern side. "I am more concerned that the warehouse right next to us is *on fire*."

With that, the man who had been listening ran to see. "What!?"

He spun unexpectedly and spotted Rubriel hovering on the stairs. "You must fetch an elementalist at once," he said to the woman. "I'll round up some guards to secure the area. And you," he barked at Rubriel, "go upstairs and inform the High Warden at once!" He pushed past her as he hurried down.

The woman scowled at her hesitation to do as he said, leaving Rubriel no choice but to ascend higher still. Her heart pounded as she climbed, forced deeper and deeper into the heart of the citadel, further and further from where she wanted to be. Perhaps she could duck out of sight at the top, just long enough to use her milestone. It pained her to leave Scoe behind, but she had to trust that he would do the same in her situation and had used his own by now.

The landing was smaller than the previous ones and empty, save for a set of double doors resting open, the crystal lamp hanging from above glinting red on the strange metalwork patterns covering their surface. She gulped and pushed onwards, into another long hallway full of other doors. She peered left and right. To the right was a semicircular room with three identical sets of double doors leading off it. The passage to the left was long and straight, with more sets of closed doors on each side.

Two figures walked away from her towards the other end. She darted to the right, quickly ducking into the shadow of a corner in the room beyond... only to rush headlong into the cold embrace of a spirit. She gasped as it wrapped around her - just briefly - before it hissed and shot away, slipping under a door. The encounter left her shaken. She reached inside her coat for her milestone. Then - a door opened right outside. Voices in the hall, almost near enough to touch.

Please, let them go another way, please... Her heart nearly leapt out of her chest as she willed them to leave. Her hand grasped her sword hilt, thinking she would have no choice this time but to fight. Then, just as she was about to spring, the footsteps carried the voices away. They were taking the stairs.

She shuddered. That was much, much too close.

She steadied herself, straining to listen over the sound of her own breathing, and reached again for her milestone. Suddenly a crash sounded from below, followed by the clang and scuffle of fighting, and shouts.

Scoe, she thought painfully, rushing back to the stairs, her first instinct to run and find him. She hesitated, and then-

Thud.

The doors at the very end of the hall suddenly flung open. She whirled and froze, inexplicably feeling there was not enough distance between her and the vast, red-lit room at the end of the passage. The hair on the back of her neck stood erect.

"Come in, Rubriel. I have been waiting for you."

22

Made to Fight

Meanwhile, Scoe stood at the bottom of a ladder and waited. After setting the blaze, he'd fled the warehouse and dropped back down into the aqueducts, thinking it the most likely place Rubriel would go while he finished, having bought him extra time. Finding no sign of her under the trapdoor, he'd even explored the tunnels a little more in case she'd wandered off, though it seemed unlikely. They had agreed to stick together.

Worried, he returned to the ladder up, waiting to make sure the way was clear before venturing back out onto the street. Thick smoke wafting out from around the back door of the warehouse confirmed his efforts were successful, but where could Rubriel have gone? Looking around, he noticed the servant's entrance to the citadel had been left slightly ajar. *Surely she hadn't...?*

Against his better judgement, he went to the door and nudged it open a little further to peer inside. He would've been relieved to see it was only a laundry, if it weren't for the trail of wet footprints leading all the way down the hall and up the steps at the end. They were grimy, just like his own boots. Reluctantly, he followed them.

A sudden scuffling from behind, and two guards fell on him and knocked him off his feet. Larger and stronger than them, he wrestled them off and sprang, shoving one of them roughly against the wall and managing to draw his knives before they recovered. He made a lunge for the exit. They blocked the way, each wielding a dagger of their own as they came at him again.

Fighting toe to toe, they drove Scoe back towards the steps, until he kicked one of them in the groin and sliced through the biceps of the other. He finished them off quickly, only to find that a dozen laundry attendants now stood between him and the way out, brandishing whatever weapons they could find; all washing paddles and washboard shields.

He ran in the other direction, surprising a guard in the next room and slitting his throat before he realized what was happening. He carried on to the end and up to the next level, finding it strangely empty. Hurriedly, he scanned the office room for any sign of Rubriel, not daring to so much as whisper her name in this place. Nothing.

He could - and would - milestone out of here, but he was torn. Was Rubriel in trouble? Had she already left? Three more armed men raced down from above, taking the decision from him as he found himself surrounded.

The Great Hall of Imul'dene was the largest room Rubriel had ever seen. Its dark floors, polished and marbled with veins of crystal, reminded her of the abandoned mines, glowing faintly underfoot. The high, curved ceiling sloped upwards to its full height at the back of the room. A monstrous chandelier hung low in the centre, a great metallic hand gathering a cluster of red crystals. They bathed the room in a bright yet oppressive ambience.

Two fireplaces burned in the walls on either side within stone surrounds. In between, panels of metalwork wrought in the same manner as the doors stretched from floor to ceiling, depicting their strange scenes.

At the back, three steps led onto a semicircular dais. The entire room was devoid of furniture, save for the throne at its apex.

Rubriel could've turned and bolted down the stairs. She could've used her milestone. She meant to. But in that instant, she stopped. A deep, guttural feeling came upon her, the uncanny certainty that everything had been leading her to this room, this confrontation, from the moment she set foot on Langlythian soil.

Reason screamed at her to flee, but something else drew her forward. Her heart thudded against her ribs. Grim determination echoed in every step as she walked the length of the hall to at last come face to face with the one she believed, deep down, was truly responsible for all her suffering.

"The journey here has cost you much."

Zildred's cold, hollow voice echoed through the empty room. He stood from the throne, the folds of his brilliant red coat spilling around him like blood. Fine embroidery decorated his chest, up to his broad, layered mantle lavished with gold and rubies. "What is it you seek, Rubriel? You will not find Molindra within these walls."

"Do not speak her name to me!" Her fists clenched tight at her sides as she squared her shoulders to confront him. "You used her, betrayed her, and now she pays for your treachery while you wage war without provocation!"

"So you believe Bantria is above reproach," he replied. Almost idly, despite the heat of her accusations.

"They have done nothing to you!"

He stepped down from the dais, so that he stood only a few feet in front of her. "And what, precisely, do *you* hope to accomplish? With what do you intend to bargain? What could you possibly offer me that is worth permitting the stain that is Bantria to grow upon the world? You cannot truly expect to defeat me in my own hall!"

Behind her, the huge double doors slammed shut as suddenly as they had opened. She flinched, but she wouldn't back down, even as her mind raced at the absurdity of her own demands.

"Call off the invasion. I know all about the World Gate. So does Bantria. Already they send word to the King of Esmara for aid." She stepped forward. "Meet with the Prime Minister, and with Elder Berren of Celessil to negotiate. There need not be a war." A knot tightened in the pit of her stomach. Her pulse quickened as she fought to control her nerves, her hand hovering near the hilt of *Persistence*.

"So bold; so naïve. You understand very little. No blade will harm me. You cannot best me in a duel of swords."

"Perhaps not!" She spat, enraged now. "But I challenge you, nonetheless." Grim determination steadied her hand. She had little choice. But if he thought she would surrender without a fight, cower in her folly and beg for mercy, he was sorely mistaken. She *wanted* to fight him, she realized. No, more than that - she was *meant* to. She felt it in her bones.

"What is this?"

The whole room seemed to darken. "I command both the living and the dead; I wield the power of both shadow and spirit. Not in two hundred years have I been challenged thus."

Rubriel bristled at his arrogance. "I do not fear death and I do not fear you. I am the last champion of the Celessilian League and you *will* face me in battle." Her words were like daggers themselves.

In her mind, she travelled back to another arena in another time and place. *Her* arena. Her domain. She had lived for this, once, and she had never encountered an opponent she could not best. *Persistence* practically lept into her hands as she drew it, instinct taking over. The well of pain that had weakened her these past few weeks now gave her strength. With it, she would destroy him.

Slowly, Zildred drew a sword of his own from a scabbard at his side that had not been there a moment before. "Your determination intrigues me. Come, then; let us see how well that courage serves you."

To her surprise, he raised his sword in a formal salute, as had been the custom before any competitive duel in years past. She returned it with a flourish; ready, baiting him as she slid into her combat stance. Her eyes sparkled with conviction.

They circled one another, neither willing to strike first. His piercing glare could have burned a hole through her skull, but she knew better than to be intimidated by theatrics. She twirled her blade impatiently, assessing him. He seemed far too at ease.

She made an experimental advance. He sidestepped smoothly, but she rebalanced herself just as easily. She attacked again from the opposite angle. He blocked her and spun away for a second time, the clang of steel ringing through the hall. She backed off, flourishing her sword, light glinting off the metal.

He closed the gap between them, daring her to try again. She moved to strike from the right, then pivoted mid swing to slice down; this time he fought back, exchanging a series of quick, crisp blows. Her blade caught every one of them, retaliating just as swiftly through any hint of an opening, until he broke away so fast she barely saw him move.

"So you have some skill," he mused. "What else will Celessil's finest bring to the fight?"

"Come and find out."

They clashed again in a deadly dance of steel and controlled fury, testing each other, yet holding back. She hardly broke a sweat. Her blood boiled with anger, urging to be released. He was playing with her and she knew it.

Aggravated, she lunged again, forcing him to defend as her eager blade searched for an opening. He held his ground, repelling her attacks with greater fervour to match her own. Abruptly, he shifted behind her some-how, and she almost fell forwards under the weight of her own thrust. She turned her stumble into a pirouette, quickly reorienting herself to defend as he thrust for her exposed side. She deflected it–just–and he drove her back, but she made use of the space to steady her defence.

His pace quickened, each blow as precise as her own, but he could not break through her guard, nor would she allow him to catch her by surprise with his ability to move without visibly *moving*. Whenever he disappeared to flank her, she would roll, dodge and retaliate before he could score any true advantage.

But she grew angrier and more and more frustrated, aware of a strange, unhinged feeling in the pit of her stomach - a realization that she had never genuinely wanted to kill someone the way she did now. That rage surged inside her, fuelling her strength as she lashed out again and again in a flurry of motion.

She lost any sense of how long they fought. All that mattered was the rhythm, the positioning, the clang of steel against steel, the anticipation of the next potentially fatal move. Her muscles burned with over-exertion. On and on they fought. He was faster than her, but when she struck, she struck *hard*. The impact reverberated in her bones.

How could they be evenly matched, as feared and powerful as he was? If he had been holding back in the beginning, she didn't think he was now, but there was no time to consider what that meant.

He shifted away again, taunting her with how easily he slid beyond her reach. She adjusted her grip in that split second, forcing herself to ignore the growing heaviness in her sword arm. Without the limitations of living flesh, Zildred was truly tireless; he would outlast her unless she ended this–and soon.

This was a mistake.

The dread of defeat loomed over her, even as she fought through it; even as the raging torrent of battle swept her beyond breaking, beyond limits. She shuddered as she absorbed each blow. Her whole body throbbed in protest, yet still she kept on fighting, stroke after stroke, parry, dodge and lunge until she feared she would lose the strength to stand.

Even then, she knew she would keep fighting from the ground, until her own weapon became too heavy in her hands. It was he who stole Molindra's future. *He* broke their sisterhood. *He* was the reason they had sent her back. She would never surrender to him—not even if it cost her life.

The doors remained sealed against friend and foe alike. She could only hope Scoe made it out safely. As if on cue, a loud bang sounded somewhere below. It took her a moment to register.

That must be what a gunshot sounds like. Scoe had resorted to firing one of his precious bullets.

The thought interrupted her flow. Zildred shifted and attacked from behind; she whirled and blocked in time, but lost her footing under the blow and rolled out of the way. With a desperate burst of determination, she stumbled back onto her feet. Her blood was on fire.

Not like this. I will not die like this!

She surged forward in one last swift and powerful assault, moving faster than the eye could see from one stroke to the next. Her resurgence surprised him. She drove him back with a ferocity she didn't know she possessed, like some otherworldly force had taken over in her moment of need. She fought him all the way back up onto the dais, glowing with intensity, until finally, *finally,* she broke through his guard and her blade found its mark. It thrust deep through his abdomen, buried right to the hilt. Zildred shuddered violently and shifted backwards, away from the blade, beyond her reach.

There was no blood. His clothing gaped open and torn; the edges looked almost *burnt.*

"Enough," he said, quite unharmed, and simply tossed her aside with an unseen hand of kinetic energy. She flew clean off her feet and landed in a crumpled heap nearly twenty feet away. Her head swam with the impact against the stone floor.

She could not get up.

He recovered smoothly. "Congratulations. Never before have I been gainsaid in my own hall. You impress me."

She shut her eyes tight and flinched as his sword-tip pressed against her throat.

"Of course, I cannot be killed by weapons alone. I did warn you."

"Finish it," she croaked.

"Ah, yes; a clean, honourable death. You deserve that much, do you not?"

A trickle of blood ran down Rubriel's neck. She stifled a whimper, telling herself to be brave.

"And yet..." He paused for what seemed like an eternity, considering her. "What *are* you, Rubriel?"

He lingered over the odd choice of phrasing as though *she* were the one who had harmlessly taken a blade to the gut. "You may yet be of use. Live - for now - and appease my curiosity."

His blade fell away. She half sat up, clutching instinctively at the wound on her neck that dribbled a steady stream of blood between her fingers. How deep was it? She had never been so tired in her life; didn't think she would survive another day, another hour, whether he commanded it or not.

Just then, the doors to the great hall swung open and a man strode in, flanked by two others of lesser rank. His garb placed him as an official of some kind; aristocracy, or perhaps military. He wore a stern countenance and brisk demeanour that suggested he had a great deal to do and very little time in which to do it. He bowed crisply from the waist.

"You sent for me, Master?" His eyes flicked briefly to Rubriel while his companions kept theirs lowered.

"This is the one who broke in and released the dam."

Rubriel shuddered, realizing the extent of his reach. As far as she knew, he'd been occupied with her the entire time, yet he had already seen the flooding in the city below and knew its cause. Whatever had she been thinking, challenging him to a duel?

"We caught one already. Foreign, fought like a beast and killed one of ours with a strange device that went off with a bang and fired a projectile straight through his forehead."

"Ah yes, the Esmaran."

Apparently he knew about Scoe, too. Had he truly been watching elsewhere, even while they fought? *But Scoe will be fine,* she told herself. *He will milestone out of here as soon as he is alone, as will I.*

"We have him locked up, and we have confiscated the device for further study," the man continued. "Shall we...?" He glanced down at Rubriel.

"Indeed," Zildred confirmed. "Take *all* her belongings and stow her away while the damage is assessed. And unlike the Esmaran, do not *lose* her, Muldeve."

Muldeve paled. His two companions visibly quaked, but snapped into action when he barked out a terse order. They leapt forward and stripped her of her remaining daggers and her outer layers of clothing. They searched her for concealed weapons, pins, or anything that could be used to pick a lock, and withdrew the small flat stone from its hidden pocket. The guard who found it briefly stared at it in confusion before Muldeve snatched it from him.

"Shall I destroy this, Master?" he asked, failing to conceal the hint of fear in his voice.

"Keep it safe until we learn who sent her. Perhaps I will use it myself and pay them a visit."

Zildred regarded him rather coldly. Rubriel had the impression Muldeve would not get off lightly for his apparent carelessness.

It means Scoe is safe, she repeated to herself over and over, determined to focus only on that and not acknowledge what was happening to her as a result. Then the guards clamped shackles on her wrists and hauled her out of there, winding down stairwells and corridor after dark corridor. She tried to memorize the route but lost track of the number of corners turned and flights descended. Her night vision didn't help, as everything looked the same.

They came to a halt in a hallway that held a long line of windowless cells and shoved her forward into one of them. She noted briefly that they probably couldn't see inside without a light source, thinking vaguely that information might be helpful at some point, before they slammed and bolted the door and she was alone. Her eyes could see perfectly, however. The room was extremely small; a few feet wide and only slightly longer. A bucket and a raised sleeping platform were the only furnishings.

She sat gingerly on the edge of the latter, resting her head in her hands and taking deep breaths to quell the rising panic in her gut, her mind racing through a thousand possibilities and very few of them good. Exhaustion won in the end, and she lay down awkwardly on the bench and fell asleep.

23

The Blood Oath

"**I** need to speak with the Elder. Please."

Molindra appealed to her guard for the fifth time in as many weeks. The stout, curly-haired man was a decent enough fellow, if rather poor company. He rewarded her with the same noncommittal response as always.

It was comfortable as prisons go: she had a proper bed, a privy in the corner, and a table at which to take meals - or write, when they granted her requests for pen and paper. The walls were built of great white slabs of smooth stone. The gleam brightened the room despite the lack of windows. She could do a lot worse.

Escape was an idea that crossed her mind from time to time. They limited her access to water and never brought flame within her reach, but there was little they could do to stop her from using the natural moisture or heat from the air.

"These bars are resistant to extremes of heat," her guard had informed her, "and penetrate deep into the stone foundation. They will not melt, or buckle under pressure. I'm sure you expected that, but just to be sure."

It wasn't the superior bars that stopped her from trying, however. An escape attempt would do nothing to help her reputation, and she was desperately trying to claw back some measure of trust. She missed Scoe's visits since he and Rubriel returned to Langlythe. He had been somewhat impartial, practical, and willing to listen; she never minded answering all his questions. Few people came to visit now, other than to bring her meals and exchange letters. It was a solitary, reflective existence.

Of course! Rubriel would say. *That is the purpose of being in prison: to keep you out of trouble and force you to think about everything you've done wrong.*

She wondered how long she would have to think about it before a council meeting was called to decide her fate. It wasn't long after supper when her guard returned unexpectedly with a glass of damper drought. Her nose wrinkled at the distinctive smell of the magic-smothering brew; something she had hoped never to taste again.

"The Elder intends to visit with you in an hour," he explained, "on the condition that you drink this first."

She steeled herself. It was a show of good faith, if unnecessary - she would never harm the Elder, nor anyone else here in Celessil. She conceded, downing the liquid and shuddering at the prickling sensation and dullness that followed.

Then, in all seriousness - "you'd best bring me another glass, if you want this to be fully effective."

He only scowled at her boastful - though honest - remark. She doubted even the strongest brew would be enough to block her raw energy now. It felt like trying to dam a river with a handful of stones, the muddied sensation of her energy pushing through a barrier somehow worse than blocking it altogether.

The hour passed with a painful slowness. She paced anxiously, running through in her mind all the things she needed to say, over and over again. Unkempt hair fell to below her shoulders now, the unnatural change in colour from her auburn roots to her bleached ends all the more pronounced. It had been a long time since she last saw a mirror, but she didn't need one to know she must look a mess.

The Elder's arrival was preceded by her regular guard, who opened the door for him before silently taking up watch from an unobtrusive distance.

"Elder Berren." She bowed deeply at his approach.

"You have written to me many times over the past weeks." He strode over to the visitor's chair but refrained from sitting down. "Now you have my attention, though I am not sure what you hope to gain from it. I will not pardon you. Could not, even if I wanted to. There is too much at stake. What is it you want from me, Molindra?"

She'd spent hours upon hours planning this meeting, but now that he was here, it was so much harder than she anticipated. "There is a side of my story I have not yet told. I didn't tell Scoe because it wasn't what he needed to know. I was so desperate to use my knowledge to help and so ashamed of what happened that I neglected to share the how and the why of it all. Perhaps if I had, I would not have caused Rubriel so much pain."

"Go on," he said reluctantly.

"I never meant to hurt anyone when I went to Langlythe. I was frustrated, bitter, resentful perhaps - but never malicious. I believed only what I wanted to believe, that I could extract the secrets of a foreign land and not pay the price. They played me for the fool I was."

She told him the story of her harrowing journey through the lesser caves of the Gloaming Mountains, her near-defeat by the gloom spirits and subsequent encounter with the Master of Imul'dene. How he offered her what she wanted most - to practice as an Elementalist - and threatened her if she refused. How she hoped at the time to absorb as much as she could from the training and then somehow flee, not realizing how deep a net she'd already fallen into.

The Elder listened intently, frowning slightly. "And what of the people of Tabethwick?"

She grimaced. "I did not understand the magnitude of the ice melt, or - or the implications downstream, until it was too late to stop." The excuse seemed pitiful.

"You were a team of eleven elementalists," he pointed out. "Surely if that amount of power was needful, you would have taken that as an indicator of scale."

"I don't know what I thought!" Her dismay burst through, feeling all the more foolish.

"I am not sure it would have made any difference if I had refused. Those mages would have melted the ice with or without me. I was only needed because..." She stopped. "There was a stone."

"A stone?"

"It didn't seem all that important at the time, but now I understand; it was the very darkest of gems, solid black like obsidian and unnaturally cold. It drew the spirits to me, but I could also draw upon it enough to push them away if I wanted. A horrible, lifeless type of energy. Now I see that Zildred gave it to me because I needed it to open the vault at the Roof of the World, alongside my sildion pendant."

"Do you still have it now?" The Elder stiffened.

"No. He took it back at the end, along with the key." His brow lifted with relief, but she frowned. "Why?"

"Ludion is equal and opposite to sildion. Had you brought it here, you would risk upsetting the balance."

She gasped. "Ludion... the substance of the great stone at the summit of the Lone Peak, in balance with our *Vanassildion?*"

He held a thoughtful finger to his lips. "I have never seen the Lone Peak, but I do believe that is true, yes. The ludion infuses everything around it with its own energy, much the same way our Vanassildion influences us. It's the reason the land and climate of Langlythe is the way it is. You are fortunate to be rid of it, and we even more so that you did not bring it here."

Molindra fell silent, seeming to coil in on herself at this new revelation, and with fear of just how close she had unwittingly come to causing even further harm. "I was so naïve. I am ashamed."

At last, the Elder took a seat. "I think we can assume the only way Zildred could obtain a sildion with which to open the vault was through one of us. Your arrival provided the perfect opportunity. As a being consumed by lucrial energy, he could not simply take it from you and use it himself."

Mol brightened. "So you agree he manipulated me."

"I do not doubt that. You are a blundering fool, but an honest one, at least."

She lowered her eyes, mortified.

He sighed. "Nevertheless, the fact remains: many lives were lost as a result of the deliberate ice melt at the Roof. Bantria, in its grief, wants someone to blame. The only name they know is yours. If it were up to them, you would be hanged."

"I need not ever return to Bantria," she protested.

"It is not that simple. How do you think Bantria would react, should they learn that Celessil harboured you and allowed you to go unpunished? It does not matter if my Council finds you innocent."

"Then send me back. Exile me to Langlythe. I should be with Rubriel and Scoe; put an end to the monster I helped create."

"You think Langlythe would welcome you?"

"No! They already left me for dead once." A tear rolled down her cheek. "I would rather die young trying to make things right than live for a hundred years in confinement."

"Would you take an oath?" His tone grew darker.

She sat up straight, waiting for him to elaborate.

"Would you forsake your sildion pendant, and swear the blood oath to oppose Langlythe until your last breath; never to return from beyond the Gloaming Mountains?"

"I..."

She shuddered. Her insides shrivelled at the thought of being trapped there should she fail. Worse, even if she saved Rubriel - and Rubriel forgave her - they would still be parted. Perhaps that was a fair price to pay for her mistakes.

"Yes," she agreed, with as much courage as she could muster. "I would give anything to have gone in her place. She never wanted this. Please, let me bring her home."

The Elder stood and fixed her with a solemn expression. "I will think on it. If the Council is willing, you may receive the chance to plead your case before them."

"Thank you." She bowed. "Thank you!"

The next morning, she received a summons to appear before the Council three days hence. She asked her guard if she might bathe before then and tidy up her appearance. He agreed, affording her a few minutes to soak in a round tub half-filled with lukewarm water. Evidently, they still felt limiting her access to the elements was a necessary precaution. A maid brought fresh clothing, and she felt altogether more human afterwards.

"Miss?"

The maid paused, looking a little surprised. "Yes?"

"Would you mind... trimming my hair, please?"

She hesitated, then nodded. "Sit here, please."

She directed Molindra to a stool. A comb lay on the table beneath the window, and she produced a pair of scissors from the pocket of her apron. She cut away the long bleached tails of Mol's hair, leaving short red waves that hung just below her ears. Thick wefts of ash blonde hair littered the floor when she'd finished.

The result was shorter than most women would wear it, and she could no longer braid it back out of the way. She didn't care. Once, she had rejected her natural colouring - as she had rebelled against a great many things in her earlier years. Now she welcomed it. It wouldn't do to be recognized so easily.

Three days stretched out like three seasons. It was all Mol could do to keep from pacing up and down, anxiously practicing what she would say in front of the Council. What she wouldn't give for a lawyer to advise her, as was the way in Bantrian courts! Justice in Celessil was... irregular in its proceedings, partly due to the country's small population, partly because of how infrequently the system was called upon. This could work in her favour; it meant the rules were flexible.

This would be her second hearing. Her first had not gone according to plan. She'd frozen up in the booth, forgetting everything she had meant to say when questioned. Her story came out as a jumbled mixture of facts and pleading. With no witnesses present to either defend or incriminate her, she left with an "indeterminate" sentence. They had no idea what to do with a case like hers, so would contain her until they found a solution. There was no telling how long that could be.

Determined to put her best foot forward this time, she donned the muted olive jacket and plain walking skirt provided for her outing. Not that she had far to go, for the courtroom was just upstairs in a different part of the building.

The most 'normal' outfit I've worn in a long time, she thought with a sly chuckle. She must control her emotions and appear level-headed if she was to stand any chance of convincing the Council that she had the courage to go through with her own suggested punishment.

Fear rose further and further in her throat as they escorted her to her place in the courtroom, all thirteen Council members facing her with stoic expressions. Celessil's idea of a jury - that is, interested citizens who wished to observe - filed in behind, occupying seats along the back wall. A few introductory exchanges, and all too soon the eyes and ears of the room fell upon her.

She may as well have turned to stone in that moment. No words came. But instead of panicking, she shut her eyes tight and pictured Scoe's face, sitting in the simple chair by her cell and listening with an easy thoughtfulness. She forced herself to breathe, focusing on that image, and told her story.

It seemed to her that she spoke for quite some time, but no one interrupted her and so she continued; objectively, honestly; ending with her final wish to save Scoe and Rubriel, righting her wrongs in whatever ways she could. A heavy silence followed. For one heart-rending moment, Mol wondered if anyone had been listening.

Then, "Thank you, Molindra. Are there questions for the accused?"

Molindra waited, nervous still, yet with a sense of relief from having spoken her truth.

"You beseech us to exile you to Langlythe, but how do we know you will not simply forget your vows and join their ranks as soon as you cross the Gloaming Pass?" Mol had never met the woman who addressed her, but she had introduced herself as Xyria.

"I betrayed Langlythe in my intent to take the key and run," she reasoned. "They were counting on me to try something like that and used it to their advantage. Nevertheless, if they did not trust me then, they certainly will not trust me now."

"And if they seek to manipulate you again; exploit your hopeless situation for their own purposes? What then?"

Molindra's fist clenched the folds of her skirt. "Then I will do what I should have done the first time. I will refuse, and die for it if I must."

A few murmurs followed, the words inaudible. Whether of approval or distrust, she couldn't tell.

"Please understand; Langlythe is the very last place on earth I would choose to spend my days - a worse fate than any cell of this court. I do this not for myself, but on behalf of those I have wronged. Of people I love."

"We spoke with a member of your family - your father, I believe. He said they disowned you twenty years ago, for your reckless behaviour brought them shame. He refused to attend your hearing. What do you make of this?" It was the Council scholar who challenged her, a man who, unfortunately, had been present when she blew up the university's auditorium.

All she could do was nod. "My family's rejection is the reason I left Celessil originally. Life in Bantria was hard, but in Rubriel I had found a sister. She tried to take care of me when no one else would."

"It seems to me you have a long history of careless, impulsive acts to the general detriment of whatever society was cursed with your presence."

"Eroth," the Elder warned.

Eroth spread his arms wide to encompass the room. "I am merely pointing out that the accused has shown consistently poor judgement thus far. What is to say her plea for exile is not the latest in a line of ill-informed, impulsive actions that backfire horribly?"

"If she is a curse upon society, I say we let Langlythe have her," grumbled another.

"Enough. If there are no further questions…" The Elder paused, looking from one Council member to the next. "Then the accused is dismissed. We will convene and regroup here in three hours."

Those were the longest three hours of Mol's life. Yet she carried herself from the room with pride, a quiet calm settling in her stomach. She'd handled herself well; done everything she could, though she would never escape her past. There was little more to do but wait.

Eroth had been right. Her sole focus was to find Rubriel and use her inside knowledge to sabotage the impending invasion, well aware that she may die in the process, but she had given no thought to what would happen if she succeeded and lived. Rubriel and Scoe would return home, but she would remain an outcast even with her final purpose fulfilled. The frost tribes would be of no help - her group had wronged them too. Her shortsightedness was more a defence from the truth than a lack of consideration.

Nerves and nausea heightened with every minute she sat waiting, her head throbbing in time to the pounding of her heart. She might have fainted there and then when the attendants summoned her back to the courtroom, had she not paused to lean against the doorframe on the way out. The Council watched her arrive with the same unreadable expressions. The eyes of those gathered to watch pierced her from behind, eagerly awaiting the verdict. Feeling exposed, she bowed deeply, keeping her eyes lowered as much to assuage her own anxiety as in deference.

When the Elder spoke, he spoke calmly. The room fell silent. "The Council has deliberated. While the vote was divided, we have reached a decision."

He paused, turning the page in front of him. "Molindra?"

"I am ready, Elder," she managed.

"This is an exceptional case, the likes of which our fair court has never before seen. While you have committed no crime against Celessil directly, under Bantrian law - coerced or otherwise - your actions constitute treason. Thus, you are guilty of endangering the alliance upon which our national safety relies. Do you understand this?"

"I do, Elder." Her heart sank.

"However."

She tensed.

"You ask not for us to pardon you, but to send you into danger, where you may yet do some good. The Council has deemed your immediate exile a fitting resolution. Swear your blood oath before us, and let the court bear witness to its sealing."

Relief flooded through her. She bowed again. "Thank you, Elder. I am honoured to give it."

A covered pedestal stood before her. With these words, they pulled the cover back to reveal pen and paper, an ornamental knife, and a silver bowl. Further attendants brought a pail of water and a hot iron. Molindra knew what to do. With a reverence befitting the act, she stepped up to the pedestal, taking the knife in her left hand as she recited from the paper.

"I, Elementalist Molindra of Celessil, do solemnly swear before the Council to leave these lands in payment for my crimes; to pass beyond the Gloaming Mountains, there to faithfully oppose the enemy of our allies; to stifle the threat I helped create, to the utmost extent of my ability."

She drew the blade across her palm, swallowing the pain as her blood pooled in the silver bowl. "From this day henceforth, I renounce my citizenship, my right to the sildion gift, and humbly accept my status of exile, until the Council may forgive me, or death takes me. May this oath thus bind me. Spoken in faith, sealed in fire, and signed in blood."

And instead of grasping the hot iron, she gathered flame in her hand and sealed the wound with her magic, tears slipping down her cheeks as she fought the urge to cry out while the flesh blistered and dried. Then she dipped the pen into the bowl and signed the page in her own blood.

"It is done," said Elder Berren. "Place your pendant on the table. The guards will return your other possessions. I will arrange an escort to Langlythe forthwith."

She bowed silently, trembling as she removed the delicate chain from around her neck with one hand, the tiny sildion's glow pooling innocently on the wood amidst those bloody implements.

Two fellow mages took up her escort the following morning, travelling swiftly on horseback to the edge of the Gloaming Mountains. On Molindra's advice, they took her not to the pass, but to the entrance of the minor cave system she had used to enter Langlythe previously.

It seemed a lifetime ago that she stumbled through those caves, so unsure of herself and her own abilities. The gloom spirits would not trouble her now, for she knew their secrets; they were nearly blind and afraid of bright light. With flames at her side, they would avoid her unless compelled otherwise.

24

Fondest Disregards

Rubriel saw nothing and no one in her confinement, the passage of time marked only by the semi-regular appearance of a bowl of gruel and the swapping of one refuse bucket for another. Those who tended her cell never spoke to her, nor allowed her to see their faces. Otherwise, she was completely alone.

With all that had happened in the city, she had by and large been forgotten - thanks to her own efforts to sow chaos. She took some small comfort in knowing that she and Scoe had succeeded in their overall mission, even if she had not observed the aftermath for herself. It was clear the city was preoccupied with *something*, for when they finally did retrieve her from her cell, the interlude was extremely brief - and for a most peculiar purpose.

She fully expected to be interrogated at some point. Indeed, she had spent many hours preparing herself for that eventuality, thinking through exactly what she would and would not say in order to appear *slightly* helpful without actually giving away anything of use. Instead, the High Warden's men seated her in a brightly lit chamber and called forth a mage to examine her.

The mage - a woman with thinly plucked eyebrows and an extremely brisk manner - gave her a cursory look over before pulling out a clunky glass syringe and sticking the needle into the crook of Rubriel's elbow. She yelped in surprise and jerked her arm, causing the whole area around the needle to balloon even as the barrel filled with her blood. The woman nodded her satisfaction and left, taking the overly generous blood sample with her.

"What was that for?" Rubriel asked of her captors, but they did not answer; merely took her back to her cell where she spent the next hour awkwardly gripping her elbow in the hope of preventing it from swelling any further. It was quite some time before she could bend it properly.

For the first time in her life, she had no control. Feelings of frustration - of being trapped in one miserable situation or another - had plagued her for years back in Tunswick, but she had never truly been without options. There had always been other paths to take; ways to set change in motion - even if she had not been able to see a way out at the time. Now it occurred to her that the financial, societal cage that held her and Molindra had perhaps been more of her own making than anyone else's.

Their means of earning a living had been a constant source of anxiety. Keeping a roof over their heads had meant straddling the line between what is lawful and what is not. Molindra practiced as an unlicensed elementalist, to whomever was willing to pay under the table for whatever competitive advantage they could derive from having a mage behind the scenes. Rubriel had tolerated an endless string of deplorable employers and their requests, which usually started off reasonable enough but almost always ended up crossing a moral boundary.

A man with her skillset might find himself employed by the city guard, or as security on board the steam trains that now ran between Tunswick and the port of Ornage. As a woman, it served only to push her right off the spectrum of respectability. The only reason she'd never been raped, or killed in a back alley somewhere, was thanks to the very same skills that damned her in every other regard. She and Molindra had been greatly unprepared when they left Celessil for the stark gender inequity considered normal in Bantria.

She'd dealt with it at the time by building walls around herself, swallowing her feelings and blocking out the memory of anything unpleasant. She'd also grudgingly accepted her role as a victim. Only now that she was locked away and isolated from the world did she find the courage to fight back. She would own her fate, whatever it may be.

It wasn't long before her new resolve was tested. The door opened suddenly and one of the guards delivered a bucket of cold water and a scrap of cloth.

"Clean up," he ordered. You are wanted above."

She did as she was told, taking the opportunity to wash the dried blood off her neck and hands, shivering as she dragged the rough cloth over her skin. She finished up quickly, unsure how long before someone would return to collect her. If she was to stand any chance of getting out of this alive, she needed information. She needed to understand what they wanted from her, what leverage she might have - and that was going to require persuading someone to actually speak to her. It was time to set changes in motion.

High Warden Muldeve descended the dimly lit stairs to the prison wing, the guards under his command acknowledging him with a brisk nod as he passed. The celair hanging from his belt cast long shadows as he walked along the corridor of locked doors, each unmarked, the knowledge of who lay where rooted only in his brain and that of those he kept stationed throughout the warrens under the citadel. Rubriel was at the very far end - on purpose, since her door was the most visible from a distance, and she would have the furthest to run should she try to escape.

And she must not escape. He had returned on that fateful day to find her companion's cell empty, without so much as a trace of him. The door was even still locked. A milestone was the only logical explanation, and it was not an oversight he had any intention of making twice. He'd stripped Rubriel of everything right down to her undergarments and ensured she was separated from *her* milestone before leaving her unattended - yet he still wasn't taking any chances.

Satisfied that the three guards posted at the other end of the corridor would be sufficient, he unlocked her cell. He heaved the door open and froze, for she was nowhere to be seen in the gloom beyond. But no sooner had he taken a step over the threshold than she leapt on him from the corner, wrapping the chain of her shackles tightly around his throat.

"You'd best give me some answers," she hissed in his ear as he struggled and kicked, "else I'll-"

He reached up and grabbed her by the shoulders and ducked forwards, hurling her right over his head.

Choking, he stumbled while she scrambled from the floor. She recovered faster.

"Don't," he croaked as she lunged for the door, which had rolled shut on its own; her night vision easily finding the mechanism as though in daylight.

"Please don't!"

She hesitated.

"You will not get far. There are guards posted all along this corridor and spirits everyw-"

She huffed and grabbed the latch. "You're right. I won't. But I will get far enough to ensure every one of them knows you failed - again."

"No! Wait." He started forwards, clasping her arm. "There is no point. Would you ruin my life as well as your own?"

She shook free of his grip. "Do you really think I care what your master thinks of you? What will he do to you, hmm? Perhaps we shall be neighbours down here."

"And what of the lives of all those below, who will perish due to the flooding? Have you no remorse at all?"

Rubriel scoffed. "Playing mind games, High Warden? I have had my fill of those already."

"No... No, I swear not. High Warden or no, I am none too proud to bargain with you if I must. Do not leave this room unaccompanied. Please." His face twisted with the word as though it tasted foul.

There was genuine fear in that voice - fear, and anguish. It caught her off guard.

"Why? Why would you of all people want to bargain with me - and after I just tried to kill you. What would you offer me in return?"

"Just step away from the door."

He stared her down until she partially relented and let go of the latch. He swallowed gingerly. "If I let you escape, my life is as good as forfeit. My family will be torn apart."

"So you are asking me to exchange this and any subsequent chance of freedom for the lives of people I know nothing about, who may or may not even exist," she said, annoyed. "That is low indeed."

"What chance do you think you have, anyway? You are in the heart of Imul'dene. Every entrance, every stairwell, every minute passage has been locked down. No one enters or leaves without clearance and I assure you - whatever devious means you used to get here have been closed off, if not outright destroyed - *by you*. Do as I say, and I will ensure your wounds are tended and your needs are met. It is better than you deserve after all you have done to us."

Rubriel was unimpressed. "You are not going to guilt me into obedience. This conversation is pointless."

"It is you who has no purpose here!" he snapped. "You burned half a year's worth of supplies while the Lower Tiers was flooded and swept over the fells, taking our people with it. Do you honestly think the Master will continue to let you live?"

In truth, she hadn't realized the full extent of the damage she and Scoe had wrought upon the city. They hadn't looked back; there wasn't time. But she said, evenly, "We are at war. That was my mission. I did what I was sent here to do."

"You did your job too well. Don't you see? You were a small price to pay. You already completed your task and no one is going to come looking for you *because they don't need you anymore.*"

His words stung. There was no response she could make that didn't feel like a lie.

"Sit down, Rubriel. I will make sure you are well-treated, as far as my position affords, in exchange for your full cooperation for however long you remain in my care."

That brief opening had passed. He'd succeeded in stalling her long enough to miss her chance to slip away, and she was annoyed with herself for falling for it. He *had* told her a little of the outside world, even if only to manipulate her. She sat, grudgingly. There was a tense silence as they weighed each other, both pointedly aware that she hadn't exactly agreed.

"I cannot take you anywhere like this." He gave a reluctant sigh and finally turned away, dissatisfied, leaving her alone with a hundred frustrations.

Why, why had she hesitated? She was ruthless. She did what had to be done. What did she owe to this man, or to anyone in this wretched place? Disgruntled, she paced her cell while her thoughts spun around and around until they ran out of steam and she flopped unhappily on the hard, empty bench.

Two others accompanied the High Warden on his next visit, and the one after that. They came only to check on her, wherever he had planned to take her that day seemingly forgotten. All three of them were armed in a way she found to be excessive and oddly flattering under the circumstances.

She noticed the High Warden wore a scarf to cover the bruising she'd left on his neck. He clearly wasn't taking any chances, though she saw no further opportunity in their brief interactions. Without her milestone, she would never find her way out of the city, even if she was somehow lucky enough to make it out of the citadel.

It was another week before he came and collected her, flanked by two others just as before, and marched her upstairs. She didn't know where he was taking her, but the higher they went, the more nervous she became. Again she tried to memorize the route, and again lost her sense of direction, but she did manage to count the number of floors - five, starting below ground and arriving on the fourth. They were standing outside the Great Hall.

Inside, a table and a single chair stood alone in the vast expanse. The furnishings did not belong there at all; too small, too plain and unassuming. He brought her to sit in the chair while his companions stationed themselves by the entrance. There were other people in the room as well, including the mage who had taken her blood. They were all staring at her. Spirits looked down from above, floating up near the ceiling. At the far end, Zildred rose from his gilded throne.

"As requested, Master," the High Warden announced, bowing.

Rubriel kept her eyes lowered, her hands clasped in her lap.

Zildred paced the floor between them, pausing only to address her. "You climbed up from below, released the reservoir upon the Lower Tiers, jammed the valves, then set fire to a High Tiers warehouse."

"I did," she said flatly.

"At whose behest?"

She didn't answer. The truth would give Langlythe every reason to go after Celessil in retaliation - the exact situation she had been sent to try to avoid. She could implicate Bantria instead, even though they knew nothing of the plot - but if word ever reached the Bantrian government, that could just as easily ruin a centuries-old alliance between them and Celessil. No; the only way to avoid political consequences was to take the blame entirely upon herself. Her eyes darted around the room, counting the faces awaiting her response. Could she convince them?

Zildred stopped his pacing and stood across the table from her. "Who sent you?" he repeated icily.

Rubriel steadied herself with a deep breath. She looked up. "My actions are my own. I work for no one."

"And the Esmaran?"

"A friend, who would not allow me to go alone."

He seemed to accept that - for now. "Your milestone - where is it bound?"

"A cave, far to the north... east," she corrected herself. "Near the Ice Divide." She had, after all, lived in such a cave for a while. She could describe it in detail to prove it.

"Unfortunate for your friend, wounded as he was."

She tried not to react, but the stab of worry was impossible to conceal.

"An act of war, she called it," said the High Warden, speaking for the first time. "She said it was her mission, that she did what she was sent here to do. I do not believe she worked alone."

Blast him! Of course he would use that conversation against her.

"A flood for a flood," Rubriel said quietly.

The High Warden's eyes narrowed, but she wasn't talking to him.

"You sent your elementalists to the Roof and brought a hundred-year flood down upon Tabethwick. There is not a soul to the southeast who does not wish you ill after that. I may have acted according to others' desires, but it was my choice to go through with it." The words felt heavy on her tongue. Whether that heaviness was the weight of truth, or the strain of a lie, she could not tell.

"I do not believe a single word that falls from her lips!" the High Warden exclaimed.

"Quiet." Zildred dismissed his protest with barely a glance in his direction. "You speak neither truth, nor lies," he said to Rubriel, "but rather weave a path between the two that will lead us nowhere. Those who serve only themselves are opportunistic by nature - and fickle in loyalty. Perhaps if it were made worthwhile, you would tell a different tale?"

When she answered, every word was true.

"There is nothing I want that you can give me, nor withhold from me. You cannot break a heart that is already broken. You cannot crush a dream that never took shape. I have nothing left to lose, and that is what makes me fearless. You have less power over me than you think."

Perhaps it was a kind of madness that gave her courage. Perhaps part of her had already died the day she walked out of Molindra's cell.

"We shall see."

He shifted, suddenly standing right behind her. She jumped. "I had thought you may assist willingly, but it seems I was mistaken."

His cold hand gripped her shoulder, the silver tips of his gloved fingers bruising the skin through her chemise, but that wasn't why she cried out. An immense pressure expanded inside her head; pain that clenched every muscle in her body in seizure-like rigidity. Then, after what seemed like an age, he let go of her and the pain ceased instantly. She slumped forward against the table, breathing hard.

"Interesting," he said. "Karina?"

"Yes, Master?" It was the mage who had taken the blood sample.

"The test results."

"All negative," she said quickly, a little flustered. "We retested three times to be sure. There was no trace of raw energy in her blood at all."

"Try again. Something is amiss."

"If I were a mage," said Rubriel dryly, "do you not think I would have used magic against you by now?"

"And how does a Celessilian become as skilled as you are without a drop of raw energy in your veins?" he countered.

"I have been asked that question a thousand times in my life. Whatever talent I have was acquired, not born. I do not know why the usual gifts of my race bypassed me."

Her answer had been completely honest, yet they took no notice of her reasoning. The mage called Karina drew another blood sample from her arm before the High Warden and his escort took her back downstairs. His men peeled off when they reached the prison corridor and he dragged her to the end, shoving her roughly into her cell.

She did not intend to fight back, not really, but she elbowed him firmly between the ribs anyway as he let go. He grunted, absorbing the blow. Rubriel fell onto the bench and glared coldly in the dim celair light, angry and hurting all over as though bruised on the inside.

"It is somewhat disappointing that you are still alive," he said bitterly. "I had sincerely hoped today would be the end of you. You are a problem I am forbidden to solve."

"If it irks you that much, why not assign someone else?" she retorted.

"Someone who underestimates you, whom you can easily catch unawares?"

Rubriel snorted.

"I am responsible either way. Better to deal with you myself."

"I could've killed you already," she said flatly.

"Then why did you not?"

"Because you fed me a lie that stalled me until the moment passed. Or was that meant to be a rhetorical question?"

"A *lie?*" He emphasized the word distastefully.

She frowned deeply, waiting to see if he would say more.

"I have a son of fifteen years and a daughter of twelve. She will become a mage, like her mother. I told no lie." The words came out all in a rush, uncomfortable in a way she had not seen before. Agitated, distressed even. Mentioning his family seemed to have brought him close to the edge.

"Why are you telling me this?" she asked, confused and impatient.

He said nothing.

"Muldeve?"

She had learned his name on the first day and never used it.

Surprise brushed his troubled face, and a little of the tension left his brow. "I should not have told you anything. Your companion already escaped my guard. A second chance is rare enough."

"I suppose it is only natural that you would do your utmost to get me executed." She tried to fold her arms across her chest, then remembered she couldn't.

"I should not have referenced that conversation," he admitted, surprising her. "You could also have turned that against me, yet you did not. For that, I am grateful."

Maybe it was the pain talking, or maybe it was merely the idea of a hot meal and fresh water, but she found herself feeling a grain of sympathy for this man, who suddenly seemed less of a monster and more of an ordinary father and husband. He hated her, but only because she could ruin him.

"I will do as you ask," she said. "I will... cooperate, in exchange for fair treatment. But I also want information. I need to know what is going on, and why everyone thinks I should be a mage. I do not trust you, but

I will try not to get you in further trouble." She fluttered a weak smile that didn't reach her eyes.

"I cannot promise to tell you anything. Information is dangerous..." He sighed. "Here. As a show of good faith..." He bent and removed her shackles.

"So I can't strangle you with them, you mean."

He shook his head dismissively, then paused, noticing the red bands on her wrists, the skin rubbed raw and weeping. "I will return shortly," he said, and left.

Rubriel could not be sure that his interest in a truce wasn't part of some greater manipulation, but she sensed she may be able to reason with him, perhaps even gain his trust in time. As long as she did not allow herself to get too comfortable around him, it wouldn't hurt to have the ear of the man most immediately responsible for her captivity.

Alone, she slept fitfully, dreaming strange dreams that felt close enough to memory to be real. She dreamt of Andorlai and Shavon, only the town fell away and before long they were in a deep mine. Muldeve was there also, covered in soot and swinging a pickaxe furiously at a faint shimmer in the rock. She turned to avoid him and instead collided with Scoe! She threw her arms around him in a tight embrace, but he pushed her away and urged her to hurry. They ran up a tight staircase to find a huge iron lever.

"It's stuck! Help me!" Scoe was throwing all his weight behind the mechanism.

She knew this part. But in her dream, she hesitated.

"Come on!" said Scoe.

She shook herself and ran to help. The lever crunched and ground its way to the floor and the roaring rush of water filled the chamber. They dashed for the way out. There was so much water, rising so fast. She didn't think they would make it this time. She felt the sensation of being underwater, thrashing around and disoriented, then Scoe pulling her out of the tunnel onto a muddy street. Blinking, she looked up and saw to her horror they were not in Imul'dene at all. It was Tabethwick before them, and it was a flooded ruin.

Gwendolen's voice screamed in her head. "Rubriel! What have you done..."

She awoke drenched in a cold sweat, the terror of the nightmare still palpable in her mind. She stretched her limbs and rolled her shoulders, wincing at the sharp pull on the wound at her throat. It was swollen and painful to touch. Sweats, vivid dreams - the first signs of infection? People of Celessil rarely suffered disease, but if a wound was left untreated? No one was truly immune. The cut had been small, but she had lost all track of time since it happened.

Muldeve returned with a salve, which she massaged gingerly into her various wounds. The time after that, he brought a strong-smelling broth instead of the usual gruel, which he claimed would promote healing and ward off infection. Its foul, bitter taste somehow left her even hungrier, but grateful. She thanked him, albeit awkwardly. Neither found it easy to adjust to the peculiar shift in dynamic between them.

He never lingered long enough for her to ask questions, though she found herself wanting more and more to ask about the damage to the Lower Tiers, the flooding, the death toll. For the nightmare returned, always the same, and she had begun to believe there was truth in it. Molindra had brought ruin to an entire community. So had she.

I may have acted according to others' desires, but it was my choice to go through with it.

Her own words haunted her, for she meant them to be true, but could no longer tell if they were a lie or not. Could she have chosen another path? Could Molindra? Regret became her grim companion as her thoughts spiralled closer to despair. Elder Berren hadn't threatened her, but he *had* forced her to carry out his assignment through fear and a sense of duty. What would he have done if she'd run away like her instincts told her? She had to believe that her actions were justified; a lesser evil in a pool of many.

Because if they weren't... Rubriel and Molindra were monsters both; both now imprisoned to await their fate. She hoped Molindra was faring better.

Days turned to weeks. Rubriel grew numb; whether from the persistent underground chill or the pain in her heart was difficult to tell. She woke with a start to find Muldeve standing over her, the light of his celair stinging her eyes as she looked up. She knew at once he brought bad news for her, as he wore an unreasonably cheerful demeanour. He let the door roll shut behind him and spoke in hushed tones, not bothering to keep the relief out of his voice.

"The mages tested you for raw energy - again - and found no trace for the second time. It seems there is nothing remarkable about you after all, save your audacity and apparent disregard for human life. You are being sent to Scarlet Arena. It is fitting, I think."

And you are no longer my problem, he didn't need to add.

"Well then," she said, standing. "Lead the way."

He scoffed at her sarcasm. "You have no idea what is coming for you."

"Your mood says it all, High Warden. I trust this is goodbye."

"It most certainly is," he agreed.

She stretched to ease the stiffness from her back. She hadn't left her cell since the Great Hall, and her joints complained at the sudden activity.

Muldeve glowered at her impatiently, keen to be rid of her and the peculiar relationship they shared.

"Please accept my fondest disregards," she said with mock sincerity and a final nod.

He shook his head and hauled the door open, releasing her into the hands of the armed men waiting to bring her to whatever grim fate awaited her next.

25

Above and Below

I mul'dene's High Tiers were split into east and west sides by the river and connected by two substantial bridges from one side to the other. Scarlet Arena sat on the far western side; an imposing oval construction four or five storeys high. Rubriel was taken not into the arena itself by the public doors, but underground via a side entrance that led down into the pits below.

Law-breakers and renegades occupied the chambers, sentenced to gladiatorial combat for their misconduct. Morbid, curious faces peered at her from behind bars as she passed. The cells were large and open to those neighbouring, as many as four or five people in each. Rubriel shared with two others; a skinny boy of no more than seventeen, and a woman who sat in the corner and did not look up as she entered.

As soon as the guards left, the whispering started. People across the room pointed and strained to get a good look at her. She sniffed and wrinkled her nose in the stale air, wondering what the keen interest was about, until a grizzled man addressed her from the cell adjacent.

"They say you are responsible for the flooding of the Lower Tiers," he said gruffly. He looked to have seen one battle too many. His arm was bandaged and covered in dried blood; his unshaven face carried bruising on his cheek and a cut on his forehead. He had a grim, resigned look about him that reminded her a little of Adam.

"My reputation precedes me," she said.

He huffed. "They also say you challenged the Master himself." He shook his shaggy head dismissively. "So you are a fool, or a spectacle; probably both."

"You seem to have quite the opinion of me, given that we have only just met."

He only grunted. She turned her back to him and sat cross-legged on the dirt floor.

"Is it true?" the boy asked her in a timid voice.

"Which part?"

"That you... that you fought the Master in a duel - with swords, not magic - and he spared you." His voice trembled slightly.

"It is true."

"But why?" He seemed both horrified and impressed.

"I have often wondered that myself," she admitted, more to herself than to him. She turned to get a good look at him. Blue-yellow bruises surrounded his left eye. His clothes were torn. Remnants of dried blood clung to his short clipped hair. "What is your name?"

"Amlin. 'Amlin of the forge', they call me - or used to." He winced.

"You work with metal?"

"My father does."

She offered him a smile. "I used to work with metal too, a long time ago. I forged weapons for competition - and learned to fight with them, too."

Amlin perked up. "You know how to fight?"

"With traditional weapons, yes. I am no modern soldier, and definitely no mage," she said, thinking of how redundant her craft had become in the south, yet realizing even as she said it that things were clearly very different here.

"Can you teach me? Will you help us survive?"

She started. The whole room was looking at her now. Even the woman who had been weeping in the corner was paying attention. She saw the desperation in their eyes. They were all the worse for wear, battered and injured to varying degrees; young and old, male and female. The arena's overseers apparently did not discriminate. She didn't answer Amlin directly; instead, she stood, went to the bars and addressed the room.

"What happens up there? How do we fight - and against whom?"

"We fight according to the whim of the overseers," one man answered.

"They design the competitions to please the audience. Entertainment - at our expense," said another.

"The arena is meant to provide training for the military. It is a proving grounds for those who would assert their strength and will to lead; a rite of passage to knock the fear out of those newly appointed, under live combat conditions," said an older woman.

"'Live combat?' the first shot back. "More like live executions."

"We fight against trained soldiers?" Rubriel interjected. "Surely not unarmed, and poorly equipped as we are."

"They give us weapons, albeit inferior ones, but it hardly matters," the second man said. "Too few of us know how to use them, and they don't spare us - not after more than a few rounds."

"You see?" said Amlin beside her. "Perhaps if we learn to defend ourselves better..."

"There are no survivors here."

The scornful remark came from the shaggy man in the neighbouring cell. Now that he moved towards the light, he seemed to scowl more deeply than ever. "None who are sentenced to the Scarlet Arena ever leave it. I have won my last four battles in a row. The most recent was meant to be my last. Instead, I turned the tide and landed the newly appointed captain on his back, though I took this gash to my arm in the process. It does not matter; when I go up there again, it will be to face a fight I cannot possibly win."

He glanced from face to face at those who had spoken before. No one was willing to say differently. He shook his head. "The overseers stack the odds against you to ensure that no one from below ever triumphs for too long. Being skilled will not help you here. It is a death sentence."

Rubriel pondered this as the conversation died. Hopelessness settled over these people like a smothering fog, yet there was fight in them still. Under the right circumstances, they could perhaps be rallied. As for her own fate, she knew well that Muldeve did not expect her to survive. Maybe Zildred thought it fitting that she should meet her end against overwhelming odds in so public a setting. Maybe he simply wanted to see what she would do. It didn't matter. The arena wanted a show, and she would give them one.

She stood up and stretched her arms high above her head, back straight and breathing deeply. Her arms opened out wide, and she bent down to touch the floor - first to one side, then the other - beginning a series of exercises that belonged to her old warm up routine. Amlin observed keenly as she rolled her shoulders and swung her torso from side to side, then bent double, sliding her hands down the front of her legs until they rested on top of her feet.

"Teach me," he said in a small voice as she straightened up. "Please?" His light brown eyes brimmed with desperation.

She started her routine from the beginning, pausing between movements so that he could follow along. His attempts felt stiff and awkward, and he almost fell over several times.

"Don't rush it," she advised. "Practice little and often. Flexibility will come."

He flopped down on the floor and hugged his knees. "I'm not sure how much time we have."

Rubriel finished her own routine by stretching out on her stomach and propping up on her elbows, a pose that opened the chest and flexed the spine. "It never hurts to be prepared," she said from her cat-like position. "Even if you cannot win the battle. There are other ways to win besides merely surviving."

"I don't understand."

"I must see inside the arena for myself." She thought it best to evade further questions for now.

Amlin practiced with her from then on. His stiff, gangly limbs couldn't match her fluidity, but he never gave up. Slowly, he began to improve. Some inmates watched their antics with interest; others stared steadfastly away, too consumed by their own misery.

The guards came for them all too soon - sometimes an individual, sometimes in pairs or larger groups. There seemed no pattern to it. Not all of them returned. Those that did came back with bruises, cuts or more grievous wounds, moaning softly while others tried to comfort them.

Rubriel bore witness to several rounds of this before they took her, alone, to a large, bare chamber right beneath the combat floor of the arena. Guards stood every few feet around the perimeter, each with chainmail visible beneath their overcoat and a sword strapped to his or her side. A barrel at one end of the room held blunt poles; the only weapons permitted to combatants from below. She already knew those from above would be substantially better equipped.

First priority, then, would be to swap her weapon for one of theirs as soon as the opportunity presented itself. She was given a simple leather tunic and pants, which offered little protection against anything besides the cold, and allowed a few minutes to practice.

Murmurs from a gathering crowd filtered down, muffled, from a hatch in the ceiling. The guards ushered her onto the platform beneath it. The creak and grind of machinery followed, and it lifted off the ground. As the hatch opened, she realized she would be entering the arena blind - and from the most vulnerable position in the centre of the open field. The lift moved slowly, but still gave her only a few seconds to orient herself before the hatch closed beneath her and she was fair game to any waiting opponent.

From inside, the arena seemed smaller than it had from outside, but much taller. Tiered seating rose steeply to form an imposing oval that encircled the barren, dusty ground of the combat area. A high stone wall separated onlookers from the fighting. On one side, heavy gates closed off a staircase that led into back rooms inside the upper floors. Overseers, easily distinguished by the fearsome spikes on their mantles, observed from a high booth situated beside the stairs. The stands were about two-thirds full, occupied mostly by the red and gold of the upper class.

There was no sign of Zildred. There were, however, plenty of spirits, which she supposed was almost the same. If anything untoward happened, he would know.

The gates opened, and a lone challenger entered from above. A young man strode confidently into the arena, drawing a longsword as he approached. He stopped twenty paces from her, his chest puffed out, seemingly ready for anything.

Rubriel, partly out of habit, and partly to contrast her opponent's arrogance, saluted graciously. A potent horn sounded from the overseers' booth. She raised her pole, just slightly, as her opponent immediately leaped in to attack. He swung at her haphazardly, all bluster and bravado, missing as she dodged easily. Annoyed, he lunged again - and again he missed. He was overconfident, clearly thinking she didn't stand a chance. She almost felt sorry for him.

"Come at me you coward!"

He seethed as she nimbly evaded him, failing to land even a single blow, until she swiped at his exposed shins and knocked him on his arse with her pole at his throat before he knew what was happening. The crowd gasped in surprise. She held him there a fraction longer to make her point, then retrieved his sword and allowed him to stand.

Looking around, the audience seemed... intrigued. She thought a few of them might even be laughing behind their hands. Rubriel merely bowed humbly before walking back to the platform and standing on it expectantly until they lowered her back down.

The inmates peered at her through the bars as she returned, whispering excitedly when they realized she was completely unscathed.

"That was... quick," said her grizzled neighbour with the wounded arm. "And you are still in one piece." Whether he was impressed or disappointed, she couldn't tell.

"What happened?" asked Amlin, rushing over.

"I suppose that was just a warmup, but the fight was one-on-one, and my opponent was both arrogant and ill-prepared. Not a good combination."

"Did you kill him?" sneered her neighbour.

"No, of course not!"

Several people exchanged glances. Clearly, they felt she should have.

"What?" she demanded of the room. "Out with it."

"You should have gutted him," one woman burst out. "Show them a taste of their own medicine!"

There were several cheers of agreement.

"They show us no mercy! Why should we show any to them?"

Now the place was in an uproar, grumbling and hurling insults at Rubriel, at the overseers, and at life in general. She glanced at Amlin. The boy just looked confused. The other woman in her cell remained silent in her corner. She waited calmly for the protesting to cool.

"I didn't kill him," she said to the room as the din settled, "because he didn't deserve it, and because that wasn't the point."

"It is exactly the point," someone shot back.

"Who has all the power up there?" She pointed through the ceiling.

"The overseers!" they replied unanimously, thinking it obvious.

"*No.*"

They stared.

"The overseers decide who we fight and when. They control the odds, it is true. But." She paused, looking from one cell to the next. "Their purpose is to please the masses. It is the audience who holds true power. Win the audience, and you win the whole arena."

From the sea of puzzled expressions, it was clear most of them did not understand what she meant. However, from that point forward, a few of the others shyly joined in whenever she and Amlin ran through their exercises. She transitioned to teaching him basic unarmed combat; stance, balance, how to deflect a blow, and when and where to strike back most effectively. The boy's confidence grew. She was explaining to him how to modify what he'd practiced for use with a pole when the guards came for all three of them.

Rubriel, Amlin, and the corner woman - whose name she still didn't know - were ushered into the holding chamber. Immediately, she grabbed a pole for each of them and used what little time they had to show them how to hold it and block. Poor Amlin was terrified, his knuckles white as he grasped the pole like a lifeline. The woman seemed too numb to move. All too soon, they were pushed onto the platform.

"Stay behind me and watch my flank," she said to Amlin. "I'll look after you."

The three of them stood back to back in the centre of the arena. Four soldiers entered from above, similarly equipped to her previous opponent, and spread out to opposite corners, surrounding them. The horn sounded its ominous bellow and the four circled them like prey, making Amlin and the woman all the more jittery.

Rubriel assessed each of them, measuring who would attack first and who would likely make the easiest target. A big man with a sword and shield ran in first from her left, followed closely by a stout woman with a curved blade who went straight for Amlin. He charged for Rubriel with his shield raised, meaning to intimidate her, but she used his size against him, ducking beneath his guard and thrusting out with her pole, forcing him to stop short. He brought his own weapon down to knock hers aside. She rotated and caught him awkwardly with the other end, unbalancing him and sending him careening into the woman to his right.

Amlin, to his credit, took the opportunity to land a solid whack to the woman's head, and she stayed down. Rubriel grabbed the man's fallen sword and whirled to intercept the second man's blade as he swung for Amlin's exposed side. They clashed heavily, giving Amlin time to skitter out of the way.

She stole a glance at her other cellmate as they fought. The usually timid woman surprised her, facing off against a masked woman with two daggers and matching her blow for blow with unexpected viciousness. Rubriel soon outmanoeuvred her opponent and ended him quickly. She shouted for Amlin to take his weapon.

Meanwhile, the big man had picked up his comrade's curved blade and was back in the fight - more cautiously now that Rubriel and Amlin both had real swords. Amlin hung back at first, but the man was so focused on Rubriel that Amlin inched forward and took a wild swing for his arm. He missed, but it was enough to give Rubriel the opening she needed to run her opponent through.

She turned as he fell to find that her female cellmate had downed her attacker all by herself, but had taken a deep gash to her side in the process. Rubriel ran to her and hoisted her to her feet, blood seeping between the woman's fingers as she clutched at her side. The crowd cheered. She saluted briefly before dragging her companions back to the platform, the woman gritting her teeth in silent agony and Amlin white with shock.

"What is your name?" she asked as they were lowered back down, the movement causing the woman to lose her balance. Rubriel held her, sitting, and applied pressure to the wound.

"Niera," she rasped. She was losing too much blood.

"Amlin, help me." They lifted Niera between them, the guards sparing them no rest before pressuring them to return to their cells. Everyone rushed forward to peer at them through the bars, their eyes gleaming with curiosity and excitement.

"She is badly wounded," Rubriel called out to the guards, who it seemed were perfectly content to leave them unaided. "We need bandages, a blanket, sheets - anything. Please."

One of them stopped, only to look back at her like she was crazy before following the others outside and bolting the door behind them. They lacked even a cot upon which to lay her.

"They mean for us to die," Niera whispered as Rubriel sat with her propped against the wall.

"Not if I can help it," she said. "You surprised me up there. I didn't know you could fight. You were very brave."

Niera smiled weakly.

"Boy! Give her this."

Amlin shuffled closer and handed Rubriel a scrap of cloth, passed through the bars from one of their neighbours. It wasn't much - likely torn off a hem or sleeve - but she accepted it and scrunched it up, pressing it firmly over the gash in Niera's abdomen until the bleeding finally stopped. She fell asleep, pale and exhausted, her skin papery.

Rubriel yawned, noticing Amlin as her head tilted back. He sat in the corner hugging his knees, staring blankly at the blood that still stained his fingers after his attempts to wipe it off.

"Are you alright?"

He nodded stiffly, seeming anything but. He wouldn't meet her eyes.

"You did well today," Rubriel told him, scooting over to sit beside. "You should be proud of yourself."

"I - I've never..." His small voice quaked.

"I know." She laid her hand overtop of his.

He flinched, his eyes wide with shock and desperation. "I was supposed to be a soldier." He spoke so quietly even Rubriel had to strain to hear him.

"I wanted to be an engineer, or to work with metal like my father, but with the war coming... I was terrified they would send me away to fight in the south. I should have been braver. I should have done my duty. 'A soldier has no quota to fulfil, until the day he must give his life in service of our country' - that's what they say. But I couldn't do it. I ran away, but they caught me and punished me as a deserter."

He sucked in a shuddering breath. "I am ashamed. And the worst part is, I will die in battle anyway - only now it will be meaningless."

"Today you were brave." Rubriel squeezed his fingers. "And you'll be brave again tomorrow, and the day after, and the day after that. There is still time now for you to fight as you wish you had then."

"They will never let me out of here," he sobbed.

"But they will remember you. Rest, Amlin. Try not to think too much."

She lay down, struggling to get comfortable on the bare floor, yet thinking nonetheless that she should take her own advice. Overthinking had been her constant companion of late.

Niera passed a few hours later. She never woke, having lost too much blood too quickly and without proper care. Rubriel knew there was nothing more she could have done, but she mourned all the same. The mood down below grew exceptionally grim. Not because Niera had been especially well known or liked, but because every death brought the hopelessness of their situation bubbling to the surface. Despair coated everything, slick and oily, leaving their motley community damp and downtrodden.

She steeled herself. It would not do to wallow, for despair was a slippery slope into a hole from which it would be difficult to climb back out.

She stood, easing herself into the first pose of her warmup routine, even as her stiff joints and jaded mind protested. After a few moments, Amlin joined her, committing to each movement with a fervour that was new to him. Here and there, others from adjacent cells tentatively joined the routine, having silently observed many times hence. Participation grew, the regular routine becoming a symbol of defiance and of unity that gave strength and purpose.

Battles became more frequent. They took Rubriel alone the next three times in a row in what felt like as many days, each time pitted against a higher calibre of opponent. She bested them all - and she bested them with style, until cheers from above rattled the ears of those who languished below.

If Rubriel had been allowed to keep the weapons she claimed from the fallen, she would have enough to equip a small army by now, but of course the guards confiscated them before the platform even reached the ground, leaving her to outwit and disarm her way to a proper weapon at the start of every new fight.

That didn't stop her training the band from below how to use them. Her exercise routines morphed into combat drills, until nearly everyone but the wounded and Brent - her grizzled neighbour - joined in the practice as a group.

Brent continued to scowl, muttering his disapproval to anyone in earshot whether they listened or not. His injured arm seemed to be getting worse, and part of her could not blame his moods in light of how much pain it likely caused him. Still, she mostly ignored him, for the rest of the group valued her leadership, feeding off a positivity she didn't know she possessed.

Her stomach clenched as the door opened, she and the others halting their practice and scurrying to the corners, but not before the guard's beady eyes caught what they were doing, the thrum of activity still palpable in the air. He called six of them out to fight; one from each cell, including Brent, who was by himself, and Rubriel, who pushed herself to the front in the hope of sparing Amlin.

On the platform, she assessed each of her companions. They ostensibly chose the more capable combatants this round, which could only mean their opposition would be great. Taelis, a surly miner from Klein; Marcetta, a ferocious demon-eyed woman of small frame and quick temper; Quan, whom they nicknamed 'the bloody baker'; and Lynter, whose crimes were that of deceit and insubordination. Each had survived at least one previous round on their own. Now, they looked to Rubriel to lead them to victory.

Two groups of four filled the ranks from above, uniformed men and women wielding short blades and spiked gauntlets. The arena fell into silent anticipation. Rubriel's group formed a semicircle facing the troops, who had split to attack from two sides. As the horn blew, they hunkered down, using their poles to keep distance between themselves and their opponents.

Tall, broad Taelis took the brunt of the assault from the left, Brent fighting one-armed at his outer flank. Rubriel fought shoulder to shoulder with Quan and Lynter, together keeping their four assailants at bay. Marcetta disappeared, slipping beneath notice as the fighting intensified. Rubriel didn't have time to worry about her. Keeping out of reach of the enemies' blades consumed their full focus. They were getting nowhere.

Quan deflected a sharp thrust to his abdomen, realizing too late his mistake as a spiked fist crashed into his skull. At the same moment, Rubriel's opponent howled and dropped to his knees. Marcetta had rammed him from behind with her pole. She stepped back to face Lynter's opponent, who backed up and turned to fend off both of them. Rubriel knocked hers unconscious and plunged his knife into the leg of the woman facing Lynter. She whirled to intercept the last of the four.

"Help Taelis!" she yelled over her shoulder, Marcetta and Lynter running off to where Taelis was pressed on all sides, being driven further and further back. Brent's movements were growing sluggish; he wouldn't hold out much longer.

With the odds evened, Rubriel went on the offensive. Quan's blood stained her opponent's gauntlet, and he snarled at her even as her longer reach got the better of him. She hurried across the arena, barrelling into a red uniformed woman just as Brent staggered and Taelis took a slash to his arm. Taelis roared as the man who wounded him moved to press his advantage, but Lynter intercepted while Rubriel spun her pole and cracked his skull with a sickening thwack. She looked around wildly for Marcetta, finding her cornered by the last of their enemies. They wouldn't get to her in time. Rubriel seized a knife from the fallen and hurled it at the back of the big man bearing down on Marcetta, landing it firmly between his shoulder blades.

The crowd erupted. Shouts and cheers bellowed from the stands, their words lost in the roar of approbation. The normally tenacious Marcetta stared open-mouthed at the corpse sprawled before her, the knife protruding from its back.

"You saved my life," she said numbly, as though she had expected less.

"We saved each other," Rubriel corrected. "We train together, we work together and we beat them. We lost Quan today, but he fought and died bravely. There is no more to ask of ourselves than that."

But then she looked up, a single word drifting down from the crowd - a name, standing out against the roar. *Her* name. The well-to-do people of the High Tiers gathered to watch their troops tear apart the lawless and destitute, but now they cheered for Rubriel instead. For some reason, that sent a foreboding chill down her spine, and she hastened her companions out of the arena. Brent could barely stand. He had sustained no further wounds that she could see, but his face held a sickly pallor, and he stumbled even as he refused assistance.

As soon as they were alone, the cell broke into lively chatter, an odd eagerness to hear all the details from the returnees overtaking those who sat waiting below. Amlin was no exception, proving particularly in awe of Rubriel's knife-throwing skills. She promised to show him how.

She spared a concerned glance toward Brent, who slumped against the wall, scowling as usual, his breath laboured.

"How is your arm?"

"You have no idea what you've done."

The room hushed.

"What do you mean?"

"This can only end *badly* - for you, and for all of us!" His proclamation boomed through the stone chamber. Rage and pain flashed in his eyes, even as the feverish sweat beaded on his forehead.

No one responded, as they seldom did to his outbursts, though Rubriel knew exactly what he meant. She sat and massaged her arms, wincing as she did so. The battles thus far had left her relatively un-scathed, but every muscle in her body ached with the strain of combat over and over, compounded by malnutrition and the lack of a proper bed. Being the crowd's favourite would not save her if her strength failed. No doubt the people would enjoy watching her downfall as much as they enjoyed her ascent.

26
Bitter Blood

Brent did not return from his next battle. Rubriel doubted anyone would miss his doomsaying and insults, yet ironically his sense of foreboding spread throughout the group more thoroughly in the wake of his death than it had when he was alive. She saw it when they practiced. There was a desperation to their training; they pushed themselves too hard, until Rubriel had to insist they rest. Not one of them had the strength to keep going like this.

Rubriel herself had been afforded a rare break from the arena. Not that she could be grateful, when it seemed the overseers had purposely excluded her in order to thin the numbers from below. No sooner had Brent's cell emptied than they filled it with three more people. Was their survival rate so high of late that the overseers now had a backlog? She thought it likely.

Her intent from the start had been to break the system. By keeping the band from below alive while winning the crowd's favour, she backed the overseers into a corner. She had watched attendance grow to the point where the arena was full for every battle. The overseers needed that attendance, but they were also meant to be operating a convenient way to 'dispose' of excess prisoners - and in that, they were failing.

"You look worried," said Amlin.

She replied with a smile that didn't quite reach her eyes. "Hard not to be."

"Everybody is on edge. What do you think is going to happen?"

"I don't know." She shifted uneasily, unsure whether to speak her mind. She lowered her voice so that only Amlin could hear. "I think my time here may be coming to an end. The overseers know they need to get rid of me."

"But you have beaten everyone they sent against you!"

"Exactly. They will have to change the odds…"

"You have to keep winning. We need you."

She said nothing more, opting to try to get some sleep. She must have drifted off after a while, because the next thing she knew was Amlin shaking her awake.

"Rubriel! The guards are coming."

More guards than usual. She bolted upright just as eight armed men marched into the room. They ignored Lynter and Taelis and took four others from the first two cells instead. From the next set, they chose four more, bypassing those who stood ready and seeking out the people who hid at the back. They ignored the three newcomers altogether and took Rubriel and Amlin both.

Ten from below. This was by far the largest group to be fighting all at once, and several of them were in bad shape. They only just fit on the platform. Rubriel glanced from one frightened face to another. Half of them looked too scared to move.

"Take your poles," she urged, grabbing several from the barrel and thrusting them into empty hands. "Take them! Remember your training." The noise from above was deafening. Why were they cheering already? Someone almost lost their balance as the platform jerked into motion. Amlin grabbed Rubriel's arm to steady himself.

"Rubriel…" His voice was pure terror.

She turned to face the entrance from above as her companions gasped and instinctively backed away from the horror that awaited them. A small army assembled at the far end of the arena.

Axe-wielders occupied the front row. Behind them sat two small catapults, each loaded with a barrel of something that would shatter on impact. At their center, a bullbeast shook its head dangerously, its huge tusks forcing its brethren to stand at a safe distance. Muscles bulged in its rider's arms as he tugged on the reins, fighting to keep the beast in check. Archers sat two abreast in the saddle behind him. And the crowd… those were not cheers of approval. They were angry shouts and jeers of protest.

The horn bellowed. Immediately, the catapults released their payload.

"Spread out!" Rubriel yelled. People ran in all directions as the barrels crashed into the ground and spilled their tarry black contents. One of hers found himself too close to the impact and slipped. The rest fell into total disarray as the bullbeast charged and the axe wielders took to each side of the arena.

Rubriel lunged out of the bull's path and landed within reach of an axe. She raised her pole instinctively, but the heavy weapon cleaved it in two and knocked her to the ground under the impact. She rolled as the man swung again for her head, managing to kick him in the shin and knock his balance. He pounced on her like an animal, leveraging his bulk to strangle her even as she kicked again and again. She fumbled and grasped one of the broken pieces of her pole and thrust the splintered end into his neck. Rolling out from under him, she scrambled to her feet and grabbed his axe in both hands.

"Amlin, watch out!" she screamed as an arrow skimmed past his ear. He was fighting for his life against an axeman, his pole next to useless as he struggled to dart out of the way of his opponent's deadly swing. Rubriel ran straight for him, forcing his attacker to turn and face her. Amlin threw his full weight behind his pole and slammed the end into the back of his knee, allowing Rubriel to break their deadlock and finish him.

A shriek pierced the din as Rubriel whirled to see the bull trample two of her comrades, a third taken down by an arrow.

"That bull needs to die."

The large circles of slippery tar splashed on the ground made the arena difficult to navigate, but they were as much a hazard to their enemy. Enraged by the throng and smell of battle, the bull's rider could scarcely control the beast. It charged for whoever was unlucky enough to catch its attention, swinging its lethal tusks at friend and foe alike.

"We have to get its attention!"

They ran across from it, putting a thick patch of tar between themselves and the bull. Amlin picked up a piece from a smashed barrel and hurled it towards the beast's head. It fell short.

"Mind the archers," Rubriel called out as its riders noticed them and swiveled to point bows in their direction. Amlin took off at a sprint, running straight for the bull. He waved his arms and shouted until its head reared dangerously and it charged. Amlin tore across the arena as fast as his legs would carry him. The bull was faster. It almost caught him as he reached the edge of the tar. He took a flying leap, landing right in the middle of the slippery stain and sliding the rest of the way.

The rider jerked hard on the reins, realizing too late what was happening. The bull plunged straight into the tar and lost its footing, barrelling towards Rubriel at speed. At the last second, she dropped to the ground and planted her axe into the beast's chest under the force of its own momentum. It roared and reared, its passengers thrown off, before it keeled over to the side and flattened its rider. Amlin descended on the archers, defenceless without their mount or their bows. Two others from below ran to join them. They were the only ones left.

Now the men who had been manning the catapults entered the fray, drawing swords and abandoning their machines.

"With me," said Rubriel, and charged.

She powered through the oncoming attackers, the heavy axe even more deadly in her hands. Her companions fought in her wake, stalling those who would try to flank her as she cut down one enemy, then another. A scream issued from her left as one of hers went down. Amlin cried out to her right. She spun in time to see him withdraw his blade from the gut of one attacker as another tackled him from behind. She stopped short as the man turned to reveal his sword pressed under Amlin's jaw.

"You cannot save them all," he snarled, and before she could react, he slit Amlin's throat.

Her scream of fury echoed even as the crowd erupted with a rage of their own. She drove him back mercilessly, her body on fire with anger and exhaustion until she cleaved his arm below the shoulder and beheaded him where he stood. Blood and tar stained her from head to toe. Alone now, she threw her axe aside and ran to Amlin's side.

"Amlin!"

He spluttered, wide-eyed, as he clutched desperately at his neck. A boom sounded from the gates. She looked up as the chief overseer himself rode into the arena astride a second bull. Plate armour covered much of his torso; pads protected his shins and thighs. A fearsome spiked flail dangled from its chain as he raised the weapon with a gauntleted hand. Fighting broke out in the stands as officials tried to subdue those who would rush forward, maddened. Some people looked ready to jump into the arena themselves.

Rubriel gathered a sword in each hand. The overseer rode to within ten paces of her.

"Surrender, and I'll make it quick." His gravelly voice seethed with hatred.

"Look around," she shot back. "It is you who should surrender."

Spirits gathered overhead even as she spoke.

"No scum from below can conquer Scarlet Arena!" His eyes flashed. The bull tossed its head, smaller than the previous beast but just as deadly.

"I'm not *from* below." She raised her dual swords, planting her stance wide and ready to spring in either direction.

He kicked the bull into motion, driving it in a wide arc around the far edge of the arena, knowing better than to tread near the treacherous pools of tar. He steered towards her and spurred the beast again, charging head on. There was little Rubriel could do against such an onslaught. She lunged out of the way, ducking as she landed to avoid the flail, his weapon's reach much longer than her own.

Scrambling to her feet, she thought wildly as he lined up for a second charge. She dove to the opposite side. The overseer couldn't heave his flail across quickly enough. She slashed a trail of blood right along the beast's side. It bellowed and bucked wildly, narrowly missing her with its hooves as it thundered past, the overseer wrestling to stay in the saddle.

He urged it to turn, but the beast had forgotten its rider, forgotten whatever training it had as the pain and stench of battle drove it to a frenzy. With a sideways buck, it unseated him. He landed heavily and abandoned the beast to face Rubriel on foot.

He swung the flail around. Its spiked ball landed in the dirt where Rubriel had stood not a moment before. She lunged as he whirled it again from the left, but she couldn't get within striking reach. It was all she could do to avoid the hunk of metal and the chain attached to it.

The battle sapped her strength. With each leap and dodge, it grew harder to keep her footing, until her legs failed her and she didn't jump back far enough. The end of the flail caught the underside of her left wrist with a sickening crack. She yelled, dropping the sword as pain shot through the broken bones, but the overseer was relentless. He came at her again and again, though she could see even through the bloody haze that he too was tiring.

An overhead swing gave her the opportunity to roll under his guard. Inside his reach, she stabbed her remaining sword up into the unprotected flesh of his outstretched armpit. He dropped the flail and staggered. She threw herself on top of him, driving the blade further in until he stopped moving.

Chaos reigned in the stands as people fought their way towards the overseer's booth. They would tear it down in their rage. Others seemed determined to jump over the wall into the arena. To what end was difficult to say. Rubriel stood slowly, her mangled arm dripping blood as she stumbled to where Amlin lay.

"R... Ru..."

"Shh. It's alright," she croaked, collapsing beside him. "You did well." She grasped his hand, squeezing tight. His desperate breaths came as a series of rapid gasps, but all he inhaled was blood. Tears burned in her eyes. "I'm proud of you."

But then Amlin tensed, his panicked face even more frantic as he tried to speak, looking at something over her shoulder. A thundering of hooves, and Rubriel turned just as the bull barrelled into her, its thick tusk smashing against her chest and sending her flying. The world spun. She spat blood into the dirt, struggling weakly onto her knees to see the beast sizing her up one last time. She could only watch as it charged again, knowing she was finished.

The blow never came. The bull collapsed mid stride as a strange blackness collided with it, silently and instantly ripping the life from it. Quiet fell over those in the stands, their struggles halted as their attention was once again drawn to the arena. The whole building seemed to darken, the rage and hatred from moments before evaporating like mist.

"Stand down, immediately."

Zildred himself now addressed them all from amidst the field of devastation. He barely raised his voice; he didn't have to.

"On your knees, every one of you. This chaos will end." He glanced at Rubriel, still kneeling where she fell.

"You should've... let it finish me," she managed.

"And make a martyr of you? I think not," he said, his cool dismissal for her ears alone.

"Out of my way! That's my *son!*" A man burst through the subdued ranks of observers, hurling himself over the wall and running heedlessly to where Amlin lay. He sobbed, oblivious to them all in his grief.

Zildred signalled to someone above, and several overseers jumped down as well. They seized Amlin's father and dragged him back, kicking and swearing in protest. Rubriel's heart ached for him, ached for the boy who had become her friend, who had counted on her to protect him, just as all the others had latched onto her, believing that she would somehow - impossibly - save them.

"Every aspect of what happened here is unacceptable," Zildred said to the masses. He looked from the people kneeling in the stands, to the crumpled body of the chief overseer, to the bloody carnage surrounding them. "No one has the right to so blatantly abuse the system. Henceforth, the arena shall be closed to all but military personnel. The remaining prisoners will be executed swiftly - behind closed doors. For the rest of you, anyone who engaged in rioting, vandalism, or challenge to authority will be punished accordingly."

"And you-" he turned to Amlin's father "-will serve as an example."

Rubriel started. The overseers hurriedly let go of him, and the same blackness that had torn life from the bull ripped the spirit from Amlin's father. A blood-curdling scream pierced the arena. It came not from him, but from Rubriel, as something hot and visceral burst all around her. Intense light and searing pain blinded. People gasped at what they saw. Then the blast faded; all turned to night, and Rubriel slipped into oblivion.

27

Burden of Stone

A grinding sound startled her awake. Her head swam as she tried to raise it, her pulse pounding in her temples. She moaned. Blood had already seeped through the bandage wrapped tightly around her mangled wrist. The pain made her dizzy. She squinted as light shone through the cell door, the familiar face of the High Warden surveying her latest accumulation of injuries by celair light.

"You again," he said with an incredulous blink. "What exactly did you do to end up back here?" Disappointment showed clearly on his face.

Rubriel heaved herself upright against the wall with a gargantuan effort. "What did I do? Heh."

Her huff turned to coughing, jarring her broken ribs. She wiped a smear of bloody spittle on her sleeve. "I trained the people below how to fight. I evened the odds. I won the crowds. I broke that wretched system and exposed it for what it was: a senseless massacre of your own people." She sounded like Brent in her bitterness - a thought that brought tears to her eyes as she remembered all those who hadn't made it.

"And the ball of light that engulfed you and blinded everyone in the vicinity before you passed out?"

Her face contorted. "What? I saw no such thing. Whatever you think you saw had nothing to do with me. I remember nothing after... after..."

"The Master thinks otherwise."

"He *allowed* this to happen," she seethed. "At any time, he could have stopped it. I will not be responsible for any of those deaths. It is not my fault. I won't let it be my fault. I can't..."

Muldeve, if he was at all moved by her outburst, did not show it. "You must not say such things. Your bandage needs changing, but I cannot send anyone here with you like this." And, as always, he left quickly; not affording himself time to hear any more from her or dwell on the things she said. It was better that way, lest he find himself next in the line of which to be made an example. Bad enough that she had somehow found her way back to burden him.

Alone, she crumpled. Sobs wracked her body, even as she tried to stifle them and the wave of pain that accompanied each one. She still believed her intentions had been good. *Make the best of a bad situation and bring others with you if you can* - that had been her motto for years. Her actions *had* resulted in the arena being shut down. Did that end justify the sacrifices? Why did she care what happened in Langlythe beyond the scope of her own fate?

But she already knew the answers to these questions - answers that simmered beneath notice, only now breaking to the surface and demanding to be acknowledged. She had allowed herself to care for her fellow prisoners, slowly unravelling the many layers of defence wrapped around her heart.

Because they are just people, trying to live their lives, just like anywhere else in the world.

That realization magnified her guilt a hundred-fold, and she wished bitterly to have never been part of this, to have never accepted the Elder's mission or had anything further to do with Langlythe, the war, or politics in general. She thought back to the argument she had with Molindra a few days before Solstice, their last conversation before the miserable exchange over the burning fence.

Perhaps most of all, she wished they had only sat down and had a different conversation - one in which they acknowledged how utterly miserable they both were with their lives and resolved to start down a new path.

Such hindsight would do her little good now. She drifted in and out of a fitful sleep, until Muldeve returned with a nurse to replace the dressing on her wrist. She sat in determined silence through it all, grimacing through clenched teeth as pain lanced up her arm from the swollen flesh. The wrappings held tightly, immobilizing the joint. Her fingers tingled with the onset of numbness.

An armed escort came next to bring her upstairs, though they need not have bothered with weapons. They ended up supporting her under each arm as they walked, for she had not the strength to climb so many stairs in her condition and fell halfway up the second flight. For the third time she found herself in the Great Hall, devoid of furniture once again, the warmth of its twin fireplaces a stark contrast to the underground cold.

Zildred waited for her beyond the threshold. She recoiled at the sight of him, remembering how coolly he smothered the chaos in the arena and brought the entire building to order in his brutally efficient way.

"Leave us," he said.

The guards released her and bowed, retreating through the doors that swung shut on their heels. She flinched at the boom of their closing.

"So, you are not a mage."

"Congratulations," she interjected, scathingly. She could scarcely persuade herself to even look at him.

He ignored her, speaking more to himself than to her as he paced the glowing floor tiles. "You are not a mage, but your blood is extremely magically conductive - ten times more so, to be precise, than the highest records the academy has on file. A peculiar trait, for one who does not have any raw energy."

Rubriel had no idea what he was talking about. She was tired of being at the centre of whatever strange research they were doing, tired of them testing her blood and questioning her about it when her complete lack of magical ability was one of the few things she had never even thought to lie about. She had assumed that line of enquiry ended with her being sent to Scarlet Arena.

"However," he went on, "it would appear that under certain circumstances, you are able to channel raw energy from another source. Specifically, your sildion pendant."

She started. Her hand flew to her chest and felt the small stone hanging beneath the thin fabric of her chemise. This... was something new. Something she had no reason to doubt. And if her pendant was the one small thing that might've given her an edge-

"Of course, Celessil's minute sildion gift is only a minor source, but if it were to be replaced with something else..."

He moved faster than she could react. Shadows lurched and tightened around her gut. She doubled over and fell to her knees. He shoved her roughly backwards, the impact eliciting a sharp cry of pain from her broken ribs. He tore open her collar and snatched the fine silver chain from around her neck. His fingers scraped like icicles against her bare skin.

"No! You wouldn't dare. It is sacred!"

He held the pendant at arm's length as though repulsed by it. The tiny bright stone shook violently and began to emit an eerie, high pitched ringing. The whole room darkened for a moment and shuddered, then with a loud crack, the stone imploded into dust.

She gasped in horror. Sildion was supposed to be indestructible; ancient beyond measure and harder than the purest diamond. There was nothing left of it at all. The broken ends of the chain lay disfigured and useless on the floor. She tried to get up, but he pushed her back. She struggled harder, but he ignored her, his other energy - kinetic - pinning her in place.

He studied another gem, this one blacker than obsidian and seeming to *glow* with darkness, if such a thing is possible, as though it were actively emitting shadows as opposed to merely casting them.

"Do you know what this is?" he asked softly.

"Ludion," she said, her heart pounding with the sudden realization of what he intended to do.

He wore no gloves or gauntlets; his thin fingers curled like shadows themselves, idly twirling the spindle-shaped stone between them.

"Sildion's twin, equal and opposite in every way. Where sildion fosters the living, ludion fosters the dead. The spirits of Langlythe thrive upon it, as do I. As will you..."

"No. Please-"

Be still.

His voice slid through her mind as he gripped her shoulder. She went rigid with pain and terror as an intense wave of his power wove itself tightly in and around her, poised to rip her spirit clean out of her body if she so much as moved an inch. Her eyes widened in shock as the sharp point of the ludion pressed against her chest, sliding in between her ribs, through layers of muscle and sinew. She felt it puncture her lung. The scream died in her throat.

Then he twisted that shard in a most excruciating way, leaving it buried horizontally between her most vital organs. There was no blood; no visible wound when he withdrew his empty hand. Only the shock and agony of something sharp scraping against her insides. Each shallow, rapid breath stung like inhaling a mouthful of metal filings.

Hot tears ran down her cheeks. The pain was so startling she feared she might vomit, and the clenching of her insides would drive the stone into her heart. Bravely, she rolled onto all fours and crawled forward, crying out sharply as she did so. She rested her forehead against the cold stone, trembling with the desperate effort to continue drawing breath.

"Painful, isn't it?"

The bitterness of his remark would sour an orchard. He watched in his idle, disinterested way, unfazed by the suffering he inflicted, the better part of his attention no doubt focused elsewhere.

Rubriel remembered little of the hours or days that followed. Her mind dropped in and out of consciousness, fleetingly aware of someone making her drink water from a cup, or offering food which she hadn't the strength to accept. All she could think of was the pain. The empty net of unconsciousness was her only reprieve.

She lost all concept of time and awareness, spiralling feverishly from one terrible moment to the next. Nearby voices dragged her awake again, and she peered through hooded eyelids to find two mages conversing about progress to repairs in the Lower Tiers - and how they couldn't reach the valves on account of the flooding. She was still in the great hall. The snippets she overheard brought a dull, grim satisfaction: the damage wrought by her efforts was still being dealt with after all this time. Their mission had served its purpose.

The pair strode from the hall at Zildred's dismissal. Rubriel flinched at the sound of his voice so close by and realized she was lying beside the throne, secured via a chain looped around her waist to the wrought iron lattice work on the wall behind her. The detailed metalwork covered the entire back wall but for a narrow door on the opposite side of the throne, hidden behind thick red drapery. She guessed that it most likely led up into the highest reaches of the citadel's tower.

Keeping still and quiet to avoid attracting attention, she filled the short spell of lucidity with trying to make sense of her situation. Whatever cruel experiment - or punishment - she was now a part of, apparently it was important enough that Zildred saw fit to oversec it personally.

She did not understand what nature of tests Imul'dene's academy had been performing with her blood, and she had never heard the concept of "magical conductivity" before, but the intent was clear enough; he expected her to be able to draw energy from the stone inside her and use it as a born mage would channel their own native raw energy.

Attempts to transfer raw energy from one person to another had always ended badly in decades past. The ill-favoured folk of Tunswick's underground had once engaged in a practice called siphoning, which involved passing a large amount of energy from one mage to another, through a non-mage. The non-mage was said to receive a small portion of one or both mage's abilities.

Benefits, if any, were extremely short-lived and wore off within a few days, leaving the subject severely ill - or dead. The full extent of the underground operation was eventually discovered and shut down by the Bantrian government in 1884, sixteen years ago. There had been no further attempts since - legal or otherwise.

At least not in Tunswick. While some aspects of Langlythian society were comparatively primitive, they were considerably more advanced in the area of arcane science. Biology, too, from what Molindra had said. They knew a great deal more about the body and its relationship with raw energy than the handful of registered elementalists at Tunswick's own university.

She watched the empty hall through glassy eyes. The massive doors remained closed, silent but for the sound of her own laboured breathing. Murals covered much of the side walls, their scenes depicted not in paint, but a combination of metalwork, carved stone and crystal; she viewed them sideways from where she lay.

The nearest showed a man kneeling in a broad field, surrounded by spirits. His thin frame leant on a staff the way an older man's might, though he seemed otherwise young. He extended a hand out to the spirits swirling around him - a gesture of friendship, she thought, and a far cry from how spirits were treated now. She wondered just how old the city of Imul'dene really was, and if it had once been a very different place.

She fell asleep thinking about it, until a strange tremor jostled her awake. The whole building shifted for a moment as though the ground had shrugged its shoulders from beneath the foundations. It passed as quickly as it came, and when she pushed herself up to look around nothing seemed amiss, but she did not think she had imagined it. She sagged down on her elbows and coughed, the resulting spear of pain jolting through her torso like lightning.

A cold hand fell on her shoulder, and she was startled to find Zildred beside her.

An earthquake, he said into her mind. *Common enough in these lands. The citadel has withstood many.*

She shivered and pulled away, but he pressed her down against the floor, his other hand holding her skull.

It is old indeed, he said, seeing her recent line of thought. *Almost as old as Morkile-ne-Nect, and built in his honour.*

He pushed deeper into her memory before she could stop him, to the conversation she had with Daelin on the way to the Ice Divide, when she had first heard the name *Morkile-ne-Nect*. She saw that moment unfurl as though she was there all over again, the Lone Peak and its ludion looming over her with its unsettling aura.

But there was more to that conversation than merely what was spoken. She'd thought about it in silence for a long while after; the strange similarity between this structure and the tower of Celessil. The stones were equal and opposite, yes - but with a symmetry between the two. Both were constructed in a similar way; both affected the environment in a large radius around them. Both had been built at approximately the same time–the Great Segregation in the first counted century.

Her intuition on the subject intrigued him - she *felt* his intrigue; an unwelcome, foreign intrusion against the current of her fear and anger. She shrivelled and retreated into herself, tucking her thoughts away behind a tightly woven shell where he couldn't see them. The vision disappeared. She willed her mind to stay blank, suppressing any thoughts before they could take shape, focusing only on the floor beneath her, grounding herself with its solidity.

His power touched that shell, gently at first; skimming over the surface for a crack in her defenses. The pressure increased and she clenched herself tighter, blood pounding in her temples. Her nails dug into the palm of her hand. She shuddered all over at the horrid feeling of his consciousness grating against hers, prodding and squeezing her shell so hard she feared he would crush her.

Do not fight me, Rubriel. This need not be painful.

No. Leave me!

He had already taken her pride, her friends and her future; she wasn't going to give up her past as well.

How much of your past do you really own?

It was all the opening he needed. She was in Celessil's grand library. Elder Berren's stern face glared down at her. She fumed at their argument.

"We raised you here as one of our own," the Elder said.

As one of our own...

She flashed through dozens of other encounters, all with a common thread of emotions - the Elder's concern, a slight sense of disapproval, and a burden of obligation that her younger self did not fully understand.

"...this I ask of you in return..." the Elder said in that hallway. The ask that sent her back to Langlythe. The foul taste of resentment rose in her throat. She hadn't questioned his right to treat her that way, nor had she noticed the unsettling implication behind those words.

But Zildred did. *He made an exception for you, and held you indebted for it.*

A protest tried to form in her mind, but he snuffed it out before it could take shape. She plunged further back in time, to the Moonwood cottage where she grew up before moving to the city proper. She practiced archery in the forest with a bow she'd made herself, bringing home a brace of rabbits for supper - only fifteen at the time. Gwendolen stirred a pot of stew over the old stove. She could almost smell her sister's cooking...

She struggled again, fighting to block out the memory and earning another jolt of pain. Her sister didn't need to be part of this. Gwendolen was innocent, and far away - it felt like betrayal to allow her memory to be tarnished so. Rubriel ignored the physical pain. Determined, she shoved with all her might against Zildred's presence in her mind.

But she no longer had the strength to break his hold over her. She was losing control. The scenes of her early life flashed by almost too fast to comprehend until she arrived at the end - or the beginning, really. There was a clothesline strung between two low branches behind the cottage. Gwendolen wrung out the linens and hung them while Rubriel sat in the grass, playing thoughtfully with a handful of buttercups.

"If you're my sister," she said with a child's curiosity, "then we must have the same mother."

"That is true," said Gwendolen.

"Where is she?"

Gwendolen gave an awkward smile. "I've told you before, love. She died when you were born. I know you don't remember."

"Oh." Her face fell, but she persisted. "What was she like? What about our father? Why don't we live with him?"

Her sister didn't answer at first. Child-Rubriel didn't understand.

"He's gone too," Gwendolen said finally. Rubriel grew upset. "Come, let's not talk about this. Help me carry the peg basket, will you?"

"But I want to know," Rubriel said miserably. She did as she was told, following along sadly. Feelings surfaced - feelings that adult-Rubriel kept buried and spoke of to no one. The disappointment, the longing and loneliness which Gwendolen had chosen to ignore, left its mark. She had been seven years old. This was her earliest memory - and all her life she elected *not* to remember it. She felt it all again as though it were yesterday. But she loved her sister dearly. The two of them had been enough. Until...

Stop, she pleaded. *There isn't any more. I remember nothing more. I cannot prove I was born in Celessil. You're right, but what difference does it make?*

Zildred ignored her. He continued to rake through the earliest roots of her memory for clues of her origin, but found none. There were none to be found. Rubriel could not have kept that knowledge from him had it existed in her memory, nor was there any thought or feeling he couldn't reach - even if she herself chose not to acknowledge them. She knew that for certain now. It was the ultimate violation of her sense of self, and she reeled from it long after he released her.

Her mind exhausted and sluggish, she could barely string two thoughts together. Yet it was her heart that ached the most. A heavy weight of hopelessness settled in and stole away what remained of her will to survive.

28
Righter of Wrongs

The company sat huddled around the brazier, their hands wrapped around hot mugs of weak broth. They said little. Scoe stared into the flames, almost mesmerized by the glowing coals, his thoughts elsewhere. The twin scouts played a game with five tiny stones, throwing one in the air and attempting to scoop up the rest before catching it again.

Adam looked especially miserable. His leg healed too slowly despite Grace's careful nursing, and not being a patient man, he was prone to making it worse by putting weight on it when he shouldn't. Scoe had returned with a leg injury of his own, having taken a stab wound to the thigh during the fight in the citadel. Fortunately, it hadn't damaged anything vital, and he too was on the mend; barely limping now.

They all shared a sense of unease and indecision. Food grew scarce as their pilfered supply of peas dwindled. Edible mushrooms and swamp crabs would only go so far, and the former required them to roam further and further afield to pick out the blooms that were safe to eat. They would have to leave - and soon, but to do so would be to give up on Rubriel. The brazier would only continue burning for so long without their tending.

Scoe knew Adam already believed her lost; it must have been weeks now since Scoe returned without her. But his leg still prevented them from travelling south with any speed - as his niece frequently reminded him - so he couldn't very well insist they move on. Daelin and Dornir voiced no opinion on the matter. Scoe admired that about them - how they lived in the moment, adapting to whatever fate served them next without complaint.

His own feelings were torn. The wisest course of action would be to leave as soon as possible, but he couldn't bear the thought of leaving Rubriel behind in that place. He knew she may well be dead, but somehow his heart refused to believe that; she was too clever, too strong a survivor.

A knock sounded.

Everyone froze. They exchanged puzzled looks, almost thinking they had imagined it when the tapping sounded again, quiet, but unmistakably coming from the well room.

"Are we discovered?" said Dornir.

"What manner of enemy would do us the courtesy of knocking first?" whispered his brother.

"Shh!" said Adam. "One who believes these ruins are occupied by someone, or something, entirely different. Arm yourselves. And stay *quiet.*"

There was a rustling, scraping sound of someone outside.

"Wait," Scoe whispered.

Adam looked up.

"Rubriel might. What if she lost her milestone and walked all the way back? Let's at least be sure of who it is before we pounce on them."

Adam pulled himself to his feet. "Come on," he said, hobbling as discreetly as he could for the entrance.

Scoe held up a hand, volunteering to go first with Daelin and Dornir close behind. Another knock, louder this time.

"Who is it?"

"Scoe, is that you?" A muffled voice filtered through the cracks.

His eyes widened. He opened the door just a sliver, his dagger at the ready.

"I'm alone - and on your side."

It took him a moment to recognize the red-haired woman before him, the olive green of Celessil partially concealed beneath a black cloak, the hood pulled back and mask lowered to reveal her face.

"Molindra."

The others tensed at the name, but she raised her hands in surrender and stepped back.

"What are you doing here?" He blocked the doorway with his body, as much to keep his own companions at bay as to keep her beyond the threshold.

"I have come to get you out of here. I feared I would not find you, that I would be too late..." She peered around Scoe, trying to catch a glimpse of their faces. "Where is Rubriel?"

Adam pushed into view. "I do not know you, Molindra, but your *deeds* are known to me. Why should we trust you? How did you find us?"

"I do not blame you for your distrust. It has taken me days to find this place. I knew only the vague whereabouts of these ruins, and hoped that Scoe took my advice and made camp here." She withdrew an envelope from her skirt pocket. "If you will not believe me, I can only hope you will believe this."

Adam snatched it from her and thumbed open the wax.

"That is Elder Berren's seal," Scoe said. "I have seen it only once before; on the letter granting me permission to enter Celessil as a foreign visitor. There is no other like it."

With tense fingers, Adam pulled out and unfolded the note within, retreating to the light of the fire to read:

Rascovor Garvin Mytholi of Esmara;

If you are reading this, you have by now encountered Elementalist Molindra, who was to stand trial by the Council of Celessil for her misdeeds in service of Langlythe. After much deliberation, I write to inform you that the Council has sentenced her to exile in the north, bound by blood oath to aid you as she may, until her wrongs are righted. You need not fear her intentions, for the oath is unbreakable, and she is skilled enough to travel without detection. May this letter reach you safe and whole.

Elder Berren of Celessil.

"Is this some trick?" Adam growled, having read the letter aloud.

"I never told Molindra my whole name; why would I? I hate it. Only Rubriel and the Council knew it in full, and perhaps a handful of officials at the port of Ornage from when I landed. The letter is real."

Scoe stepped back from the door. Molindra removed her glove and held her right hand into the light, turning her palm upward for him to see. A thick, raised scar traced across her palm, from the base of her index finger to just below her wrist. They gathered closer to peer at it.

"I shall not betray you. I am here to help - I truly mean that."

Adam grunted, then nodded finally. They made room for her to step inside properly and sealed the door behind her.

Molindra scanned the faces of those she did not know. "You must tell me, I beg you; where is Rubriel?" The fear in her voice was unmistakable.

"We don't know," Scoe answered heavily. "She and I were separated and somehow got lost within the citadel. I was wounded and captured but managed to milestone out. I wish I knew more, but I did not see or hear anything of her after she left me at the warehouse to create a diversion."

"No..." Molindra covered her face with her hands. She sniffed, pinching the bridge of her nose to stop the tears from coming.

"It has been weeks," Adam reminded them. "We need to face the fact that Rubriel is not coming back and focus on our own survival. You said you could get us out of here?"

"No!" Molindra's shout echoed uncomfortably in the hollow space. "I will take you to safe passage out of Langlythe if that is your wish, but I am exiled here for a reason, and I will not rest until I know her fate for certain. You cannot expect me to give up that easily!"

"We haven't all been introduced," Grace interrupted. "You have travelled a long way, and we could all do with some tea and getting to know each other a little before we face such heavy topics. Please, may we sit down?" She threw a pointed look at her uncle.

The twins had already dropped back to their cross-legged position by the fire. Molindra and the others joined them, though she sat a little further back from the group. Grace, Adam and the twins exchanged introductions. They made awkward small talk, not yet trusting each other enough to discuss anything important.

"You must be tired," offered Grace, bringing an end to the tense conversation. "I will prepare one of the other rooms for you. It isn't much, but it is dry, and we've made use of some old bedding we found when we got here."

Molindra rose and followed her.

"Someone should keep an eye on her door, make sure she doesn't try anything while we sleep," Adam murmured once they were out of earshot.

"Fine," Scoe replied at once, volunteering primarily for the opportunity to talk to her one on one. There was no shortage of rooms and passageways branching off the two larger spaces they used as common areas. They had gradually explored them all, finding that most either came to a collapsed dead end or led to a mineshaft that was best avoided. Knowing there was no other exit to the surface besides through the well room made them feel safer, though they kept most of the excess space shut off anyway to conserve heat.

Scoe waited until the others had settled into their respective chambers before knocking quietly on Molindra's door.

"I'm sorry about that reception," he said as her surprised face peered at him from the dimly lit chamber.

"Oh. It went about as well as it could have, I suppose. At least your companions didn't throw me out." She forced a smile.

"Adam is a good man, but he has grown bitter after too long spent watching Langlythe prepare to invade his home. His leg has only made him more resentful."

"What happened to him?" She backed into the room and sat on the cot.

Scoe leant against the opposite wall, lowering his voice further. "He took a bad fall and likely fractured it, based on how slowly it is healing. No cure for that but time, which only makes him more impatient."

"I may be able to speed up the healing process. I doubt he will ever trust me enough to let me try though." Her eyelids fluttered shyly.

Scoe shook his head. "I wouldn't. If you heal him, he will expect you to lead us out of Langlythe right away. The only reason he has allowed us to wait for Rubriel this long is because his leg prevented him from travelling on foot with any haste. It's not that I would prolong his suffering," he added quickly, seeing Molindra's expression, "but in truth, I am as loathe to give up as you."

"What about you?" she ventured, indicating his own leg wound.

"I'm fine. Just a scar to add to my modest collection."

She nodded. "I am scared, Scoe. It all seemed so clear to me back in Celessil, but now that I'm here, and Rubriel is missing... I do not know what to do."

"Neither do I. We cannot blindly go looking for her without first knowing if she is alive and where she is being held captive, if that is indeed the case. Nor are we achieving anything by hiding in these ruins." He sighed. "Sleep on it. We will talk more in the morning, or... you know what I mean."

"Scoe."

He turned to look back over his shoulder.

"Thank you."

He smiled and nodded, closing the door softly behind him.

Alone in the small, makeshift bedroom, Mol unlaced her boots and undressed from her outer layers, shaking out the cloak and draping it over the bed for extra warmth. No sooner had she done so than she buried herself under it and cried herself to sleep.

Mol rose to find Scoe snoring propped against the wall outside her chamber. He jostled awake as she almost tripped over him, his bleary eyes gazing up into a puzzled expression.

"Sorry," he mumbled. "Adam wanted someone to keep an eye on you while we slept. Obviously, if I believed that was necessary, I would be more, umm, awake."

She waved off his explanation. "I cannot tell you what a relief it is to have found you here, willing to trust me."

Scoe yawned and stretched to his feet. "The others only know what most people know; your involvement and its consequences. They weren't there to see how you suffered for it. You have paid for your mistakes in triplicate already. It is not my place to make things any worse for you than they have to be."

Her eyes lit up. She looked for a moment like she would hug him, then thought the better of it as sounds of life clattered from the mess hall. One of the twins let out a curse, followed by a watery plop of something being dropped in a pot.

"Swamp crabs are easy pickings this hour," Dornir announced. "Look at all these!" He pointed to the large cooking pot, in which five angry crabs clamoured awkwardly over one another, trying to scale its walls. "They are on the move, heading for the deeper pools."

"And exceedingly grumpy about it," Daelin complained, nursing his thumb where one of their pincers had caught him.

"Great," said Scoe, trying not to look sheepish as he wondered if the twins had seen him snoring in the thoroughfare when they went out gathering.

"I saw a well on the way in here," said Molindra. "I should very much like to wash, if possible - after the journey and all."

"Of course! Water is no problem. Not much we can do about the temperature, though. We only have one cooking pot, one fire... and it is currently occupied."

"I can take care of that," she said brightly. When they returned lugging the heavy bucket between them, Molindra dipped her fingers in the water. Tiny bubbles formed on the bottom, and within seconds the water grew pleasantly tepid.

"You can stay," Daelin called out, seeing what she'd done.

"It is nothing," she said to Scoe. "I can warm the water for each of us."

Warming bathwater was not the only way Molindra made herself useful around the camp, determined to earn her keep - and their trust. She accompanied the twins on their excursions to find food, her elementalist abilities allowing them safer access to the more treacherous parts of the bog. Adam even permitted her to examine his leg in due course, though he stopped short of allowing her to perform any healing. Still the brazier burned steadily, with no sign of Rubriel's return.

Tensions mounted as the camp grew more and more divided on the matter. Even the twins voiced their concern about staying any longer, as despite Molindra's help, they seldom brought back enough food to go around. The crabs had moved into unreachable, deeper water. When Adam urged the group again that it was time to leave, they reluctantly agreed, though the prospect of life in the vastly different world beyond the Gloaming Pass frightened the brothers more than they cared to admit.

Scoe saw the wisdom in the decision. He longed to return home, to the sunny days and vibrant green of Esmara. He knew if they waited much longer they may not have the chance. Still, his heart ached at the thought of leaving Rubriel - and for that matter, Molindra - to their fates. So it was they reached a solemn agreement; they would rest up, gather what supplies they could, and travel east as soon as they were prepared.

Molindra grabbed Scoe's arm and dragged him aside.

"You are not really leaving, are you?"

"I... I am, Mol. I'm sorry. My life isn't here; it is waiting for me back across the sea, where my betrothed must surely think I have abandoned her. I do not wish to die here needlessly. Though, I will likely be sent straight back, if Bantria calls upon Esmara for aid in the coming war."

Molindra looked as though she'd been slapped. "So that's it, then? You do not care about us; you re-evaluated in the face of death and decided we are not worth it?"

"That is not what I said, Mol-"

"Look me in the eye and tell me she is not worth it!"

"Wh...?"

"You privileged folk are all the same." She scowled. "You would sooner run off with the shoes of the less fortunate than walk a mile alongside them."

"Where is this coming from?" Scoe burst, exasperated. "I am sorry; I know you cannot leave with us. I know you are bound to your oath, even if what you pledged to do is beyond hope. I don't blame you for not wanting to face that alone."

She brushed a tear from her cheek. "For a while there, I thought..."

"I know. I understand."

"No, you *don't.*"

Scoe stood helplessly, quite at sea with her behaviour. He could do nothing but wait for her to calm down.

"No, it - it doesn't matter." She sighed, though the bitter aftertaste of her words remained. "It is my fault. It should have been me - up there. I cannot ask you to share this hopeless fate with me."

"It could very easily have been me," Scoe reminded her. "I was with Rubriel all the way up to the High Tiers. If I'd taken another route, if we hadn't been separated... who knows?" Bravely, he rested a hand on her shoulder. "My father always said there is no point in wasting away over what could've, should've been, because one cannot go back to find out the answer. We can only move forward, and make the best of the path we tread."

Slowly, Molindra nodded. "I should go." With another sigh she went off to bed, suddenly aware of just how tired she was.

Scoe called to her as she reached the doorway. "Rubriel loves you, Molindra. Eventually, she will remember that."

"If she's alive," Mol whispered, then disappeared into the dimly lit room beyond.

29

Shuddering Earth

Fifty-two years is a long time over which to accumulate memories, Rubriel thought, especially when forced to sort through them systematically, like files in a great dysfunctional archive arranged more like a spider web than a linear timeline. She had become little more than a repository of places, people, conversations; a source of information to be mined until nothing remained unknown.

Of the present, she saw very little. Zildred continued to raid her mind throughout most of her waking hours. She resisted, of course, but her ability to do so declined with every attempt, as though the pathways he forged through her brain remained open permanently once formed.

That, and the compelling incentive not to fight back, for when she inevitably gave in, he took away her pain. So much so that she came to not only welcome the relief, but to crave it - and she hated that most of all. She fell into a kind of trance, disconnected from her own memories, as though observing all the details of her life through the eyes of another - which, in a way, she was. Those sessions usually left her unconscious. For how long at a time, she could not gauge.

No clocks chimed in the halls of Imul'dene. If such public timekeeping mechanisms existed here, they were silent - unlike the tolling bells of Celessil's clock tower, or the sprightly chirping of the bedside alarm clocks to which Bantrian businessmen woke each morning. The people in Andorlai carried pocket watches - complete with twenty-six hour markings - but she hadn't found the opportunity to study a clock since she first encountered their peculiar design in Mornik's visiting house.

He observed her Bantrian years in detail. She sensed his interest was purely practical; it was her knowledge of Bantrian life, law and government that held value more than her personal experiences, but that didn't stop her reliving the emotions tied to each moment in their full spectrum of colour.

Some memories seemed only vaguely familiar to her, like the trip aboard a steam train to Ornage she and Mol had taken in their earlier years, before their financial situation deteriorated. The sight of the great passenger ships anchored in the harbour, the jittery travelers and crew lugging suitcases up the ramps, marked the birthplace of their dream to sail for Esmara themselves, making a new life in the "land of excess," as Bantrians were fond of calling it.

Others returned vividly, like the day the blacksmith's shop shut down and left her without work, or the humiliation of meeting Vesner about the contract Molindra had signed, asking him for help after the morally degrading way he'd treated her over the years. She sensed that Zildred despised Vesner as much as she did, though she lacked the context to understand why. He never allowed her to ask questions of her own, and she thought that whatever snippets of meaning she managed to glean from him were more side-effect than intent on his part.

Not even Molindra knew the full extent of her suffering at the hands of men who sought to take advantage of her in one way or another. As an unlicensed mage running with the wrong crowd and practicing illegally, Mol had abundant problems of her own. Rubriel built walls around her heart, sealing away the hurtful memories behind a veneer of stone where she could choose to forget them.

Now they laid bare in front of her, the ugly truths of a life spent looking over her shoulder, lived from one day - one disaster - to the next. Zildred spared her no shame, his inquiry relentless.

He watched her build the growing house in Andorlai, posing as one of his people. He watched her chase Molindra to the Roof of the World, then shun her friend even as she brought her home; except now Rubriel blamed only herself, and she accepted that blame with the weight of a thousand faults. He saw the tumultuous mix of respect and resentment for Elder Berren as he sent her on the quest that led her to the ruins at the edge of the Painted Bog, where her friends guarded a brazier of flame under Mount Yel'ent and waited.

Suddenly, her awareness jerked. The rest of her memories didn't matter. But this - if he knew where that cave was, there was nothing to stop him hunting down Scoe and the others. He knew their names, their faces - he could have spirits searching for them within the hour, and living soldiers on the march as soon as they were found-

You still seek to protect them, he said into her thoughts, and she struggled more forcefully than she had in countless days.

Leave them out of this. They would not still be here if Scoe and I had not intercepted them. They were never part of our plan.

Likely they left already.

She panicked, lashing out at the threads of his consciousness woven through and around hers like roots. She may as well have thrashed around in space for all the good it did.

He remained inexorably calm, perhaps even faintly amused by her outburst. *No one ever planned to rescue you, Rubriel. You were expendable; dead to them the moment you set foot in my halls with only a milestone to save you.*

The ground seemed to sway beneath her. She didn't want to believe him, but the very fabric of her being trembled, the world as she knew it shaking itself apart. Somehow, she forced her eyes open. The world was indeed shaking; the ancient walls of the citadel moaned, the floor rose and fell like a great wave. Metal clanged as the double doors toppled free of their hinges.

Zildred released her, casting her aside as the earth rebelled. Shouts could be heard from beyond the Great Hall. Above them, the hand-like chandelier swung violently on the end of its chain, until its fixture snapped and it crashed down from the ceiling. Hundreds of red crystals spilled from its grasp as it fell, smashing into infinite glowing fragments that scattered across the floor like a rain of exquisite hail.

They saw the water ripple first. The bucket sat beside the stove, filled to the brim with hot water. Grace peered into it, frowning. Curious vibrations rocked its contents. Then she heard it.

What started as a distant rumbling drew closer and more menacing. The others came running at once.

"Is that a-"

A jolt from the ground interrupted Daelin's question and he stumbled forwards, grabbing onto the table for balance. Tools clattered and fell where they leaned against the wall as the cavern shook.

"Find cover!" Adam braced himself against the doorframe while the twins crawled under the table and held onto its legs.

Scoe grabbed hold of Grace and backed into the entrance to the well room, watching in horror as a crack snaked its way down the rock wall.

But Molindra pushed past Adam and rushed to the centre of the room, planting her feet wide and looking up even as dust crumbled in the corners and a terrifying boom echoed from the mine. Instinctively, she raised her palms towards the ceiling, as though to physically hold it aloft.

"What are you doing?" He shouted over the roar of the earth and the rumble of rocks as they shifted and cracked.

Mol ignored him. Her face set in concentration, her power stabilized the cavern while the mountain tried to tear itself apart all around them. The shaking seemed to last a lifetime. They could do nothing but hold on and hope the wrath of the quake would spare them. Then at once the rumbling passed, fading like a breath of wind. Slowly, Molindra lowered her hands, panting slightly. The cavern remained firm.

"Did you call the earthquake?" asked Dornir, aghast.

Molindra exhaled heavily. "You flatter me. The earth does not shake on my command." She strode towards the entrance. "I did, however, shield this cave system from collapsing on us." She unbolted the door to the well room and yanked it open with some difficulty. The hinges had bent slightly.

Beyond, she breathed a sigh of relief to find the well still intact. Lighting the way with a small flame in her palm, she ventured out into the corridor, stepping over piles of debris as she went. Her magic only extended so far. The further she went, the more extensive the cracks in the walls and ceiling.

Another quake of that magnitude would bring the whole system down on their heads, with or without her help. However reluctant she had been before, there was no doubt in Molindra's mind now; they had to get out of there as soon as possible.

She rounded a bend and froze, looking back over her shoulder in case she'd taken a wrong turn. She stoked her flame higher, spilling light throughout the corridor.

Or what was left of it.

Before her stood nothing but a mass of rocks and dirt where the way out should have been. She tore away some loose stones, fear mounting as she found no sign of a way through. She gathered air and pushed it against the blockade, searching for any weak spot.

"That's... not good," said Scoe behind her.

She turned to face her companions, not knowing what to tell them.

"So now you've trapped us here," Adam said darkly. His accusatory tone struck a nerve.

"I prevented us from being crushed, but only in the immediate area. I am not strong enough to hold an entire cave system together against the will of nature."

"Or held together just enough while allowing our escape to collapse."

"Adam, *shut up*."

Scoe had never looked so stern. "Accusations are not going to help us get out of here, and I am sick to death of the two of you fighting. We are *all* going to starve unless we work together to dig through that."

The two men stood barely inches apart. Scoe towered over Adam, his jaw set. Adam glared hotly in return, fists clenched at his sides. None of the group had ever raised their voices to him until now. He stormed off, still fuming.

Grace made to go after him, but Dornir held her back. "Let him go," he said sagely. "Let him cool off."

"I need a minute," said Scoe, walking away as the rest of them surveyed the collapse in dismay.

"If I could have prevented this, I would," Mol said, low.

"Of course you would," said Daelin. "You're not stupid."

Mol only shook her head, saying nothing.

Little did they know how the earthquake had saved their lives. Saved by sheer luck; by a whim of nature and Molindra's quick thinking, from the true threat of which they knew nothing.

She lay curled in the dark. It was over - truly over. She fought for so long to protect those she considered blameless, often at her own expense, just like she'd fought to shelter Molindra all those years. In the end, she'd betrayed the identity of the last few people she cared about without even realizing it until it was too late. Whether her mission significantly postponed the war or not, eventually Zildred would launch an invasion of Bantria - and he would do so with *her* knowledge of the land and its people.

She had utterly failed them all.

The shard of ludion stabbed painfully inside her. Knives filled every breath; she cried out more than once in the bitter cold of the cell, unable to bear the pain any longer. An unfamiliar face had dragged her down there in the wake of the earthquake. No one had come to her since.

When someone finally did, she jolted awake with a start, swallowing the agony in her chest and wheezing frightfully. She yelped as Muldeve's boot crushed her hand. His pale celair light failed to illuminate her lying on the floor. Jumping back, he almost dropped the bowl he carried, spilling some of its contents. He said nothing, crouching beside her and offering her the bowl.

Slowly, she lifted her weary eyes to meet his through the blurred patchiness of her vision. He looked weary in his own right; dark, puffy circles betraying the stress he was under, no doubt exacerbated by the recent quake. She trembled with the effort of staying upright, but she held her captor's gaze, himself a captive in so many ways. Still he said nothing, but she saw the apology in his face, and something else—a look she couldn't quite place.

"You do not mean to eat," he said at last. He set the food aside.

She couldn't speak. Her lips moved without sound, and she sagged against the side of the bench.

"Perhaps you do not mean to live," he said more quietly, pulling back. Was that sorrow she sensed in his voice? Disappointment? He tensed as if to stand, then changed his mind. "I do not blame you. I would... want the same, if..." He trailed off, unable to finish. He sat with her for longer than he needed to, perhaps wanting to say more.

He didn't have to. Rubriel recognized that expression well enough, the pain in his eyes, the hopelessness.

"I will tell you... what I would tell myself, if I could go back." She forced the words from her throat. The voice of a ghost - or close to one. "You can... choose... another way. There are always... other paths, even when you cannot... see them."

"But I will not," he croaked, fighting the unwelcome feelings stirring inside him.

She spluttered, struggling to stay conscious. "I think... you are a good man, inside. You deserve a better life. A world... without the shadow of fear, without..." She gasped. "Remember..."

She fell into coughing then, the conversation taking its toll; rough, painful tremors that shook her whole body.

And it took every ounce of willpower Muldeve possessed to turn his back and leave her like that.

"I won't risk it."

Muldeve paced the living area of his house. His wife rested her palms on the back of an armchair, a mixture of disapproval and sympathy in her sharp features.

"It's not *worth* the risk. She's just-"

"What *is* she to you, Muldeve?"

He stopped and faced her. "What is she to any of us? She is supposed to be the enemy. The broken valves, the flooding, the fire in the warehouse - that was all her doing. But I saw her fight in the arena. I saw her rally those people and hold more power than the overseers, even in the moment of her defeat. How can anyone be so broken and so strong at the same time? How can-"

He swallowed, the sudden wave of emotion surprising them both. It was unlike him to speak of such things. In all his years as High Warden - and as a lesser warden before that - he had never come home to vent like this. It frightened him to say what he admitted next. "I have never seen a person endure so much, yet somehow still find a shred of good in this world."

He lowered his voice. "She told me I deserve a better life, that there are always other paths to choose, whether we see them or not. That is not our way, but I *believed* her, Lucillia. Maybe that makes me the fool, to be led astray so easily. But I cannot stop imagining that maybe..." He faltered, falling into the armchair with his head in his hands.

"Do it," Lucillia said quietly.

He twisted to look up at her, his face stricken. He shook his head. "She's dying, and... it is not worth the risk. If I were caught, if there was even a whisper of suspicion, if another of the wardens thought to advance their position by exposing me... You know what would happen. I will not take that chance."

"Your guilt is written all over you. The earth itself moves against us; people are tired, afraid, and fed up. The guilt of doing nothing will condemn us as surely as your physical betrayal would, sooner or later."

She leaned forward to whisper in his ear.

"Do it."

"Why?" He frowned.

"Because I've imagined it too."

30

Luck for the Ill-Fated

She could not count the hours or perhaps days that passed while she slipped in and out of consciousness, her waking moments brief and sometimes delusional. She imagined several times that someone came to get her, but each time she forced her eyes open to find the cell empty and silent.

Finally, she heard real footsteps approaching from outside. The door opened and a strong pair of hands grabbed her and dragged her out into the hallway. It wasn't Muldeve. Only when they reached the door of the bathing room did she catch a look at the stern-faced woman, whom she had never seen before. The woman said nothing; only stripped off Rubriel's filthy, bloodstained clothing and pointed at the tub, already full of lukewarm water. Clothes hung off large racks standing upright against the walls. Some were dripping.

Is this a laundry or a bathroom? she thought numbly as she half-climbed, half-fell into the water.

The woman cussed at the splash she made, grabbing a brush and roughly scrubbing her from head to toe, paying no heed to the blackened bruising that covered most of her upper body, or the angry, swollen flesh of her fractured wrist. Rubriel sat rigid through it all, gritting her teeth against the pain, thinking that she would very much like to knock some manners into this cruel woman, who made no effort to hide her resentment of playing handmaiden to a prisoner.

"Get out," the woman barked.

Rubriel grasped the edge of the tub, or tried to. Her maimed left hand would not obey. She heaved, but she could not lift her own weight over the edge. The woman snatched for her injured forearm and carelessly yanked; Rubriel made a sound halfway between a growl and a yelp and lunged towards her, knocking the woman onto her backside and sending a wave of dirty water flooding over the rim of the tub.

"Bitch!" the woman shrieked, crabbing backwards as the water soaked her and Rubriel tumbled onto the floor. She made to lash out again, but Rubriel scrambled behind one of the racks, knocking it over. It hit the woman on the bridge of the nose and she fell back, dazed.

"Get your hands off me," Rubriel growled. Her arm throbbed. She grabbed a cloth to dry herself off and spied a fresh set of plain grey clothing by the door, which she put on shakily; running on desperate, borrowed energy. On impulse, she wrapped her corset back on over the top, struggling to fasten the busk one-handed. She would've done away with it, except that the support took some of the strain off her injuries and helped with the pain a little.

The dull, worn skirt was too loose on her; she made to pull the cord tighter across her too-thin abdomen. That's when she felt it. A lump, an object. There. Flat and hard inside the waistband, but most definitely there. She pulled her hand away quickly. Could it be...?

There was a heavy pounding on the door.

"Time's up, Ashyn," said an impatient male voice. "What is going on in there?" He pounded on the door again before two of them came barging right in, surveying the chaos in the room with disgust.

Rubriel only glared at them as they looked from her, to the wet floor, to the woman moaning against the wall and clutching a bleeding nose.

"You are a fool, Ashyn," the second man scowled, not bothering to assist.

"You!" he demanded of Rubriel. "You are wanted in the Great Hall. Come." They grabbed her arm in arm and hauled her out of the room.

Her heart beat faster and faster as she pieced together what had just happened, silently praising Muldeve for his cleverness and subtlety. If he had truly returned her milestone, now all she needed was to be alone long enough to use it. Ironically, what she needed now was the dank solitude of her cell, but they were marching her in the opposite direction.

She stumbled up the four flights of stairs, her captors practically carrying her most of the way, and she dreaded what was at the top far more than usual, because now she had a *new* secret. One that she was determined to keep at all costs.

There were no lights in the Great Hall, save the two ever-burning fireplaces on each wall and the glowing crystal veins snaking through the black stone underfoot. The chandelier that fell in the earthquake had been removed and swept clear, but not replaced. The huge, reinforced door, however, had somehow been lifted back onto its hinges, and it opened of its own accord to admit them.

They dragged her weak and breathless into the room and dropped her at the base of the dais. She landed awkwardly, her fractured wrist not able to support her weight, and she clutched it against her body as she fought back a fresh wave of pain and dizziness.

"I have news for you."

Zildred stood atop the dais where he had not been a moment before. She made no reaction. She rarely spoke to him these days; not when he could extract from her thoughts whatever reply he wished.

"The earthquake caused considerable damage to the central plateau. Much of the old mining village in the area was demolished by landslides, and the abandoned buildings set into the mountainside finally collapsed. It seems your fellowship of Bantrian spies is no more."

He took a step towards her. Two.

She swallowed and slowly raised her head to confront him. "You're lying," she said. "My friends will have left Langlythe by now. They could not stay for me; it has been too long. You said so yourself."

"Everything I have told you is true," he snapped. "There is nothing for you to go back to."

"Go back?" she said, a little too quickly. Surely he didn't know already...?

But he made no further response. Instead, he circled around behind her and prised her injured arm away from her chest, his fingers like a cold iron band against her swollen flesh.

How did that happen? he asked directly into her thoughts, and she involuntarily recalled that fateful day in the arena, the overseer's spiked mace slamming up into the underside of her wrist with sickening force.

She cried out and jerked away, feeling it again just as acutely in the present as she had then. He studied her a while longer. Had he the ability to wear an expression, she was sure it would have been a deep frown. He flashed through her memory again, rapidly, the way one might flick through a stack of papers looking for something in particular.

She could not glean what he was looking for, however, and the torrent of images rushing past made her world spin such that she lost her balance. Even as his pace began to slow she dared not try to open her eyes, for it seemed the universe had tilted on its axis and she could not tell up from down.

Gradually, he brought the engine of her mind to a stop, but did not relinquish control. He wiped it clear of thoughts and held her in emptiness as he spoke once again.

You carry a shard of pure ludion inside you, yet I see no evidence of you having channeled its energy, voluntarily or otherwise. You have had ample opportunity - and reason - to do so.

She did not know what he meant, or what he expected her to have done, but - horrifyingly - she lacked the ability even to convey *that*; his hold on her mind was so tight she couldn't access it to form thoughts of her own. She winced at his hand on her chest, pressing lightly over where the stone was buried. Pain lanced through her ribs. Underneath, a strange coldness radiated from within her core. It seemed to slide through thickly, roughly, stinging the inside of her veins like coarse, icy sand.

Her body fought it even if her mind could not. Every inch of her seemed to constrict as she rejected the dark, foreign energy, but the pressure only increased as Zildred ruthlessly drove it further and further in. She cried out in agony, convulsing and writhing on the floor, but he wouldn't stop, and she was breaking, breaking...

Suddenly, she regained some measure of control over her own mind. She slammed her will against the power that gripped her. She could isolate the feeling of his consciousness threaded through and around hers and she clawed at it, tore at it harder than ever. *You can't break me!* she screamed mind to mind and knew he felt it. *I will die before you make me anything other than myself!*

At that moment, her body seemed to give out. The convulsions stopped. Her lungs turned to stone. She struggled fitfully to draw breath until the pain disappeared and even the desperation for air faded away. There was nothing to feel at all, save the blanket of energy that engulfed her fully and held her very still, and she knew that she was dying; her spirit destined to reside in Imul'dene forever like all the others.

But then she was awake, and coughing violently; not one but two mage healers leaning over her as a great lump of dark, clotted blood spilled from her upon the floor.

"The bleeding has stopped, for now," she heard one of them say, "but the damage is severe and it may easily start again."

"It is enough," Zildred replied. "Mend her wrist as well. Then you may go."

They worked a while longer, easing away the swelling and knitting the fractured bones back together, sealing the skin over the top until all that remained was a thick white scar on the underside of her wrist. They hustled from the hall, leaving Rubriel where she lay, Zildred looking down at her as though she were an object of some perplexity.

"Many will say they would rather die, but very few will see it done," he said, and Rubriel thought that none could tolerate such a painful proceedings, even if they were agreeable to it. She had not the strength to say as such, so her thoughts remained her own, for once.

She could make little sense of it all. He had almost killed her this time, yet he spared her - again - and went so far as to summon healers to tend her, though they treated only the bare minimum to keep her alive. They continued to check on her over the hours that followed. She did not understand what made her worth the trouble, after all the hateful things she'd done and every last scrap of intelligence already drawn from her memory, that he still sought to imbue her with the ludion's energy and make of her something more. Had she not long since served her purpose here?

She slept fitfully, plagued by the sharp, twisted versions of reality that had become her constant companion. She felt the hardness of the milestone under her, still lodged safely inside the waistband of her skirt. A fine help that had turned out to be! She wondered if it would still work if the abandoned buildings at the other end had collapsed in the earthquake and destroyed the brazier. Perhaps it would only serve to trap her beneath a mound of earth and debris. She considered bitterly if that might still be an improvement over the current situation.

It mattered not; she could not use the milestone in the Great Hall. They never left her truly unattended, minded by spirits or human door guards if not by Zildred himself, and even if she were to somehow grasp the stone and hold it aloft without catching the eye of her observers, it was not enough just to think the inducing words; she would have to speak them aloud, convincingly and without interruption. If someone was to grab her before she finished, it would transport them with her.

She remained curled on her stomach, her arms folded beneath her to keep her chest raised off the floor. It was the only way she could breathe, as though her lungs were still filled with lead and crushing her. The effort of that alone was exhausting.

She dreamed again, this time of a place she did not know - a great city built of bricks and shingles. From a mossy rooftop she looked down over tree-lined streets and saw a face she recognized amidst the throng of people meandering about their day. It was Scoe, and this was Esmara, she thought - or at least how her feverish brain imagined Esmara to look, since she had never been there.

She wanted to call out to him, but the sun blazed down from above, too bright and too scorching. She shielded her eyes and retreated, until shadows surrounded and engulfed the brilliant green of those foreign streets.

Now she was back in Langlythe, but a part she did not recognize. A pedestal stood before her, holding a twisted glass cylinder half filled with grey sand. Its base was hung with red drapery and surrounded by a carpet of brilliant red flowers - *flowers!* - their petals soft and thick like crushed velvet. No such plant could grow in that blighted earth, yet here they were, a stark contrast against all that blackness.

She looked up and saw to her amazement that the sky was clear. The emerald lights had lifted and snow fell from a veil of soft white cloud. It was impossibly beautiful. She wanted to stay in that dream, feeling the snowflakes kiss her face with the tiniest brush of cold. But the euphoric calm soon fell away and she woke again, her eyelids fluttering open to see only the black stone of the Great Hall's floor and its crystal veins glowing demurely.

Food had been left there in case she found the strength to eat; some kind of gravy or broth. Her stomach had no desire for it. Instead, she reached feebly for her milestone. Perhaps if she just held it, perhaps...

There were spirits in the room, and they stirred at her movement. She felt a moment of envy for them, how they floated and drifted lightly, feeling nothing; though of course they had no real freedom here. Maybe she would yet become a spirit herself.

Abruptly, she jostled fully lucid. Cold enveloped her as Zildred wrenched her upright from behind, a hand at her throat holding her rigid.

You must not starve, he scolded her.

Leave me alone, she returned weakly. She choked and struggled, trying feebly to unlatch his fingers.

To her surprise, he slackened off after a moment. He pulled the bowl of brown-coloured gravy towards her. *Eat, Rubriel.*

The command rattled through her. She hesitated, not wanting to reach for the bowl but finding it difficult not to.

I have better things to do than force feed you, or send my best healers up here just to keep you alive, he said into her mind.

You made me like this! Either kill me or heal me properly, and perhaps I will be less of an inconvenience! But she shuddered and conceded, shakily taking up bowl and spoon. She wolfed down the meal as rapidly as she could. She didn't know what she was eating; just wanted it gone so that he would leave her. *Let go,* she urged again.

As you wish. He released her.

She lacked the strength to support herself and crumpled against the side of the throne. Her breath came shallow and rapid, aching bitterly against each inhalation.

Zildred lingered beside her a moment longer before he turned to walk away. "You will not find respite in death, Rubriel," he said aloud. "Your spirit will not pass beyond the Weave, but remain here and serve with the rest. Better to live, and grow powerful."

Rubriel's whisper was barely audible even in the silent room. "Why? Why would you give me power to rival yours? I would challenge you... if I could. You must know that." Talking made her cough, sending a piercing lance of pain through her chest.

"You will aid me in taking the Eastern Continent."

"But you already have my knowledge," she rasped. "What more..."

He paused, as though deciding whether or not to elaborate.

"Knowledge of places, and of the land; its strengths and weaknesses, yes. But those people know you and will welcome you back to live among them as a hero, escaped from Imul'dene after a daring sabotage. Their leadership will listen to you now, even look to you for counsel. What better position from which to bring about their downfall?"

"Whatever ills I suffered in Tunswick, it is not enough to warrant that. I will never turn on them." She ground out the words as forcefully as she could against the frailty of her own voice.

"That will not be your choice to make," he said quietly.

Rubriel backed away, frightened. He never spoke to her like this; had never once answered her questions, nor conversed with her aloud as an equal might. There was no malice left in his voice, no further reproach. The candidness with which he spoke was somehow more frightening than his usual admonishment. He bent down to her and released the chain from around her waist.

"You do not understand the true nature of Iudion and that which afflicts you," he said. "Come, I will show you."

He picked her up, sweeping her up off the floor in one fluid movement. She yelped and hung limply, too weak and too shocked to struggle as he carried her through that mysterious door to the left of the throne and into the dark passage beyond.

She'd thought about that door often enough, the one that never seemed to be used, wondering if it might hold some form of escape. There were no windows or crystal lamps to light the way. The steep, tightly curved stone staircase went up and up and up, and she soon grew disoriented as they climbed higher and higher into the uppermost reaches of the citadel; the spire they called the Tower of Longing.

A trapdoor flung open of its own accord with a thud. Cold air rushed in and scoured a path through her aching lungs. She shivered. The world spun. So high–it was so impossibly high. The air seemed too thin, the emerald forks that lit up the sky much too close. The tower's circular roof space felt much too small against the vast, open view of the city and lands far beyond, its hip-height walls not secure enough to stop her from falling into the abyss. Her dizziness made it worse. She couldn't get enough air.

Zildred put her down and she collapsed under her own weight. He pulled her upright again, pinning her against the wall.

Look to the southeast, he told her.

Far out on the horizon, beyond the Plains of Kalakat that lay between Imul'dene and the Jagged Labyrinth, the dark prominence of the Lone Peak could be seen where it touched the sky.

Morkile-ne-Nect is the oldest and most concentrated source of dark energy in the world. The energy within is self-sustaining, and its sphere of influence enfolds the entire country. The land and all who dwell here are touched by it, altered by it.

Rubriel found her gaze unwillingly transfixed upon the distant shape of the ludion; its horrible, endless darkness drawing her in. She could not turn away. It pulled and tugged at her as though she were connected to it, and it would not let go...

The shard of ludion inside you is no different. Its energy persists in your blood as an elementalist's raw energy is carried by theirs. Whether in years, or perhaps months from now, you will indeed become my equal - but at the expense of your free will. You will never have the freedom of mind to challenge me. The ludion remains connected to its original creator - and you with it. He peeled her gaze from the distant peak and sank with her onto the floor.

Darkness engulfed her. She trembled with fear.

I cannot wait for the stone's influence to change you over time. I will spare you the slow torment and finish it at once.

She felt it already - the ache in her chest grew bolder and thin slivers of icy pain began to radiate through her torso. His hand pressed down on her sternum and she struggled to dislodge him, finding that she did not have the strength to do so. *I will not survive,* she thought desperately.

You will, he returned softly. *You will...*

The shard seemed to bite into her. She cried out. *No, no,* she begged. *Zildred, please...*

There was no compassion in him at all; he did not care for her pleas, or her pain. But he was also a master of his craft, holding back just enough so as not to exceed her threshold of tolerance and push her any closer to death.

The pain came in waves, freezing her from the inside out. Tears sprang to her eyes and rolled down her pale cheeks. The energy stung in her veins like a thousand needles piercing all over her body and she wished only for it to end, all the while a strange pressure building in her core, as though her very essence was being compacted and crushed.

It was worse than before; worse, because she could *feel* the dark energy taking root, and she was terrified of it - terrified that she would become the thing she hated most - that she would be an agent of the same destruction she fought so hard to prevent. The pressure within became unbearable. Something *cracked* inside her.

There was an explosion of light, an audible snap, and energy of a different kind burst from her.

Zildred dropped her and backed away as though scalded by its brightness. Rubriel gasped and threw herself towards the wall, managing to get a leg up and heave herself onto it. On her knees, she spun, turning her back to the sheer drop below. Her fingers found the cool, flat surface of the milestone hidden inside her waistband.

"You cannot escape your fate."

She gripped her milestone fiercely and met his faceless stare with defiance.

"Today I will," she growled, and threw herself backwards off the tower.

She spoke the words of induction as she plummeted towards the earth. Bright light engulfed first her outstretched hand, then her whole body, mere moments before she hit the ground. And then she was gone.

31

Reunion

A loud crackling from the brazier drew Grace's attention from where she sat, mending a hole in the sleeve of her dress. She leapt to her feet with a start.

"Uncle?"

The flames swelled higher and roared. A bright light blinded Adam as he rushed through the doorway to see a human figure materialize on the floor, her outstretched arm still clutching the used milestone high towards the ceiling.

"Rubriel!"

Molindra heard him and pushed past before he could say more, flying to Rubriel's side.

She lay there rigid; her glazed eyes wide with shock and panic, the spent milestone clutched so tightly that her knuckles were white and her arm was shaking.

"Rubriel, are you alright?" Mol said. "What has happened?"

Rubriel didn't seem to notice her.

"Look at me," Mol urged, taking her shoulder and shaking her a little. "Look where you are."

This time she *did* see, and a look of startled recognition came over her. "Mol, how? You cannot..." Then she fell into a fit of coughing and gasping, such that her whole body convulsed with it.

"Oh my goodness!" Mol took one look at the speckles of fresh blood that escaped her and panicked. "Rubriel, what's wrong? Tell me! Tell me so I can help."

But Rubriel couldn't speak, and she flinched at Mol's hand upon her back. By now, Scoe, Daelin and Dornir had all gathered around.

"Heal her, Molindra," Scoe said urgently.

"I'm not sure how!" Grappling to recall knowledge from her brief months of training, she found in her panic that she couldn't remember any of it.

"She can't breathe!" Adam said impatiently.

"Hurry."

Breathing. Air. Yes, she could do that. She shut her eyes tight and blocked out their cajoling, focusing instead on getting clean air in and out of Rubriel's lungs. She thought she met resistance, and remembered that she knew how to staunch a bleeding vessel or quell inflammation without having to see it or understand the cause. With her focus on soothing the airways, Rubriel's ragged gasps calmed and evened out. Her eyes blinked and moved from one anxious face to another, as though seeing them properly for the first time.

She glanced at the milestone still clenched in her fist and said, "I am really here, and you are all here, though... There was an earthquake and this place collapsed. I do not understand."

"Not all of it collapsed," Scoe said. "Molindra was able to hold the earth above us intact, though the way in and out is blocked and we have been trapped in here since. How did you know about that?"

"You have been gone a long time. We kept the brazier lit for you, but feared the worst when Scoe came back and you did not," said Grace. She didn't mention they had been about to leave when the place collapsed.

"Scoe, you were wounded," Rubriel suddenly remembered. "Are you alright?"

"I was, but it has healed just fine. That was three months ago."

"And Mol... How can you be here?"

Molindra looked down at her palm, where the long diagonal scar ran across. "I was exiled under blood oath, to find you and atone for my sins by halting the war I helped to create. I did not come through the Gloaming Pass, but via another passage further north, and crossed the main road right before the army spilled into the plains. I was too late on both counts." Her tone of regret brought a deep silence to the group, the gravity of their situation laid heavily upon them.

"Alright, give her some space," Adam said, standing. "Rubriel needs to rest, and we must not burden her with our troubles when she likely has a great many of her own."

Mol glared at him resentfully.

Scoe carried her into another room. The far corner collapsed into nothing but a pile of rubble, but the other held a bed of sorts, with clean blankets and a thin pillow. Rubriel settled onto it gratefully. Grace brought in a pitcher of drinking water and set it beside the bed. They retreated to let her sleep, except Mol, who lingered a moment longer, uncertain.

As their only option for a healer, she knew she would need to examine her condition more thoroughly, but she was afraid Rubriel would blame her all over again and send her away, and even more afraid that she would die during the night, and all that needed to be said between them would remain unspoken forever. But she did turn to leave, reluctantly, for there was nothing more to be done at present.

"Mol," Rubriel whispered.

Mol looked back anxiously. Their eyes met across the room.

"Stay."

She let out a sob and ran to the bedside. "I've missed you so much."

Rubriel embraced her with some difficulty, flinching a little. "I've missed you too. I wasn't there for you - not in the way you needed. I am sorry."

"You were always there for me," Mol countered, sobbing. "Even when I was behaving like a hot-headed lunatic. And you were usually right. I should have listened to you."

"Not this time," Rubriel said sadly. "I was blind and self-righteous and I could not see what really mattered. But I have seen terrible things since you left - I have... caused... terrible things. I judged you harshly, but I am no better myself."

"Rubriel, I love you. You are a sister to me - the only real family I have. There is nothing I cannot forgive. Nothing!"

Rubriel smiled weakly through her tears - stiffly, as though the muscles in her face had forgotten the movement. She wanted to say more, to tell Mol they would start over with all forgiven, but the sharpness in her chest stopped her and she lay back, very still. Mol watched over her anxiously, disappearing only briefly to fetch her own blanket and a chair from the other room. She slept fitfully, but Mol could not, for the sound of Rubriel's laboured breathing frightened her terribly and kept her awake.

They were disturbed in a few hours by the sounds of cooking from the other room; Grace would be preparing some broth out of what little supplies they had left. Rubriel jerked awake and sat up, then caught sight of Mol beside her and blinked confusedly for a moment before she fell back into the pillow. "Sorry," she muttered.

"It was bad, wasn't it."

Rubriel said nothing. Her sunken eyelids held a glazed, haunted look; the look of one who had knocked on the very door of death and found even that pathway barred to them.

"I will need to examine you properly. I know some healing techniques, but I did not have much time to study the more complex aspects of diagnostics and treatment. I will need you to tell me where it hurts, how it happened - I will heal as much as I can. I promise."

Rubriel swallowed hard. "Thank you."

Mol frowned, deeply concerned at the change in her. Only a few hours ago she had seemed... exhausted and weak, yes, but relieved too and pleased to see them all. Now it was just a shell of her friend lying there, as though something consumed her from within. "Will you have some breakfast? There isn't much left, but it is hot at least."

Rubriel just shook her head.

"Alright," Mol said suddenly, pulling the blankets down to her waist.

"What are you - doing?" Rubriel spluttered in protest.

"I need you to talk to me, but you can hardly speak at all and your chest rattles and heaves like an old bellows. You would tell me to get on with it, and figure it out for myself; so I will do exactly that, but do not hate me for healing only what I can see. I cannot know everything that befell you just by-"

Mol stopped short of what she had been about to say, because it was suddenly all too obvious. "You weren't just locked away somewhere, were you? You knew about the earthquake, you knew Scoe had been injured - because Zildred showed you. I'm sorry; I should have guessed. He only did that to me once, but I have never forgotten how awful it felt to have my mind violated like that, even briefly."

"I... fought him," said Rubriel. "The effort nearly killed me. I wasn't strong enough."

"I have no doubt that you did, and to your own detriment. Three of your ribs are broken and not healing properly, because the bones are misaligned. I can mend them, but I shall need Grace's help. It is going to hurt, I'm afraid."

Mol grimaced. The bone shafts hadn't pierced the skin, but she could see through the bruising that they were not straight. Grace would have to hold them in place while she knit them together.

"Actually..."

"Hmm?"

"That was a bull."

Mol blinked. The remark took her completely by surprise. "What?"

"A bull's tusk. It charged. I did not get out of the way fast enough."

"Oh Rubriel." She sighed. "How on earth was there a bull involved?" But she smiled too, for that was a little of the old Rubriel showing through.

"Scarlet Arena." She shut her eyes tight and shuddered at the memory of that fateful day. She could still hear the riots, the screaming...

Grace appeared in the doorway. "I heard my name. Did you call for me?"

"In a bit," said Mol. "We should have some of whatever you're cooking first."

They sipped watery broth and talked a little, until they could put it off no longer. Grace fetched some clean water and cloth. Molindra tried her hardest to reassure Rubriel that everything would be fine, when really she was more terrified of performing the procedure than Rubriel was of receiving it. It was painful, it was messy, and somewhat unorthodox with Mol apologizing repeatedly throughout, Rubriel telling her to get on with it, and Grace acting the most calm and nurse-like of them all, but they managed it.

They mended her ribs, though not at all tidily, and she had three knuckle-like protrusions of misshapen bone to show for it. Nevertheless, the pain subsided considerably after that, with the swelling gone and most of the bruising healed; though she still coughed and shuddered in doing so.

She slept long and deeply when they had finished. Mol was relieved to see it, though it left her with too much time to think.

Do not waste away over what could've, should've been, Scoe had wisely warned, but how could she avoid feeling that what happened to Rubriel was her fault? It had been her decision to go to Langlythe; Rubriel had been strongly opposed, but followed her there anyway out of fear and fierce loyalty that she had not truly appreciated until now. She had been the one to set off the flood and find the key to the World Gate, but it was Rubriel who went back to make things right.

"Mol."

She looked up.

"What are you thinking about?"

"It is my turn to sit and brood."

She sighed, stretching her legs out in front of her. "I was found guilty and I deserved my punishment; yet somehow you still paid the greater price. It isn't fair."

"I made choices too," Rubriel said gently, "and had others make them for me. I went back to Langlythe and spread chaos in Imul'dene at Elder Berren's behest. I didn't want to. I wanted to run - to get away from it all and I felt cowardly for wanting that, but I did not think it was my fight. The Elder made me believe I had no other choice. And honestly... I do not think it is all that different from... from how Zildred manipulated you into retrieving the key from the Roof of the World."

Horrified by her own words, she searched her friend for reassurance. "Oh Mol, is it terrible of me to say that?"

"I think the Elder did what he believed was best on a larger scale, as a leader must, but unfortunately, he did so at your expense. It probably was not an easy decision for him, having known you all your life," Mol replied thoughtfully.

Rubriel still looked troubled.

"What?"

Rubriel tried to put into words what had happened in Imul'dene, everything she had seen and re-lived, yet with an altered perspective that continued to play tricks on her. There was not a single memory she could recall without questioning its accuracy, or her own interpretation of it, and trying to understand what it all meant was exhausting.

Mol was a good listener, as hard as it was to hear. "I'm so sorry. And I feel stupid saying that because it is both unhelpful and woefully inadequate as a response. It is tearing me apart to see you like this."

Rubriel swallowed and reached out to hold her hand. "It tore me apart when they took you away." Her voice was thick with emotion. "I never even asked you for your side of the story. We travelled side by side all the way from the Roof to Celessil and I never reached out, not once. Out of everything I regret that the most. Please, Mol; tell me everything."

They talked for hours over the days that followed, in between periods of rest at Mol's insistence, and their ongoing but futile attempts to dig their way out of the collapsed tunnel. Every so often, a minor tremor would shift the stone a little, giving everyone a renewed determination to break through; they would dig and pound against the blockage with gusto, dislodging a bit more of the rock each time, until they once again reached a solid unyielding mass and gave up.

"If it were dirt, I could manipulate it; moisten it so it is easier to dig out," Molindra had explained to the frustrated group. "But I cannot work with these solid rocks. Only a kinetic could lift or push them out of the way."

"What we need is a few decent pickaxes," said Dornir.

"Or a massive earthquake," Daelin added unhelpfully, "although that would be just as likely to collapse the rest of this place on top of us."

"This is an old mining village; one would think there might be a few lying around in here somewhere. But no - at least not anywhere we can reach."

Nevertheless, the mood lightened considerably, despite the grim situation. Aided by Mol's healing, Rubriel recovered remarkably quickly. They fell back into an easy companionship. Not at all the worse for their time apart, they mused over tales and old memories and found the strings of humour in it all between the trials.

The cavern sang with their infectious laughter. Even Adam and Grace found their spirits lifted, baffled as they were; as though they sat on the fringes of some great joke just outside their reach, the only option to laugh along and be merry for reasons they couldn't fathom.

Molindra beamed with contentment, her cheeks flushed and eyes bright. She seemed older, too, Rubriel thought; older and more centred. The trust and respect they had for one another deepened by the day, and this unlikely happiness they created between them was a better tonic than any magic or medicine she'd ever tasted. Their rations were stretched so thinly it could scarcely be considered a meal, but fresh water remained plentiful enough thanks to the well, and Rubriel drank deeply at Mol's insistence that it would speed her recovery.

She stretched regularly, gently exercising to rebuild her strength. She made good progress with her sword arm. Her left hand, unfortunately, remained weak due to partial loss of movement in the outer two fingers.

They spent long hours sitting and talking while Mol massaged away her aches, plotting their journey home and other far less practical things, too. How they would sail to Esmara with Scoe to attend his wedding to Lady Morgrian, Rubriel dreaming up a feast of all kinds of full flavoured foods while Gwendolen played love songs and Mol kept the weather sunny and perfect.

How they would demand their compensation from Vesner - and then some - and build an academy of their own for underprivileged mages, where Mol would train anyone who wished it whether they had coin or not, and in exchange the students would work on tasks Rubriel set out for them between their studies. She could run almost any business venture she liked this way, they decided.

Never mind Mol's banishment, or that the entire scheme went completely against Bantrian law, or that the country was deep in its preparations for war. Those were some of the happiest days either of them could recall.

They were asleep when the earthquake came again, bolder this time and more frightening, as a new crack opened up across the ceiling and down one of the walls. The cave integrity continued to hold - for now - as did the pile of rocks blockading them in, though the first thing they did as the shaking eased was run to see if the rubble had shifted any.

Disgruntled, Adam sent them all back to bed for a while longer.

Molindra returned to check on Rubriel and found her sitting bolt upright on the mattress, backed into the corner and staring into space.

"Rubriel?"

She broke out of her trance, wide eyed and startled. Her reaction was pure instinct, and after a few moments she blinked and caught Molindra's shocked expression.

"I'm sorry." She slumped back into the mattress, pressing her forehead into the pillow and taking several heaving breaths.

"I didn't mean to frighten you," said Mol apologetically. "Shall I get you some broth? There's a few drops left."

"Not yet."

Molindra frowned. "Aren't you starving?"

"Not for lack of trying." She made a sound halfway between a cough and a snort.

"*Trying* to starve? Oh, do not say that, Rubriel! That is a terrible notion!"

"I gave up, Mol. I couldn't... I wanted it to end."

Mol knelt beside her and squeezed her hand. "But you got out, alright? Your time in Imul'dene is over, and as soon as we break through the rubble, you're getting right out of Langlythe too. You need your strength."

But Rubriel only leaned back and sighed heavily - a sigh which caught in her chest and set her coughing again.

Mol shuddered in sympathy, worried and sad and suddenly fearful as a haunted, faraway look took hold of her friend. Her eyes seemed to darken to a stormy grey, and her face hollowed with grief. She seemed not to see Mol at all for a long moment, until at last she gulped and swallowed with it the truth she could not yet bear to utter, as though giving voice to it would make it real.

She tried to shut out everything Zildred had said. It would do no good to dwell on his words, spoken only to feed her despair and manipulate her for his own purposes. Yet she did not think he was lying about the ludion eventually consuming her. She got the impression their mind to mind exchanges worked both ways; it had been impossible for her to conceal the truth from him, but she also thought that he could not lie to her either, that she would have sensed an untruth as easily as he did.

Mol stared at her like she was possessed.

"I'm alright now," she said, as the ground beneath them trembled again, and the men rushed to the entrance to push and heave once more. A whoop of triumph echoed through the chamber.

"A breeze! Fresh air!" Adam's triumphant whoop rang through the caverns. "We are beginning to break through. Have at it, fellows; this tremor may have loosened it enough."

"See?" cried Mol. "We are almost out! A little longer and we can leave this place for good. I will lead us to one of the smaller tunnels through the mountains. There is one straight to the east; where the Gloaming Mountains meet the Ice Divide. It is empty apart from gloom spirits, which would sound problematic except I learned they are not *human* spirits; they fear light and are completely blinded by it. As long as we light the way, they will not attack us, nor recognize us as enemies. Adam, Grace and Scoe can go home, and we..."

She grew serious for a moment. "My sentence is for life. I can never return to Celessil, and if I was discovered in Bantria I would likely be killed. But there are wild lands to the east where neither will ever look for me. You will make a living more easily in Celessil than you did in Tunswick, and at least we can see each other. I am not sure how long my lifespan will be since I renounced my sildion gift, but I am only forty. We will still have time."

"I'm... not sure I do, Mol."

"What do you mean?"

Mol's face fell as she noticed something that had eluded her until now. "Your pendant is missing too. Where is it?" She hesitated.

"It's gone. Destroyed. I know we were taught that sildion is indestructible," she added before Mol could interrupt. "I watched it disintegrate."

"What!? But... how? Why?"

"They thought I was channeling energy from it somehow. I told you how they ran tests on my blood over and over because they were convinced I was a mage. Turns out they were measuring something called 'conductivity', and I have the highest readings they had ever seen."

"I had that test too. I think all mages do in Langlythe. They can measure both raw energy potential and how much a person can use before reaching overexertion. But why destroy the pendant instead of simply taking it from you?"

"Equal and opposite," Rubriel murmured, almost to herself.

Mol's eyes searched her face, desperate for answers.

"I am sorry, Mol. There is something I have not yet told you. You said that you had to channel through a shard of ludion in order to open the vault at the Roof of the World..."

"I held both ludion *and* sildion at the same time. It made me feel physically ill." Mol shivered at the memory.

"I have a shard of ludion inside me," Rubriel said finally. "In the absence of any raw energy of my own, Zildred means for me to draw from ludion as he does. Eventually, I'll become like him and have as little control over my own actions as the spirits do. I am so sorry, Mol."

Her voice broke a little at the distress all over her friend's face. "I am not even sure I can follow you under the mountains. The gloom spirits will not see you in the light, but they will sense *me* and bring doom to us all. I should have told you before, but... we were together finally and at ease with each other, happy. I wanted us to enjoy those few days dreaming about the future, one last time."

Mol sank back and sagged against the wall, defeated. "Dreaming is all we have. All we ever had. There is no future in which we're both free."

"You may still be free someday. You are exiled from Celessil - and from Bantria by association - but there is nothing to stop you from taking to the seas. Find your way to the east coast. Set sail."

"You want me to become a pirate?"

"I think that rather suits you."

"No!" Mol sniffed, shaking her head vehemently. "I'm not going anywhere without you."

"Zildred will come for me sooner or later, and-"

"I'll kill him!" Mol raged. "I'll tear open the sky and turn the rain to fire! I'll... I'll-"

Rubriel rolled off the bed and crawled to where Mol sat on the floor. She put her arm around her shoulders and held her like that until they both ran out of tears.

"We will lead the others to the way out," Mol said slowly, her throat rough from crying.

Rubriel nodded. "We can do that much to help, at least."

"But when we get there, I will not go through. I am staying with you, no matter what happens." She cupped her forehead in her palms and tried to massage the heavy weight from her brow. Never in her life had she felt quite so defeated as she did then.

Rubriel said nothing. She conceded to Mol's desire to stay without objection, for in truth, there was nothing she wanted more.

Mol groaned and stood, pacing from one side of the small room to the other. "I did not think it would end like this. I really didn't."

"You were always the optimist of the two of us. I admired that about you; how you could wear your heart on your sleeve and always find something for which to be hopeful. It was your wild dreams for the future which kept me going. And I *didn't* resent you - you were never a burden. I knew you couldn't help it, but sometimes I was so tired and miserable that I lashed out. We lived in our dreamworld for too long and forgot to attend the present."

"Hindsight can be a curse. What good is it to learn where you went wrong if you do not get the chance to correct your mistakes?"

Rubriel frowned slightly.

Mol reached into her pocket and offered back the simple metal spiral, the twin ring to her own. She slid it back onto Rubriel's finger. "It is not over quite yet. We will show the others the way, and then we will fight back in whatever small way we can." She gasped as a tremor ran through the ground beneath them. Another aftershock.

They sat in silence for a few minutes, poised in case there was more shaking to come. When none came, Mol had an idea.

"I wonder if it is possible to climb right to the top of the Lone Peak, where the really huge ludion is," she thought aloud, a tangible shift in her tone from the heavy sorrow of earlier to the pensive, mischievous note she took on whenever she was plotting something.

Rubriel almost laughed. "The 'really huge ludion' is called *Mork-ile-ne-Nect* -and Mol, why oh why would we want to do that? It is the very last place on earth I wish to see up close."

"Because it is the centre. The spirits are different there. More solid, more *present*. Like it brings them closer to who they really are, or were when they were alive."

"It makes them stronger," Rubriel said doubtfully.

"Yes, but quite possibly more vulnerable, too. If they are more present, might that not also mean more affected by any energies directed at them?"

"Alright. Perhaps. But the spirits are still not going to help us, no matter how 'alive' they are. I doubt they have any free will at all, and I would've thought that being close to the 'centre', as you put it, would make the binding stronger, not weaker. You can't possibly mean to *fight* them... do you? I'm confused."

But Mol wasn't listening. She was on her feet, pacing again.

"I think that may apply to Zildred as well. No man made weapon can kill him - you've seen that already - but maybe the elements can under the right circumstances."

"I am not sure about that. You said you thought the mage Gal'denan would overthrow Zildred given the opportunity, but if he were capable of doing so, why betray you? He could have played that very differently."

And then it was her turn to stop and grow thoughtful. She didn't hear what Molindra said next. The pieces began to click into place, and she thought that maybe she understood something which had been bothering her for a while.

"Wait," she interrupted. Mol ceased her pacing and spun towards her, her eyes alive with hope and defiance. In that moment, Rubriel felt that her friend's wild spirit was the most beautiful thing she had ever seen. The ice inside her thawed a little. "I think I know what to do," she said, "but if I am wrong, this will end extremely badly."

"I think we are already signed up for a bad ending, so let's make the most of it, shall we?"

32

Wind and Fire

The tremors continued. The men took turns prying at the blockade with any tool they could find to lever rocks out of the way. Only the unmistakable signs of progress kept them going, for their bodies ached with the gruelling combination of physical effort and malnourishment. They could finally see through a small hole to the outside, and not a moment too soon. It had been days since they tasted anything more than weak mushroom broth.

While the tremors helped loosen more of the rubble, each one brought the renewed threat of further collapse. Molindra remained on guard, ready to step in and stabilize the cavern whenever the earth shuddered. With her left arm still weak, Rubriel busied herself with packing up anything they could use on their journey - blankets mostly, and a few crystal lamps for the passage under the mountains. She filled every pouch and bottle they had with water, for they would have to walk across empty plains for many miles before the next opportunity to refill them.

"What weapons do we have?" she asked of the group. "I lost mine in Imul'dene."

"Me too," said Scoe. "Fighting is unlikely to be our best option whatever the circumstances, but if we have no choice..."

She and Mol exchanged glances. They still hadn't told the others what they were planning.

Adam straightened from where he bent over the rubble, wincing as he did so. "Most of us still carry our knives, but that is all. We found a couple of old swords when we arrived here, but the blades were dull and pitted. I doubt they have seen use in over a hundred years."

"Show me," said Rubriel. "I may be able to improve them."

Adam opened his mouth and closed it again.

"I used to be a blacksmith, remember?"

His face contorted with the effort of picturing the pale, half-starved woman before him swinging a hammer over an anvil, until he shrugged and gestured for her to follow him. He walked stiffly, but his leg had vastly improved since Rubriel and Scoe first arrived, the limp now only subtle.

The swords were in bad shape, covered in dust and grime. All she could really do without the proper tools was clean and sharpen them, but they would have to do. She gave the heavier of the two to Scoe and kept the shorter, lighter one for herself. Guiding the blade through a few experimental moves proved stiff and awkward; the techniques she'd practiced for most of her life came sluggishly to her weakened body. She grimaced. Her slowness made her vulnerable, and the design of the pommel reminded her of Scarlet Arena.

"Rubriel?"

Molindra burst in to deliver the news, but stopped short when she caught Rubriel's troubled expression.

"I'm fine." She dismissed Mol's concern with a wave.

A triumphant whoop sounded from the cave entrance.

"I was coming to tell you that we have a hole big enough to crawl through. It is time to leave."

"That it is." Rubriel gave a firm nod. "I prepared what I could. We are as ready as we'll ever be."

"When are we going to tell them?"

"Soon." She drew close enough to whisper. "I worry that Scoe will try to follow us."

"He will see reason. He…" Mol swallowed. "He came to that conclusion himself, right before the earthquake. I was mad with him at the time for leaving you behind, but he was right in wanting to get out of here while we could."

"So the collapse really is the only reason they stayed," said Rubriel, taking on that haunted tone again as the hairs on the back of her neck stood up. "No. It does not matter." She shook herself out of it. "Let's go."

One at a time, they crawled through the tunnel painstakingly cleared through the blockade over many hours of hard labour. Daelin and Dornir went first, gasping with relief as a faint breeze ruffled their clothing.

"Ugh, it stinks!" said Daelin. "Never thought I would be so pleased to inhale that smell." The ground trembled again. "Quickly; get everyone through before something else collapses."

Adam went next, followed by Grace and Rubriel. Mol and Scoe brought up the rear, passing their meagre supplies to the other side before climbing through themselves.

"It does smell worse than I remember," Scoe agreed as they made their way downhill on unsteady legs.

Grace and Adam held onto each other for balance. Rubriel lunged to grab Mol's arm as she lost her footing and threatened to slide into a mud pit.

"Careful," Scoe warned.

Steam rose from the surface of the mud. A bubble burst in the middle every so often with a thick *plop*, like the stickiest molasses. The stench of sulphur was almost unbearable. Rubriel gagged on it.

"Hold up," Scoe called out to the twins, who led the way.

"I'm alright," she said. "Let's just get away from here."

They clung to the outskirts of the bog as best they could, taking the most direct route around the base of Mount Yel'ent and away from the central plateau. They hadn't gone much further when the twins stopped in their tracks.

"Crabs," Dornir said, almost salivating at the sight of them - many of them - leaving their pools and scurrying up onto dry rock.

"What are they doing?" Rubriel frowned. "There's so many of them."

The brothers were not about to let the crabs' odd behaviour get in the way of the first meat they'd tasted in weeks, and neither was Scoe. They rounded up as many as they could carry.

Adam assessed the situation. "We are all weary with hunger. As unpleasant as the bog may be, we are alone out here - and relatively safe. We would be wise to eat while we can."

No one saw fit to argue. They made for some dry ground at the top of a small rise, a tall rock sheltering them from the south.

"If only we could find some dry kindling," Grace moaned.

"I'll take care of it." Mol jumped in, eager to assist. She crouched and brought her hands together, close to the ground, igniting a small golden flame between her palms. Slowly she drew them apart, the flame growing larger as she did so, until they had a small campfire burning away on the bare rock all by itself.

They took turns at skewering a crab and holding it over the heat for as long as their patience permitted, then cracked open the shells and wolfed down the meat as though it were the best meal of their lives. Molindra ate last, and Rubriel made sure they saved her a larger helping. She said nothing, but Rubriel knew raw energy had to come from somewhere. Her expenditures on healing and holding out against the earthquakes would have cost her dearly without proper nourishment.

Scoe leaned back against the rock, gazing absently at the emerald swirls overhead. He closed his eyes. "I cannot wait to lie in an open field of grass, lush and green as far as the eye can see, and look up into a blue sky with the sun warming my face as I watch the clouds roll by."

Adam sympathized with a rare smile. "Aye, I could do with that."

"Soon," said Grace.

Daelin turned to Rubriel beside him. "Is the sky really blue where we're going?" he asked. His brows quirked in the middle.

"Yes," she said, yawning. "Unless it is nighttime, or very cloudy."

"And the grass... does not sound like the grass we have."

"Grass is everywhere, bright green."

"Like our sky?"

"Brighter. Richer than that." She closed her eyes and fell silent.

Daelin looked like he wanted to ask more but thought the better of it. He shared a befuddled glance with his brother.

They enjoyed a few moments of rest, knowing it may well be their last this side of the Gloaming Mountains. Adam groaned as he ushered them to their feet all too soon. Everyone wanted to be on the other side, but no one was keen to make the journey, fortified with crab meat or not. They trudged south, the sogginess underfoot retreating as they left the outskirts of the bog behind to be replaced by dust and dry rock. Darkness enfolded them, making their already frayed nerves all the more twitchy and irritable.

Dornir held up a hand. "Stop here a moment. There is a lookout spot not far, from where we can see down to the road. Daelin and I will scout ahead before we go further."

They huddled together between the rocks as the twins disappeared from view, fighting to stay awake. Their makeshift beds in the ruins already seemed a lifetime ago.

"We may have a problem."

Rubriel sat upright, reaching for her weapon.

"No - no one saw us," Dornir said quickly, "but soldiers march along the road as far as the eye can see, heading southwest. They stand between us and the Gloaming Pass."

"We are not aiming for the Gloaming Pass," Molindra reminded them. "We will skirt around them to the north instead. Langlythe's troops are not infinite in number; there must be an end to the army you saw."

He shook his head. "I could not see far enough to say. They are like a dazzling river of lights that plays tricks on the eyes."

"Just how far is this alternative pass, Molindra?" asked Adam.

"Do you know of Ashpul?"

He nodded.

"Our path lies to the northeast of there, almost directly east of our current location. Here," she said, handing Adam her compass. The needle spun wildly until the device settled in his palm, then swerved to point steadfastly east. She suppressed a small sigh of relief. "It is a difficult path, to be sure, but a discreet one."

As quietly as they could, they moved parallel to the road, keeping the ridge between themselves and the open plain below. From the lookout, they understood what Dornir meant; each soldier carried a celair from his belt, making the army appear from a distance as a glacier of tiny stars flowing slowly but inexorably from one side of the country to another.

"Rubriel... can you see where it ends?"

She peered into the distance, squinting beyond the lights to make out where the rows of human shapes ended. "No. It is too far. We will have to go a long way to cross behind them."

"We have no choice it seems. Keep moving," said Adam.

Sick with fear, they hurried on. Whatever time Scoe and Rubriel had bought Bantria to prepare for an invasion, it had run out. Hearts sank as they realized what no one dared to voice: *their trials thus far were only the beginning.*

A deep rumble tremored beneath them, reverberating in their bones. They froze. Transient aftershocks had become a regular occurrence, but this one kept on going, and the rumbling grew stronger. As if it were alive, the earth reared to throw them off their feet. They fell, grasping at one another and lunging for cover as loose stones tumbled down the hillside toward them. Grace shrieked as a sizeable rock narrowly missed her head.

"What is this?" Mol cried, her raised voice drowned out by the roar. "So much energy. I can't..."

A great boom shook the land. Streaks of fiery orange spouted forth into the sky from the summit of Mount Yel'ent, an immense cloud of thick smoke billowing and unfolding like a great, looming menace that shrouded the emerald aurora. A second explosion tore at the mountainside, the wall of its crater collapsing and falling in an avalanche of ash, mud and molten rock towards the plains.

"RUN!" Mol screamed. "Run!"

They took off blindly, lurching and stumbling away from the volcano as fast as their legs would carry them across the unstable earth, all thoughts of stealth forgotten as they fought to put as much distance between themselves and the path of the deadly landslide as they could. The ragged terrain forced them closer and closer to the road, but the army, realizing they spanned the lahar's path, had split in two, the two halves fleeing in opposite directions.

Ash fell from the sky as they came to a stop, breathing hard and wild with adrenaline. Lava painted the cone of the wounded peak like tracts of fiery blood weeping from the core of the earth. The crater's collapse took out most of the route they'd travelled and washed down over the road, debris spreading out over the dusty plains. They crouched numbly, able to do nothing but watch and thank their lucky stars they had managed to get far enough away before the eruption.

"I had only read of such events before now," Rubriel said to Mol. "It is almost as though this land is dying, like nature itself could end it all for us…" She grimaced.

Mol laid a healing hand on her back, willing her to stay strong.

"As luck would have it…"

Everyone turned to stare at Scoe. A half crazed smile washed over his face as he gazed towards their destination, the road now empty and silent. "Come on. We won't get a better opportunity than this."

Something in his voice renewed their spirits. They followed him down onto the plains, across the cobblestone road that had crawled with soldiers less than an hour ago. With the area deserted and surer footing, they made haste towards the mountain range. Swirling ash caught in their throats, leaving a bitter taste in their mouths and reducing visibility even further than normal, but for the Lone Peak on their left, standing solemn and stalwart as ever where its ludion touched the aurora, even as ash and smoke swallowed everything else.

They passed close to the Jagged Labyrinth, the ground sloping down to their left into its maze of rocky protrusions. Ahead, the dark border and its hidden tunnels beckoned them to relief. Rubriel and Molindra hung back. The group came to a stop.

"This… is where we part ways," Molindra said.

The others threw her a series of bewildered looks - all except Rubriel, whose face sagged with remorse.

"What do you mean, 'part ways'?" Adam grumbled. "We are still far from Bantria."

"I thought you were going to guide us through the caves?" Daelin quipped, displeased.

"The way through isn't far from here. Once you reach the mountains, turn south and follow it until you reach a staircase. It is very narrow, but once you climb it you'll have a view out over the plains, with Ashpul in the distance. The cave behind you is the way out. Follow it down into the wide open cavern with shallow water, then up onto a ledge and through its twists and turns until you find the exit. You have celairs from the ruins; the gloom spirits will not bother you so long as you wield the lights. That is your way home. But I am not going with you."

"And neither am I," Rubriel said softly.

"What!? But... why?" Scoe searched their faces, disbelief in his voice.

"We are bound for the Lone Peak," Mol continued, "to end it all. To challenge Zildred."

Daelin coughed. "Might you have inhaled a little too much ash? There are simply no adequate words in either language to express how badly that went last time."

"I had no idea what we were dealing with. Neither of us did," Rubriel said. "Now we do - and we know that none of this will truly stop while he remains in power."

"This is a suicide mission," Scoe urged. "*Worse* than suicide. You mustn't. You've done enough..." His voice quavered.

"Scoe," Rubriel stopped him, taking his arm and leading him to face her. "Scoe, stop. Look at me."

He tried to avoid her, but she followed his gaze until it settled reluctantly on hers.

"You've got to go home, Scoe. Rally Esmara; prepare them to support Bantria in the days to come."

"I can't just leave you behind - again!" he protested, his sadness coming out as anger. "You don't get to do something stupid while forcing me to be reasonable. I'm coming with you."

"*No,*" she said, planting a firm hand on his shoulder. "You *are* reasonable; you are courageous, intelligent, loyal to a fault - the world needs more men like you, and that is why you have to go." She winced suddenly, a sharp pain in her chest stalling her.

"I am broken," she admitted, "and the only thing left for me to do is provide the diversion Molindra needs-"

A dreadful screech pierced the air right above them.

"Bats! We must move," Molindra urged them.

Rubriel tore herself away. "Run," she said, backing towards Mol as she hurried into the cover of a jagged boulder.

Scoe couldn't move.

"RUN!"

She turned away as Adam grabbed Scoe's shoulder and shook him to his senses. She didn't have time to watch them go as she and Molindra bolted, darting from the shadow of one rock to the next, disappearing down into the maze and out of sight.

Mol peered upwards as the shrieks faded. "Did we lose them?"

"I doubt it. We're too exposed here; keep moving."

They hurried further in, seeking an overhang from which to make their stand. A bat dove for Rubriel; she ducked just in time and Mol spun around and shot a thin stream of flames after it. It screeched as it swooped away, alerting its fellows. Mol ushered Rubriel ahead towards an alcove in the rocks, guarding the rear. Between an upright boulder and a wall of cut earth where the ground fell away, they were shielded on two sides, meaning the bats would be forced to come at them from only one direction.

Rubriel drew her sword, ready to fight, but Mol held her back. "Save your strength. I'll handle this," she said. "Be ready if one breaks through."

Rubriel nodded. In the distance, the bats were regrouping, five of them in all. They circled high, flying right over their hiding place before turning sharply in line for a direct attack. Molindra stepped forward, seemingly vulnerable without any visible weapon. Rubriel hoped she knew what she was doing. She let the bats get alarmingly close, baiting them.

As one, the five bats surged for her. They were met with a sudden blast of wind that halted their flight, wings flapping fiercely against the force of a gale. Two of the smaller ones were overcome and swept away. The largest of them with the size and strength of an alpha let out a blood-curdling shriek, painfully high pitched and echoing. Mol's concentration did not falter, a slight adjustment allowing the bats to gain a little ground, bringing them closer together. Sensing an opening, the alpha lunged with renewed vigour. Mol responded with heat as she expertly transformed her winds into white hot flames, incinerating the bats.

"Nicely done," said Rubriel. "Let's move on before the other two come back."

Spurred on by Mol's display of prowess, they made good progress towards the base of the Lone Peak. Several stragglers tried to catch them unawares; Molindra blasted them away with ease. Rubriel took a lucky swing at one and severed its wing clean off.

"There. My contribution," she said triumphantly.

Mol grinned.

The gigantic spire loomed ahead, paradoxically rising from the lowest point in the ground, the valley floor all sloping towards its base. It was like one of the jagged rocks had been gripped and stretched violently skywards, elongating it to an impossible height. Now that they were closer, they could see man-made stairs winding up around the sheer face, partially set into the rock. It looked frightfully narrow.

"There is only one way into that spire," Mol said. "Unless you can fly."

"Is that the entrance?" Rubriel pointed to where the rocks were packed down and flattened into a climbable slope that led to a huge arch.

"Yes. The doors could be guarded. We need to move around and get a better look."

They crept around to the front, choosing a hiding place that offered a direct view of the entrance. The air had gone so still and quiet. Rubriel felt they were making too much noise as the dust scratched under their feet. Even their breathing seemed too loud.

Molindra cursed under her breath. "It's shut. I see no guards, but that doesn't mean there are none."

"Have you any idea what we'll find in there?"

"A handful of scientists, perhaps. They are the only long-term inhabitants, as far as I recall. We should be able to handle it, as long as they don't have mages with them."

"If there are guards, we should blow the doors and draw them out. Blast them open; we make our stand on the ground floor, before it gets too narrow further up."

Mol nodded, then hesitated.

"What is it?"

"It suddenly occurred to me that in all this time, I've never actually fought alongside you. I have watched you countless times; I have fought alone when I had to, but never this. Never together."

Rubriel squeezed her shoulder. "You and I are capable of far more than we were ever permitted to express. There are no rules anymore, no consequences for us beyond today. We do this our way."

She readied herself. Molindra returned her squeeze and gave one last burst of generalized healing; her pains faded to little more than a muffled ache.

"On the count of five, we run. Ready?"

Mol nodded.

"Five."

They shifted into position.

"Four."

Smoke curled under the doors.

"Three."

The metal glowed.

"Two."

Shouts from inside.

"One."

The doors exploded.

Rubriel charged, bypassing the two interior guards thrown aside in the blast, through the gaping arch into the dark chamber beyond. She clashed against a surprised scholar, who yelled in alarm, but he was ill-prepared and went down easily. The room was a long, half-moon shape with a high, ragged ceiling; as though the inside of the Lone Peak had been roughly hollowed out. She positioned herself across from where the tight spiral staircase spilled into the atrium, diagonally opposite the entry.

A stifled shout signalled the guards' demise at Molindra's hands; she'd raced down to finish them off before she hurried inside to find Rubriel fighting three to one as more men tried to pile down the stairs and overwhelm her.

"Rubriel move away!"

Rubriel dodged a blow and leapt back as Mol sent a stream of flame into the narrow opening. The band of scientists screamed and died; others scrambled hurriedly back up the stairs and out of range. She sucked all the warmth from the room. Rubriel shivered as Mol sent wave after wave of scorching heat up the spiral ascent, pushing it further and further to clear the way.

Until she met resistance. She felt her flames dissipate against some form of shield. Someone was blocking her.

"Another mage," she whispered, motioning Rubriel to duck around the corner out of sight. Blades were of little use against mages - unless caught off guard. If Molindra distracted this one, perhaps Rubriel could take him by surprise while he concentrated his energy elsewhere.

"I know you're there," Molindra said. "Show yourself!"

A cascade of broken objects answered her. Cracked pots, bent weapons and broken bits of wood crashed against the walls and tumbled down, littering the base of the stairs. She backed away and frowned.

"What is all that?"

"I don't know." She raised her voice. "Our foe declines my invitation and sends us trash! An insult." She moved forward, sidestepping one of the bodies. "Yet all he has managed to do is provide me with additional kindling."

"Be careful, Mol. I smell a trap." Rubriel was nervous. Something was off here.

"I wouldn't do that if I were you." A man in the red garb of a mage stood before them, taking in the scene disdainfully. Mol looked ready to burn, but he held up a hand and she hesitated.

"Elementalist Molindra," he said. "So this is what became of you. So much promise, now turned traitor - and fool."

Mol knew this man. She'd seen him at the academy in Imul'dene and somehow knew he was important. He'd never visited her department that she could recall. That meant he wasn't an elementalist. But something in his bearing and the way people had always deferred to him now gave her pause.

"You're wrong," she said. "To call me a traitor implies that we used to be on the same side." Imperceptibly, she gathered energy from the room. It was colder now and there wasn't much left. She reached backwards,

outside, searching for heat, moisture, anything - even earth - from which
to draw upon.

His face twisted into a snarl. "We of the High Tiers made you what
you are. You owe us everything!"

"Yes." Her eyes narrowed. "I took what I wanted, but I never intended
to stay."

He snorted. "That makes you all the more a fool." His eyes roved the
litter-strewn room. "And only a fool would confront a kinetic in such a
cluttered space."

All around, the debris rose against gravity. He lifted it without touching it, then sent it shooting down at Molindra with a flick of his hand.

She shielded with a current of air, but most of the objects were too
heavy. A reflex duck protected her head with her arms as the barrage
slammed into her. She cried out in pain. The blows didn't stop coming.
He simply picked up the same objects and hurled them at her over and
over in a tempest of table legs and broken plates. He was so intent on
beating her that he didn't see Rubriel leap from behind him.

She dodged a flying pot and her thrust missed, but she jabbed the hilt
of her sword back into the side of his head. He softened the blow with
magic and retaliated, throwing Rubriel across the room. She hit the wall
with a groan.

Molindra sprang to her feet and incinerated a good two-thirds of his
arsenal in one enraged burst of power. He threw her backwards too, but
she was ready - she pushed hard with air against the opposite wall. It
was like being squashed between two invisible barriers, but she held. He
couldn't toss *her* around like some discarded, broken object.

But he only smirked, and abruptly let go, sending her flailing towards
him under the force of her own air current. She crashed into an invisible
wall and fell at his feet. He grabbed her by the throat, choking her, but

she reached up with both hands and set his clothing on fire. He cursed and rolled off her, rolling and rolling to smother the flames.

"Rubriel!" Mol dashed over and hauled her to her feet with a flare of healing, restoring her strength.

She looked Mol up and down. "Heal yourself," she said incredulously.

The kinetic groaned where he lay. His chest was badly burned, his robes in blackened tatters.

Mol held fire in both hands. "How many more of you upstairs?"

He crawled backwards, attempting to throw Mol off her feet, but he was much weaker now, and she braced herself against the invisible force.

She hurled a fireball at the ground, missing his face by mere inches.

He cried out and shielded himself with his arms.

"I said how many!"

"Spirits, many spirits. They will recognize you, they-"

Rubriel silenced him with a sharp blow to the temple. "Let's go."

They climbed the stairs, picking their way over fallen bodies and debris into the chamber above. Tall bookshelves lined the walls on three sides. An aisle of pedestals held curiosities, engravings, weapons; they looked to be hundreds of years old. The air held a thick scent of dusty, crumbling tomes mixed with lingering smoke.

"The reliquary," said Mol, catching Rubriel's look of awe. "This place is ancient. And full of spirits. Some believe the relics themselves are possessed."

"Is that even possible? To contain a spirit within an inanimate object?"

"I have no idea. Come on."

The exit on the opposite side of the room brought them outside, onto a steep climb curling up around the outside of the spire. The air was still. They stepped lightly, but the scuffle of their boots still seemed to echo across the valley. Mol led the way until the stairs ended in a small landing with another door leading through the centre of the spire. It stood ajar enough to squeeze through, and silent. She was about to swing through the doorway when Rubriel grabbed her and jerked her back.

"Spirits," she said. The upper rooms teemed with them. She could *feel* them, somehow, feel them swarming the tower, searching. "We cannot go that way."

The stairs to the pinnacle were on the other side of that room, straight across from them. Wordlessly, Molindra pointed to a narrow ledge in the wall. It ran around the circumference, barely wide enough for a human foot.

They were mad - utterly mad, Mol thought as she volunteered to go first, hugging the wall to her back and inching carefully, carefully sideways. She kept her eyes focused straight ahead, not daring to look up or down, trying desperately not to think about what she was doing at all.

Rubriel followed behind, even more slowly. She was dizzy enough without a sheer drop in front of her, and kept her eyes tightly shut, feeling her way around the wall.

Mol made it to the platform on the other side. She reached out to help Rubriel, who was struggling to make the last few steps. Her foot dislodged a few small pebbles. She froze as they clattered down the wall and smashed somewhere far below, trying not to imagine falling like that. Gritting her teeth, she forced herself to keep moving, just a bit further and a bit further, until she opened her eyes and grasped Mol's hand and tumbled with her onto the relative safety of the platform.

They were under the very eaves of the pinnacle, between one last curved flight of stairs and the tower wall.

"Rest a bit," said Mol. "I do not know what we will find up there, but we should gather what strength we can before we face it." She crawled and sat against the wall, taking a few sips from what was left in her canteen and offering the last of it to Rubriel.

But Rubriel couldn't take it. She hunched over, tense and trembling, her face bone-white. She moaned in pain. "It's so powerful, Mol."

"What? What is?"

"The ludion. It's so heavy, pressing and pulling at us. I can't..." She clenched tight against it, that massive, oppressive force from above. It was seeking her like it had all the way from the Tower of Longing, wanting to grip and pull. Her skin prickled horribly. Worst of all, something inside her *responded* to it, an involuntary and oddly familiar recognition even as she rejected it with all her might.

"I don't feel anything, Rubriel," Mol said helplessly. She could only watch her gasp and struggle, fighting an enemy she couldn't see or hear.

Rubriel cried out once, sharply.

Mol seized her shoulder and shook. "Not now," she growled. "You must break this and come back. You are here with me and it cannot have you. Not now. Not today. We are almost there. Fight it, Rubriel. *Fight it!*"

Rubriel shuddered hard, but her wide, fearful eyes locked on Mol's face and she pulled herself towards it, out of the shadow's reach. She lay on her back, chest heaving up and down, slowly recovering. Tears slid silently down Mol's cheeks.

"I'm alright," Rubriel said, after a time. "It has passed." It hadn't, not entirely, but her mind was her own again, firmly planted in her own skin and aware enough to move on. The ludion's power slid thickly over and past her, but couldn't latch on again. She stood up slowly.

"There is nothing to gain from waiting any longer," said Mol. "We have to go up there."

"I know. Ready or not, we have to end this now as best we can, else our efforts thus far will be for naught."

All around, the air sat thin and silent, despite the volcano billowing in the distance. The sky pulsed overhead in brilliant green flashes, bold and powerful here at what she belatedly realized was the source. She realized something else then, too; something she couldn't put into words. This was a trap that could spring both ways. If they made the wrong choice now, they would be caught on the wrong side of that trap.

The air chilled as Mol slowly pulled energy from her surroundings. There was precious little moisture to be found, and the air hitched dry and rough in her throat. She reached further and further out, seeking more.

"Mol, wait." Rubriel swallowed hard, sagging against the wall. "Wait here."

"What?" Mol's concentration broke, and the air warmed around her.

"Wait here. I will go first."

"No! I should be the one who-"

"I have to go up there alone," Rubriel bit out. "Else… else he will not take the bait. We cannot destroy the ludion; our presence here is not a threat. It is me he wants; I think… I think he expects me to be lured here, by and by. *You* are still unseen, and far, far stronger than I am. He will come only to find me, and you may catch him unawares." She sounded braver than she felt, though she knew with grim certainty there was no other way.

Mol sobbed once and threw her arms around Rubriel, who winced painfully but hugged her back, tears in her eyes, too.

"I won't let him take you back there," she said fiercely, pulling back and gripping Rubriel's too-thin shoulders, pouring healing energy into her.

But Rubriel pulled away after a moment. "I know." She put herself between Mol and the stairs, herding her away from the ascent. "I know, and I trust you."

Mol looked ready to explode, or scream, but she closed her eyes and nodded once. Then Rubriel turned away, put one foot on the bottom step and looked up. The ludion tugged at her still; that fine, invisible line hooked onto something deep inside and demanding her attention. She adjusted her stiff-fingered grip on her sword hilt and climbed.

33

Lightning and Shadow

With heavy legs and heavier hearts, Adam's company of five began the gradual ascent into the foothills of the Gloaming Mountains. No one spoke. Grace looked close to tears. Even the twins were unusually quiet, going through the motions of scouting ahead and watching the group's flank, mercifully seeing nothing to cause alarm. Onward they trekked, slower than they should, but Adam had not the heart to push the pace, not when everyone's thoughts remained far behind their footfalls. He stopped, realizing they suddenly numbered only four.

Scoe stood a few paces behind. "I can't do this," he said.

"What?" Adam signalled the others to hold up.

He shook his head. "This is wrong. We can't leave them behind. I will not leave Rubriel behind again."

No one knew how to respond.

"This fight is ours - all of ours. We should be *together*, to whatever end. Not like this. This is not right."

A sob escaped Grace; she hid behind her hand. Adam hung his head and frowned deeply. It was Dornir who spoke for them.

"Scoe's right," he said, striding back toward the centre of the group. "We've all been through so much, making our escape seems like the easiest thing to do. But... but this is our home, and Rubriel is our friend. Fleeing is not the answer. Because once you start running? You never stop. Daelin and I know that better than anyone."

Daelin clapped his brother on the shoulder in solemn agreement. "Adam, please. Uncle...?"

All eyes fell upon him. "Rubriel and Mol left to give us a fighting chance. We must honour their sacrifice by making every effort to get out of here alive. The knowledge we've gained will be invaluable in the war to come. It must not be lost."

"Mol left because she had no choice!" Grace exploded. "She is exiled; bound by a blood oath. Rubriel is in no shape to fight but she followed Mol anyway because she could not bear to be parted from her!" She startled them with her outburst, normally the mildest and most rational of the group.

"When I return to Esmara," said Scoe, "I will marry the heir to the throne and take responsibility over many lives of men; to lead, to protect. That terrifies me, but not as much as living with the choice to abandon my friends when they need us most. Adam, you are right about the war effort - take Grace and make haste into the mountains. But I am not coming with you. Not yet. Because if Rubriel and Mol were to slay the Master of Imul'dene, there would be no war at all. That is a risk worth taking."

Adam nodded slowly. "We will wait for you at the edge of safety. You have a week, then we must move on."

"Understood."

"We're coming with you," said Daelin, both twins bounding to Scoe's side. "This country is in serious need of a change in leadership."

If the great ludion had felt oppressive from below, up close its presence was nothing short of withering. Rubriel kept her gaze averted, fighting to quell the fresh wave of anxiety that rose at the sight of it, and that terrible notion of something stirring inside her that she couldn't control. It was three times the height of any man and broader at its teardrop base than the trunk of the oldest oak. That same aberrant blackness roiled inside of it, seeming to oppose all things living and natural by its very existence.

All was still but for the sound of her own heartbeat. Not even the distant rumblings from the volcano could pierce the veil of emptiness surrounding the pinnacle. For a few horrible moments, she fell to thinking that their trek all the way up here might've been for nothing.

But Rubriel knew what she had to do. She couldn't quite explain *how* she knew, but she'd seen enough during her time in Imul'dene to understand that every spirit in Langlythe was connected by that strange, unnatural energy - and unfortunately, so was she. And so, against every rational impulse, she closed her eyes and allowed herself to feel that coldness inside of her, to acknowledge the link between her and the looming presence before her.

She felt the spirits in the tower below her, felt their recognition - and confusion - before a sharp screech snapped her awareness and brought her painfully back to where she stood.

A great bat circled the tower, larger than any she had fought before. It eyed her thirstily, lining itself up to snatch her from the roof. She followed its movements, ready and waiting as it circled closer. It banked steeply, stalling its flight and extending its clawed hands and fanged snout in a sudden dive. Rubriel ducked at the last second and swung her sword upwards with both arms. The old blade sliced roughly through the bat's neck and its body fell in a gruesome lump at her feet, twitching.

She backed away. She couldn't let its weird, bloodless corpse distract her. Something else entirely tugged at her senses. There was no time to worry about how, or why, or the insanity of what she was about to attempt.

"You know I'm here," she said, "so face me."

"As you wish," Zildred's cold voice replied. He stood before her now, shadows rippling off him in waves and pooling at the hem of his coat. He carried no visible weapon, but Rubriel knew he didn't need one - not here, at the full height of his power.

"I am not surprised to find you here, though the timing of your return is curious. Do you already hear the spirits' voices? Feel the incessant tug of the ludion on your mind so soon?"

"Those who sent me here have left me behind." She eased to the side, so that she was facing the stairwell where Molindra hid behind him. "There is no place for me in the cities to the south. Not any more. I have come to reach an agreement."

Very deliberately, she knelt and placed her sword on the ground. "Vesner, Berren, Adam - I owe them nothing, and they are nothing to me." Bitterness soured her words; her expression held only contempt. "I will draw from the stone inside me willingly - aid you in taking the Eastern Continent - on one condition. My will remains my own." She stepped forward boldly, her features set in grim resignation. In the background, Molindra signalled her readiness.

"That's what you want, isn't it?" she continued. "You need me to infiltrate Tunswick and prime it for collapse, because you know you cannot win a war staged from the Gloaming Pass alone. And with the portals destroyed, there is no alternative."

Zildred regarded her coolly. "A bold proposal, convincingly delivered; but you are stubborn and proud to the bitter end. I do not believe you."

She offered her bare hand. "Then come; see for yourself. I cannot lie to you."

Rubriel knew her ruse would be over the instant he touched her skin, but it didn't matter. All she wanted was to hold his full attention until the opportune moment. He took her by the wrist. Several things happened at once.

Molindra bounded onto the platform, wreathed in flame and crackling with heat. Distracted, Zildred's assault on Rubriel's mind faltered. Rubriel thrust her free hand inside his chest with all her strength. Her hand spasmed painfully, but her stiff fingers managed to grasp the ludion shard she gambled on finding there before Zildred realized what she was trying to do and shoved her bodily away from him. She wrenched the shard free and tumbled backwards over the edge.

Molindra screamed as Rubriel fell and hurled fire at Zildred, who blocked with a shadowy shield and answered with a projectile of his own. She dodged, the sliver of shadow taking a slice out of the flames protecting her as it flew past her shoulder. The fire snuffed and smoldered; she felt the cold against her exposed side and drew deeper from the air to replenish it.

Her flames fanned out in front of her just in time to absorb a second blow. She almost missed it. The raw energy Zildred fought with was nearly invisible but for the dark ripple in the air as each disturbance streaked towards her. His assault was relentless, seeming to come from every direction. He forced her to maintain her shield as a sphere around her body, taking every last drop of heat and motion from the air just to hold it steady. But the air was too still and cold up there already. Molindra rapidly depleted what little environmental energy was available to her; she'd have to act fast or she would have no choice but to draw on her own reserves.

She leapt across the platform, diving behind the ludion as cover, and dropped her flames. Zildred hissed as she blasted the platform with a violent gust of hot air. He sent darkness spinning around the base of the stone, but she was already moving. She sent fire in a stream across the ground; more hurtled as a ball of flame through the air. He deflected both and answered with a great billowing wall of shadow that she barely managed to absorb.

The effort left her momentarily unprotected. She needed more energy - now - but where could she get it from? The air was too still, too empty; the volcano too far away. The ludion was vast and limitless, but she had only herself. And so she did the one thing Gal'denan had warned her never to do; she dipped into the well of energy flowing in her own veins and focused it. The anger and fear and love trapped in her heart bubbled and seethed to the surface. She came alive, blue fire igniting all around her as though her very skin were aflame.

Zildred channeled from the ludion, the shadows that whirled about him gathering strength until they took on an almost solid form. Darkness raged towards her. White-hot flames seared through the air. The two collided with an audible roar in one endless blast, the two of them locked in a battle of pure strength.

Molindra glanced up. The clouds. The emerald lights - it was a shield, a shield that blocked out the sun, the stars; blocked out the true nature of the sky above. It flashed and spasmed, as though the disruption below had momentarily weakened it. Above that shield, the sky held cloud, rain, wind and sun; just like anywhere else in the world.

Those elements were hers. She had to break through.

Her shield blackened, straining to absorb the onslaught of shadow that slowly pushed her backwards. The ludion's well of power remained steady, while her own ran dry so very quickly. In her mind she reached above, calling to the forces of nature that passed overhead, and pulled.

Zildred's torrent of darkness slammed relentlessly against her. He knew she couldn't hold out much longer. He let the darkness eat at the centre of the flames, gradually consuming the heat and light. All the while, Molindra pulled and coaxed the storm brewing just above the emerald lights, amplifying it until that unnatural aura began to crack. The bright green edges of it sizzled menacingly where she forced them apart.

Clouds spiralled through, dark and electric, growing bolder and bolder as she sucked them downwards with rapidly increasing intensity. The ludion crackled in warning, and then another sound joined the roar of darkness and fire; a high-pitched hum, opposing forces grating against one another like metal on granite.

Molindra screamed in defiance. The storm bellowed in answer, the monstrous black clouds spinning fast and racing down towards them. At the last moment she dropped the fire, sent the last of her energy into the sky, and the greatest bolt of lightning the world has ever known struck the tower. Light blinded. Thunder boomed and shook.

The storm evaporated in seconds. Molindra struggled to push herself up off the ground. The lightning had cleared away the shadow and left Zildred crumpled on the ground as well, but the tail end of the dark torrent had hit her in the moment she dropped her shield, leaving her cold and strangely detached from her body. Soot stained the pinnacle in a ring around where Zildred knelt, crippled and struggling to rise, his mantle singed and his coat in tatters.

But he was alive, and so was she, and the fight still wasn't over. She forced her limbs to move and hurled a feeble firebolt, rolling aside to escape his answering, much diminished, slice of shadow. She tried again, her second firebolt finding its mark as she collapsed from the effort.

He hissed in pain, but finally stood and approached. He drew an ordinary dagger, concealed until now, from beneath what was left of his coat.

She was on all fours. She needed to get up, but she couldn't - her body wouldn't obey, as though it no longer belonged to her. Her vision shuddered with motion, yet she remained frozen, numb. She wondered if she would even feel the killing blow.

"You have been a worthy opponent, Molindra," he said quietly, "but it seems the final stroke will still be mine."

"NO!"

He turned.

She was bleeding from her forehead, gripping her sword awkwardly in both hands, battered and broken and yet somehow... glowing.

"It is mine." Rubriel's skin sparkled with the light of a thousand moons as she raised her sword.

"You're a-"

She drove the blade deep into where his heart should've been. It seemed to stick, and an unseen force rippled up her arm and blasted her backwards.

Zildred screamed an otherworldly scream. He grasped at the invisible wound, his shadowy form seeming to condense and shrink around it, until he finally dissolved, all that remained of his power reabsorbed by the ludion - exactly where it belonged.

Molindra fell to the ground.

Rubriel heaved herself onto her stomach. She crawled, inch by inch, clutching her uselessly numb right arm against her body while her left arm pulled her towards where Molindra lay. Pain surged beneath her ribs. Every muscle and bone in her body ached and threatened to give way as she moved.

"Mol?" she called weakly. "Mol..."

Molindra lay on her side, her breath coming in irregular, pained gasps. Her eyes flickered when she saw Rubriel, and the corners of her mouth turned upwards in a weary smile.

Rubriel groaned as she used her good arm to roll Molindra onto her back and lift her into an embrace, her head resting on Rubriel's shoulder.

"I have never... seen anything like that. Your magic... the intensity, the control you had... I am so proud of you, Mol."

Molindra leaned her head back and gazed up into Rubriel's tired eyes.

"It... it is... over..." She gasped, a strange, vacant smile blooming on her pale lips.

Rubriel smiled and kissed her forehead. "We made it," she whispered. They held each other's gaze, savouring that moment of peace between them. One perfect moment of stillness and light amidst all that blackness, when all wrongs were forgiven and all hurts washed away, and Rubriel wished for nothing more than to stay like that forever.

But Molindra's expression sorrowed. When she spoke again, her voice was barely above a whisper. "I'm... sorry. So sorry..."

"Shhh." Rubriel stroked her hair. "Don't."

"Th-thank you... for giving me the chance... to make it up to you, to... make amends... for leaving... f-for..." She gasped. "Thank you, for believing in me... here, at the end... where it... it mattered... most..." Her strength failed her. The words would not come.

"Shhh, rest Mol. No more guilt. No more," Rubriel said quietly, her own voice trembling. "It's over. What are you apologizing for?"

Molindra closed her eyes for a moment. She drew a deep, shuddering breath. "Rubriel... I feel... strange."

"It's alright." She touched her cheek tenderly. "We'll get out of here. I will find someone who can heal you. You'll be alright," she promised. "I know you'll be alright."

Mol shook her head. "There is... nothing to heal. My body isn't broken... my... spirit is. I used... so much energy... I..." Her voice faded.

"Wh- what?"

Mol shuddered. "C-cold," she stammered. "I'm cold..."

Rubriel held her closer, tears brimming in her eyes.

"No..." she whispered, "No Mol, no..." She swallowed hard. It wasn't right. She wasn't going to lose her friend, her *sister*. Not here. Not like this.

"I am going to save you," she said stubbornly. "You're going to grow strong again. You're going to keep learning and growing until you're the best mage in all of the Eastern Continent."

Molindra smiled weakly.

"No, wait - you *are* the best mage in the Eastern Continent! We'll sail away from here - far, far away from here - and build a house in Esmara, with a huge garden, a laboratory, a forge..."

But Molindra held a glazed, faraway look, as if already drifting off to that home of their dreams.

"I... can't... lose you," Rubriel sobbed. "I love you more than life itself."

At that, Molindra looked up at her one last time.

"You've got to go on, Rubriel. We have secured... a future... full of hope... another chance... new beginnings..."

Rubriel squeezed her tight.

"...But that... future... is not... mine."

And then she was silent.

Rubriel shook her head, open-mouthed in shock, stroking the hair away from Mol's beautiful brows, refusing to believe that she would never speak again.

"Mol..."

She was so still. So cold and empty. Just... gone.

Rubriel shattered. Harrowing howls of despair took her. She couldn't stop. She held Molindra tightly, hugging her close and rocking back and forth in a desperate, bitter plea. Her whole body shook with violent sobs, the cruel combination of grief and exhaustion. Her physical wounds were meaningless. She'd pushed herself far beyond the boundaries of what any living being should. It didn't matter. Nothing would ever be the same.

She cried into the empty void, a broken woman in a broken land. Cried until her eyes ran dry. Cried until every spirit from miles around gathered by her side on the cold cracked stone, at the pinnacle of a lone peak under an emerald sky.

Epilogue

Scoe and the twin scouts hurried through the Jagged Labyrinth, following the smell of smoke emanating from the tower at the bottom of the valley. Even from afar, the great flash had been blinding, the thunderclap moments later loud enough to rival the volcano. They feared they were too late. Smoke thickened as they reached the tower's gaping maw, its doors blown to pieces and burning beneath a heap of bodies and debris.

Bile rose in Scoe's throat. The twins coughed, but they masked their faces and dashed up the stairs. Scoe swore and pushed after them, dripping with sweat as he forced his way up to the second floor and outside. The twins already climbed the pinnacle. He steeled himself and made a run for it through a room that resembled the inside of a furnace. Wheezing, he staggered up the last few steps.

The sight of the ludion filled Scoe's heart with dread, held untouched in its grand setting. All was quiet. His eyes briefly flicked to the corpse of the great bat, beheaded and lying awkwardly, before he spotted Daelin and Dornir crouched before the soot-stained scorch mark covering a third of the platform. They stood as he approached.

"That thunderclap earlier... the chaos below. This was quite the battle, but it is over. We are alone."

Scoe stared at the mark, crestfallen. Though they searched every inch of the pinnacle, they found no trace of Rubriel nor Molindra - and no witness, living or dead, to tell the tale.

"Look down there," he croaked, tears in his eyes as he pointed to the sea of soldiers in the distance. Their tiny lights turned around and marched back towards Imul'dene.

"Ah, Mr. Carter!"

The estate agent waved in greeting as the cart pulled up outside Adam's old home. He disembarked and took his niece's arm before accepting the moustached man's handshake.

"Welcome back! Things are... mostly as you left them. We replaced one of the windows; looked as though there had been a break-in at some point, though nothing was ever reported stolen." He paused as his hand rested on the freshly painted gate. "Oh, and the fence is new. Unfortunately, your tenants set fire to it somehow, then up and left the following day."

"Indeed?" Adam raised a brow.

"Very peculiar." The agent nodded enthusiastically. "They paid for the damage and everything."

Inside, the house was, indeed, exactly as *somebody* left it - right down to the photographs on the mantelpiece.

Grace let out a small squeak as she recognized one of the pictures and thrust it into her uncle's hands.

"You didn't know our tenants when they signed the lease?" she said excitedly.

"No; never met them."

"You do now. Look!" She pointed to the black and white figures gazing out of the small frame.

A stunning dark-haired lady sat in the front, done up in all her evening finery. Jewels draped across her delicate collarbone, and a single lock of curls escaped her updo to caress her cheek. Behind her on the left stood a woman with light-coloured hair braided around her head, looking rather smart but for the top button missing from her bodice. And on the right, a face they knew well; Rubriel stood proudly behind her sisters, her cheeks full and her eyes sparkling even through the black and white photo.

"This was their home too, for a while. We should keep the pictures."

Adam nodded and hugged her, tenderly setting the frame back in its place.

At the station, the platform bustled with activity. Scoe leant against the wall, rubbing his hands together in the crisp autumn air as he waited to board the train that would take him to the port of Ornage - and a ship home to Esmara. The twins, overstimulated by the frenzy of foreign sights and sounds, had wandered off somewhere to look at one of the engines. He hoped they made it back to the platform on time. Travelling with those two was going to be... interesting, to say the least.

A commotion further down caught his attention. A small crowd gathered around a woman in royal blue. He could see straight away why she attracted attention. It wasn't just her appearance; she seemed to radiate a kind of invisible energy that felt almost familiar.

"Just one photograph. Please, Miss," called a young man from behind a camera, struggling to find an unobstructed view of his subject as another man with spectacles scribbled on a notepad and peppered her with questions.

"Gentlemen, please." She graciously posed for a single photo before giving a polite incline of her chin and making it clear she would accept no more fuss. As she glided down the platform, a piece of paper slipped from her pocket.

Scoe picked it up and pushed after her. "Excuse me, Miss!" he called, straining to be heard over the throng of people.

She whirled when he got close and threw him an irritated look.

"Sorry to bother you, but you dropped this."

"Oh, how kind," she said, taking the paper from him with a gloved hand. "Thank you." She smiled, and the resemblance in that moment was too striking to ignore.

"You're Gwendolen Starsinger," Scoe blurted.

She swatted away the recognition with polite shyness, but before she could say anything more, he stopped her cold.

"You're Rubriel's sister."

She gasped, studying his face properly now. "How do you know my sister?"

He took a moment to answer, unsure how much to say - how much she knew of her sister's fate. He opted for the truth. "I met her in Langlythe. I saved her life, and she mine. Without Rubriel and Molindra, I would never have made it back." He smiled, meeting Gwendolen's bright, silvery eyes. "She was the most remarkable woman I have ever met."

The End.

****

Thank You

I am thrilled that you chose to read my work and sincerely hope you enjoyed it! If you did, please consider leaving a review for this book on Amazon and/or Goodreads. It only takes a moment, but makes all the difference. Your support means the world to me as an indie author. Thank you!

Rebecca Holmes used to think that inventing entire worlds and cultures in her head was something everybody did in their spare time. Then she realized this may or may not be a talent she should put to good use. When she isn't trying to decide if they're peas or lentils, she is probably playing video games, sewing, reading, or taking a nap. (Seriously–naps are underrated.) She lives in Vancouver, BC, Canada with her mum and her dog.

Follow her author page on:

- Goodreads

- Amazon

- Tiktok